"There is not one reason why this book isn't a winner! Everything about it screams success. The book is masterfully written with a tightly woven plot, visually detailed settings and well-developed characters."

—*Rebecca's Reads*

Praise for *White Tombs*

Named Best Mystery of 2008 by *Reader Views*

"Valen's debut police procedural provides enough plot twists to keep readers engrossed and paints a clear picture of the Hispanic community in St. Paul."

—*Library Journal*

"*White Tombs* is a superb police procedural starring a fascinating lead detective. Santana is a wonderful new addition to the subgenre."

—*Midwest Book Review*

"Santana is an intriguing character. St. Paul readers will enjoy Valen's sense of place."

—*St. Paul Pioneer Press*

"Christopher Valen addresses a very wide range of extremely relevant social issues in *White Tombs,* and this book goes well beyond being just a detective story. The characters are fantastically well developed . . . the writing is solid an elegant without unnecessary detours. Any lover of solid writing should enjoy it greatly. *White Tombs* also screams out for a sequel—or better yet, sequels."

—*Reader Views*

The John Santana Novels

White Tombs

The Black Minute

Bad Weeds Never Die

Bone Shadows

Death's Way

The Darkness Hunter

Also by Christopher Valen

All the Fields

Praise for *The Darkness Hunter*

"A taut story full of mystery and tension . . . with a pertinent message interwoven into a thrilling plot."

—*Reader's Favorite*

"Christopher Valen is where it is at when it comes to police procedural thrillers. The mysteries are complicated but believable. The characters are well drawn and realistic. The dialogue and action is crisp and intense. I highly recommend *The Darkness Hunter* and Christopher Valen to anyone looking for a solid mystery novel."

—Phillip Tomasso (Author of *Damn the Dead* and *Extinction*)

Praise for *Death's Way*

"Valen is a master of words, of plots and subplots, and subplots within subplots. In *Death's Way* Valen has once again crafted a spellbinding tale of mystery, murder, intrigue and the unexplained. His readers, both old and new, will not be disappointed."

—*Rebecca's Reads*

"This carefully plotted police procedural deals with the sex trade from Costa Rica, drug trafficking, a wrongly convicted murderer, and murderous drug cartels. There are numerous turns and twists in this carefully plotted police procedural. Secrets and the meaning of life and death drive this intriguing and fast-paced mystery."

—*Reader Views*

Wow! Christopher Valen has done an extremely good job of making sure his latest offering, *Death's Way,* keeps you glued to the book till the end. The methodical way in which John Santana goes about piecing together the evidence in the case holds the reader's interest all the way. The author has researched his story well and ties up all the loose ends beautifully. Kudos to Christopher Valen for having come up with a character like John Santana."

—*Reader's Favorite*

"The tightly wound story moves at a fast pace, with each chapter ending on a cliffhanger so that the audience will want to keep reading . . . this novel represents a gripping offering from an award-winning author."

—*Foreword Reviews*

Praise for *Bone Shadows*

Midwest Independent Publishers' Association 2012
Best Mystery of the Year

Named Best Mystery of 2012
by *Reader Views* & *Rebecca's Reads*

"*Bone Shadows* is guaranteed to hold readers' attention until the last page . . . Valen's highly moral Santana character is golden."

—*Library Journal*

"With a compelling and believable hero and a colorful cast of supporting characters, this turned out to be another superbly written tale of convoluted motives and surprising twists and turns. I would highly recommend Christopher Valen's *Bone Shadows* to anybody who enjoys a well-written, contemporary story."

—*Reader Views*

"*Bone Shadows* has a well thought out plot that is up to date with today's society and current social issues. Valen writes with an easy to follow style, and he is adept at keeping his tale interesting, intriguing and exciting. I appreciated the many convoluted twists and turns of the story . . . I am also certain that this book will elicit at least one or two gasps of shock/surprise . . . *Bone Shadows* was a great read."

—*Rebecca's Reads*

Praise for *Bad Weeds Never Die*

Named Best Mystery of 2011 by *Reader Views* & *Rebecca's Reads*

"The latest John Santana police procedural is an excellent investigative thriller."

—*Midwest Book Review*

"Christopher Valen's third novel, *Bad Weeds Never Die,* continues the story of John Santana, a homicide detective in St. Paul, Minn., who was introduced in *White Tombs* and whose story was continued in *The Black Minute.* The three novels are all great police procedural stories . . . I have thoroughly enjoyed reading Valen's novels."

—*Bismarck Tribune*

"*Bad Weeds Never Die* . . . delivered on all fronts. Once again I enjoyed Mr. Valen's well-plotted and intriguing mystery for all the obvious reasons: flowing and well-paced storyline, great dialogue, multi-layered and vivid characters, a great sense of place and time, relevant issues and believable events."

—*Reader Views*

"This is the first of Valen's books that I have read in the John Santana series and surely will not be the last . . . Valen's novel is gripping, fast-paced and will have you guessing until the end. The characters are intriguing, and there are many plot twists and turns. It is a true page turner in every sense of the word."

—*Rebecca's Reads*

Praise for *The Black Minute*

Named Best Mystery of 2009 by *Reader Views*

Midwest Book Award Finalist

"Santana—an appealing series lead, strong and intelligent . . . Readers who enjoyed *White Tombs* will settle easily into this one; on the other hand, it works fine as a stand-alone, and fans of well-plotted mysteries with a regional flair . . . should be encouraged to give this one a look."

—*Booklist*

"As in *White Tombs,* Valen writes well about St. Paul and surrounding areas. He gives just enough sense of place to make you feel like you're there, but he never loses track of his story's fast pacing. And he does a super job of keeping the suspense going as the action reaches a crescendo."

—*St. Paul Pioneer Press*

"The second John Santana St. Paul police procedural is a terrific thriller . . . Christopher Valen provides the audience with his second straight winning whodunit."

—*Midwest Book Review*

"*The Black Minute* grabbed me from the first page on and pulled me into a complex world of evil, violence, deceit, bravery and a search for justice . . . While the plot is complex and anything but predictable, his storyline stays comprehensible and easy to follow. The characters are well developed, very believable and constantly evolving. The setting of the story is vivid, detailed and engaging."

—*Reader Views*

SPEAK FOR THE DEAD

A John Santana Novel

Christopher Valen

Conquill Press
St. Paul, Minnesota

This book is a work of fiction. Names, characters, places and incidents either are products of the author's imagination or are used fictitiously. Certain liberties have been taken in portraying St. Paul and its institutions. This is wholly intentional. Any resemblance to actual events, or to actual persons living or dead, is entirely coincidental.
For information about special discounts for bulk purchases, contact conquillpress@comcast.net

SPEAK FOR THE DEAD

Conquill Press
387 Bluebird Alcove
St. Paul, MN 55125
www.conquillpress.com

Cover Design: Rebecca Treadway

Library of Congress Control Number: 2017940080

Valen, Christopher
SPEAK FOR THE DEAD: a novel/by Christopher Valen—1st edition

ISBN: 978-0-9908461-9-2

Conquill Press/October 2017

Printed in the United States of America

10 9 8 7 6 5 4 3 2 1

For my brother, Captain John (Jack) Peterson,
Northwest Airlines (Ret.)

"It has become appallingly obvious that our technology has exceeded our humanity."

—Albert Einstein

Prologue

Angel Estrada walked among the low rolling hills and broad lawns that comprised the city of the dead.

Among the forest of headstones sat elaborate crypts, low-walled family garden plots, and service roads that divided *el barrio de los acostados,* the sleeping neighborhoods. But many families had chosen to bury the remains of their loved ones in niches in the walls of communal mausoleums.

In the distance a burial service was in progress. Cars were parked along a curb. Brown tarps covered mounds of grave earth. Mourners attired in black dresses and suits sat stoically in rows of folding chairs set up on the grass, oppressed by the heat and grief, and perhaps, by a sense of their own mortality.

Angel Estrada stopped in front of a grave with a large headstone. The ground beneath his feet felt soft from the fall rains in Cali, Colombia. A breath of hot air whispered in the trees. Dark clouds veiled the sun.

The name carved in the headstone read ELENA CEPEDA.

Angel Estrada nodded at *El Lobo,* who squatted beside the headstone. With a forefinger the Wolf touched *la dormilona,* or the sleeping plant, growing near the grave. The small green leaves of the plant folded inward and drooped at the touch, as if it were dying. But it was only protecting itself from harm until the danger passed and the leaves opened once again.

El Lobo smiled and stood.

There was nothing remarkable about the Wolf—except for the eyes. No emotion. No light. Looking into the deadness was like looking into two bullet holes. Estrada realized that the Wolf's eyes were the last things victims saw before they died. Before the light expired in their own eyes. And unlike *la dormilona,* the victim would never return to life.

El Lobo wore many disguises and spoke English, Spanish, French, and Portuguese. Rumor had it that the Wolf was fluent in Russian and Eastern European languages as well.

But the key to the Wolf's success, Estrada thought, was the way in which those targeted died. It always appeared as if their deaths were accidents or suicides—never murder.

"This is the man I want killed," Estrada said, holding out a black-and-white photo.

The Wolf did not look at it or ask why. Estrada would get around to it. They all did—sooner or later.

"This man murdered my stepbrothers, Emilio and Enrique, and my father, Alejandro." Estrada nodded at the grave. "And my sister, Elena."

The Wolf knew of Alejandro Estrada, the former head of the Cali cartel. The old man had drowned in Lake Guatavita near Bogotá. Elena Cepeda's death was a mystery, as were the deaths of the others. But these facts did not concern the Wolf.

Estrada pointed at the photo. "This man has also killed those who have gone before you." He paused, waiting for a reaction. When none was forthcoming, he added, "He is a dangerous and resourceful man." Estrada felt the sudden heat of embarrassment in his face. His heart thumped. "Of course, no one is as dangerous and resourceful as you." He forced a smile.

El Lobo could see the sheen of fear in Estrada's eyes.

"The man you must kill is named Juan Carlos Gutiérrez Arángo," Angel Estrada continued. "But he goes by the name of John Santana."

Chapter 1

The skeletal hand reached out of the soil inside the cave as though clawing for life.

A foot-long, black-handled dagger through its palm pinned it to the ground. The dagger had a seven-inch blade, a cast metal pommel, and a sculpted outstretched dragon talon guard.

St. Paul Homicide Detective John Santana dropped to his knees and brushed away the winged seeds lying cold around him. The air smelled of wet stone and was damp and cool, despite the sunlight streaming through the cave entrance.

The bony hand triggered a flashback. A sharp pain knifed through Santana's heart. He shook his head, trying to erase the dark memory, forcing himself to concentrate on this crime scene and not on the scene that would forever haunt him.

The ground had been overturned, as if an animal had been rooting around in the soil. Santana could see fire remains near the cave entrance.

Two young men had gone into this cave earlier in the day, entering through a narrow passage, where they had spotted the hand and alerted police.

Along the Mississippi River bluffs, there were nearly fifty manmade sandstone caves that had once been used for growing mushrooms. Many others had been naturally carved out of sandstone or limestone and were wide and high enough for anyone to stand in easily.

This cave was approximately twenty feet high and thirty feet wide, narrowing like a cone as it tunneled deeper into the sandstone. It was part of a larger network that lay across the Mississippi River from downtown St. Paul and extended for miles. Most of the entrances had been sealed off from the public due to the deaths of two teenage girls years ago. But with so many entrances, it was impossible to completely seal off all of them or to know where they were all located.

The teenage girls had died from carbon monoxide poisoning from burning campfires, the most common cause of death in the caves. A "NO TRESPASSING" sign had been posted warning of the dangers. Beside it was a memorial plaque commemorating the girls' deaths.

A well-worn path led past numerous entrances, many showing evidence of the city's attempt to seal them with plywood and piles of sand. But as the young men had demonstrated this morning, a determined person could find a way in.

Santana had gotten call-outs about bones before, especially during Halloween and in spring when the snow melted and animal bones appeared. But this was different. This hand was human. He used a small Maglite to study it. Then he gently ran a latex-gloved hand over the bones.

A young patrol officer named Rick Paukert squatted beside him. "Thought the hand was a fake at first. Like maybe someone stuck it in the soil as a practical joke."

"Greasy feel," Santana said. "Green bone."

"What's that mean?"

"Freshly skeletonized. It's no joke."

The officer's face reddened. He nodded in agreement.

Santana could see a slight depression where the body was buried. He knew that as time passes the soil in a grave compacts and lowers, especially over the torso when the organs decompose and the rib cage collapses. He wondered how much of the rest of the body would be found beneath the topsoil.

Given the slim size of the hand, he figured it belonged to an adult female, possibly a homeless person who had sought shelter in the cave. But this wasn't a person who had built a fire and then died from carbon monoxide poisoning or through natural means. And even with the wind whistling through the cave entrance, it would have taken years for the soil to cover the body.

Someone had driven the dagger through her hand and murdered whoever was buried here.

Santana made a quick sketch of the scene. Then he took out his department cell phone and snapped a photo of the dagger. He tried to frame the picture so that the hand didn't show, but he couldn't completely hide it and still get a good shot of the dagger.

As both men stood, he asked Paukert, "What about the two young men who called it in? Are they still here?"

Paukert lowered his gaze. "I let them go."

Santana released a frustrated sigh. "Did you get their names?"

The young officer looked at Santana again and smiled. "Sure did." He held up his notebook. "Names and phone numbers."

"Okay." Santana handed Paukert his car keys. "Get some crime scene tape out of the trunk. Wrap it around a series of trees to cordon off the area. There's a clipboard with a crime scene log in the trunk. Make sure everyone signs the log before passing under the tape."

"You got it, Detective."

According to SPPD protocol, all personnel entering a crime scene had to also prepare a written report detailing why they were there, what they did, and what they observed. Santana felt that oftentimes, despite advances in technology, he could spend most of his days typing reports and filling out forms.

Paukert hesitated.

"Something else, Officer?"

"Uh . . . I'd like to become a homicide detective one day. Any advice?"

Find another career, Santana thought. But instead of crushing the young cop's aspirations, he said, "Listen and learn."

Paukert smiled again.

"The crime scene tape?" Santana reminded him.

"Oh, right," he said. "And I'll make sure everyone signs the log."

Santana watched Paukert hurry off and remembered when he was a young officer. Eager. Excited. Wanting to please. Hoping that one day he would have a gold shield. Never figuring how much it would cost him.

Gina Luttrell, the SPPD district supervisor, nodded at Paukert as they passed each other. Her short dark hair complemented her narrow face and slim body. She wore a black pants suit and light leather jacket. Her gold shield hung from a lanyard around her neck.

"Never seen anything quite like this before, John."

She took out her cell phone, dialed, and gave him a thumbs-up, indicating she could get a signal inside the cave. Once she'd notified the SPPD's watch commander of the situation, she disconnected and looked at Santana.

"FSU will be here soon," she said, referring to the SPPD's Forensic Services Unit. "I'll check the perimeter. It's your scene now, Detective. *Buena suerte.*"

Though Luttrell's mother was Puerto Rican, she wasn't fluent in Spanish, but she knew enough to carry on a basic conversation and to wish him "good luck."

Moments later, Santana's cell phone rang. It was Reiko Tanabe. He recognized the Ramsey County medical examiner's number. Santana detailed the crime scene. Then she asked, "You're sure this isn't a BLR or a BLS?"

Santana understood that the anthropological acronyms stood for bonelike rocks and bonelike sticks. "I'm sure."

"Okay. I'll contact the bone detective. He should be there to supervise the disinterment."

Tanabe was referring to anthropology professor Rob Wallace, the state's only board-certified forensic anthropologist. He was qualified to conduct or participate in the recovery of human remains and perform osteological analysis, which meant he had the ability to determine such things as age, sex, height, and stature, and provide any information that might explain the death based on bones alone.

"I have to bring him in on this, John," Tanabe said.

"I know. But I don't have to like it."

"I'll gather my team and be there shortly."

It was a forty-minute drive from Rob Wallace's lab located in the Midwest Medical Examiner's Office in Anoka, Minnesota.

Santana disconnected and called his partner, Kacie Hawkins. While he waited for her to arrive, he flicked on his Maglite and walked to the back of the cave, where he entered an eight-foot-by-five-foot tunnel that burrowed into the wall. He could see footprint impressions in the sandstone floor leading into and out of the tunnel. Forensics would need to take dental stone castings of the footprint impressions.

Did the footprints belong to the two young men who had discovered the skeletonized remains or to someone else? And where did the tunnel lead? Was there another entrance to and from the cave?

Santana kept going, following the beam of light, making sure he didn't step on the other footprints, and noting how the tunnel narrowed and shrunk as it wound deeper into the darkness, forcing him to duck his head.

Just as he thought it would come to a dead end, the tunnel split into two larger branching tunnels, one to his left and the other to his right. He focused the Maglite beam in the one to the right. Twenty yards ahead he saw a pile of rough debris, where the footprints appeared to stop. The remaining space between the pile and tunnel wall was quite narrow, making passage difficult, if not impossible.

He turned into the left tunnel, following it and a set of footprints as it curved to the right and then dead-ended. He retraced his steps back to the body.

Kacie Hawkins was waiting when he returned. Staring down at the bony hand and then at Santana, she asked, "How you doing, John?"

"Fine. Why?" His response had sounded confrontational. He immediately regretted it.

Hawkins placed her hands on her slim hips and cocked her head. "Just asking."

Santana imagined his partner was remembering the same scene in her mind now as he'd pictured the moment he saw the bony hand in the soil.

He hadn't slept well for weeks and considered offering it as an excuse for his attitude, but then thought better of it. He knew what the real cause was.

"Interesting-looking knife," she said, shifting the conversation, letting him off the hook.

"I'll check and see who sells this type of dagger," Santana said. "Maybe we can get lucky and trace the buyer."

"What do you want me to do?"

"Divide the secondary area into smaller quadrants and assign officers and canine units to carefully search each section."

Santana believed the recovery of human remains was no different from any other investigation. He still had a possible crime scene that needed to be examined for physical and testimonial evidence and a possible victim. In processing a crime scene, he was just as concerned with the secondary areas or avenues leading to the victim as he was with the primary area, where the victim was located.

"Will do," Hawkins said.

"And get the names and phone numbers of the two kids who found the remains from Officer Paukert."

"The cute guy with the crime scene log?"

Santana saw the sparkle in his partner's brown eyes. "Yeah, that one. I'll wait for Tanabe and Wallace."

"Wallace?"

"We're dealing with bones here."

As Hawkins strode away she said, "Have fun with Hollywood." She used the disparaging nickname Wallace had acquired among homicide personnel since becoming a consultant for one of the numerous CSI shows on network television.

Wallace's moniker wasn't simply a result of jealousy, Santana thought, a feeling he understood but didn't share with his colleagues. Rather, it was emblematic of Wallace's insufferable ego that seemed to inflate like a balloon the more trips he made to Hollywood.

By the time the forensic anthropologist arrived, the scene looked like a bivouac. Media vans filled a nearby parking lot. Helicopters from local television stations circled overhead. Forensic techs and dig team members dressed in white jumpsuits photographed and mapped the scene on a grid, took impressions of the footprints in the cave, and screened the soil in the burial site, looking for something that might help ID the body. Using soft brushes, they gradually exposed the skeletal remains and remnants of clothing.

Santana acknowledged Wallace with a nod.

"Detective," Wallace replied, dipping his double chin. He placed his hands on his ever-expanding hips and surveyed the scene, like a director appraising his actors before calling "Action."

He crossed his arms and gazed at the skeleton, tapping an index finger against his lips, a mannerism he'd adopted after watching the actor who played the forensic anthropologist in the TV series. "Appears to be the skeleton of a female, based on the size of the pelvis." Wallace fixed his gray eyes on Reiko Tanabe, the ME, and offered an encouraging smile.

Tanabe looked at Santana. "The pelvis itself is larger in males, as is the coccyx and the angle in front of the hips. The opening between the hips is larger in the female for birthing."

"The chin is squarer in the skull of a man than that of a woman," Wallace added, looking at Tanabe as if she was unaware of that fact. "Women tend to have a slightly more pointed chin. The forehead of the male slants backwards. The female is slightly more rounded. Males seem to have brow ridges, whereas females don't."

In all the years Santana had worked with Tanabe, he'd never seen her lose her cool. But he saw her cheeks darken, and behind her wire-rimmed glasses, he saw her eyes flash with anger. She touched the *café au lait* mark on her neck with the fingers of her right hand, a habit she had when under stress.

"We'll get some photographs," Wallace said. "No soft tissue left to examine. I'll X-ray the bones and set aside a femur, rib, and tooth for DNA testing for the BCA."

BCA stood for the state Bureau of Criminal Apprehension, which investigated both criminal and civil cases and provided lab and record services to local agencies.

Tanabe squatted beside the remains and gently turned the head slightly to the left. Santana immediately saw the damage to the skull.

"Blunt force skull injuries to green bone sometimes leave some identifying marks of the weapon used to inflict the trauma," she said. "In this case, I'd say a blunt, oval-shaped club."

"I concur," Wallace said.

"Something just under the body," Tanabe said. She leaned forward and, using a forefinger and thumb, picked up what appeared to be a jagged piece of paper approximately 3 ½" by 3 ½" that was wedged beneath the edge of the pelvis and the dirt. She peered at the paper a moment, then handed it to Santana.

"Looks like part of a pawn ticket," he said. "Given the smooth edge on the top and right side, I'd say it was the top half of the form." Santana held it up in his gloved hand so that Tanabe and Wallace could see it. "The item number is listed in the right corner. See the maturity date and amount here?" He pointed to a partial red box. "Six months ago."

"There's a 'LUX' showing near the torn edge," Wallace said.

Santana nodded. "Probably a partial name of the company."

"The ticket could've belonged to the vic," Tanabe said.

"Or to the perp," Santana said.

Chapter 2

While Kacie Hawkins remained at the crime scene, Santana logged into the Automated Property System from his office computer at the Law Enforcement Center and typed in the item number listed on the pawn ticket.

The APS is an online listing of items sold to Minnesota and Wisconsin pawnshops and is owned and operated by the Minneapolis PD. The SPPD and other departments throughout the state pay a fee to access the information. Each night pawn stores in dozens of cities upload transaction information—which usually includes a person's photo and driver's license data—to APS computers. APS then checks serial numbers of pawned items against stolen property listed at the National Crime Information Center. A list of hits is sent daily to police in the city where the possible theft happened.

Santana remembered that before the APS, law enforcement agencies had to physically check inventory taken in by pawnshops and then check the inventory against recent stolen property reports to see if there was a match. It could take hours. And pawnshops lost whatever they paid for stolen property confiscated by police. Though pawnshops across the state had initially fought the establishment of the system, they soon realized that dealing in stolen property was bad for business. They didn't want stolen items in their stores. Because of APS, pawnshops were now one of the worst places to bring stolen goods.

Santana wasn't sure if the partial pawn ticket found underneath the body in the cave had been written for a stolen item, or if it would lead him to the murder victim, to the killer, or to both. But it was the only lead he had.

According to the APS, six months ago a man named Trevor Dane had pawned a Rolex watch that matched the item number on the pawn ticket at a shop in Bloomington, Minnesota. Santana logged off and drove to the north side of the Mall of America in Bloomington.

Luxury Loan was located on the second floor behind a set of smoked glass windows. A long counter case held gleaming bracelets, rings, and watches. Glass framed artworks hung on the walls.

Standing behind the counter was a tall, thin man with razor-cut silver hair and a carefully-trimmed silver mustache. He wore a gray pinstriped suit and pale gray tie with a lavender shirt and pocket-handkerchief, and a pair of gold cufflinks. To his right was an Apple laptop computer. On a shelf behind the man was a solid gold hourglass. Instead of sand trickling through the narrow neck, what appeared to be small diamonds dropped from the upper to the bottom bulb.

"This doesn't look like any pawnshop I've ever seen," Santana said.

"The term 'pawnshop' tends to conjure up mental images of a seedy strip mall storefront dealing in antique jewelry," the man said. "That's why we don't use the term to describe the company."

Santana gestured toward the hourglass on the shelf. "Those real diamonds?"

"Yes, sir, they are. Thirty-five carets' worth." He touched the top of the hourglass with a manicured hand. "It's made by Cartier. Are you interested in the piece?" He spoke in a soft voice, without inflection or excitement, as though he were selling a package of gum rather than something worth thousands of dollars.

"Something else," Santana said, opening his badge wallet.

The man looked at the badge for a second and then at Santana again. His eyes were the color of dark chocolate. "My name is Thomas, Detective Santana. How can I help you?"

"Is Thomas your first name or last?"

"I'm Thomas Renslow. I own the store."

Santana took a copy of Trevor Dane's contract from an inner pocket of his sport coat, placed it on the counter, and turned it 180 degrees so that Renslow could read it. "You took in a Rolex watch six months ago."

Renslow's eyes shifted off Santana's face to the paperwork on the counter. Santana waited until Renslow looked at him again and then tapped the agreement with a forefinger. "Do you remember anything about Trevor Dane, the man who pawned the watch?"

Renslow peered at the photo ID on the contract for a moment and then shifted his gaze to Santana. "Yes, I believe I do recall him." Renslow's fingers raced across the computer keys. A few seconds later he said, "About ninety percent of our clients pay off their loan and reclaim their merchandise within the period of the contract. Mr. Dane was among the ten percent who did not. Some never intend to pay off the loan. They just need the money. I can't tell you why he failed to reclaim the watch, only that it was a woman's watch."

"A woman's watch?"

"Yes. Perhaps it was a gift for a wife or girlfriend. Perhaps the relationship didn't work out and the watch was returned to Mr. Dane. We take in quite a few engagement and wedding rings and resell many of them."

"You wouldn't have the lady's name in your records?"

He shook his head. "No. I'm afraid not. You'll have to ask Mr. Dane why he chose to sell the watch."

"I intend to. Do you still have the watch?"

"Unfortunately, no. It was sold a few weeks ago."

"Who was the buyer?"

"We pride ourselves on discretion, Detective."

"I can come back with a warrant."

Renslow took some time processing the thought and then looked at the computer screen again. "The watch was sold one month ago." He smiled at Santana. "If we don't receive a payment for sixty days, we're allowed to sell the merchandise. It's the law."

"I know the law, Mr. Renslow."

"Of course you do. But perhaps you're unaware that we offer loans from fifty dollars to one million dollars. In most cases, taking a loan on the merchandise is cheaper than selling the valuables outright. If you sell an asset, you lose thirty percent of the value in the costs of selling. The Rolex in question was one of the less expensive ones. Mr. Dane took a loan of forty-five hundred dollars."

"The name of the buyer who bought the Rolex."

"Oh, yes." Renslow wrote the name on a piece of paper and handed it to Santana.

Santana wasn't sure that he would need the name, but now he had it, just in case. "Thanks for your time, Mr. Renslow."

"One moment, Detective."

Santana waited.

"What kind of detective are you?"

"Homicide."

"Was Mr. Dane murdered?"

"I hope not."

"But someone was. Someone connected to the watch."

"Have a good day, Mr. Renslow."

* * *

After Santana left the pawnshop, he called Hawkins and briefed her on the information he'd found regarding Trevor Dane. Then he asked, "You get the names of the two guys who found the body in the cave?"

"One second."

Santana could hear Hawkins flipping pages in her notebook.

"You want both?"

"No, pick one for me. You can interview the other one."

"Try Albert Greer." Hawkins recited his address and cell phone number. "I'll take Cory Brown."

Before meeting with Greer, Santana checked the Computerized Criminal History (CCH) System, which is the state's central repository for data on persons arrested for felony, gross misdemeanor, and enhanced misdemeanors—previous charges and arrests for the same offense that can bump a defendant up a degree if charged again.

What Santana discovered about Albert Greer surprised and intrigued him.

Greer answered his cell and agreed to meet Santana at the towing and service company in St. Paul where he worked. A half-hour later, they sat across from each other at a wooden employee picnic table out back.

Greer was a stork-like young black man with large ears and a weak chin and handshake. His hair was razor cut on the sides and short on top. A label with his name was stitched above one pocket of his work shirt. Grease had collected under his fingernails.

Long afternoon shadows smudged the green grass. Dry leaves blown by a light wind scraped across the parking lot, like bony fingers on a casket lid.

"How long have you worked here, Albert?"

"Well, two . . ."

Santana watched him figuring the calculation in his head.

"No," he said. "I take that back. Almost three years now."

"Where did you work before your job here?"

"A couple of fast food places after high school. But I've always liked cars."

"What kind of car do you drive?"

"An older Chevy Camaro."

"Fast car."

"It's a classic. Purrs like a kitten. Babes love it. But I don't plan on working here much longer."

"Really."

"Yeah. I'm going to college." His eyes flitted back and forth like bugs under glass.

"Where?"

"Not sure just yet. I figure I'll get a scholarship 'cause I'm pretty smart. Scored high on my ACTs. I used to let the good-looking girls copy my homework."

"That right?"

"Yep," he said, not making eye contact.

"Why didn't you go to college after high school?"

"Wasn't sure what I wanted to study."

"But you know now."

"Sure do."

Santana waited.

"Engineering," Greer said.

"Railroad?"

Greer laughed. "You're a funny guy. Like a civil engineer. You know, the people who build things. I'm good with my hands."

"You like working with your hands."

He held them up for Santana to see. "Sure do. These are a man's hands."

They *were* large for his size. Probably could hold a basketball in one of them—or someone's neck.

"Where do you live, Albert?"

Greer's gaze slid off Santana's face. "At home with my mother," he said softly. He stared into space for a time before his eyes met Santana's again. "But I'm getting my own place soon. Guy my age shouldn't be living with his mother."

"What does your mother do?"

"Oh, she's a surgeon at Regions Hospital. She wanted me to become a doctor, too. I probably will someday."

"What about civil engineering?"

"Guy can have two careers in a lifetime, right?"

"I suppose."

"Bet you've always been a cop."

"I have."

"Ever think of doing something else?"

Santana had been thinking about a career change recently, but he didn't confess that to Albert Greer. "I'm good at what I do."

"Hey, Detective, I'm good at what I do, too. Doesn't mean I'm always gonna to be doing it."

"Your father doesn't live with the two of you?" Santana said, changing the subject and re-taking control of the conversation.

"He's an asshole. Left home when I was five. Don't know where he is now and don't care." Greer's lips were pressed together in anger.

"How old are you, Albert?"

"Twenty-three."

"How long have you known Cory Brown?"

"A few years."

"High school pal?"

He shook his head. "There's a club called the Underground Explorers. I found it online and joined. Cory is a member. We've been in most of the caves and tunnels that run under St. Paul and Minneapolis."

"You're aware of how dangerous that can be?"

"Sure. But danger increases the thrill of it."

The way Greer spoke about it—and the nearly rapturous look he had on his face—suggested that the explorations were the highlight of an otherwise dull life.

"What does your friend Cory do for a living?"

"He's working at a fast food joint and going to technical college." Greer fixed his eyes on Santana. "You've been in the tunnels under the city?"

"I have."

Greer perked up. "Where?"

Recalling a murder case he'd once worked involving a terrorist plot, Santana said, "Under the streets of St. Paul."

"Oh, yeah. Cool." He stared off into space, as if remembering or imagining.

"What were you doing in the cave the day you and your friend found the remains buried in the sand?" Santana asked.

"Exploring."

"You do that often?"

He nodded.

"Which one of you discovered the body?"

"I saw the hand first. We thought someone was playing a joke, you know? We didn't think there was a whole skeleton buried there. But we decided to call the police."

"You did the right thing."

"Sure did. We got our picture in the *Pioneer Press*. You see it?"

"I haven't."

Greer looked disappointed. "Oh. Well, with Halloween coming up soon, the talk shows in town have invited us to come on. Never been on television before. Never had my picture in the paper either. It's like being a celebrity." He grinned with excitement.

"Anything else unusual you noticed that day?" Santana asked.

"Like what?"

"That's what I'm asking you."

Greer appeared to be thinking about it. Then he shook his head. "Nope. Nothing else."

"Ever been in that particular cave before?"

Greer looked away. "Don't think so."

Santana waited, figuring Greer would be uncomfortable with the silence.

Finally Greer shrugged and made brief eye contact. "Lotta caves look alike. Could've been in that one before. But if I was, I didn't see any hand sticking out of the ground."

Santana looked at his notebook and what he'd written down while searching the CCH database. "You have an interesting history, Albert: burglary in the fourth degree, possession of marijuana, resisting arrest, domestic assault with a firearm."

"Hey, I had an argument with my mother. She overreacted and called the cops. I forfeited the weapon. The burglary and dope arrests happened when I was younger. I'm a changed man now."

"Perhaps you are," Santana said. "But you were also charged with criminal sexual conduct."

Greer's mouth hung open for a moment before he ran his tongue over his dry lips and anger replaced the shock on his face. "I was eighteen. We were dating. I didn't know she was fifteen at the time. Thought she was sixteen. They sent me to treatment is all."

In Minnesota the legal name for the crime of rape and sexual assault is "criminal sexual conduct." The state has five degrees, or levels, of criminal sexual conduct that vary based on the unlawful sexual activity and the age of the victim.

Albert Greer had been charged with fourth-degree criminal sexual conduct and could have been sentenced to imprisonment for not more than ten years or to a payment of a fine of not more than $20,000, or both. Mistaking the victim's age is not a defense. But if the court had deemed that Greer and the complainant had had a "relationship," the judge could stay the prison sentence and/or fine and require him to complete a treatment program, which Greer had done.

"You're a registered sex offender, Albert."

"That don't mean I killed anybody."

True, Santana thought. The charge itself was no proof that Greer had become a killer. But it, along with Greer's fascination with women and fast cars, created suspicion in Santana's mind.

He handed Greer a business card. "You let me know if something occurs to you."

"Sure, Detective," Greer said.

Santana handed him his notebook and a pen. "Write down your work number."

Greer picked up the pen with his left hand and wrote it down. As he passed the notebook and pen back to Santana, he said, "That woman we found. She was murdered, huh?"

"We believe so."

"How'd she die?"

"Can't say."

"Then how is it a homicide?"

"Thanks for your time, Albert."

Greer looked at the card in his hand and then stood up. "Always here to help, Detective."

* * *

Santana returned to the LEC and sat down at his desk to write his preliminary report. Pinned to a partition that separated his desk from those of his colleagues was a photo of Santana and his late girlfriend, Jordan Parrish, taken on his boat at the St. Croix marina in Hudson, Wisconsin. She was sitting on his lap with an arm around his shoulder, her head tilted against his. They were both smiling, unaware of what fate had in store.

Santana still had her phone number in his contact list. He could not bring himself to delete it.

There were also photos of murder victims from unsolved murder cases pinned to the partitions on three sides of his desk. They were a constant reminder of unfinished business and justice not yet served.

As investigating officer, he began filling in the IO's chronological record. The CR, along with his preliminary report, summaries of interviews, death investigation and autopsy reports, evidence inventories, and crime scene photos would become part of the murder book, if the victim's remains could be identified and if she had, in fact, been murdered.

When possible, he wrote his preliminary report the same day as the incident, or within twenty-four hours. Keeping good notes made the process easier. Waiting made it harder to remember all the details.

Computers and computerized reports had greatly improved the speed and efficiency of a process that had once involved handwriting or using a typewriter and white-out to complete a report. But computers and spellcheck couldn't improve a grammatically incorrect and poorly-written report. Having referenced murder books compiled by other detectives over the years, Santana understood the importance of being concise and accurate.

And while technology could be helpful, he knew through experience that clues leading to the killer, and to the solution of the murder, were often buried somewhere within the pages of the murder book, and that instinct and old-fashioned police work usually led to the perpetrator's capture.

Chapter 3

Santana awoke abruptly before sunrise, the sheets balled in his fists, calling Jordan's name in the darkness. He'd come out of the nightmare with the scent of her perfume fresh in his mind, but he could not hold that fragrance, leaving him with the sour smell of his night sweat and the memory of her tragic death.

He'd fallen into a familiar pattern—a pattern he'd periodically experienced since the age of sixteen—in which tortuous nightmares invaded his sleep. Reacting defensively to the terrors that awaited in sleep, his mind kept him awake for long stretches until, exhausted, he fell into a deep sleep, only to be jarred awake again by a nightmare.

Karen Wong, the private therapist who worked with the SPPD in officer-involved shootings and who had counseled Santana in the past, would tell him he needed to assuage the guilt he felt in his waking hours over Jordan's death. But that was easier said than done.

He waited until his heart slowed and then got out of bed and went to the glass door that opened onto the second-floor deck of his home. The house sat on two heavily wooded acres of birch and pine on a secluded bluff overlooking the St. Croix River, the natural boundary between Minnesota and Wisconsin.

Light from the full moon glossed the river's flat surface and the ragged shapes of the trees. Only the icy, distant glimmer of a few stars was visible. He'd been in such a daze of desolation for the past two months, moving through life like a sleepwalker through a dream, that he'd taken little notice of the world around him.

He saw life now as a journey from one empty blackness to another. Raging against a God he believed did not exist was as futile as screaming in the void of outer space. He could see no meaning in the suffering that was so much a part of the human experience. Anger was the engine that drove him. Anger not only for all that he'd lost in his life, but anger because he hadn't saved those closest to him.

He'd always believed that he would die young. But to his surprise—and regret—it was those closest to him who had died. He was left alive, unable to justify his survival. Yet he feared death no more than an animal fears it. Such a fate seemed like a welcome relief.

For years, finding justice in an unjust world had kept him moving forward. Solving each mystery presented to him was his mission, his purpose, and perhaps, even his redemption. He'd hoped that directing his anger against those who had murdered the innocent would offer some relief, but it had not. He would always carry with him the unspeakable things he'd seen and experienced as a homicide detective. The dark memories were the price he paid for being skilled at his job, for choosing this profession.

Now he felt as if this burden was too much, that even his search for justice could not save him from the terrible hollowness of incomprehensible loss, could not save him from the darkness and the angry caged demon inside him that sought vengeance. He feared what he might become, the ease with which he might embrace vengeance and call it justice.

When the dawn broke, Santana changed into a running suit and shoes and took his golden retriever, Gitana, or "Gypsy" in Spanish, out for their morning run. He'd adopted her after her owner had been killed during an investigation. She'd saved his life on at least two occasions and seemed to sense Jordan's loss and the deepening darkness in Santana's soul. Always one to stay close to him, she rarely let him out of her sight now. He welcomed her companionship and emotional support, her unconditional love, and the laughter she often drew out of him. Outside of his sister, Natalia, who lived in Spain, Gitana was the only family he had.

After his run, Santana showered and ate an *arepa* with scrambled eggs and hot chocolate. He'd just arrived to his desk at the LEC when his department cell phone rang.

"I've got an ID on the skeletal remains," Rob Wallace said. "The vic's dental records were entered into NamUs. I believe we've found the remains of a woman named Kim Austin."

"I'll be there soon," Santana said.

Santana disconnected and logged on to NamUs, the Department of Justice's National Missing and Unidentified System. Medical examiners, coroners, law enforcement officials, and the general public can search the free online system. There are three databases. The Unidentified Persons database contains information entered by medical examiners and coroners. Deceased persons who have been identified by name, but for whom no next of kin or family member have been identified to claim the body, are entered into the Unclaimed database. Santana was interested in the Missing Persons database. It contained information that could be entered by anyone, but before it appears as a case on NamUs, the information has to be verified. When a new missing person or unidentified decedent case is entered into NamUs, the system automatically performs cross-matching comparisons between the databases, searching for matches or similarities between cases.

Santana found Kim Austin's name in the missing persons database along with her photo. She'd been a very attractive African-American woman. A few weeks after Austin's disappearance, a woman named Elisha Austin had entered information—

including dental records—into NamUs. Santana figured she was Kim Austin's mother, or perhaps a sister.

He ran a copy of Kim Austin's photo. Then he called Kacie Hawkins and gave her the information. Hawkins told him she would run a background check on Austin and let him know what she found.

* * *

Santana drove to Rob Wallace's lab located in the Midwest Medical Examiner's Office in Anoka, Minnesota. Color framed photos of Wallace with Hollywood actors and actresses hung on his office walls, along with his diplomas and newspaper clippings of big cases he'd consulted on.

As they stood beside the skeletal remains now lying on the autopsy table, Santana said, "You have an educated guess as to how long the body was in the ground?"

"Well, we know that exposure to climate accelerates the PMI," Wallace said, alluding to the postmortem interval, or the amount of time from death to decomposition. "When I was studying at the Body Farm in Tennessee, we had bodies in the summer heat that were skeletonized in as little as two weeks. But in the cave, the body was protected from some of the elements." Wallace paused and held a smile on his face, offering Santana an opportunity to be impressed.

Santana had also been to the University of Tennessee's Forensic Anthropology Research Facility, better known as the Body Farm, but unlike Wallace, he didn't wear it as a badge of honor. Forensic anthropologist William Bass had established the facility in 1980 in order to study the rate of decomposition of human corpses under various conditions. His findings were crucial in driving forensic investigation into unsolved deaths.

"It was a shallow grave in the cave, and there were no other bodies," Wallace continued, his face registering disappointment at Santana's failure to be impressed. "The fewer the bodies, the faster the rate of decomposition." Then, in the way of an explanation, he added, "In mass graves, where bodies are usually packed very tightly and there's little oxygen to promote the growth of organisms and decomposition, the bodies can stay well preserved."

Santana recalled that Wallace had begun his career working with the ICMP, or International Commission for Missing Persons, in Bosnia-Herzegovina, exhuming bodies from mass graves. Thousands of remains had been recovered. Identifying the deceased and returning them to grieving families had been difficult given the lack of documents, distinctive clothing, or personal belongings. So Wallace and others had relied on DNA as the chief means of estimating age and gender.

Santana imagined the experience had left its mark on Wallace, as death had left its mark on him. But it had also given Wallace training and skills that few possessed. The experience had added additional hot air to the inflated balloon that was his ego.

"The wound to the skull measures approximately four inches high by five and one-half inches wide," Wallace said. "Injury appears to have resulted from a single blow administered to the posterior of the head, delivered at an approximate ninety-degree angle to the occipital bone. The bone breakage patterns are similar to antemortem trauma but show no healing. Because the bone was still green, or fresh, when the trauma occurred, the fracture edges are sharp and clean. Dry bone fractures typically have more jagged or torn-looking edges with random patterns of breakage. The fracture edges of postmortem breaks also look lighter in color than perimortem injuries because they've been exposed for shorter periods."

"So the injury to the head occurred at the time of death," Santana said. "And the blow was hard enough to kill her."

"I believe so."

"Was there any evidence of torture?"

Wallace shook his head.

Santana wrote the information in his notebook.

"There's also a chauffeur's fracture to the distal radius of the right arm," Wallace said.

"Chauffeur's fracture?"

"People who used to crank their cars to start the engine sometimes received a blow to the wrist when the engine backfired and the crank whipped around in the opposite direction and whacked them on the wrist. A fracture like this is associated with severe trauma."

Wallace pointed to the skeletal left arm. "Antemortem trauma is also evident in the shaft near the distal, or far end, of the left radius."

Santana could see that the larger of the two lower left arm bones was crooked, several inches from the top.

"The broken bone has completely joined back together, indicating that the break happened long before Austin died, probably when she was a child. The information about that injury was also in the NamUs database."

Wallace fisted his hands on his hips, his belly straining against the buttons of his lab coat. A big smile was pasted on his flabby face. "You solve the vic's murder, Detective, it'd make a hell of an episode on the series I'm consulting on. I might even be able to snare you a small role. Good-looking guy like you, who knows? Could be your ticket to a whole new career."

"Thanks, but no thanks. Working homicide, I've met enough perps that were great actresses and actors, enough to last a lifetime."

Chapter 4

After leaving Rob Wallace's office, Santana called Kacie Hawkins and asked her to run a background check on Kim Austin. The next person Santana wanted to interview was Trevor Dane, the man who had pawned the expensive woman's watch.

According to the driver's license information on the Luxury Loan contract, Trevor Dane lived in Minneapolis. Before driving to the residence, Santana ran a Google search on Dane and was surprised by the amount of information available.

Trevor Dane had graduated from Northwestern University with a degree in economics and a minor in mathematics. He moved to Tokyo, Japan, to join a Japanese securities house as a research analyst, where he became fluent in Japanese. Two years later he was appointed the Tokyo correspondent for the *Economist* magazine and the *Financial Times*. For the next five years Dane published articles about the economies, companies, and leaders of Asian countries. He interviewed a number of major figures in the region, including China's premier, the prime minister of Japan, and the president of the Philippines.

Dane then moved to New York as the US editor of a major business magazine. After three years with the magazine, he was hired by a large investment bank to build a new division in international equities. Later, he was promoted and transferred to London to head up the sales and trading of Japanese equity derivatives in Europe and the Middle East. Two years later he left to set up a brokerage firm in Minneapolis, which became a top performer in the industry.

Dane's residence was located in a century-old four-story factory building. A decade ago the aged brick and wood floors had been meticulously restored and the building converted from industry to expensive condos and business offices.

The receptionist on the ground floor asked Santana if he had an appointment with Mr. Dane. Santana showed her his badge. She made a quick call and then directed him to the top floor. He took the stairs rather than the elevator for exercise. The steps creaked despite the renovations.

When he reached the fourth floor, he came to a set of wooden double doors with glass panels. A plaque on the wall to the right of the doors displayed the words:

DANE BROKERAGE FIRM

Santana walked into a large office suite, where a second woman in an expensive pinstriped pants suit met him. In the outer office there were four desks. Young men talking into headsets occupied three of them. Their sleeves were rolled up to their elbows, and their suit coats hung over the backs of their chairs. *Working hard* was the obvious message.

Santana assumed the empty desk belonged to the woman. Given the address on Dane's license, it was clear that he lived and worked in the same building.

"This way, Detective," the woman said.

They walked between two desks to a thick wooden door. The woman opened it and stepped to the side. Santana entered.

Trevor Dane was seated cross-legged on a light blue sofa in front of a glassed-in fireplace. A large black leather ottoman served as a coffee table. On an end table was a sculpted, white stone Buddha.

Dane was nodding as he listened to a phone conversation on his cell. He was lean of frame and wore a silk shirt, open at the collar, a pair of expensive-looking suit pants, and black loafers with no socks. The sleeves of his white shirt, like those worn by his colleagues in the outer office, were rolled up to his elbows. His suit coat was draped over the back of the couch.

Sensing Santana's presence, he turned his head.

Santana held up his badge wallet. He was certain Dane couldn't read the ID from where he sat, but he could see the badge.

Dane covered the phone with one hand and held up an index finger, indicating he would be just a minute.

Santana's eyes scanned the dark hardwood floor and exposed brick walls. Surrealistic artwork hung on a white wall that stretched twenty feet from the top of the fireplace to the beamed ceiling dotted with spotlights.

One of the surrealistic paintings intrigued Santana. It depicted the silhouetted back of a man walking toward a blazing campfire in the clearing of a forest. He was wearing a trench coat, talking on a cell phone, and carrying a briefcase. The top halves of the pine trees were tall skyscrapers reaching toward a full moon in the nighttime sky.

Hanging on the opposite wall was a large hunting bow Santana estimated to be at least six and a half feet in length.

Dane finished his call, rose to his feet, and gestured toward the sofa. "Have a seat, Detective . . ."

"Santana."

"And you're with the Minneapolis PD?" Dane said.

"St. Paul."

Dane waited until Santana sat on the sofa across from him before he sat down. "Mind showing me your badge again?"

Santana held up his badge wallet once more.

Dane leaned forward, his gaze locked on the ID opposite the badge. Then he sat back and said, "So what can I do for you, Detective? Interested in an investment?" He gave a silent chuckle as if laughing at his private joke.

Santana took his notebook and pen out of an inner pocket. "What exactly does your brokerage firm do, Mr. Dane?" Santana asked, taking control of the conversation.

"We facilitate the purchase and sales of financial securities between a buyer and a seller. Our clientele consists primarily of investors who trade public stocks and other securities, usually through one of the firm's agent stockbrokers." Given Dane's bio, it appeared that he was doing very well financially.

"Was there something else you wanted to see me about, Detective?"

Santana placed the copy of the pawnshop document on the ottoman. "Six months ago you pawned a Rolex watch at a shop in the Mall of America."

The statement appeared to surprise Dane, judging by his raised eyebrows and wide-eyed look. "Yes, I did," he said. His dark eyes remained fastened on Santana. They reminded him of the glass eyes in a stuffed, mounted animal.

"Who did the watch belong to?"

"It belonged to me."

"A woman's watch?"

"Well, initially I purchased it for my girlfriend at the time."

"And what was her name?"

"Kim Austin. But we broke up six months ago. She returned the watch."

"Is that normal?"

"How do you mean?"

"When you break up with a woman, does she usually return the jewelry you bought her?"

"I wouldn't know. I don't always buy my girlfriends jewelry."

"Had quite a few girlfriends?"

"I've had my share," he said with a smirk.

Santana moved on. "You said Kim Austin returned the watch you bought for her."

He shrugged. "We had fight. She was upset."

"You never spoke or saw each other after your breakup six months ago?"

"Never did. But even when we were dating, we often didn't see each other for long stretches."

"Why was that?"

"Kim lives in DC. I'd see her when she was in town or whenever I could get to DC."

"What did she do for a living?"

Dane paused and stared at Santana. "You just asked me what Kim *did* for a living. Now you're here questioning me. What happened?"

"We believe her remains were discovered yesterday."

Dane said nothing, just stared into space, his face an emotionless blank slate.

Santana never knew what to expect in these situations, so he wasn't completely surprised by Dane's response—or lack of one. People reacted in different ways when told of the death of a friend, a loved one, or in this case, a former girlfriend. Still, he watched Dane closely, looking for tells, before asking his next question.

"What did Ms. Austin do for a living?" Santana asked once more.

Dane didn't reply.

"Mr. Dane?"

His gaze reconnected with Santana. "She worked for the NTSB."

"The National Transportation Safety Board."

"Yes. That's why we didn't see each other often. Besides living in DC, she traveled quite a bit."

"How did you two meet?"

"She was here in town visiting her mother."

"Where in town does her mother live?"

"In St. Paul, I believe. I'm not exactly sure where."

"How long were you two dating before the breakup?"

"A little over a year."

"You dated for over a year but don't know where your girlfriend's mother lives?"

"Never was invited to her house."

Santana thought that was unusual. Then again, not all mothers liked the men their daughters or sons were dating.

"You find that strange, Detective?"

"I do."

"I'm a Buddhist. Kim's mother is a strict Catholic. She didn't approve of our relationship."

"Is that why you broke up?"

Dane started to answer and then stopped. "I don't have to answer that, Detective."

"You don't have to answer any of my questions, Mr. Dane."

He suppressed a smile. "But if I don't, you'll consider me a suspect. Right?"

"I didn't say Ms. Austin had been murdered."

"Well," Dane said with a nervous laugh. "You're a homicide detective. What am I supposed to think?"

"Would you happen to have a recent photo of Ms. Austin?" Santana asked, ignoring Dane's question.

"I'm afraid I don't."

"What was her mother's name?"

"Elisha."

"Elisha Austin?"

"Yes." Dane's gaze shifted to the pawn ticket on the counter and then quickly back to Santana. "Where did you get the pawn ticket?"

Santana had no intention of telling Dane a piece of the pawn ticket had been found at the crime scene—at least not yet.

"A Rolex is a very expensive gift, Mr. Dane."

"Kim liked nice things. I tried to impress her. It was my mistake."

"Why did you pawn the watch?"

"I needed some quick cash."

"You never bothered to buy it back."

"I told Kim I would."

Dane's comment piqued Santana's interest. "She knew that you'd pawned her watch?"

Dane let out a long breath. "It wasn't her watch."

"But you gave it to her as a gift."

"I did. But she gave it back when we argued. A couple days later we got together and talked. I thought things were smoothed out. And then, when she asked where the watch was, I had to tell her I pawned it."

"What happened?"

"I showed her the pawn ticket and told her I'd buy it back. She got real angry. The ticket tore when she grabbed it out of my hand." Dane paused as his dark eyes lit with recognition. "That's how you found out about the pawn ticket, isn't it?"

"How's that?"

"You must've found a piece of the pawn ticket on Kim's body."

Santana remained silent, waiting for Dane to fill in the conversation void.

"That's why you're here. You think I killed Kim."

"I never said that."

"You don't have to, Detective. I get it. But I had no reason to kill Kim."

"Sometimes things get out of control when lovers argue, Mr. Dane."

"And most of the time they don't."

Dane's gaze continued to focus on Santana. Then he said, "You're not originally from the States. I'm guessing somewhere in South America."

"Colombia."

"Ah," he said with a satisfied smile. "The home of Fernando Botero, one of my favorite painters."

Santana gestured toward the white wall above the fireplace. "I see you also like surrealistic art."

"I do." He made a sweeping gesture with a movement of his hand, indicating the walls. "Modern artists rather than the masters like Dalí painted these. I'd love to have one of his paintings hanging on my walls, though some of these young artists are very good."

"I understand you speak Japanese?"

"I'm a bit rusty. I need to get back to Japan again soon and brush up."

Santana's eyes drifted to the large bow on the wall. "You into archery, Mr. Dane?"

Dane tracked Santana's eyes. "I was when I lived in Japan. I studied the martial art of archery, or *Kyūdō*. The bow you're looking at is called a *yumi* in Japanese."

"Were you any good?"

"I wasn't bad. But to the Japanese, *Kyūdō* is more than just shooting an arrow at a target. The goal is to reach a state of *shin zen bi*. Truth, goodness, beauty."

"And how do you achieve this goal?"

"By giving oneself completely to the shooting. *Munen musō*. No thoughts, no illusions. In *Kyūdō*, true shooting is that of no deceit."

"So every shot is devoted to getting closer to the truth."

"Yes. Exactly."

"You buy your girlfriend a Rolex watch. You collect art and, by all appearances, have lots of money. How do you square that circle with Buddhism?"

"You've studied Buddhism?"

Santana shook his head. "Just picked up a few things in my experiences, such as the belief that you can't attain real happiness from things that are impermanent."

"Ah, yes. Craving for pleasures produces karma. Thus, the endless cycle of death and rebirth."

"Takes longer to reach nirvana that way, huh, Mr. Dane?"

"Have you reached it, Detective?"

"Not in this life."

"Then perhaps you shouldn't judge others."

"I generally leave the judging to the courts. But I do understand that no matter what religion you practice, killing is wrong."

"Are you accusing me of killing Kim?"

"Not unless you'd like to confess."

Dane offered a half-smile. "Let me ask you something, Detective." He pointed to the paintings on the walls. "Is beauty objective or subjective?"

"I consider myself an objective person."

"I assumed that given your profession. Facts are objective rather than subjective. But there's more to truth than just the facts. Truth often depends on a person's perspective and experience. Just because you believe something is true doesn't make it so. I'm sure, given your profession, you totally understand that."

"What I understand is that facts can answer the questions of where, when, and how, Mr. Dane. Only truths can tell us why."

* * *

Before driving home, Santana stopped at a shop called Mr. Knife Guy on St. Paul's East Side. Paul Munson, an Iraqi War vet, owned the store.

Santana had first met Paul Munson in a homeless shelter while investigating the murder of another Iraqi War vet. At the time Munson had had a thick black beard and scraggly long hair, which hid much of his handsome face. He'd kept the beard, though now it was neatly trimmed and much shorter, as was his dark hair. Santana had known the previous owner of the shop and had gotten Munson a job. When the owner retired, Munson had purchased the business and kept the name.

"Hey, John," Munson said with a wide grin as Santana entered the store. "Good to see you. It's been a while."

"It has," Santana said. "You doing well?"

"Business is good. Life is good."

Gone were the wind-burns on Munson's once weather-beaten face and the empty look in his eyes that had seen more tragedy and death than most men twice his age had seen. Gone, too, was the nervous tic in the corner of Munson's mouth, as though he were making a half-smile. Still, the ghosts that haunted Munson's soul would always be with him, as were the ghosts that haunted Santana's.

"What can I do for you, John?"

Santana took out his department cell phone and showed Munson the photo he'd taken of the dagger impaled in Kim Austin's hand. "You sell anything like this?"

Munson peered at the photo and shook his head.

"Know anyone who does?"

"I'm sure you can buy it online. But I've never sold a dagger quite like this." Munson peered at the photo once more. Then his eyes found Santana's. "That's a real hand it's stuck through, isn't it?"

Santana nodded. "Anything you can tell me about the dagger?"

Munson held up the phone and expanded the size of the photo with a thumb and index finger. "It's looks like tantō."

"That a type of dagger?"

"Uh-huh. The blade can be single or double edged, generally between six to twelve inches. The dagger was designed primarily as a stabbing weapon, but it can be used for slashing as well."

Munson set the phone on the counter, so Santana could see the photo, and ran an index finger along the blade. "They're usually forged without a ridgeline and are nearly flat. Samurai carried them."

Santana looked at him. "It's a Japanese dagger?"

"Yes," Munson said.

Santana recalled his recent visit with Trevor Dane and their discussion of Buddhism and Japanese archery. He wondered if Dane had a collection of daggers, too, and if one was missing.

Chapter 5

It had rained briefly just before dawn, and the city streets were still cool with morning shadow. Santana could smell the wet pavement and the dank odor of the brick and concrete buildings as he walked into the Law Enforcement Center and took the elevator to the SPPD's Homicide and Robbery Unit on the second floor of the Griffin Building, just northeast of downtown. A skyway connected it to the Ramsey County Sheriff's Department. The two buildings were referred to as the LEC.

The detectives assigned to the Homicide Unit each had a separate desk. All were located in a large common work area, which was separated from the rest of the floor by sound partitions. Only the most senior detective and the commander, Pete Romano, had separate offices.

Santana was the last of the homicide detectives to arrive for the weekly murder meetings led by Romano. The detectives sat at a large rectangular table in the center of the room, murder books and files and cups filled with coffee set out in front of them. Each detective in turn would update the cases they were working.

Murder meetings were the brainchild of the previous homicide commander, Rita Gamboni. She now worked as a liaison to the FBI, but Romano had recently reinstituted the practice.

Santana nodded at Kacie Hawkins as he sat down beside her.

"Good morning, Detective," Romano said, a tight smile on his face.

A clock on the wall behind Romano read 8:05 a.m. Santana knew that under normal circumstances, Romano would chew him out for being even five minutes late. But since Jordan's death, he and the rest of the detectives had been tiptoeing around him as though he were an eggshell.

He hated this awkwardness in his partner and his colleagues, the pity he saw in their eyes, though he realized it came from a genuine sense of compassion. His colleagues were kind to him, but he wondered sometimes if they also felt uncomfortable around him because he reminded them of their own mortality.

He'd never been a joiner, never been one to cultivate many friendships. Still, he knew he'd become more isolated than ever since Jordan's death, refusing all offers of dinner and companionship outside of the job.

Romano called on the first detective to his right and then worked his way around the table until he came to the last two detectives, Santana and Hawkins. "I believe the skeletal remains found in the cave near the Mississippi yesterday belonged to a woman named Kim Austin," Santana said.

"How did you arrive at that conclusion?" Romano asked.

Santana explained that Kim Austin had been missing for six months. Austin's mother had uploaded her daughter's dental records to the NamUs database. Rob Wallace had used that information to match the teeth in the skeletal remains. Under the "body details" section, her mother had added that Austin had also broken the radius bone in her left arm when she was younger, which made identification easier.

Romano clasped his hands over his paunch and stared at Santana. "What do we know about Kim Austin?"

"I ran a background check," Hawkins said. "She was born and raised here in St. Paul in the Mac-Groveland neighborhood.

Graduated from the University of Minnesota with a degree in mechanical engineering. She got her private pilot's license, became a flight instructor, and was eventually hired by Blue Skies Airlines. She flew for them for five years and then took a job as an accident investigator with the NTSB.

"Six months ago Austin attended a security conference here in the city. The day the conference ended, she checked out of the downtown Sheraton. She had a return ticket on Delta and a rental car."

"We ever locate the car?"

"The rental was found a day after she checked out of the hotel," Hawkins said. "It was parked in the lot near the cave where her remains were found. Keys were in the ignition."

"I assume it wasn't checked for trace evidence."

"No one suspected Kim Austin had been murdered."

"Okay," Romano said. "What else?"

"When Kim Austin never returned to DC, her mother had her declared missing and entered the data into NamUs," Hawkins said. "A Google search told me that Austin worked for the NTSB as an accident investigator. I called the NTSB and asked to speak to one of Austin's colleagues. They gave me the name of Cathy Herrera. She didn't answer her extension at the NTSB, so I left a voicemail with the number for Homicide."

Romano looked down at his notes and then at Hawkins and Santana. "What about the dagger?"

"It's a Japanese tantō," Santana said. "Austin's former boyfriend, Trevor Dane, once lived in Japan and has adopted some of their culture."

"You think Dane could be good for the murder?"

"I'll take another run at him," Santana said. "See what I come up with."

"Check with the security conference organizer as well. He might remember talking to or meeting with Kim Austin." Romano looked around the table. "All right, let's hit the streets."

When Santana and Hawkins returned to their desks, Hawkins said, "I'll start with the conference organizer, see where it leads."

"Good. Ask if he has a list of conference attendees. Call the airlines, too. Find out what flights arrived from DC the day before and the day of the conference and what flights departed for DC the day the conference ended and the day after. We need the passenger information lists."

"You think whoever killed Austin flew here from DC?"

"Maybe. We'll cross-check the PILs with the list of conference participants. Might find a match or two."

"I'm on it," Hawkins said.

Santana's desk phone rang. "Homicide. Detective Santana."

"Oh," a voice said on the other end of the line. "I was returning Detective Hawkins' call. My name is Cathy Herrera."

"I'm her partner, Ms. Herrera. Are you calling about Kim Austin?"

"Yes."

Santana motioned to Hawkins and then pressed the speakerphone button so that she could hear the conversation.

"Can you tell me what happened, Detective Santana?"

"We don't know for sure, but we believe Ms. Austin was murdered."

"I was afraid of that."

"What do you mean?"

"I . . . I was just afraid that after all this time, something terrible must've happened to her."

Santana thought Cathy Herrera's initial response suggested something else, but he let it go for now.

"What's your position with NTSB?" he asked.

"I'm an accident investigator."

"Was Ms. Austin also an investigator?"

"Yes."

"So you worked together often."

"No. We're assigned on a rotational basis to respond as quickly as possible to the scene of the accident."

"So you never worked with Ms. Austin?"

"I didn't say that."

Santana waited.

"We, ah . . . did work together recently on the Blue Skies crash."

Santana remembered hearing something about the crash, but he couldn't remember the details. "How long ago was that?"

"Eight months."

"What caused the crash?" Santana asked.

"Well, the final report hasn't been released yet. But the supposition is the plane ran out of fuel."

"Ran out of fuel? How does that happen?"

"It was way off course," she said. "They had to ditch in the ocean. It didn't go well."

"So the pilots were at fault."

She didn't respond.

Santana thought for a moment that they had been disconnected. "Ms. Herrera?"

"Like I said, Detective, the final report hasn't been released yet. But I suspect the crash will be blamed on pilot error."

Santana thought he heard doubt in her voice. When he looked at Hawkins, she was shaking her head in disbelief.

"How many accident investigators were there?"

"Well, I don't remember the exact number. But we're usually separated into teams based on our expertise."

"So how many members were on your team?"

"Four."

"Is that fairly standard?"

"Not necessarily. The team can have more than a dozen specialists from the board's headquarters staff in Washington, DC. The groups are sometimes also staffed by representatives of the parties to the investigation."

"Who might that be?"

"The Federal Aviation Administration, the airline, the pilots' and flight attendants' unions, and airframe and engine manufacturers."

"You and Kim Austin make two of the four members of your team. What are the names of the other two team members?"

"Why do you want to know?"

"Kim Austin was likely murdered, Ms. Herrera. This is a homicide investigation. Maybe one of your team members has information that can help us."

"You think one of the team members murdered Kim?"

"I didn't say that. But I'd like the names."

She let out a sigh. "Barry McCarthy and Paul Westbrook."

"Was one of the four in charge of the team?"

"Yes. Paul was our group chairman."

"So he led the whole investigation?"

"No. That would be the IIC, the investigator-in-charge."

"And what was his name?"

"Terry Powell."

Santana was taking notes as he listened. "So how many groups were there?"

"Well, there was one for operations, structures, power plants, systems, air traffic control, weather, human performance, and survival factors. So eight total."

"And to which were you assigned?"

"Systems."

"What was your specific role?"

"We investigated the plane's hydraulic, electrical, pneumatic and associated systems, together with instruments and the flight control system."

"I understand the responsibilities for the groups in charge of weather, survival factors, air traffic control, and now systems. What's the role of operations?"

"They investigate the history of the flight and crewmembers' duties for as many days prior to the crash as appears relevant."

"What about structures?"

"Documenting the airframe wreckage and the accident scene, including calculation of impact angles to help determine the plane's pre-impact course and attitude."

"Power plants have to do with engines?"

"Yes. That group examined the engines, propellers, and engine accessories."

"And human performance?"

"They studied the crews' performance and all before-the-accident factors that might be involved in human error."

"Such as?"

"Fatigue, drugs or medications, medical histories, training, work load, and work environment."

"Do the members of your group all live in or around DC?"

"Yes, we do."

"You wouldn't know Paul Westbrook or Barry McCarthy's addresses or home phone numbers?"

"Sorry. I don't."

Santana wasn't certain he believed her.

"But you could call the NTSB," she said. "They'll have Barry's number."

"What about Paul Westbrook?"

"Paul resigned."

Santana and Hawkins exchanged a quick glance. "How long ago was that?"

"Five months."

"So he resigned from the NTSB a month after your colleague, Kim Austin, disappeared."

"Yes."

"Have you spoken to him at all since the crash?"

"No. I'm not sure where he is."

"How did Paul Westbrook know Ms. Austin?"

"Through work."

"Would you happen to have a photo of Mr. Westbrook?"

"I might have one with him and other members of the team on my iPhone."

"I'd appreciate it if you'd send it to me."

"All right."

Santana gave her his SPPD cell phone number and then asked, "How long had you known Ms. Austin?"

"Three years. Kim and I were both from Minnesota."

"Where in Minnesota are you from?"

"Grand Marais, not far from the Canadian border."

"Your parents still live there?"

"No. But my brother and I inherited the family cabin outside of town."

"Does your brother live in Grand Marais?"

"Yes. He owns an outdoor supply store in town."

"Did you talk to Ms. Austin about her breakup with Mr. Dane?"

"I didn't know they had broken up. Have you talked with Trevor?"

"I have."

"Then ask him."

Santana didn't think it was necessary to tell her that he had. "You ever meet Trevor Dane, Ms. Herrera?"

"I never did."

"Is Kim Austin's mother named Elisha?"

"Yes."

"Did Ms. Austin ever mention close friends she had?"

"Not that I remember."

"How about enemies?"

She paused before responding. "I don't know if Kim had enemies. But she was killed in St. Paul, not in Washington. Shouldn't you be looking for her killer there?"

"Believe me, we are, Ms. Herrera."

"Yes, of course."

"Anything else you can tell me that could help us?"

"No. I'm afraid I can't."

Santana wondered if *can't* meant she couldn't or wouldn't. "I understand Ms. Austin's mother lives here. Has she made any attempt to contact you?"

"No, she hasn't."

"Was Ms. Austin having financial problems?"

"How would I know?"

"You were her friend."

"Maybe you talk about your financial situation with your friends, Detective, but I don't."

Hawkins silently mouthed the word, "Ouch."

"Did Ms. Austin own a Rolex watch?"

"Trevor Dane gave one to her. Why?"

Santana ignored her question. "You have the number here, Ms. Herrera. If you think of anything, please give us a call."

"Certainly," she said and disconnected.

Santana hung up and turned to Hawkins. "What do you think about Herrera?"

"Something's off. She sounded like she had some doubts about the cause of the Blue Skies crash. And she's not the friendliest woman on the planet."

"We should notify Elisha Austin of her daughter's death."

"Hold on a second," Hawkins said. She got up, went to the printer, and returned with photocopies of a *St. Paul Pioneer Press* article. She handed Santana a copy and kept one for herself. The front-page headline read

BLUE SKIES AIRLINER CRASHES IN PACIFIC
ALL 217 ABOARD FEARED DEAD

"The Internet has a number of stories about the crash," Hawkins said.

Santana nodded and read the article.

"Running out of fuel," Hawkins said when she finished reading. "How do you make that mistake?"

"Maybe whoever fueled the plane screwed up?" Santana said. "The NTSB recovered the black boxes, which means they have the flight data recorder and a cockpit voice recorder. That should give investigators a clue as to what went wrong."

"What's next? The mother?"

"Let me make a call to Metropolitan Police Department in DC first," Santana said. "See if we can get a homicide detective to search Kim Austin's place."

* * *

The Macalester-Groveland area in western St. Paul is a mix of single-family homes and apartments with corner stores and commercial corridors. Students from Macalester College, the University of St. Thomas, and St. Catherine University populate the neighborhood. Scenic pedestrian and bicycle trails extend throughout the area and along the Mississippi riverfront.

Elisha Austin lived in a small bungalow on a tree-lined street in the heart of Mac-Groveland, as it's known. The house had a long sloping roof, two dormer windows, and a wide porch across the front of the house. Evergreen bushes hid the foundation, and crimson leaves from the maple trees along the curb were scattered across the small lawn.

The air smelled like the cut lawns and fresh soil of summer, rather than the shorter days of autumn. There were beds of dead flowers in front of a shaded porch. The shades were drawn over the windows facing the street. A Neighborhood Watch decal was stuck to one of the windows.

Santana knocked on the door. He and Hawkins waited.

After a short time, Hawkins said, "Maybe she's not home."

Santana pressed an ear against the door and listened. He could hear what sounded like a television or radio playing inside. He knocked, and they waited some more. When there was no answer, he tried the doorknob. It turned.

The air inside the house smelled strongly of feces.

"Backed-up toilet?" Hawkins asked.

"I don't think so."

"Me neither," she said.

Elisha Austin's body was in her bed, the covers pulled up to her head on the pillow. Only her face was visible. She'd defecated after death.

As they stood over her, Santana looked down into the void in her bloodshot eyes and then at her face, frozen with rigor. Her mouth was slightly open. Her lips were stretched and tense, with the corners drawn back. Santana recognized it as the death mask of terror.

"You thinking what I'm thinking?" Hawkins said.

Santana nodded. He understood that his partner was referring to the lighter skin around her nose and mouth, which was in contrast to the bluish discoloration of the rest of her face.

"Better call the watch commander," he said. "I'll get some crime scene tape."

Chapter 6

While Reiko Tanabe, the ME, and her crew examined the body and took photos, Santana and Hawkins searched the house. Everyone was wearing Tyvek coveralls, gloves, and booties. Some of the techs were wearing masks or using Vicks under their noses to cover the smell of feces.

Framed photos of Kim Austin as a child, teen, and adult hung on the walls of her mother's bedroom. Santana saw no photos indicating she had a brother or sister. There were no photos of a father on the beige walls. If he were still alive, he'd either not played a significant role in his daughter's life or her mother had no desire to recognize him.

Pinned to the wall beside the photos were newspaper clippings describing Kim Austin's disappearance and the futile search that had followed.

Santana slid open the closet door. A puff of sandalwood and rose greeted him and momentarily cut the stench of feces in the room. Definitely not the scent of an older woman, he thought. There were blouses and pants and simple dresses on hangers. Summer clothes were already wrapped in plastic bags. Near the back were a shoe rack and hamper for dirty clothes.

Before leaving the bedroom, Santana saw Reiko Tanabe make a small incision in the upper right abdomen of Elisha Austin's body and pass a thermometer into the tissue of the liver to get an accurate reading of the body temperature.

In the bathroom medicine cabinet Santana found blood pressure pills and assorted toiletries and makeup. The shelves under the sink held large refill bottles of soft soap and cleaning supplies. Everything was neat and orderly, even the second bedroom that was used as a scrapbooking office.

Santana pushed the message button on the answering machine. *Hi, Elisha. It's Sharon. Just wanted to thank you for the wonderful dinner last night. You're still the best cook in town. I hope you hear something positive concerning Kim's whereabouts. You're both in my thoughts and prayers. See you again soon.*

The woman named Sharon had left the message yesterday. The same day Kim Austin's body had been discovered. Santana could feel hot blood surge inside him as he listened to the message. Whoever had killed Elisha Austin had no idea that she enjoyed scrapbooking and cooking, or that she and her friend had had dinner together, and didn't care. Elisha and Kim Austin had lost their lives too soon. Santana wanted justice for them—and maybe some revenge.

He sat in a desk chair and looked through Elisha Austin's mail, bills, and bank statements. Nothing jumped out at him.

Santana found Kacie Hawkins in the living room, where the light brown carpet was worn in spots, the country-style furniture well used.

"Nothing appears out of place in the basement or kitchen," Hawkins said, standing beside him.

They slipped off their booties and placed them in a paper sack that would later be processed at the crime lab in case they had any evidence on them. They disposed of their gloves and coveralls in a bag labeled "biohazard." All items would be saved until it was determined they were not needed. Then they headed outside.

Reiko Tanabe joined them in the front yard, along with Gina Luttrell, the SPPD's district supervisor. The sun had disappeared behind dark clouds, blanketing the landscape with shadow.

"I'm getting tired of seeing you two," Luttrell said to Santana and Hawkins. Turning toward the reporters and their camera crews from the local news stations who had gathered along the curb behind the crime scene tape, near the ME's van, she said, "And I'm really tired of seeing them."

Pete Romano parked on the opposite side of the street and got out of his sedan. He slipped a suit coat over his white shirt, straightened his tie, and waved away reporters as he ducked under the crime scene tape and strode across the yard.

"Detectives, Reiko, Gina," he said with a nod to each of them as he joined their small circle. "What'd we have?"

"I'd say she was smothered to death," Santana said.

Romano rested his hands on his hips and shifted his gaze to Santana. "You know homicidal smothering is extremely difficult to detect."

"There's cyanosis and petechiae of the face, Pete. Petechial hemorrhages in the eyes, as well."

"And the area around her nose and mouth is pale," Hawkins added. "Probably from the pressure of a pillow."

"Well," Romano said, throwing up his hands as he looked each one of them in the eye. His gaze finally settled on the ME. "You might as well take off, Reiko. Seems my detectives have done your job for you." The sarcasm in Romano's voice was obvious.

With her hands resting on her hips, Gina Luttrell said, "Let's not get ahead of ourselves, Pete."

Santana looked at Tanabe, waiting for her support.

"The autopsy may reveal asphyxia," she said. "I'll look for saliva, blood, and tissue cells on the pillowcases and high levels of carbon dioxide in the blood. If a hand were used rather than a pillow, I'd likely see scratches, distinct nail marks, or laceration of the soft parts of the face. I'd expect to see pericardium around the heart if she was smothered with a plastic bag. I didn't see any bruising or lacerations of the gums and tongue.

But obstruction applied with skill might not leave any external signs of violence."

Romano said to Tanabe, "So you're saying there may not be any corroborative medical evidence to prove she was murdered."

"There's no evidence of violence at the death scene."

The smile on Romano's face was one of satisfaction, as if Reiko Tanabe's response had proven his point.

"But there's a bland bruise on her chest," Tanabe said.

"Meaning?" Santana said.

"I'm hypothesizing now, so don't take it at face value."

"We won't," Romano said. His hard gaze moved from Santana to Hawkins and then softened as he made eye contact with Luttrell.

"You like to attend boxing matches, John, so you know how a face can bruise after a solid punch," Tanabe said.

Santana nodded.

"The body's first response to a solid blow is to hemorrhage within an hour," she continued. "After an hour, the body sends in white blood cells, or inflammatory cells. But if a person dies before an hour has passed, there will be no response, hence the term 'bland bruise.' If that's the case, all that I'll be able to see under a microscope at autopsy is fresh red blood cells in the bruise on her chest."

"So what exactly are you saying?" Luttrell asked.

"Someone could've put a knee on her chest and a pillow over her face and smothered her."

Luttrell nodded.

"Estimate of time of death, Reiko?" Santana asked.

"Well, there's rigor in the facial and upper neck and shoulder muscles. Lividity is about fixed. Her body temperature reading was ninety-two point six degrees. Figuring the room temperature is stable inside the house and she's lost a degree and a half per hour, I'd say somewhere between four and six hours."

"That would make the TOD this morning," Santana said.

"So Elisha Austin is murdered the day after we find her daughter's body," Hawkins said. "Quite a coincidence."

"That indicates the killer is here in town and trying to cover his tracks," Santana said.

Romano squeezed his eyes shut for a moment, as though a cord were twisting inside his head. "We don't know for a fact that Elisha Austin was murdered."

"But we do know there are very few coincidences in homicide," Santana said.

* * *

Santana and Hawkins took the houses to the right and left of Elisha Austin's house. They assigned patrol officers to interview the rest of the neighbors on the block and across the street.

A white man Santana estimated was in his fifties was seated in a wheelchair on an open porch that looked out on the street as Santana approached. His face and hairless head had been severely scarred by burns. The man wore a long-sleeved denim shirt, khaki pants, and thick-soled shoes. His hands were scarred and ridged with blue veins, the skin as thin as tissue paper over the bones.

A small black bag was draped over one shoulder. One end of a clear tube was connected to the portable oxygen concentrator in the black bag, the other end to a nasal cannula in the man's nose.

Santana walked up to the top step of the porch and showed the man his badge.

"Detective, huh?" he said in a raspy voice.

Santana nodded. He could hear the sucking sound of the compressor with each breath the man took.

"Quite a commotion," the man said.

"Your name?"

"Morgan. Glen Morgan."

"You know your neighbor, Elisha Austin, Mr. Morgan?"

"I did."

"So you know she's dead."

"Figured as much."

"Know her well?"

He shook his head. "Not well. But she was a good neighbor. She kept an eye on things."

Santana recalled the Neighborhood Watch decal in Elisha Austin's window. "You lived here long, Mr. Morgan?"

"Over twenty years."

"How long did Elisha Austin live here?"

"She was here when I moved in."

"Was she married?"

"I don't believe so."

"Did you know her daughter, Kim?"

"I did. She . . ." Morgan paused and looked away. His eyes were wet and focused inward, possibly on some distant memory, Santana thought. Then his eyes found Santana's again. "I saw this morning's paper. Her remains were found in the cave along the river."

"Yes," Santana said.

His gaze slipped away once more. He sat quietly in the wheelchair.

Santana waited.

"I met Kim when she was a young girl," Morgan said. "She used to make me homemade cookies." He laughed softly. "They weren't very good, but I always ate them. We'd sit here on the porch and talk. My scars, my condition, never seemed to bother her. When she got older and moved out of town, I'd see her occasionally. She was a sweet kid." He covered his mouth with a hand as he coughed.

"When was the last time you saw Elisha Austin?"

Morgan shrugged. "Can't say for sure."

"Did you see anyone outside her house recently?"

"I like to keep to myself, Detective," he said, gazing at Santana. "Expect others to do the same. I'm not a snoop."

"I understand."

"It's not difficult," he said.

"What isn't?"

"Keeping to myself. Not the way I look anyway."

"The war?" Santana asked.

"Accident. Broke my spine. Saw my skin melting like a hot candle. Seared my lungs. Don't know how or why I survived. Would've been better off if I hadn't."

Santana didn't know what to say to that, so he handed Morgan one of his business cards. "If you think of anything else, call me at that number. Do you have a number where you can be reached?"

"What for?"

"Something might come up, Mr. Morgan."

Morgan peered at the card for a time. Then he looked at Santana again and recited his phone number. Santana wrote it down in his notebook.

"There was something," Morgan said

"When?"

"Early this morning. When I was driving down the alley in my van, headed for my physical therapy appointment. Guy looked like he was from the electric company."

"I meant someone suspicious looking, Mr. Morgan."

"Well, that's what I just said. You should listen more carefully, being a detective and all."

"You said he *looked like* he was from the electric company."

Morgan nodded. "Guess you *were* paying attention. That's good, Detective. You see, the electric company reads the meter near the end of each month. It's early October, closer to the beginning of the month. Doesn't make sense."

"Can you describe this man?"

"Kind of tall and lean."

"Hair color?"

"He wore a cap."

"Skin color?"

"White."

"Anything else?"

"I think whoever was posing as the meter man, or someone else, broke into my house while I was out."

"You think?"

"I always latch the screen leading out to the backyard. When I came home, it was unlatched."

"Perhaps you forgot to latch it."

"For a man like me, Detective, routines and a sense of order are important. A place for everything and everything in its place."

"Was anything stolen?"

"That's the strange thing. I don't believe anything was. You're the detective. So why would someone break into my place and not steal anything?"

"I couldn't say for sure, Mr. Morgan. But if you think your place has been broken into again, you should contact the police."

Morgan thought about it and then shook his head. "But if nothing has been stolen, what's the point?"

"No one wants strangers in their home for any reason."

"I'll keep your suggestion in mind, Detective."

"Appreciate your cooperation," Santana said.

"I don't want any credit," Morgan said with a dismissive wave. "Don't want my name in the paper. I just want to know one thing."

"What's that?"

"Was she murdered?"

"I don't know."

"But you're a homicide detective."

"We investigate all suspicious deaths."

Glen Morgan nodded. "I hope she died peacefully," he said. "About all anyone can hope for, Detective."

* * *

After Santana returned home from work that evening, he changed into his running suit and shoes and took Gitana out for a run. The fall air near the river smelled of moss, fish, and smoke from a distant fire. Serpentine lines of dead leaves shed from trees scudded across the pavement. White sails on the river leaned against a wall of wind. He could hear the distant hum of a powerboat and the calls of gulls swooping over the water.

The flame-lit gold of the birch trees, the crimson leaves on the maples, the cool wind fanning the ash of a dying fire, and the honking of geese overhead were less signs of Indian summer, Santana thought, than a prologue to gray winter days and cold, snowy nights.

His thoughts shifted to this afternoon and Elisha Austin's death. None of Glen Morgan's neighbors had seen or heard anything unusual, or if they had, they weren't willing to talk about it. Still, Santana knew instinctively that Elisha Austin had been murdered and that the man posing as a meter reader probably had something to do with it. A quick call to Xcel Energy had confirmed that no one had been sent out to read the meter at Elisha Austin's house. The motive for her murder remained unclear, as often happened in the initial stages of murder investigations.

Santana pushed himself harder, trying to clear his mind of the depressing thoughts that buzzed like a nest of angry bees inside his head. He focused his mind on each step, on the sound of his running shoes thumping against the asphalt, and on the panting breaths of Gitana loping beside him, her tongue lolling from her mouth.

When he reached the four-foot stone wall in front of his house, he bent over and rested his hands on his knees and sucked in air, trying to slow his heart rate and catch his breath. Gitana plopped on the brown grass and leaves beside him and let out a heavy sigh. The red sun had reached the horizon, and the last glimmer of light was dying in the treetops as daylight bled slowly into dusk.

Santana liked living closer to nature. The SPPD did not require officers to live within the city limits, and less than a quarter of the force did. Driving out of the city after work to his home along the river gave him at least a sense of separation and allowed him to decompress.

The previous owner had been a well-known chef in town before an ugly paternity suit and lawyer fees had taken most of his money and his entire house. Santana had negotiated a price well below the market value and had used some of the large sum of money he'd inherited after his parents' death to purchase the house.

He heard the slap of running shoes before he spotted the woman jogging toward him and straightened up. The short-sleeved white shirt and shorts she wore contrasted with her tanned arms and legs. Her brunette hair was side parted and cut in a sleek bob that barely touched her shoulders; the sheared, pointed ends slicked back behind her small ears.

"I like your dog," she said as she drew closer, her teeth bright in the fading twilight.

"Thanks," Santana said.

She loped past him and then made a half-turn and jogged in place, perspiration sliding down her cheeks. "You live here?" She nodded at Santana's house, which was set back from the road.

"I do."

"I live three houses down." She pointed in the direction of the pine trees that grew along the southern edge of his property.

Gitana got up, her tail feathers fanning the air, and went to her. The woman stopped jogging in place and squatted down. Gitana licked her face.

"What a lover," she said, smiling at Santana while she stroked Gitana's back.

"She is that."

"What's her name?"

"Gitana."

She gave Gitana a hug. "I had a golden when I was kid. Best dog I ever had." She stood, waved, and jogged off.

Santana watched her for a time, noting her fluid strides, how she moved like an experienced runner with her head held high, her shoulders relaxed, her hands cupped slightly, her elbows bent 90 degrees, her arms pumping easily, never crossing the midline of her body.

Inside the house, Santana disarmed the security system, gave Gitana a large bowl of water, toweled off, and stripped down to a pair of shorts and a T-shirt with cutoff sleeves. Then he went to the guest bedroom he'd converted into a workout area, wrapped his hands with wide elastic wraps, and slipped on a pair of Everlast training gloves.

He'd let himself go for a time after Jordan's death, overwhelmed by her loss. Like a swimmer caught in a riptide, he was pulled down into the depths of a cold, dark depression. Running, lifting weights, hammering the heavy bag and speed bag, forced his mind to focus on something besides her death and his feelings of failure for not protecting her.

First he worked on the heavy bag hanging from a chain fastened to a ceiling beam, making sure he was snapping his punches rather than pushing them, letting his fists rebound off the bag instead of pulling them back after contact, hitting the bag with flowing combinations, staying relaxed as he moved around it, keeping his feet on the ground, imagining he was fighting in close, making sure he didn't lean on the bag or try to push it around with his shoulder. Shouldering the bag would only lead to poor balance, allowing an adversary to easily move out of the way, then attack him with counters.

Santana was sweating heavily when he removed his training gloves and switched to the speed bag. He kept the hand wraps on and began hammering the front of the speed bag, using both hands in random rotation, working into a rhythm, hitting it on the odd number rebounds, creating a familiar drum beat as the bag rebounded off the board.

The bag became a blur in front of him as he increased his intensity level, his deltoids burning as he concentrated on maintaining the rhythm. When he could no longer hold up his arms, he gave the bag one final whack.

He did fifteen muscle-burning pull-ups on the bar he'd installed in the reinforced doorframe. Then he showered and ate dinner.

Later, he was seated on the living room couch, strumming and picking the strings of his Martin acoustic guitar. He loved the rich sound and feel of its strings. He'd taken guitar lessons as a child and had been told more than once that he had talent. But his dreams of playing the guitar professionally and becoming a doctor had ended at the age of sixteen with his mother's murder. Now the guitar helped fill some of the empty spaces in his life.

Gitana lay on her back beside him on the couch, showing how much she trusted him. He would play the guitar for a while and then stop and rub her belly, talking to her with a smile, as if she were a baby.

He listened to a Juan Carlos Quintero CD while he got ready for bed, hoping that tonight he could get some much-needed and uninterrupted sleep. The Colombian-born jazz guitarist was one of Santana's favorites. But he lay awake for an hour, staring at the ceiling, his mind filled with unanswered questions about his current case. Frustrated, he threw back the covers and went to his computer, where he opened a private e-mail account that his uncle in Bogotá, Arturo Gutiérrez Restrepo, had set up.

Only Arturo and Santana's sister Natalia, who lived in Barcelona, Spain, and worked as a pediatric surgeon at the Vall d' Hebron University Hospital, knew the password to the account. Because of death threats from former members of the Cali cartel, Santana could not risk sending a direct e-mail to her given that it might be intercepted, thus revealing her whereabouts to those who wanted him and his sister dead. And so he and Natalia had worked out a system in which they would write each other e-mails, place them in the drafts folder, but never send them. As long as each of them had the password to open the account, they could read the e-mails.

Natalia always asked about his current case, and so he gave her some information without going into graphic detail. As her older brother, he still felt it was his duty to look out for her, to protect her from the darkness in the world, even though he lived 4,500 miles away and had seen her only once since he'd fled Colombia and the Cali cartel at the age of sixteen. Natalia had been nine at the time. But ever since she was a child, she'd been strong and brave and mature beyond her years.

Still, he knew that he was responsible for placing her life in danger by avenging the murder of their mother. Fear for her safety haunted him like the nightmares that disrupted his sleep.

Chapter 7

The next morning Santana and Hawkins drove from the LEC to the downtown office of David Knapp, the man who had organized the security conference Kim Austin had attended.

"You take a look at Knapp's website last night?" Santana asked.

"I did. As well as some Google searches."

She extracted a small spiral notebook from a side pocket in her sport coat and opened it, flipping the pages until she found what she was searching for.

"His father was a very successful plastic surgeon in Beverly Hills who later became a multi-millionaire by investing his money in California real estate. While he was in college at Stanford, Knapp worked as a volunteer intern for the Palo Alto Police Department. Later, he worked as an intern for a California congresswoman. After Knapp received his BA in business, he was accepted into the Navy's Officer Candidate School in Newport, Rhode Island."

"The congresswoman probably helped him out there," Santana said.

Hawkins nodded. "Knapp was commissioned as an officer in the Navy and went on to become a Navy SEAL. He was deployed with SEAL Team 8 to Haiti, the Middle East, and the Balkans. Then he transferred into special operations for a few years."

"What are special operations?"

"Doesn't say. After his service ended, he helped run his father's business. When his father passed away, Knapp sold the business, took the profits, and started Cyber Security Systems."

Fifteen minutes later they took an elevator up to David Knapp's tenth-floor office, which was filled with modern artwork and polished steel-and-glass furniture. Floor-to-ceiling windows revealed a light blue afternoon sky that was ribbed with strips of white clouds.

Santana and Kacie Hawkins sat in front of a large desk. Knapp sat in a high-back leather chair behind the desk, eating chicken lo mein out of a carton. "Sorry," he said between mouthfuls, "but I have meetings all afternoon. When I was younger, I used to go in hungry. Made me a little edgier. But now," he said, waving the pair of chopsticks in his hand, "all hungry does is make me irritable and cause my stomach to grumble."

He had short salt-and-pepper hair and wore a white shirt with shiny silver cufflinks, a red-and-black-striped tie, and red suspenders. His pinstriped suit coat hung on a coat rack in the corner of the room. The walls were lined with shelves filled with thick books and glass-framed college diplomas, cyber security awards, and membership certificates from organizations like IAPSC, the International Association of Professional Security Consultants.

Inside a separate glass frame was a worn circular badge depicting a bald eagle grasping a claymore, or Scottish sword. The words SEND ME were written on the blade. The Latin phrase VERITAS OMNIA VINCULA VINCIT was written around the outer edge of the badge.

While he continued to eat, Knapp studied a photo Santana had made from Kim Austin's driver's license. Then his gaze shifted from the photo on his desktop to Santana. "You said Ms. Austin's body was found in one of the caves along the Mississippi?"

"Her skeletal remains."

"How do you know it's Austin's remains?"

"We have ways."

Knapp's smile was as thin as a blade. He set the chopsticks inside the carton and wiped his mouth with a napkin. "I'm sorry, but I didn't see Ms. Austin at the conference."

"You sound certain."

"I have a wonderful memory." He leaned forward and reached across his desk to return the photo to Santana.

"Take another look," Santana said.

Knapp hesitated.

"Just to be sure, Mr. Knapp." Santana feigned a smile.

Knapp shrugged and peered at the photo again.

"Kim Austin was registered for the conference," Hawkins said.

Knapp glanced at her. "Three hundred individuals were registered for the conference, Detective. Very hard to remember them all."

"How many were African-American women?" Hawkins asked.

The sarcasm in her voice was hard to miss.

"We didn't register individuals based on their skin color, Detective."

"You've got such a good memory, Mr. Knapp," she said. "I thought you'd remember an attractive black woman. Couldn't be that many of them at the conference."

"I didn't bother to count."

"Did everyone who registered attend?"

"A few didn't."

"We'd like a list of all attendees," Santana said.

"My secretary has already prepared a list. See her on the way out."

Santana placed Kim Austin's photo in the briefcase on his lap, removed a tri-fold brochure, and opened it. "Your secretary gave us a brochure from the conference. I see the topics were all about DNA, hacking, and encryption."

"Rapidly changing fields," Knapp said. "If we're going to provide the best for our clients, we need to understand the latest developments and research. I'm sure it's the same in your profession, Detectives."

"What exactly do you provide for your clients?" Santana asked.

Knapp handed Santana a business card made of heavy linen stock and raised black lettering. Across the middle of the card were the words CYBER SECURITY SYSTEMS. Knapp's name was written in fancy script underneath the company name. In the upper left-hand corner was the image of a black fingerprint, representing the company logo. Santana slipped the card into a side pocket of his sport coat.

Knapp said, "Our specialties include digital forensics, encryption technology, risk assessments, crisis management, and emergency planning, among other things."

"Such as?"

"Sophisticated authentication systems using biometrics."

"Meaning?"

"Fingerprint, palm, iris, and facial recognition, retinal scans, and DNA prints. We deal in software that recognizes physiological characteristics such as voiceprints, eye movement patterns, walking gaits, and dynamic signatures."

"Were any of the conference sessions recorded?" Hawkins asked.

"All of them were."

"And could your secretary provide us with copies of the recorded sessions?"

"Of course. I'll notify her." Knapp typed a message on his computer and then focused his dark brown eyes on Santana.

Santana's gaze slid to the diplomas on the wall and then back to Knapp. "Ever been to Washington, DC, Mr. Knapp?"

Knapp tracked Santana's gaze and then smiled at the detective, his teeth nearly matching the brightness of his shirt. "Yes, I've been to DC, as you well know from my diploma on the wall. I graduated from Georgetown. Still have friends there."

"Been to DC recently?"

Knapp thought about it. "Not recently."

"You said earlier you have an excellent memory, Mr. Knapp," Hawkins said.

He nodded.

"So you're a pretty smart guy," Hawkins said.

Knapp's eyes remained fixed on Hawkins, as if he were weighing the seriousness of her response. "My clients seem to think so. That's all that really matters." Knapp switched his gaze to Santana. "Is there anything else? I have a busy day."

"One last question," Santana said. "Kim Austin lived in Washington, DC. Do you know if anyone else from DC attended the conference?"

"Sorry, Detective. I don't."

* * *

On the drive back to the Law Enforcement Center, Santana said to Hawkins, "What's your read on Knapp?"

"Slick," she said. "Like an oily rag."

"Doesn't make him guilty of anything."

"I want to look at the video recordings of the conference, John." She held up the discs in her hand.

When they returned to the LEC, Hawkins viewed the digital recordings from the law conference Kim Austin had attended while Santana called the NTSB office in Washington, DC, and asked to speak to Barry McCarthy, one of the four members of the systems group who had investigated the Blue Skies crash. When McCarthy answered his extension, Santana introduced himself and explained that he was calling about Kim Austin's murder.

"I'm real sorry to hear about her death," McCarthy said. "But the first and only time I met Kim was when we both were assigned to the same group."

"What can you tell me about her?"

"Like I said, Detective, I really didn't know her other than the short time we worked together."

"So the group isn't always made up of investigators who have previously worked together."

"No, it's not."

"I understand Terry Powell was the investigator-in-charge."

"That's correct. He's a good man."

"So you've worked with him before."

"I have."

"You know much about your group chairman, Paul Westbrook?"

"Well, I've worked with Paul before, but I couldn't say I know him well outside of work."

"Did you know he had resigned?"

"I'd heard that, yes."

"Has he ever tried to contact you?"

"No, he hasn't."

"Did everyone agree with the final report?"

"It's a very involved process, Detective."

"That doesn't answer my question."

"It works like this. Each investigative group, under the direction of their chairperson, develops a set of field notes. It's the responsibility of the chairperson to ensure that an accurate and complete set of field notes is compiled while the group is on-scene or during any follow-up activity. Each group chairperson is responsible for providing a copy of the signed group field notes to the IIC."

"What happens then?"

"Once the field investigation is completed and the team members return to their respective offices, reports are written regarding the findings. Each group typically drafts its own findings and analysis of the accident and submits it to the NTSB. The NTSB reviews each report and completes its own individual accident report."

"In the case of the systems group, Paul Westbrook would have given the group's field notes to Terry Powell."

"Yes. But each group member reviews the field notes for technical accuracy and affirms agreement with the contents by signing them."

"And then what?" Santana asked.

"The IIC approves the field notes before group members are released from their on-scene duties."

"What if there's a disagreement among the group members?"

"The IIC can meet daily with all of the group chairpersons. It's a means of encouraging open discussion and resolution of problems. But in the end, it's up to the chairperson to try to resolve any issues to the satisfaction of all the group members."

"And what if that doesn't happen?"

"Well, in the rare case that a disagreement of one member can't be resolved, that member is expected to sign the field notes verifying their general agreement and noting their specific objections to the disputed content in the notes."

"Was there disagreement about the cause of the Blue Skies crash among your group members?"

Silence.

"Mr. McCarthy?"

"The final report is the group chairperson's responsibility. Concurrence by the entire group is not required, Detective."

"So there was disagreement."

"Any dissent regarding the accuracy or completeness of the report should've been communicated to Paul Westbrook, and if necessary, discussed formally with Terry Powell during a technical review meeting later in the investigative process."

"Did that meeting take place?"

"Yes, it did."

"What was the disagreement about, Mr. McCarthy?"

"Prior to the NTSB's adoption of the final report, Detective Santana, only appropriate NTSB personnel are authorized to publicly disclose investigative findings. Even then, the release is limited to verified information identified during the course of the investigation."

"Do you know why Paul Westbrook resigned from the NTSB?"

"I have no idea."

"Would you say Westbrook knew what he was doing?"

"He was an experienced investigator."

Santana took his response as a yes.

"How well did you know Cathy Herrera?"

"Not well."

"What do you think caused the Blue Skies flight to crash?"

"It ran out of gas."

"Because it was off course."

"Exactly."

"So the crash was due to pilot error."

"That's what I wrote in my report."

"Did all the group members agree with your analysis?"

"I didn't read all the individual reports, only the final one."

"Did you have any discussions with your colleagues regarding the cause of the accident?"

"What are you getting at, Detective?"

"What do you think?"

"I think if you're really interested in solving Kim Austin's murder, you'll look in another direction."

"Who or what are you afraid of, Mr. McCarthy?"

"Nice talking with you," McCarthy said and hung up.

Barry McCarthy had sounded confident about his analysis of the crash. Maybe Kim Austin had had other ideas.

Chapter 8

When Santana hung up the phone, he updated Hawkins on his conversation with Barry McCarthy.

"So McCarthy disagreed with Kim Austin's crash assessment," she said.

Santana nodded. "One of them is wrong."

"Delta is sending the passenger lists I requested."

Santana's cell phone pinged. "Hold on a second."

He opened the message from Cathy Herrera that read, "Here's the photo of Paul Westbrook you requested." Santana recognized Kim Austin standing beside Westbrook. He rolled his chair next to Hawkins and showed her the photo.

Westbrook had long, reddish-brown hair. He wore a pair of wire-rimmed glasses and had fair, freckled skin, amiable chestnut brown eyes, and like the actor Joaquin Phoenix, a small dent between his upper lip and left nostril called a microform cleft, a mild form of a cleft lip. Santana estimated Westbrook was in his mid-to-late thirties.

"Well, at least we know what he looks like now," Hawkins said. She held up a DVD and slid it into a USB SuperDrive. "You need to see this."

Seconds later a large conference room filled with men and women in suits appeared on her computer screen. "I've looked through both disks," she said. "Most of the time the camera was focused solely on the speakers. But there are audience shots right before the presentations."

"So what am I looking for?"

"In about twenty seconds, the camera pans the room, stops for a moment, and then pans back again. I'll stop it at the point I want you to see."

As Hawkins had described, the camera began slowly panning the room from left to right, giving him an opportunity to observe the faces of the conference attendees.

"There!" Hawkins said, freezing the frame. "I believe that's Kim Austin."

Santana leaned forward. He recognized the face of the attractive African-American woman. "You're right. She's talking to another woman."

"The same woman appears with Austin again on another DVD. The woman is beautiful. Looks sort of Asian."

"We need to find out who she is, Kacie."

Hawkins stopped the DVD, and they scanned the list of conference attendees David Knapp had provided, separating the women's names from the men's.

"Not surprising that the men outnumber the women by two to one," Hawkins said with a disgusted shake of her head.

"Maybe men just like attending security conferences more than women," Santana said.

Hawkins gave him an *Are you serious*? look.

"Relax. I'm kidding."

Hawkins smiled. "That's good."

"What do you mean?"

Hawkins looked at him for a split second and then focused her gaze on her computer as she removed the DVD. "Nothing," she said. "Forget it."

Then Santana realized what she was getting at. "You think I've lost my sense of humor since Jordan's death."

Hawkins thought about it before her eyes met his again.

"Let's face it, John, you'll never be the life of the party, if you ever attend one."

"Thanks."

"It's true. But it's understandable that you'd be depressed after what happened. Anyone would be. I'm just happy to hear a little humor from you. That's all."

Santana felt a familiar knot of anger tightening in his chest. He knew that Hawkins shouldn't be an outlet for his outrage over Jordan's death. Prolonging the conversation would probably lead to his saying something he would regret. He didn't want to lose Hawkins as a partner or a friend. So he simply nodded, let out a breath to release the tension, and pointed to the list on the desk in front of him.

"Where do we go from here?" he asked.

"Well, we've got the names of eighty or so women who attended the conference. But we don't have their photos. I suggest we log into the DVS and cross-check the names with the photos. We might find a match to the woman who was talking to Austin."

"Only if she's from Minnesota."

"True," Hawkins said. "But we might get lucky."

"Take a picture of the woman on the screen with your iPhone, Kacie, and send it to Knapp. He might know the woman with Kim Austin."

"He couldn't remember Austin—or so he said."

"Let's give him another chance. I'll call him and let him know you're sending him a photo."

While Hawkins took the photo of the two women on the computer screen, Santana found Knapp's business card and set it on his desktop. Then he called Knapp, told him Hawkins was sending a photo to his iPhone, and asked if he could identify the woman talking with Kim Austin. Santana waited on his phone until Knapp received the photo.

"Reyna Tran," Knapp said.

"You're sure?"

"Absolutely."

Santana thanked him and disconnected. "Reyna Tran," he said to Hawkins.

"Is Tran Chinese?"

Santana leaned forward and viewed the screen. "Vietnamese, I think. She could be Amerasian. Lot of soldiers fathered children with Vietnamese women."

Hawkins searched Google for the name Tran. "You're right, John. She is Vietnamese." She clicked back to Tran's website. "Read what it says about her company."

> Tran Security Services provides protection and advice to public figures, prominent families, and at-risk individuals.

Santana wrote down the contact number on the screen and dialed it using the phone on his desk. He told the receptionist who answered who he was, and she immediately put him through to Reyna Tran.

"Good afternoon, Detective Santana. How can I help you?"

He pressed the speaker button before he spoke again. "I'm investigating the death of Kim Austin."

Santana waited for a response. When none was offered, he said, "Ms. Tran?"

"Yes, Detective?"

She spoke with little inflection, as if he'd just told her it was raining. He continued, "We believe Ms. Austin was murdered."

"I drew that conclusion when my receptionist said you were a St. Paul homicide detective."

Hawkins mouthed the word "Cold" and shook her head.

Santana paused a moment before asking his next question. "Did you know Ms. Austin was reported missing six months ago?"

"I did not."

"How well did you know her?"

"I met her at the security conference in St. Paul."

"Did you spend quite a bit of time with Ms. Austin?"

"It was only a two-day conference."

"Did you see her both days?"

"Yes. I believe I did."

"Do you remember if Ms. Austin spent time with anyone else?"

"If you mean did she talk with other people at the conference, I'm sure she did. If you mean something else, Detective, that would be none of my business."

Santana hadn't considered the possible sexual interpretation of the otherwise innocent phrase 'spent time with,' but he considered it now. He glanced at Hawkins, who had a smile on her face. Then he quickly switched the conversational direction.

"Did Ms. Austin say if she was meeting anyone while in St. Paul?"

"We only spoke for a brief time. It wasn't like we were good friends."

"I see."

"But I was wondering . . ."

"Wondering what, Ms. Tran?"

"Where you found the body?"

"In one of the caves along the Mississippi River."

"Do you have any suspects?"

"We've just begun the investigation," Santana said. "Thank you for your time."

"Of course. I hope you solve Ms. Austin's murder, Detective Santana. If I can be of further assistance, please let me know."

She disconnected without waiting for a reply.

"Well?" Kacie Hawkins said.

Santana hung up the phone. "Let's take a look at the discs again."

Hawkins swiveled her chair and slid the first DVD into the drive. Santana watched the computer screen as Hawkins scrolled ahead until Reyna Tran stepped out of the frame. Austin stood still for a time, reading the conference brochure.

"What do you think, John?"

"Leave it running," he said.

The camera panned to the right.

"Stop!" Santana said. He pointed at a man who had long, reddish-brown hair, wire-rimmed glasses, and a microform cleft lip. His clothes were disheveled. "That's Paul Westbrook."

"What's he doing there?"

Hawkins shuffled through the papers on her desk until she found what she was looking for. "Westbrook isn't on the attendee list, John. Take a look." She handed Santana the paper.

Santana perused the list. "You're right. Keep it running."

The camera began panning the room again. When it came back around to where Westbrook had been standing, he was gone.

Chapter 9

Santana left the LEC and drove to the autopsy suites located at Regions Hospital, where the ME was examining Elisha Austin's body.

Santana had witnessed many autopsies in his time as a homicide detective. From the odor of decay and formalin, to the soft hum of fluorescent lights overhead, to the cold tile walls, stainless steel tables, and sharp blades of the bone-cutting tools, the experience was much the same.

Only the victims were different.

He could have waited to learn the necessary details spelled out in the lab report, which he would receive in days, except for lab workups that often took longer. But he felt he owed it to each victim to be here and to listen to his or her silent testimony, listen as each one of them spoke to him through his or her manner of death.

In Elisha Austin's case, Reiko Tanabe confirmed through microscopy that slight bruising in the mouth and nose had occurred. Mucus was found at the back of the mouth, and a bloodstained, frothy fluid was present in the air passages. In the lungs Tanabe detected acute emphysema and edema—an excess of watery fluid in the tissues—as well as petechiae and scattered areas of atelectasis, or partial collapse of the lungs. The internal organs were deeply congested and showed small hemorrhages.

Based on this information, together with the fibers found on a pillowcase, Tanabe determined that the cause of death was asphyxia by suffocation. Manner of death: homicide.

* * *

After leaving Regions Hospital, Santana called Trevor Dane. His receptionist told him that Dane was at an archery range in Minneapolis. Santana asked her for Dane's cell phone number and then called him. He answered on the second ring.

"Detective Santana, Mr. Dane."

There was a long pause before he said, "What can I do for you?"

"We need to talk."

"Go ahead."

"In person."

Dane hesitated. "Okay. You ever used a bow and arrow?"

"Can't say that I have."

"Well, now's your chance."

Dane gave him directions to a range in the northern suburbs. When Santana arrived at the building, he was directed to the Techno Hunt video archery simulator, where Trevor Dane was waiting. The simulator had one screen that projected elk and other large game. It reminded Santana of the FATS, or Firearm Training Simulator, he'd used, though this was not nearly as sophisticated, and he was aiming at humans, not animals.

Dane was shooting blunt-tipped arrows at elk on the large screen. The simulator immediately showed if an arrow hit any of the vitals. Dane explained that when you were finished, the simulator printed out your average score and how many vitals you'd hit.

"Let's go shoot some real arrows," Dane said.

"I came here to talk."

"I only have so much time before I have to return to my office, Detective. This is how I relax. I can talk and shoot at the same time. How about you?"

"All right," Santana said.

He followed Dane to the front counter, where Dane signed them up for one of the twenty shooting lanes.

"What's your dominant eye?" Dane asked.

"My right."

"Then you need a right-handed bow." Dane handed Santana a bow on which the central parts of the limbs curved toward him and the tips of the limbs curved away.

"That's a recurve bow used to teach archery to beginners," Dane said with a hint of amusement. "And you'll need these." He handed Santana an armguard for his left forearm and a fingertab to protect the first three fingers of his right hand when he drew back the bowstring.

"And your bow?" Santana asked.

"Compound," Dane said, holding up a second bow that had a complicated-looking system of cables, pulleys, and cams that, as he explained, assisted the archer in holding a heavy draw weight at full draw without causing excessive muscle fatigue. "Still need a good deal of strength to initially draw the bow," he said, as if assuring Santana that his bow required more strength. "You can shoot up to forty yards. But since this is your first time, Detective, let's shoot from twenty."

Dane picked up a quiver of arrows, and they walked to a lane with side-by-side targets about a foot apart. "Let's see what you can do, Detective."

Santana pulled on the bowstring to gauge the tightness of the draw. Then he lined up his shot and let the first arrow go, but it was wide to the right. He made a slight adjustment in his aim. His second shot was closer to the center ring, but still to the right. His last arrow hit square in the middle of the bullseye.

"Not bad, Detective. Now it's my turn."

Dane's first two arrows hit near dead center.

Just as he was about to release his third arrow, Santana said, "You know what a tantō is, Mr. Dane?"

The arrow flew wide to the left, barely hitting the edge of the target.

"Sorry," Santana said.

Dane stared at the arrow as though he couldn't believe his poor shot. Then he shifted his gaze to Santana. "Why do you ask?"

"Curiosity."

"I think it's something else, Detective. And I think you already know what a tantō is."

"You ever own one?"

"When I was in Japan," he said. "It's a finely crafted weapon."

"How about here?"

Dane shook his head.

Santana took out his SPPD cell phone, found the photo of the dagger, and showed it to Dane. "That it?"

Dane drew back from the photo, his eyes suddenly wide with surprise and fear.

Santana said, "What do you suppose your employees would say if I asked each one of them if you ever owned a dagger like this?"

Dane thought about it for a long moment. "I did bring one home that looks like the one in the photo. But it was stolen."

"Convenient," Santana said.

"Six months ago."

"About the time Kim Austin, your ex-girlfriend, went missing."

"Yeah."

"You ever report it stolen?"

He shrugged. "How much effort are the police going to put into finding one dagger?"

"Where did you have it?"

"In my office, right beside the statue of Buddha."

"Any idea who might've taken it?"

"Maybe it was Kim?"

"Why would she take it?"

"Why would anyone take it?"

"Good question, Mr. Dane," Santana said.

* * *

Later that afternoon, David Knapp's secretary directed Santana to the Commodore, an art deco bar and restaurant that had recently been renovated and reopened. Santana wanted to find out what, if anything, David Knapp knew about Reyna Tran.

The Commodore had two lounges, two bars, and two restaurants. It was located in a quiet neighborhood in St. Paul's Cathedral Hill district, below several stories of condos. A sidewalk under a long black-and-white-striped canopy led to a set of double doors. With its metallic ceilings and ornate trim, glittering glass chandeliers, black-and-white checkerboard floors, and white leather furniture, the place emanated opulence and decadence. Santana imagined a time when the Commodore was a hotel with an illegal speakeasy frequented by authors like F. Scott Fitzgerald and Sinclair Lewis, and post-Prohibition gangsters like Ma Barker and John Dillinger.

Opposite the white-tablecloth dining room, where the walls were adorned with historical photos and images of famous actors and actresses from the Golden Age of Hollywood, Santana found David Knapp alone at a table in the lounge. Here the walls were covered in mirrors, and a gold dome lit the ceiling. Big Band music was piped through speakers.

A quick frown passed over Knapp's lips when he looked up from his meal and saw Santana standing by the table. "I take it you're not here to sample the Zelda cocktail," Knapp said.

Santana sat down in the chair opposite him.

"Have a seat," Knapp said, after the fact. He picked up a French fry from his plate and ate it. "Seems like you're always catching me when I'm eating."

"This won't take long."

Knapp glanced at his watch. "I know. I've got to get back to the office."

"Late night of work?"

"Not much down time in the security business. Same in police work, I suspect." He swallowed some white wine and said, "What's so important that it couldn't wait till I was back in my office?"

"We looked at the security conference DVDs. On one of the discs we saw a man we believe to be Paul Westbrook. He wasn't listed on the attendance list or the conference brochure as one of the presenters."

Knapp dabbed his mouth with a napkin. "Westbrook. Don't remember him. Must've been a late registrant."

"Reyna Tran," Santana said.

"What about her?"

"You're both in the security business."

"What does that prove?"

"Nothing. Yet."

Knapp ate the last French fry on his plate. "Reyna Tran and I are competitors."

"Her bio is pretty thin."

"That's by design."

Santana waited while Knapp finished the last bite of his chicken sandwich and the last swallow of his wine.

Knapp wiped his mouth with a napkin and set it beside his plate. "Ask Reyna Tran about her background, Detective, and you'll get a lot of different stories. Probably because she doesn't want anyone to know where she came from—or maybe she's just a compulsive liar—or maybe both."

"So how do you know so much about her?"

"As you said earlier, she and I are in the security business. It helps to know your competition."

A waitress stopped by the table and asked Santana if he wanted anything.

"No, thank you."

She turned to Knapp. "Would you like another wine, Mr. Knapp?"

He glanced at his watch again and then at Santana before focusing his attention on the waitress once more. "I'll need another. And bring me the bill, please."

"Certainly," she said.

After she departed, Knapp rested his elbows on the table, leaned in, and said, "Reyna Tran was born in Hanoi in 1975, just after the fall of Saigon and the end of the war. Tran's mother raised her and her four siblings. Her husband had been killed two years earlier in the war."

"Lot of Vietnamese died in that war," Santana said.

Knapp nodded. "Up to three million, most of them male soldiers who left behind wives and young children. Single mothers like Tran's supported their families with what I'd call clandestine household commerce. She raised her daughter to be equally resourceful."

"What do you mean by 'clandestine household commerce'?"

"What do you think I mean?"

"Give me a hint."

"Well, most 'household commerce' involved American soldiers and prostitution."

"So what about 'equally resourceful'?"

Knapp canted his head. "What comes to mind when you think of resourceful, Detective?"

"Ingenious, maybe, or creative."

"How about in your line of work?"

"Clever."

"Reyna Tran is ingenious, creative, *and* clever, Detective. Plus, she's smart. Scary smart."

The waitress returned with Knapp's glass of wine and the bill, and left again.

Santana said, "You were telling me about Reyna Tran."

"Right." Knapp drank some wine and set the glass on the table. "Tran came to the US in 1990, following passage of the Amerasian Homecoming Act."

"I'm not familiar with it," Santana said.

"It became law in 1988. Vietnamese Amerasians born between 1962 and 1976 were allowed to apply for immigrant visas. The application window only lasted until the spring of 1990. But when some Vietnamese women claimed American citizenship for their daughters or sons, the fathers denied the relationship by calling them prostitutes. Prostitutes were largely excluded from the program."

"So Tran's mother wasn't a prostitute?"

Knapp shrugged and sipped some wine. "You draw your own conclusions."

"Did Tran come with her mother and siblings?"

Knapp shook his head. "Alone."

Santana did some quick math in his head. "At fifteen?"

He nodded.

"She had to spend six months in the Philippines learning English and then lived here with a Vietnamese family for two years till she graduated high school."

"By *here*, you mean St. Paul?"

"Tran and over twenty-six thousand Vietnamese. She completed her undergraduate degree at MIT in two years and went back to Vietnam at the age of nineteen. Ten years later, she returned to the States and started Tran Security in Chicago. It's now a multi-million-dollar firm with offices in Chicago, LA, and Washington, DC."

"What did she do in Vietnam for ten years?"

"Never could find out."

"Where did she get the capital to start her own business?"

Knapp shrugged again. "Many ways to acquire large amounts of capital in a relatively short period of time in Southeast Asia—if you're an enterprising individual."

"Drugs?"

"Sure. Maybe gun running or sex slavery."

"Must've been better opportunities available."

"Remember the Communists run the country, Detective. They changed the Democratic Republic of Vietnam to the Socialist Republic of Vietnam. Then they implemented a so-called 're-education' program for captured and imprisoned former military officers, government workers, civil servants, capitalists, and priests. So there wasn't much capitalism going on and even less opportunity. Still isn't much today in the north. Commie system runs pretty much on personal connections and relationships."

"Lucky that doesn't happen here," Santana said.

"Yeah. It's different in Ho Chi Minh City, the old Saigon. Alongside the hammer-and-sickle flags are Chanel and Cartier boutiques. Young Vietnamese are as selfie and Facebook-obsessed as their peers around the world."

"And you know this because . . ."

"I've been there. If Tran ran a legitimate business when she was in Vietnam for ten years, no one has reported it, least of all her."

"You familiar with the Blue Skies crash, Mr. Knapp?"

His eyes skittered back and forth before settling on Santana again. "I read about it. Why?"

"Kim Austin was one of the investigators. So was Paul Westbrook. They both attended your security conference. Now Austin is dead and Westbrook has resigned."

"And you think someone at the conference had something to do with Austin's death and Westbrook's resignation?"

"Could be," Santana said.

* * *

Late that afternoon Santana drove with Gitana to the St. Croix Marina in Hudson, Wisconsin, where he kept the *Alibi,* his 37-foot mainship. The boat was only ten years old when he'd purchased it at a repo sale and had been well cared for. It had lots of space and headroom below, which he appreciated, given that he was six feet two inches in shoes. There was a wide aft deck with a wet bar area and steps up to the fly bridge that offered a 360-degree view. Walkthrough steps led to the foredeck, which meant he and any guests wouldn't have to tiptoe around the sides to go forward. The boat had a large galley and slept six, two in the forward cabin, two on a convertible dinette, and two in the aft stateroom that had a separate shower.

Santana drank from a bottle of cold Sam Adams while sitting in the captain's chair on the fly bridge. Gitana was stretched out on the wraparound cushioned seat, her ears perked, her eyes locked on a pair of mallards floating on the rippling surface of the water. The air smelled like fish and exhaust fumes and the oily film on the water's surface. He heard distant music and the calls of gulls gliding over the water.

There were fewer boats in the slips now. But if the fall weather continued to cooperate, Santana would wait as long as possible before storing the *Alibi* for the winter months. He was hoping that the longer he held it out of storage, the longer the nice autumn weather would last. It was a false hope, but hope nonetheless. Or maybe it had more to do with prolonging the ending, specifically his times with Jordan. He remembered how much she'd enjoyed the boat and the trips they'd shared cruising up and down the St. Croix River.

Unconsciously, he felt the scar through his shirt left by the knife blade that had sliced open his abdomen. Jordan had nursed him back to health while urging him not to pursue the case he was working. He wished now that he'd listened to her, listened to her warnings about chasing the darkness. Though he tried to hide it, he wore his guilt over her death like a cloak for all to see.

But he knew he could have no more given up on that case than he could change who he was. But the questions lingered longer now as the months passed. Was it all worth it? Was it worth the lives of those he cared about, the damage to his psyche? How could he justify it all?

He could never erase the images that haunted his mind and soul. He understood that the dark memories were the heavy price he paid for the skills he possessed.

Santana forced his thoughts to shift to his current case, his mind wading through a swamp of possibilities.

He'd made a second call to Barry McCarthy and Cathy Herrera, two of the four investigators in the group that had included Kim Austin and Paul Westbrook. The operator who had taken his calls had indicated both McCarthy and Herrera were in the building, but neither of them had answered their phones. Santana had left no message, figuring McCarthy and Herrera were avoiding him. If he wanted to speak to them again, he believed it would have to be in DC, where they wouldn't be expecting him. Convincing his commander, Pete Romano, to fund the trip would be another matter.

Santana drank from his bottle of Sam Adams as he recalled his phone conversation with Reyna Tran. His conversation with David Knapp had only deepened the mystery that surrounded her life.

He wanted to talk face-to-face with her, but he would have to convince Pete Romano to use department money for a flight to Chicago. Then again, he needed to renew his Colombian passport. The closest place to do that was at the consulate general's office in Chicago. Dual US-Colombian citizens had to present a Colombian passport to enter and exit Colombia and had to have a US passport to return to the States. He had no current plans to visit Colombia, especially since his last visit had nearly cost him his life, but he wanted to keep his options open.

The consulate was open only from 8:00 a.m. to 2:00 p.m. Monday through Friday. If he could book an early flight to Chicago, he could renew his passport in the morning and, hopefully, arrange to meet Reyna Tran for lunch, then return on a flight later that afternoon. And he could do it on his own time without using department money.

Santana drank more beer and switched his thoughts to Kim Austin's murder. There was something familiar about it, something about the dagger through the hand.

Like all good homicide detectives, he remembered every one of his cases. He was sure he hadn't had a similar case before, so it had to be something else, something stored in his subconscious mind. Everything that had ever happened to him, everything that he'd ever learned or read or heard, was permanently stored in this limitless memory bank. He just had to find the key to access it.

Chapter 10

Santana waited for Reyna Tran at the Signature restaurant on the 95th floor of the 100-story John Hancock Center on North Michigan Avenue in downtown Chicago. He sat at a linen-covered table for two beside the floor-to-ceiling windows that offered a spectacular panoramic view of the city and Lake Michigan. Santana wished he could enjoy the view, but he wasn't fond of heights.

Glancing out the window at the clear blue sky and the city far below, he imagined the glass suddenly breaking, the wind sucking him out of his seat, and his body falling into the void. He felt his heartbeat quicken and his palms sweat.

The adrenaline rush reminded him of the dreams he'd experienced when he came to the States at sixteen, after his mother's murder: the recurring sensation of falling that had so often occurred during the first stage of his sleep, the hypnic jerks, or muscle spasms, of his arms and legs, the sudden contractions wrenching him awake.

As a child he'd once believed the popular myth that he would die if he didn't wake before he hit the ground. But the more he studied and learned about his dreams, the more he came to realize that like so many things in life, what he imagined wasn't true. Rather, his dream of falling represented the anxiety he'd felt at the time, the overwhelming sense that his life had spun out of control, that he had nothing he could hold on to, no purpose, and no mission in life.

It was his adoptive parents, Philip and Dorothy O'Toole, who had provided a safe, loving environment. They were the only people he'd trusted enough to share the dark secrets of his past. Phil had taken Santana to SPPD headquarters, introduced him to his fellow detectives, convinced him to become a homicide detective, given him a renewed sense of purpose. He wondered now if a sense of purpose, of justice, was enough to sustain him.

He took in a breath to steady his heartbeat, stood, and wiped his moist hands on his thighs as Reyna Tran approached the table. She wore a body-hugging *ao dai* dress with a high collar and tight waist that accentuated her curves and clung to her figure as if it had been soaked in water. Her straight hair hung to the middle of her back and glistened like black silk under the lights. She moved with the grace of a panther. Women as well as men turned their heads to watch her.

"Ms. Tran?"

"Reyna, please." She offered a delicate hand and Santana shook it, noting her firm grip and bright red nail polish.

When they were seated, Santana looked around to see if anyone was watching. Satisfied, he discreetly flipped open his badge wallet and showed it to her.

"You want to keep this formal."

"We're not on a first name basis."

"Yet," she said with a sly, almost flirtatious smile. Her eyes zeroed in on his for just a moment. They were liquid, almost luminous, like her skin.

"I appreciate you taking the time to see me, Ms. Tran."

"I hope I can be of some help. But let's order first. I'm hungry." Reyna Tran signaled a waitress and shifted her gaze to the menu beside her place setting.

Santana picked up his menu. "What's good here?"

"I love the salmon Caesar salad. But I'm guessing you would like something more substantial."

Santana scanned the menu and decided to try the Angus burger with cheddar cheese and fries. He ordered a Coke. Reyna Tran chose a tea.

After the waitress had taken their orders and walked away, he said, "Tell me a little about your background, Ms. Tran."

She smiled. "I suspect you already checked my background and know quite a bit about me, Detective."

"And why would you think that?"

"It's what I would do if I was in your position."

"Then perhaps you've looked into *my* background."

"I have." She rested her elbows on the table and her chin on the backs of her hands. "I think talking about you would be much more interesting than talking about me."

"I doubt that very much."

"Your real name is Juan Carlos Gutiérrez Arángo," she said without taking her eyes off his. "You came to this country from Colombia when you were sixteen, after your mother's murder. You lived with a couple named Philip and Dorothy O'Toole. Philip was a St. Paul homicide detective. How am I doing so far?"

Santana's heartbeat had increased again. He could feel the heat in his face.

"Well, the embarrassment I see in your complexion indicates I'm on the right track," she said.

He knew that someone looking deep enough could find this background information. Still, the disclosure unnerved him, particularly coming from a stranger like Reyna Tran.

"I'm guessing something besides your mother's murder brought you to this country," she said. "Would you care to share it?"

Santana said nothing.

"Talking about it can be helpful."

His eyes locked on hers. He could feel his heartbeat throbbing in his ears.

"No?" she said. "Well, you've had quite the career as a homicide detective. But I was so sorry to hear that you lost your lady friend. How do you do it?"

He cleared his throat. "Do what?"

"Maintain your sanity."

The intensity of her gaze nearly made him blush again. He removed his small spiral notebook and pen from an inner pocket of his sport coat and flipped the notebook open. He had no intention of sharing his background or his feelings with Reyna Tran.

Disregarding her last comment, he said, "You came to the States after the passage of the Amerasian Homecoming Act."

A cloud of disappointment passed over her eyes and was gone as quickly as it had appeared. "My background is of little importance."

"Why don't you let me be the judge of that?'

"Am I a suspect in Kim Austin's death?"

"Who said anything about her?"

"That's why you're here, isn't it? To get a sense of who I am."

"Your bio is a little sketchy."

"As is yours, John."

"We're not on a first—"

"Name basis," she said, finishing his sentence.

Santana looked at his notes and then at Tran again. "Let's start with when you came to the States."

She let out a sigh and then continued. "I came with many Amerasian children who were left in Vietnam. We had to go through interviews to prove whether or not our fathers were US soldiers."

"You never knew your American father."

She leaned back in her chair and shook her head. "My mother told me he was a soldier. I had no documentation, so I had to pass the medical exam."

"Meaning?"

"If we looked Amerasian, we passed."

Reyna Tran definitely possessed the wide-set eyes, high cheekbones, full lips, clear light skin, and short nose commonly associated with Asian women. But her striking blue eyes were large and down-slanted.

"That must've been difficult, living as an Amerasian in Vietnam after the war."

"We were called *bui doi,* meaning the dust of life—or trash."

"I'm sorry."

"Name-calling never bothered me."

Santana found that statement hard to believe, yet something in her voice suggested it really hadn't.

"Later, we were called 'golden children.'"

"And why was that?"

"Not only could golden children move to the US, but so could our parents."

"But your mother didn't come with you."

"My, you have done your homework."

"I like to know who I'm talking to."

"Of course you do. Well, my mother chose to stay in Vietnam."

"What did your mother do in Vietnam?"

"She was a business woman."

Something in her tone suggested pursuing this line of questioning was a dead end. "You were very young when you came here," he said, changing the subject.

"I was mature for my age." A strand of dark hair fell like a wire across her forehead.

"You must be very bright as well."

She brushed away the strand of hair and smiled. "I'm a member of the Giga Society."

"I haven't heard of it."

"It's a rather exclusive group," she said. "There are six members in the world. Two in the US and four in Europe."

"Why so few?"

"You have to be smarter than nearly everyone to join. In theory, that means one in a billion individuals can qualify. And you have to score more than one hundred ninety-five on one of their accepted IQ tests."

The waitress reappeared with Reyna Tran's tea and Santana's Coke. When she left again, he said, "That must be difficult . . ." He let this thought linger.

She cocked her head and waited.

"Being smarter than nearly everyone," he said.

"On the contrary, I find it rather liberating."

"Yet after finishing college at MIT in two years, you went back to Vietnam."

"College bored me."

"You weren't bored back in Vietnam?"

"There are many ways to make money when you are an enterprising woman."

"What made you decide to return to the States?"

"Business opportunities. Particularly in security."

"And why security?"

"Fear is a strong motivator in uncertain times, Detective. And the times in this country and around the world have grown more and more uncertain. People see terrorists around every corner. The media helps fan the flames. Always thinking of the worst-case scenarios. Most of what they talk about is nothing but a creative exercise, not a prediction of events likely to happen. It's a waste of time and energy."

"What about contingency planning?"

"Of course my company does some of that. But it's important to put our resources where they count the most. Governments can only do so much."

"Meaning?"

"Some people are more than willing to pay private security companies to protect them and their loved ones. Companies require protection as well. That has created a need for more security service providers."

"Money to be made."

"It's difficult to put a price tag on peace of mind," she said, sipping her tea.

"You must know David Knapp."

"Ah, David," she said. "He supplied you with information on me."

"He was helpful."

"And now you would like me to be as helpful when it comes to him."

"He's your competitor."

"I don't need another reason to help you, John." She made a show of putting a hand to her mouth as if using his first name was an unintended mistake and not purposeful.

"*Another* reason?"

"I like you," she said. "That's reason enough for me."

"We just met."

"I'm a very good judge of character."

"I'm flattered."

"No you're not," she said. "But thank you for saying it."

"So what about Knapp?"

"I assume you know something about his company and background."

"I do," Santana said. "But you're apparently on a first name basis."

"We are as far as I'm concerned. Unfortunately, David has not embraced my friendship."

"And why is that?"

"I'm afraid he doesn't trust me."

"Can I trust you?"

"Have I given you any reason not to?"

"Like I said. We just met."

She smiled. "I'll bet you're a quick judge of character, too."

Santana believed that he was. But no matter how good his judgment, no matter how trustworthy a new acquaintance appeared to be, he always kept some distance. Women saw it as a flaw, particularly those who were interested in a more intimate relationship, but he thought of it as a necessity in his line of work. Now, after Jordan's untimely death, he'd added more bricks to the protective wall he'd constructed around himself.

He had no interest in Reyna Tran other than as a source for information. The wound left by Jordan's death was too fresh. It would eventually heal, but the guilt he carried because of it would leave a permanent scar on his soul.

Tran was a classic manipulator who used her beauty and brains to get whatever she wanted. Her ability to direct the conversation around to him exemplified how successful she was at it. Her skill set reminded Santana of a few jujutsu classes he'd taken through the department in which the object was to manipulate the opponent's force or the attacker's energy against himself rather than confronting it or directly opposing it with your own force.

"Knapp's bio says he was in something called 'special operations' while he was in the service," Santana said. "You know anything about that?"

"I do," she said with a sly smile. "Would you like to know?"

"I would."

"Well, our friend David once belonged to a top-secret government agency called the Intelligence Support Activity, or ISA. The Pentagon rarely acknowledges their existence. When they do, they deny any knowledge of their activities. Before it operated under the name ISA, it was known as the Field Operations Group, or FOG."

"Sounds appropriate."

"Absolutely," Tran said. "FOG was created in 1980 to rescue the American hostages held in the Tehran embassy after the first attempt failed. You were too young to remember. And you were living in Colombia at the time."

"I read about the rescue attempt when I was older," Santana said. "We do have news in Colombia."

"Of course you do."

"But I don't remember reading about a second rescue attempt."

She shook her head. "It never took place. Anyway, after the hostage crisis, the spymasters decided that FOG needed to expand and be given more resources. And the name was changed to ISA, often referred to as just The Activity. They specialize in gathering HUMINT, SIGINT, and also combat."

"What do the acronyms stand for?"

"Human and signals intelligence."

"I get the human side of it. What about the signals part?"

"ISA intercepts communications transmitted electronically through radar, radios, or weapons systems. They were part of the special operations that tracked down your countryman, Pablo Escobar."

Santana was already in the States when Escobar was killed in 1993. But he vividly remembered the chaos created throughout the country when Escobar ran the Medellin cartel.

"ISA collects intelligence in advance of missions by counter-terrorism forces like SEAL Team Six and Delta Force," Tran continued. "Not much else is known about them."

"Someone like Knapp must've had a special skill set to get into ISA."

"Probably still has some of those skills," Tran said.

"I saw a badge in a glass frame in his office. The Latin phrase VERITAS OMNIA VINCULA VINCIT was written around the outer edge of the badge."

"It means 'Truth Overcomes All Bonds.'"

"The only Latin phrase I remember is *In Somnis Veritas*."

"In dreams there is truth," she said.

Santana nodded.

She leaned in. "Do you follow your dreams?"

"Tell me about Kim Austin."

"Talking about you is far more interesting."

"Not to me."

Letting out an exaggerated sigh, she said, "All right, then. What would you like to know?"

"Did Kim Austin ever talk to you about the Blue Skies crash?"

She raised her eyebrows. "No, she didn't. But that's an interesting question."

"How so?"

Reyna Tran set her cup on the saucer, folded her hands, and placed them on the table. "Kim Austin was an accident investigator. You must think her death has something to do with the Blue Skies investigation."

"It's possible."

"Nearly anything is."

A few seconds passed in silence before Santana said, "What do you know about the crash?"

"Only what I've read."

"And what have you read?"

"That the flight somehow got off course. That the aircraft ran out of fuel and crashed in the ocean, killing everyone on board."

"Any ideas as to how the flight could have gotten that far off course?"

"Pilot error."

"It's my understanding that the captain and crew were experienced pilots."

"Everyone makes mistakes," she said.

"Even you?"

She smiled. "Rarely."

"Could terrorism have caused the crash?"

"Always a possibility. But the feds haven't suggested that was the cause. Then again, do you believe everything the government tells you?"

"Because I'm a police officer, some people see me as working for the government."

"Then I guess I shouldn't trust you, Detective," she said with a wry smile.

"Did you meet a man named Paul Westbrook at the security conference?"

"Briefly. Why?"

"He was one of the investigators of the Blue Skies crash."

"How interesting."

Santana drank some Coke and set the glass on the table. He glanced at his notes and then said, "According to your website, you created a computer program that profiles passenger lists."

"That's right. The software is based primarily on passenger information. Once that data is in the system, the program calculates the likelihood of passengers posing some kind of threat."

"Does Blue Skies Airlines use your software?"

"Unfortunately, they're one of the few airlines that don't."

"Have you profiled the passenger list on flight six twenty-four?"

"I have not."

"Anyone ask you to?"

"You mean like the FBI?"

"The FBI or any of the other alphabet soup agencies."

"Why would they if pilot error caused the crash?"

"Do you believe everything the government tells you, Ms. Tran?"

"*Touché*." She leaned forward again and whispered, "We're so *sympatico*, don't you think?"

Santana didn't think so at all.

Chapter 11

Santana caught a 4:50 p.m. nonstop flight from Chicago that landed at MSP airport at 6:15 p.m. By the time he collected his SUV from the Park and Fly lot and drove home, it was 7:30 p.m.

Once inside the house, he deactivated the security alarm using the keypad on the wall, flicked on the light switch, and hung up his bomber jacket in a closet near the front door. Santana never used the protective sticker or sign advertising the name of the alarm company. Most professional burglars had the wiring diagrams to all the major systems. They would know exactly how to pry open the control cover and cut the right wire before the alarm had a chance to send its signal.

Besides the alarm, his home security system also consisted of four high-resolution cameras, strategically mounted to give him a view of all sides of the house. The cameras recorded images in color during the day and switched automatically to black-and-white recording when ambient light was low. Infrared LED lights surrounding the lenses allowed the cameras to record with night vision capabilities up to fifty feet from the house. The cameras activated and recorded only when they detected motion.

The video streams could be viewed on his computer monitor. A large hard drive on a digital video recorder stored the footage recorded by the security cameras. When the hard drive was full, the system was configured to back up all footage to an external hard drive, thus freeing space on the DVR. The system was also capable of transferring live video feeds to any computer with an Internet connection. Santana considered his security measures preparation rather than paranoia.

As he walked into the kitchen, he sensed immediately that something was wrong. Gitana hadn't come to greet him, as she always did when he returned home. With his heart beating rapidly and his mind conjuring awful scenarios that could have befallen her while he was gone, Santana went to her food and water bowls near the back door. He could see that she'd eaten some of the food he'd left for her and drunk some of the water.

Because of Santana's odd work hours, a contractor had installed a dog door in the back wall. An electronic chip in Gitana's collar activated the door that gave her access to an enclosed dog run he'd constructed in the backyard.

He opened the back door, half expecting—no, hoping—that he would see her in the dog run, but his heart sank when he saw that the gate in the fence surrounding the dog run was open. He'd rarely opened the gate since it was installed. When he was home, Gitana entered and exited with him through either the front or back doors of the house.

Gitana had never attempted to escape from the enclosed area and had never run from him when off her leash, as some dogs were prone to do. In fact, she always checked to see where he was if she was unleashed and never allowed him to get too far away from her.

He went outside and checked the latch on the gate. After examining the latch, he thought he had the answer as to how she'd gotten out. He remembered installing the gate when it was cold and wet outside, meaning the wood would have been slightly swollen. When warm weather arrived and the wood had dried out, it had apparently shrunk some, making it more difficult to close because the gate was too far from the jamb for the latch to engage in the strike.

He returned to the house and went up to his bedroom to the computer on the desk, where he touched a key to awaken it. Then he clicked on the application for the security cameras mounted around the house. Four separate rectangular black-and-white boxes appeared, representing the sides of the house. He saw instantly that something was blocking the lens on the camera overlooking the dog run and the back yard.

He grabbed his Glock and Maglite out of the nightstand drawer and hurried downstairs and out the back door, and then out the gate and into the back yard that sloped toward his dock and boathouse along the river. It was clear and cool, with a waning gibbous moon and stars glistening like tiny shards of glass.

Shining the beam of light on the camera, he saw that a leaf was covering the lens. He then focused the beam on the ground below the camera, looking for footprints, but he saw no evidence or indication that anyone had stepped here recently.

Despite the motion detector in the camera, someone could, he imagined, stay close enough to the side of the house to place a ladder against it, climb up, and put a leaf over the lens without being detected. Santana made a mental note to adjust the angle on the camera to prevent this from happening in the future.

He got a ladder out of the boathouse, climbed up, and removed the damp leaf from the lens. Then he adjusted the camera angle so that it covered more of the area closest to the house and climbed down.

He turned toward the river, striding among the pines and birch trees that studded his yard, calling out Gitana's name. He knew she would come if she heard him—if she was able to.

He'd lost so many of those close to him that he felt he could not bear to lose another, especially his dog, his friend, his companion.

At the shoreline he wondered a moment if she'd jumped or waded into the river after a duck or goose and had been swept away. But he quickly rejected the idea. Though she loved the water and was a strong swimmer, she'd never ventured into the river after anything, sensing, perhaps, the presence of danger in the swift current.

A heavy cloak of helplessness enveloped him now as he turned away from the river and called out her name again and again.

"Gitana! Gitana!"

As he hiked up the hill and past the garage toward the road running perpendicular to his house, darker thoughts entered his consciousness. He wondered if another Colombian assassin had come for him and had killed Gitana in the first act of revenge.

Santana clenched his fists and gritted his teeth as a blister of anger burst loudly out of his mouth like an epithet. "Gitana!!"

He flicked off the Maglite, knowing that the beam would offer a clear target, and looked around him, his eyes gradually adjusting to the darkness.

Puddles of light lay below a streetlight a block to the north and another two blocks to the south. He saw nothing but a stretch of empty tar road underneath the lights.

And then he thought he heard a dog barking in the distance to the south. *It's just my imagination, wishful thinking,* he thought. But then he heard it again, coming closer.

He squinted into the darkness until he saw her racing out of the shadows down the street, her tail feathers wagging, ears perked, mouth open as if in a wide grin.

And then he saw something else, someone running behind her, someone closing in.

Chapter 12

Gitana jumped up when she reached him, pressing her paws into his chest while she repeatedly licked his face. Then down on all fours, she pushed her body against his as he squatted in front of her and gave her a hug, whispering, "How's my girl?" in her ear, as his eyes remained fixed on the approaching shadow in the distance.

He flicked on the switch and shined the beam at whoever was approaching, hoping to blind them and giving him a chance to move quickly if he had to.

"Whoa," the figure approaching said, throwing her hands in front of her eyes. "Hello?"

Santana let out a breath and flicked off the Maglite. "Sorry about that."

"I didn't mean to startle you," she said, stopping in front of him.

Santana stood. "Not at all," he lied.

She smiled. "Good."

He'd met his neighbor when he was out jogging a few days ago. She was dressed in a dark running suit now with light-reflective paneling and dark running shoes with glow-in-the-dark detailing.

"I found Gitana in my front yard this afternoon," she said. "When I didn't see you around, I wondered if she'd gotten loose somehow. I knocked on your door, but no one answered. So I took her home with me. I hope you don't mind. As soon as I saw your lights, we came over."

"Thanks for taking care of her," he said. "I was out of town. Somehow she got loose from her dog run."

"Does that happen often?"

"Never before."

"That's strange."

He was tempted to invite her in as a "thank you" for watching over Gitana, but he was tired from the long day and the flight. A shower, a comfortable bed, and some much-needed sleep were all that he wanted.

A long silence ensued as they stood looking at each other before she said, "Well, see you later."

"Thanks again."

"No problem. She's a lovely, sweet dog." She started walking in the direction of her house.

"My name is John Santana," he called after her.

She stopped and turned toward him. "Deborah Russell," she said, followed by a bright smile.

"If you're not doing anything tomorrow, come over and I'll barbeque steaks on the grill," he said.

"No need to repay me."

"It would be nice to have some company."

"Steaks would be great."

"How about one o'clock? Just come around back."

"Sounds like a plan," she said. "I'll bring a Caesar salad."

"Sounds good."

"See you then." She waved and jogged off.

Before Santana went to bed, he checked the video stream from the cameras around his house, focusing his attention specifically on the camera overlooking the dog run and back yard. He could see Gitana still inside the dog run at 11:16 a.m., tracking an elusive scrap of paper. Trees bent in the wind, and leaves blew in tornado-like swirls on the ground and off the branches of the birch trees in the yard. The gate looked as if it were closed.

Santana fast-forwarded. A few minutes before noon, a leaf appeared to land on the camera lens, totally blocking the view. Approximately forty-five minutes later, he saw Deborah Russell approach the front door with Gitana beside her. She rang the bell and waited before ringing it again. It looked as if she said something to Gitana. Then they walked across the yard and out of camera range.

Santana got up from the chair and crawled into bed. Gitana was already in the bed, waiting for him. In the past, he'd rarely allowed her to sleep with him. Rather, she'd slept in her bed on the floor or on the floor itself, depending on how warm or cool she was. But since Jordan's death, he'd loosened the rules and let her up in the bed. She'd taken full advantage of the opportunity. Now, he thought, it would be difficult—and unfair—to change the rules again.

He held the sleep/wake button down on his department cell phone until the power off slider appeared, but for some reason, when he slid it to the right, the phone stayed on.

The city provided the phones for the detectives, although, like Santana, most had their own phone as well as the department's. Santana remembered when detectives used to carry just one phone and paid the city for any personal use. But when it became an issue with the news media because it was sometimes difficult to figure out what was personal and what was business, the department went back to two phones. Santana was aware that some of the brass had their phones set up by the city IT staff that worked at the police department, but the majority of officers, including detectives, got their cell phones and replacements from the radio shop.

He plugged in the power cord to charge the battery on his department phone and set it on his nightstand.

* * *

The autumn sunlight felt warm against Santana's skin, the light northern breeze cool, as he set two plates, silverware, and cloth napkins on the picnic table in his back yard that was ablaze with yellow leaves. Earlier this morning he'd repaired the broken gate latch. Now he could smell wood smoke and cooked meats wafting in the wind. A sailboat glided over the small waves on the river as a crow rose from a crook in a birch tree branch like an ash off a dying fire.

The gas grill was already heated when Deborah Russell came around the back corner of his house a few minutes after 1:00 with a bottle of red wine in one hand and a serving bowl in the other. She wore jeans, running shoes, and a jean jacket over a black pullover.

Gitana, who had been sleeping on her side near the table, got up and went to Russell, her tail wagging as she approached.

She stroked Gitana's head and held up the bottle of wine. "I hope you like Merlot."

"It'll be good with steak," Santana said. He handed her a waiter's corkscrew. "Would you do the honors?"

"My pleasure."

He watched as she quickly opened the bottle. She saw him watching and said, "I once worked in a winery in California. Opened a lot of bottles. But caps are replacing corks."

"I've heard that."

She nodded. "Preserves the wine better. Just have to get past the snobbery that comes with uncorking a bottle."

"What do you do now?"

She filled each of the wine glasses half full. "I'm a jury consultant."

"You help lawyers pick favorable jurors."

She nodded. "So you know something about it."

"I do."

She handed him a glass. "Try it. It's from Napa Valley."

He could taste the black cherry and plum flavors.

"Like it?"

"It's good."

"It has a very silky texture. Can you taste the tannins, cinnamon, and toasty oak?"

"I'm afraid my palate isn't that developed."

She waved. "Sorry. I get a little carried away when it comes to wine."

He nodded. "How would you like your steak?"

"Medium rare."

Santana opened the grill cover and used a long fork to spear each filet mignon from a plate on a side table, the steaks sizzling as he set them on the hot grill. Behind the steaks he placed two Idaho potatoes he'd pre-heated in the microwave and then wrapped in foil, and closed the lid.

"Would you like to eat the salad before or after the steaks?" she asked.

"Before is fine."

"You're not French or Italian," she said as she sat down across the table from him, facing the river.

He shook his head.

"Well, they generally eat their salads after the main course. My father was second-generation French and my mother second-generation Italian. They kept many of their customs."

"Do you speak either language?"

"Unfortunately, no. I wish now that I had learned."

"It's good to speak more than one."

"What other language do you speak?" she asked.

"Spanish."

"You're lucky."

"How so?"

"Being fluent in two languages. I wish I spoke Spanish. It's so common here now."

"Yes, I suppose so."

She picked up the pair of salad tongs on the table and served them each some lettuce and croutons. "So what do you do for a living?" she asked.

Santana was always reluctant to respond to the question, primarily because opinions of homicide detectives were mostly garnered through unrealistic television shows and movies. Plus, he never discussed cases with anyone other than his colleagues in the department, except for Jordan, since she'd once been a police officer and then a private detective, and with Natalia. But short of lying to Deborah Russell, he really had no options other than telling her the truth, though he could shade his response a little.

"I'm a police officer."

"Where?"

"In St. Paul." He hoped she would leave it at that.

"You work patrol?"

He shook his head. "Homicide."

"Oh, you're a detective. No wonder you're familiar with jury consultants. You speak for the dead."

Her remark surprised him. He and his fellow detectives had used those same words before when describing the job, but he had no recollection of hearing them used outside of the homicide unit.

"Where did you hear that expression?" he asked.

"I have a doctorate in behavioral science and have been around lawyers and police officers for many years."

She looked as if she was in her mid-to-late thirties, but Santana had no intention of asking her age. He did notice a slight scar running just below her right cheekbone to under her bottom lip.

They ate without speaking for a time. Santana felt comfortable with the silence, but he wasn't sure how Deborah Russell felt.

"You like the salad?" she asked.

"Very much."

Santana checked the steaks and then sat down again.

"They smell delicious," she said. Her eyes wandered through the trees and toward the river. "I like how peaceful it is here. That's what attracted me to this area. I love being by the water."

"I'm afraid I don't know much about my neighbors. How long have you lived here?"

"Only about a month," she said. "Do you have a boat?"

"I do. It's docked in the marina in Hudson."

"Only so many days left to enjoy it before winter comes."

Santana wasn't certain if she was angling for a boat ride or merely making a statement of fact. "Winter's not my favorite time. Where did you live before moving here?"

"A number of places, actually, but I moved here from California."

"Is that where you're from?"

"My father was in the service. We moved a lot. I never had a place I considered home. Perhaps I'll find a place I can call home here in Minnesota along the St. Croix."

"Perhaps you will," Santana said.

Chapter 13

At dawn on Monday morning the wind blew out of the west, moist and warm and mixed with rain. Santana could not shake the images of last night's dream from his mind as he stood in his second-floor bedroom near the sliding glass door that faced the river, finishing his cup of hot chocolate, watching the current drift southward toward its confluence with the Mississippi. Gulls rose off the water, their bodies white against a gray sky.

He'd called Hawkins late last night and debriefed her on his trip to Chicago and his conversation with Reyna Tran. Then he'd fallen into a restless sleep in which he'd dreamed of being trapped in an airliner as it spun out of control and plunged toward the ocean, the sound of screaming passengers reverberating in his ears, his heart thumping in his chest. Reyna Tran was seated in the aisle seat to his left. For some reason he could not understand, he was unable to see or hear the passenger sitting in the window seat to his right, though he knew someone was there.

Tran was looking directly at him, a blissful expression on her face, her dark red lips curved in a beatific smile, her hand clasped in his. She was not screaming.

A plastic cup half-filled with wine sat on the console between them. Strangely, the wine lay perfectly still in the cup. Underneath it was a napkin stained with the blood of the grape.

* * *

Santana was the first detective to arrive at the LEC for his shift that morning. Knowing that Pete Romano was an early riser and liked to be in his office before his detectives, Santana wanted to be there to talk with him about a trip to DC. Romano's door was open. Santana was surprised to see two men he didn't recognize. One was seated in a chair in front of Romano's desk. The other was leaning against the far wall.

The men sensed Santana's presence at the door and turned to look at him. Romano's eyes followed.

"John. Good to see you so early." Romano curled his fingers. "Come in. I'd like you to meet Ted Lake and Jack Gaines."

As Santana approached, Lake stood and offered a hand. "Good to meet you, Detective."

Ted Lake had a self-confident demeanor, neatly trimmed dark hair, and boyish good looks that probably fooled most people into thinking he was considerably younger than he was. Maybe they didn't notice the little fan-shaped wrinkles beside the corners of his eyes and mouth and the few strands of gray hair that indicated he was in his early forties. Together with the dark suit, white shirt, subdued dark blue tie, and black, sturdy shoes—the standard uniform of the FBI—Lake was the poster boy for the Bureau.

Santana shook Lake's hand, making sure he squeezed just as hard as the agent squeezed his.

Romano said to Santana, "Ted is from the FBI."

"Could've fooled me."

Lake smiled. "Bet you never guessed, right, Detective?"

Santana didn't reply.

The second agent, wearing a similar suit and tie, approached Santana with his thick hand extended. "Jack Gaines," he said with a slight Southern accent. He had eyes like brown stones and gave Santana his best cold cop stare.

Gaines was more heavyset than Ted Lake, though his grip wasn't as firm. He had a beefy face and buzz cut and reminded Santana of a stereotypical drill sergeant in a Hollywood movie.

"Sit down, John," Romano said.

Santana grabbed a second chair from against the wall and sat down to the right of Lake. He was thinking that if he played it just right, agents Ted Lake and Jack Gaines from the FBI were going to make his DC trip request a lot more palatable for Romano.

Romano looked at both agents and then focused his gaze on Santana. "We were just discussing the Kim Austin murder case."

Santana's eyes shifted to Lake. "Why would the FBI be interested in her murder?"

"She worked for the NTSB."

"So the FBI investigates all deaths involving NTSB employees?"

The agent gave Santana a tight smile but offered no reply.

"What is it you really want?" Santana asked.

Lake looked at Romano. "Cooperation."

"And how would you define that?" Santana asked.

Lake kept his eyes on Romano. "Your detective is wound a little tight, Commander."

"Is that so?"

"All we're asking is to be kept abreast of the case."

"This wouldn't have anything to do with the Blue Skies crash, would it?" Santana said.

Lake fixed his charcoal-gray eyes on Santana. "Now why would you think that, Detective?"

"Oh, just a wild guess."

"Is that what this visit is all about?" Romano said, directing the question to Lake.

"Your detective seems intent on harassing NTSB employees who were part of that crash investigation," Gaines replied. "People who had no connection to Kim Austin's death."

"And how would you know that?" Romano asked.

"We've received complaints," Gaines said.

Romano shook his head. "I'm not talking about complaints, if in fact there were any. What I meant was, how would you know that these individuals had no connection to Kim Austin's death?"

"Unless the FBI knows who murdered her," Santana added.

Lake jerked his head in Santana's direction. "I take exception to that insinuation, Detective."

"Well, I take exception to you and Gaines and the Bureau interfering in my investigation."

"Take it easy, John," Romano said.

"All I'm asking is that you keep us informed," Lake said to Romano.

"And if we don't?"

"I'm sure your chief would appreciate knowing of your refusal to cooperate with the Bureau."

"Is that a threat?"

Lake stood. "Take it any way you want, Commander." He looked at Santana. "Nice meeting you, Detective. Good luck with your case." He nodded at Romano. "Thanks for your time, Commander. I expect you'll be in touch."

"I wouldn't hold your breath," Romano said.

Lake headed for the office door.

Gaines straightened up, unwrapped what Santana thought was a jawbreaker, and placed it in his mouth. As he walked by Santana, he dropped the wrapper and followed Lake out the door.

Santana bent over and picked up the wrapper. It smelled like butterscotch.

"What a couple of jackasses," Romano said.

"I need to go to DC, Pete."

"Kim Austin was killed here."

"Maybe someone followed her here."

"They'd have to know the area. Know where the caves are."

"If I'm going to find out anything about Austin, I need to talk to the people who knew her."

"You mean NTSB employees."

"Only the ones who were members of the Go-Team."

"For the Blue Skies crash."

Santana nodded.

Just as Romano was about to reply, his phone rang. He answered and listened, his gaze lifting from the murder book on his desk to Santana's face. "All right," he said at last and hung up.

Romano's eyes locked on Santana. "Looks like you and Hawkins will be missing this week's murder meeting."

"What's up?"

"Seems the body of another young woman has been found in a cave along the Mississippi. If the same perp killed both women in separate events, we could be dealing with a serial killer."

Despite Romano's anger with the FBI, Santana realized he was quoting the Bureau's definition of a serial killer.

"This changes things," Romano said.

"In what way?"

"We'll postpone the DC trip for now. I want you and Hawkins to focus on this latest murder. See if you can find a connection."

"To be officially considered a full-fledged serial killer, the perp has to commit at least three such homicides within a thirty-day period," Santana said.

"Let's hope it doesn't come to that, Detective."

Chapter 14

Santana and Hawkins followed a uniformed female SPPD officer, whose last name was Sykes, along a narrow dirt path through the woods near the banks of the Mississippi River in Lilydale Park. The path rose slightly as they neared the underbrush surrounding the entrance to the cave.

"You the first officer on the scene?" Santana asked Sykes.

"Yes."

"Who discovered the body?"

"A parks employee named Frank Dornan found her."

"What was he doing in the cave?"

"Supposed to be sealing up the entrances in the area."

"You go inside?"

"Wish I hadn't," she said.

Santana saw the uniformed parks employee named Dornan leaning against a waist-sized boulder near the cave entrance, smoking a cigarette. His hands were shaking. Standing beside him was Rick Paukert, the young SPPD officer Santana had met at Kim Austin's crime scene. When Dornan saw the three officers approaching, he straightened up, dropped his cigarette on the ground, and crushed it with his shoe.

Crime scene tape had been wrapped around a series of trees, cordoning off the area near the cave. Santana held up the tape as Sykes and Hawkins ducked underneath it. Then he ducked under and approached Dornan and Paukert.

"Detective Santana," Paukert said. His gaze slid quickly to Hawkins. "Detective Hawkins."

Hawkins flashed him a smile.

"Already set up a perimeter," Paukert said. He held up a clipboard. "Crime scene log is ready."

Santana could see that Paukert's, Dornan's, and Sykes' names were already written on the log, along with Gina Luttrell, the district supervisor.

"Where's Luttrell?"

"Inside the cave," Sykes said.

Santana signed the log and turned his attention to Dornan, the parks employee with a hooked nose and shaggy hair. "Please pick up the cigarette butt you dropped."

"Oh, sorry," Dornan said. "Got to keep the park clean."

"I'm more worried about contaminating a crime scene."

"I should've caught that," Paukert said, a look of embarrassment on his face.

"You touch anything, Mr. Dornan, when you entered the cave?" Santana asked.

He shook his head.

"Why did you go inside?"

"I always check to see if anyone is in the cave before it's sealed." He motioned over his shoulder. "But it doesn't matter."

"Why is that?"

"You come back here in a few weeks, the entrance will be open again."

"Kids?" Hawkins said.

Dornan let out a breath and nodded his head toward the entrance. "More publicity means more kids. Rather them than this."

"Are there any tunnels leading out of the cave?" Santana asked.

"None that I saw."

"Let's take a look," Santana said.

Sykes said, "If you don't mind, I'll wait here."

Santana and Hawkins looked at her and then each other.

"No problem," Santana said.

This cave was approximately forty feet high and sixty feet wide and deep, but it had the same damp smell of wet stone as in the cave where Kim Austin's body had been found.

"Sweet Jesus," Hawkins said, a horrified look on her face.

Santana slipped on a pair of latex gloves as he approached, stopping five feet from the body, where Gina Luttrell was standing, her arms folded across her chest. She gave Santana and Hawkins a nod but didn't speak.

A dagger that looked very much like the one through Kim Austin's hand had been embedded in the victim's palm. Her head had nearly been severed from her body. The turtleneck sweater she wore was pulled up to her breasts, revealing a large section of tissue that had been carved out of her stomach, exposing her organs.

The darker, looser sand around the body was smoother and more compact than the soil in the rest of the cave, as though dragged with a flat mat, like an infield on a baseball diamond.

Hawkins came up beside Santana. "What kind of sicko would do something like this to another human being?"

"Maybe he's making some twisted statement," Santana said. "But there's something about the way the scene is staged that's familiar."

"Familiar as in Kim Austin's murder?" Luttrell asked.

"Yes," he said. "But familiar in another way."

"How, John?" Hawkins said.

"It'll come to me."

"It better come soon," Luttrell said. "I want this bastard off the streets."

"There's something else," Santana said.

Hawkins looked at him. "He didn't bury the body."

Santana nodded.

"Maybe he didn't have time," Luttrell said.

"Or maybe he wanted this body to be found."

"Why?"

"I'm not sure."

"Animals haven't been at her," Hawkins said.

"This scene is fresh, Kacie."

There was a long silence before Hawkins said, "You remember the young woman who went missing from the convenience store the other night?"

"Laurie Baldwin."

"You think it might be her?"

"We'll know soon enough," Santana said.

* * *

Later that same day, after the body had been identified by the driver's license found at the site, Santana and Hawkins drove to a rambler on St. Paul's East Side.

An attractive, petite woman in a jeans and a camo T-shirt opened the front door and faced them. In the background Santana could hear the overused phrase "breaking news" spoken by a female reporter from a local television station. The reporter was describing the scene outside the cave entrance they had just come from and the discovery of a female body.

Carol Baldwin's brunette hair was graying and tied in a ponytail, though her face appeared nearly wrinkle-free. Her amber eyes were red and swollen. She held a crumpled tissue in her hand.

"Ms. Baldwin?" Hawkins said.

She nodded.

"I'm Detective—"

"I know who you are and why you're here."

Hawkins glanced at Santana and then said, "May we come in?"

When Carol Baldwin hesitated for a moment, Santana thought she might close the door on them, hoping, perhaps, that keeping them out would somehow suspend time. It was a reaction he'd seen before. But instead of closing the door or inviting them in, she turned and walked across the living room, where she sat stiffly on the edge of a couch, her hands in her lap, her eyes staring blankly at some distant point.

Santana and Hawkins let themselves in. Hawkins sat beside Carol Baldwin. Santana sat in an armchair across from them. Hawkins introduced herself and Santana in a soft, soothing voice.

Carol Baldwin inhaled a deep breath and slowly released it. "I've been listening to the news. You found my baby's body this morning, didn't you?" She looked at Santana rather than at Hawkins sitting next to her, as though holding him personally responsible for her daughter's death.

The face Santana had seen at the crime scene—even in death—looked like the face in the framed photos on the wall. Still, he needed a positive ID.

"We believe it's your daughter, Laurie," he said. "But we'll need you to come to the morgue to positively identify her body."

Hawkins slipped an arm over the woman's shoulders. "We're very sorry for your loss."

Carol Baldwin shrugged off the gesture as she would a shawl. "Why didn't you find my girl before she was killed? Why did you let this happen?" she said in an angry, frustrated voice. "My baby was only twenty years old."

Santana knew there was nothing he or Hawkins could say that would lessen her pain, in the same way he knew nothing anyone said or did could assuage the pain he felt over Jordan's death. He'd found some solace in the death of the perp who had killed Jordan, but it was too early in this investigation to offer Carol Baldwin anything but hope and his word that he would bring her daughter's killer to justice.

"We need you to help us find her killer," he said.

Her nostrils flared. "How?" she said, raising her hands in a helpless gesture. "You're the ones supposed to help me."

"You can help by telling us about your daughter, Ms. Baldwin," Hawkins said. "Who were her friends? What were her interests? Was anyone angry with her? Was she afraid of anyone? Did she have a boyfriend?"

"Yes."

"Yes, she had a boyfriend?" Hawkins said.

Carol Baldwin blew her nose and nodded. "But he'd never hurt her. He loved her. Besides, he's out of town deer hunting."

"We'd like his name and a number if you have it."

She gave Hawkins the name. "But I don't remember his phone number."

Her eyes were focused on the ceiling as her small body slumped against the couch cushions, evidence of her growing sorrow and helplessness.

"How long have they been dating?" Santana asked.

"About a year."

"Does she have other close friends?"

"A cousin. And a friend from high school."

Santana asked for their names and wrote them in his notebook.

Carol Baldwin's eyes welled up again. She wiped away the tears with the tissue and sat up. "We're good Catholics. Good people. We followed the rules. Lived a good life. Where is the reward for a good life? If God was a loving God, how could He let this happen?"

Her questions were the same ones Santana had asked himself over twenty years ago when a drunk driver had killed his father and two men had murdered his mother. Because he could find no clear answer, he'd arrived at his own conclusion and abandoned his faith.

There was no God, nothing after death, he believed. Heaven and hell were right here on planet Earth. Life was what each of us made it. And even then, fate often intervened, taking the innocent in accidents, disasters, and murder. Despite all the best efforts and intentions, victims ended up in the wrong place at the wrong time, like Laurie Baldwin and countless others Santana had come across in his investigations.

Carol Baldwin looked at Hawkins and then Santana. "Laurie was a good girl. She volunteered at the food shelf because she loved to help others. She lived here at home to save money for school and to help me out. I don't make much in my job waitressing."

"Where do you work, Ms. Baldwin?" Hawkins asked.

She gave the name of a local restaurant. Then she looked directly at Santana. "My baby didn't use drugs or drink alcohol. She was a good student. I never had any trouble with her." She clenched her fists and held them against her eyes. "This doesn't make sense."

Carol Baldwin either consciously or unconsciously believed that life operated under a set of rules. As a parent, she believed in the natural order of life—the older generation should die first. Belief in a natural order rather than chaos was her defense against the randomness of the universe and the uncomfortable idea that we were not in complete control, that it was futile to try and understand the incomprehensible, that rules were arbitrary. Her daughter's death was evidence of that mistaken belief. Her daughter would not outlive her. Having lost the foundation that helped her to feel safe and to make sense of the world, Carol Baldwin felt as if she'd lost her moorings and had been cast adrift.

"I told Laurie not to take that job at the convenience store," she said with an exasperated shake of her head. "If she'd listened to me, she'd be alive today," she sobbed.

Hawkins slipped her arm around Carol Baldwin.

Santana waited silently for a time before he said, "Did your daughter mention anyone or anything she thought was strange or odd recently?"

"Not that I recall."

"Is there a Mr. Baldwin?" Hawkins asked.

She hesitated as though she didn't know how to reply. Finally, she said, "Stu was killed in an accident just after Laurie was born."

"Any other children?"

She shook her head. "I never remarried. I'm alone now."

"Is there anyone you can call, Ms. Baldwin? A relative? A friend?"

"My sister."

"Does she live in town?"

"The suburbs."

"You should call before we leave."

"Yes. I should."

"We'd like to look in your daughter's room if you don't mind," Santana said.

"Why? What do you hope to find there?"

"Maybe a connection to the person who killed her, Ms. Baldwin."

She led Santana to her daughter's bedroom and then returned to the living room, where Hawkins waited.

Laurie Baldwin had moved on from her teen years into young adulthood. There were no boy band posters on the wall. Instead there were photos of her with a young man Santana assumed was the boyfriend Carol Baldwin had mentioned. There were photos of the young couple fishing and hunting, photos of them with a large black lab Santana thought might be the boyfriend's dog, photos of the two of them at the Minnesota State Fair, photos of them on the boyfriend's motorcycle, photos of them canoeing. Always, Laurie Baldwin was smiling.

Santana felt his blood get hot. He wanted the perp who had killed Laurie Baldwin, wanted justice for her mother. Still, he knew he had to control the caged demon inside him, the demon that demanded revenge for all the innocents who had suffered.

He inhaled a deep breath and exhaled slowly, waiting until his heartbeat slowed. Then he went to the small desk in a corner opposite the door and opened the top drawer. He worked quickly, checking each of the drawers, eliminating anything he felt was unrelated to the case.

In a bottom drawer he found a short stack of receipts held together with a rubber band. Most were gas and grocery receipts. But one stood out.

It was a receipt from a towing company dated two weeks ago. The receipt came from the place where Albert Greer worked. The same Albert Greer who had found Kim Austin's skeletal remains.

Chapter 15

The following morning, Santana and Hawkins drove Carol Baldwin to the Ramsey County medical examiner's office on University Avenue. The ME's office is located next door to Regions Hospital in a one-story tan brick building with a front door for the living and a back door loading dock for the dead. They parked in the lot in front of a sign that read

RESERVED FOR FAMILY OR POLICE

The detectives escorted Carol Baldwin to the family waiting room. They sat quietly for a few minutes until Reiko Tanabe, the ME, entered the room and introduced herself to Baldwin.

Pointing to the monitor on a table in a corner, Tanabe said, "There's a video camera on the ceiling in the suite. When you're ready, the camera will be turned on and you'll see a clear image of the deceased's face, enough to make a positive ID. You can view the image alone, or you can have one or both of the detectives remain here with you if you'd like. Take as much time as you need."

Family members were given all the time they needed to work up the courage to view their loved one, without being pressured by a detective or staff from the medical examiner's office. Afterwards, a staff member would offer to direct Carol Baldwin to grief counseling or other services should she feel she needed them.

"I don't want to see my baby through a camera lens," she said. "I want to go into the suite."

This was not an unusual request in Santana's experience. Family members often chose to enter the suite rather than ID the deceased on a video monitor. Babies were usually brought out of the clinical confines of the suite to the mother waiting in the family room so she and/or other family members could say their last good-byes.

"Are you sure?" Tanabe asked.

Carol Baldwin nodded. "I'm sure."

Tanabe led her out of the waiting room and into the suite, where she turned on the video camera so the detectives could see.

Though a solid wall separated him from Laurie Baldwin's body lying on a cold, wheeled autopsy table, Santana felt there was no distance between the two of them. Once he became involved in the case, it was his responsibility, his mission, to bring the perpetrator to justice, to provide the family with closure. He was her voice now. He would speak for her. He considered it a sacred responsibility.

After Carol Baldwin identified her daughter's body, the detectives drove her back to her house.

As Santana pulled the sedan up to the curb, Hawkins said, "Would you like one of us to walk you to your door, Ms. Baldwin?"

Carol Baldwin sat stiffly beside Hawkins in the back seat. "Her ring," she whispered as though talking to herself.

Santana turned away from the steering wheel to face her. "What ring?"

Baldwin seemed to come out of a trance. "My baby's high school class ring. It wasn't on her finger."

"Did she always wear that ring?"

"Always," Carol Baldwin said. "She never took it off."

* * *

Kacie Hawkins called the towing company where Albert Greer worked. Greer's supervisor said he hadn't come to work today. She then accessed Albert Greer's address from the DVS, and she and Santana drove to an apartment building in the Eastview neighborhood in the southeast corner of St. Paul.

A thin mulatto woman in a T-shirt and jeans answered the apartment door. Dark roots were growing out of her bleached blonde hair. Acne had scarred her cheeks.

"Ms. Greer?" Santana said, thinking the woman looked as if she'd been napping.

"No," she said. "The last name is Jones."

Santana held up his badge wallet. "I'm Detective Santana. This is Detective Hawkins. We're with the St. Paul Police Department. We're looking for Albert Greer."

"What has Albert done now?"

"We just want to talk with him, Ms. Jones. Are you related to him?"

She canted her head. "I'm his mother."

"Are you a doctor at Regions Hospital?"

Her laugh came out as a hard cough. "Yeah. I'm a brain surgeon."

"Where do you work?"

"At the Lock and Load," she said.

Hawkins gave Santana a questioning look.

"It's a gun shop," he said.

Santana had suspected Albert Greer wasn't being truthful about his family during their interview. Now he knew for certain that Greer had lied and wondered what else he'd been untruthful about.

"Do you know where your son is now?" he asked.

"At work."

Obviously, Greer had lied to his mother as well as to the police. "You mind if we look in his room?"

Her eyes focused on each of the detectives before she said, "I do mind." Then she closed the door.

"Should we get a warrant?" Hawkins asked.

"We need to find Greer first."

"Let me try his friend Cory Brown. See if he knows where Greer is. I got his number when I interviewed him."

Hawkins called Cory Brown and got his voicemail.

"Brown lives with a roommate. Let me try him."

The roommate answered on the second ring.

"It's Detective Hawkins. I'm looking for your friend, Cory Brown."

"How come?"

"If you know where he is, you need to tell me," Hawkins said.

"Far as I know, he's with Albert Greer."

"And where would that be?"

"At the cave."

"Which one?"

"Where they found the Austin woman's body."

It took Santana and Hawkins fifteen minutes to get to the nearby parking lot and another ten minutes to hike up the trail to the cave entrance.

Yellow crime scene tape was still wrapped around the tree trunks. The detectives ducked underneath and made their way into the cave. Santana and Hawkins turned on their Maglites and let the beams play across the walls and ground.

"Maybe they were here and left," Hawkins said.

A moment later Santana saw Albert Greer and another male he assumed was Cory Brown emerging from a shadowy tunnel in back of the cave. They both wore helmets with lamps attached so their hands were free. The young men froze when they saw the two detectives.

"Albert," Santana called. "We need to talk to you."

Greer spun around and took off into the tunnel.

"I'll get him," Santana said, sprinting after Greer. "You watch him," he yelled over his shoulder as he ran past a stunned Cory Brown.

Santana stooped as he ran to keep from bumping his head on the gradually shrinking tunnel, the Maglite beam bouncing in front of him like a headlight on a rough road. The musty air smelled of wet sandstone. Vapor from his breath hung in small white clouds in front of him.

Greer was maybe thirty yards ahead. Santana caught sight of him each time he rounded a corner of the twisting tunnel.

Running on the sandstone floor was like running on a sandy beach. Santana could feel his calves tightening.

When he came to two branching shafts, one to his left and the other to his right, he focused the Maglite beam on the tracks in the sand and saw that Greer had turned right.

Santana followed for twenty yards until he came to a pile of rough debris. The remaining space between the pile and tunnel wall was quite narrow, making passage difficult. Given that Greer was so lean, Santana figured he'd had no trouble squeezing through. Having explored these caves and tunnels before, he probably knew where he was headed. Santana had no idea. He only hoped there was an opening somewhere ahead. Santana's shirt snagged and tore as he wiggled past the debris and ran after Greer. After fifty yards he came upon a ladder embedded in a vertical tunnel. Looking up, he saw Albert Greer climbing the rungs above him. Santana turned away as a shower of rust flakes rained down on him.

He switched off the Maglite, stuck it in his belt, and began scaling the ladder. He focused his eyes on the wall in front of him to avoid getting rust in them. Still, he could feel flakes landing on the top of his head and see them drifting by him like tiny falling leaves.

The ladder led to another tunnel that was six feet high and just wide enough to move through. He grabbed his Maglite and turned it on. Twenty-five yards to his right was a solid sandstone wall.

Ten yards to his left he saw Greer kick open a chain-link grate attached to a four-by-four-foot hole in the wall. A second later Greer slid through the opening on the seat of his pants and disappeared. Santana went after him.

The opening in the wall led to a sewer drain ten feet below. There was a dry ledge three feet above the flowing sewage on each side of the drain. Santana shook his head in frustration. He had no desire to jump into a stinking sewer. But the fleeing Albert Greer had given him little choice.

Santana dropped through the hole and landed on his feet, then nearly lost his footing in the three inches of fast-moving liquid sewage. He could feel the sludge leaking into his shoes and squishing between the soles and his socks.

The humid air smelled like a plugged toilet bowl. The walls were made of concrete. Roaches caught in the Maglite beam fled to the shadows. Santana didn't see any rats, but he was certain they were here.

Greer was no more than twenty yards ahead of him now. Santana figured the young man wasn't in the best shape and he would soon run him down, if the footing weren't too slippery.

"Come on, Greer. Give it up!" he yelled.

Greer looked back. His eyes glistening in the beam of light were wide with apprehension—but he kept going. Santana cursed under his breath and went after him.

Bubbles rose from the decomposing waste with each step he took. The deeper into the drain he slogged, the more misty and cloudy the air became. At first Santana thought the mist and clouds were caused by condensation from the humid conditions, but the sudden increase in his breathing rate and his heart palpitations were telling him something else.

A few yards ahead of him Greer slowed and began staggering as if he were drunk.

Santana's vision was blurry. He felt sick to his stomach.

Methane gas!

If they didn't get out of the sewage drain quickly, they both would soon be dead.

Chapter 16

Santana caught up with the staggering Albert Greer, wrapped an arm around his waist, and held him up.

"Stay awake!" he yelled.

Greer slung an arm over Santana's shoulder. "Got to . . . get out . . . of here."

Santana's legs felt rubbery. His eyes itched and watered. The space behind his right eye pounded as though it were being bludgeoned with a hammer. He was sweating profusely and fighting the urge to close his eyes and to sleep. The high quantity of methane gas in the sewage pipe was depleting the oxygen level in his body. Once the level fell to less than twelve percent, he would lose consciousness.

Death would soon follow.

He stuck the Maglite in his belt and pressed a handkerchief over his nose and mouth as he half-carried and half-dragged Albert Greer back the way they had come.

He was thankful that Greer was mostly skin and bones and couldn't weigh more than one hundred forty pounds. *No way I can carry someone of considerable weight. Not with the methane gas sapping my strength.*

Santana's eyes had adjusted to the dim light, though he wasn't sure if the red-eyed rats he saw scurrying out of his way were in his imagination or were real. At this point he didn't care.

One more step, he kept telling himself. *One more step.*

Then he stumbled, nearly went down. *Don't fall in the sewage!*

He held Greer tightly around the waist as he lurched forward.

A puddle of light spilled through the open grate ten feet above them. The grate led to the labyrinth of tunnels they had passed through and eventually to fresh air and freedom. But climbing up the slimy concrete wall to the tunnel was impossible, even if he wasn't carrying Albert Greer.

There has to be another way out through the sewage drain—if I can stay conscious and alive long enough.

He plodded forward, fighting the urge to stop and rest. His feet felt as if they were made of concrete. His workout regimen sustained him.

Twenty yards past the grate, the clouds of mist thinned. His heartbeat slowed. He felt less dizzy.

He stuffed the handkerchief in a pocket of his raid jacket, took out his SPPD cell phone, and checked the signal. *No reception.*

Santana lowered Greer into a sitting position on the ledge. "Can you hear me?" he said, leaning close to the young man's face.

Greer's eyes blinked open. He nodded his head.

Santana straightened up. "You going to make it?"

"Sure," Greer said. He bent over, rested his hands on his thighs, and vomited. Santana stepped back and waited.

When Greer was finished, he wiped his mouth with his jacket sleeve and peered up at Santana. "Why were you chasing me? I didn't do anything."

"Then why were you running?"

He shrugged and closed his eyes. His chin dropped to his chest.

"Albert," Santana said.

No response.

Santana listened to Greer's breathing. It sounded labored.

Though there was less methane mist here than where they had been a few minutes ago, the rotten smell of sewage was still thick. They needed to get out soon.

Santana noted the direction the liquid sewage was running. *It has to come out somewhere.* He wished he could ask Greer if he knew the way out and how far it was.

He stood Greer up. His left arm felt numb from dragging and carrying the young man, so he switched sides and wrapped his right arm around Greer's waist. Then he slid the Maglite out of his belt with his left hand and flicked on the switch.

"All right," he said, even though Greer was unconscious and couldn't hear him. "Let's keep going."

Santana followed the Maglite beam for what he estimated was a quarter mile before he saw a side passage to his right. Shining the light into the passage, he noted that after ten yards, it led to a much larger and better-lit drain.

In less than a minute they entered a massive drain that Santana estimated was at least sixteen feet in width, with limestone walls and brick ceilings over ten feet high. Two inches of water covered the floor. The air was much better, though still not as fresh as the outdoors. He'd been trying to get a fix on the direction they were heading. He guessed—and hoped—this pipe led to the river.

He paused a moment and inhaled and exhaled, trying to clear his lungs of the methane. Then he tightened his grip around Greer's waist and kept going.

Ten minutes later he lugged Greer out of the pipe near the riverbank, where he called 911 and then Kacie Hawkins.

* * *

Later that same day, after leaving the emergency room at Regions Hospital, Santana took a long shower and changed into a clean set of clothes and shoes he kept in a gym locker at the LEC. His torn shirt and sewage-stained shoes went into the garbage. He sent his pants and raid jacket to the dry cleaner.

Albert Greer remained in the hospital, suffering from the effects of methane poisoning. Mechanical ventilation was applied. According to the treating physician, Greer's symptoms and chest radiographic findings were consistent with acute pneumonitis. He was admitted to the intensive care unit.

Hawkins obtained a warrant to search the apartment where Albert Greer lived.

Greer's mother reluctantly let them in. The apartment smelled strongly of marijuana.

"I don't see too well up close," she said as Hawkins gave her the warrant. "But my brain still works. I know my son. And he ain't no killer."

"Maybe you can help us prove that, Ms. Jones," Santana said.

"How am I gonna do that?"

"By being truthful with us."

"The truth gonna set him free, huh, Detective?"

"If he's innocent, it will. If you'll tell me where his bedroom is, Ms. Jones, Detective Hawkins will ask you some questions. We'll leave you an inventory of anything we take."

Her gaze slid off Santana to Hawkins and back to Santana again. "Gonna let the black lady detective ask me the questions, huh?"

"That isn't the way it always works," Hawkins said.

"Seems that way to me."

"Just like with your son," Santana said.

"What you mean?"

"The way things seem isn't always the way they are, Ms. Jones."

She nodded and pointed with an index finger. "Last door down the hall," she said.

The furniture in Greer's bedroom consisted of a single unmade bed and a beat-up four-drawer dresser. Colorful posters of muscle cars with sexy-looking, heavy-breasted women in various stages of undress covered the wall space.

A small television sat on a stand in one corner. Stacked on a shelf under the TV were video games with names such as *Dark Souls III, Ryse: Son of Rome, Soul Edge,* and *Chivalry: Medieval Warfare.* According to the synopses, all the games involved the use of swords.

Santana checked the drawers and then the closet. On a shelf Santana found a 4" x 6" hardbound sketchbook. The pages inside were mostly filled with drawings of cars and women, but on a few pages near the back of the book were sketches of Black Sabbath album covers. One cover featured the sinister figure of an evil-looking woman standing in front of a watermill amid a darkened wood.

Santana looked under the bed and then between the mattresses. His fingers felt something, but it was too far back to reach. He stood and lifted up the top mattress. Underneath it he saw what appeared to be a small jewelry box. Inside it was a class ring.

* * *

When Santana and Hawkins returned to the Homicide Unit, they met with their commander, Pete Romano.

"How you feeling, John?" Romano asked.

"Better."

Santana and Hawkins were seated in two chairs facing Romano's desk. The chairs were new and more uncomfortable than the ones they had replaced. The legs were shorter as well. Santana wasn't sure if Romano had deliberately ordered less comfortable and shorter chairs as a way of creating a power advantage when he met with his detectives. Santana had had his disagreements with Romano, as he'd had with Rita Gamboni and the commander before her, but he hadn't pegged Romano as petty and conniving. Then again, he'd been wrong about things before.

"You're lucky," Romano said. "I hear Albert Greer is still in the hospital."

"At least for twenty-four hours," Santana said. "We can't question him till he's off the ventilator and out of intensive care."

"That's assuming he doesn't lawyer up," Hawkins said.

"And that he lives," Romano added. He straightened a small stack of reports on his desk and pushed them aside.

Framed photos of Romano's wife and five children were neatly arranged on one corner of the desk. Hanging on the wall behind the desk were framed photos of a young Pete Romano in his class-A uniform, his eight-point cap tucked under one arm, and more recent photos of Romano shaking hands with the current mayor, one of the state's senators, and the President. Mentally comparing the earlier photo with the more recent ones, Santana noted a few wrinkles creasing his olive complexion and wisps of gray threading Romano's jet-black hair.

Romano rested his elbows on the desk and folded his hands together. "Anything interesting or incriminating turn up in the search of Greer's apartment?"

"Laurie Baldwin's high school class ring," Santana said. "I found it in a jewelry box under Greer's mattress. Baldwin's mother ID'd it. She said her daughter never took it off."

"Pretty damning evidence," Romano said. "What did the mother say?"

"She refuted pretty much everything Greer told me about his family." Santana opened his notebook and flipped the pages until he found the page he was searching for. "His mother isn't a surgeon at Regions. She works at the Lock and Load."

"Is that a bar or restaurant?" Romano asked.

"Gun shop."

"Clever."

"Father disappeared years ago. Both he and the mother were known drug users. Child protection also paid a few visits to the house where the family once lived. When Albert was seven years old, the school nurse reported finding bruises on his body. Mother said he fell off his bicycle. A case worker was assigned, but the father took off."

"Let me guess," Romano said. "No more bruises."

"You've heard this story before."

"Unfortunately, I have."

Santana continued. "Mother remarried, hence the different surname, but got divorced a few years ago. Albert dropped out of high school his senior year and, to his mother's knowledge, never took the ACT test. A check of his student records indicated he was a below average student at best, and not the 'smart' kid he described to me."

"Sounds like he's hiding something," Romano said.

Hawkins nodded. "Or he's got an inferiority complex."

"He drives a late-model Chevy Camaro," Santana said. "We had it towed to the impound lot. Forensic techs will check the car for blood spatter, hairs, or fiber we can connect to Laurie Baldwin. Greer also has a collection of video games involving swords. Laurie Baldwin was nearly decapitated."

"You find a sword?"

"No," Santana said. "But when we searched Laurie Baldwin's bedroom, I found a receipt from the towing company where Greer worked."

"So we've got a possible connection between Greer and Baldwin. Any connection between Greer and Austin?"

"We're looking. Forensics will run the blood on the dagger in Baldwin's hand. The blood on the dagger found in Kim Austin's hand belonged to her. Some of the foot impression evidence in the cave where Austin's remains were discovered belongs to Albert Greer and his friend, Cory Brown. Other prints haven't been identified."

"Lots of kids in that cave," Hawkins said.

Romano nodded. "Any connection between Kim Austin and Laurie Baldwin?"

"Nothing yet."

Romano's gaze shifted to Hawkins and back to Santana. "You two think Greer is good for both killings?"

"I'd like to question him again," Santana said.

"Then we all better hope he wakes up," Romano said.

Chapter 17

Laurie Baldwin's naked body lay on the stainless steel table in an autopsy suite. Reiko Tanabe, the Ramsey County medical examiner, stood beside the table. She was clothed in scrubs, an apron, a scrub cap, and elbow-length gloves. Her face shield was on the autopsy table.

Santana stood on the opposite side of the autopsy table. He was not wearing scrubs.

"There's severe bruising in the upper right back area, in the right chest area, on the muscle of the upper left shoulder, and inside the muscle of the right side of the chest," she said, pointing to each area of the body as she spoke. "The second and third ribs in the right side of the chest are broken. The middle of the muscle in the right hand is bruised, along with injuries to the inside of her lower lip and bruises on her face."

"She was beaten before she was killed."

"That's my conclusion," Tanabe said. "I also examined the deep knife wounds to her neck under a low-power stereomicroscope. There are sharp force injuries to the cervical vertebrae. Also a point mark from where the blade sunk in the vertebrae. From the bone wounds I estimate that the width of the blade was between one and one quarter to one and one-half inches. The length was between seven and eight inches. The blade had a non-serrated cutting edge. This wasn't a thin-bladed kitchen knife. This was a heavy weapon that could cut through thick bone."

"Like the dagger stuck through her hand."

Tanabe nodded. "There was no evidence of blade chatter."

"Meaning?"

"The cutting pattern. When a thin blade jumps around slightly from side to side, it's called blade chatter."

"What about manner of death?"

"The knife wounds were postmortem," Tanabe said. "There's a contusion in the scalp suggesting she was struck with an object, but I don't believe that's what killed her either." Leaning over the body, she pointed to the small wound in front of the right ear. "Nearly missed this, John. An ice pick, or something similar, perforated the vertebral artery. Laurie Baldwin died of massive cerebral edema."

* * *

Early that evening Santana knocked on the door of Joe Wesley's home on Big Carnelian Lake, five miles north of downtown Stillwater. Wesley had degrees in psychology and criminology. Prior to his retirement, he was a former Minnesota Bureau of Criminal Apprehension crime scene investigator, as well as an FBI special agent and criminal profiler.

Wesley had made a name for himself profiling and tracking the infamous Edward Bastion, who was suspected of raping and killing over twenty young women, many of them hitchhikers he'd picked up along US Highway 93, which stretched from Jackpot, Nevada, through Idaho to Lost Trail Pass in Montana. Bastion was eventually killed in a shootout with FBI agents in the Bitterroot Mountains of Idaho, but not before he'd killed two FBI agents and severely wounded Joe Wesley. Soon after his recovery, Wesley had retired from the FBI and disappeared from public view.

The man who answered the door in a rumpled red flannel shirt and blue jeans, a cane in his right hand, looked nothing like the handsome Joe Wesley Santana had admired when he was an SPPD patrolman and Wesley was a crime scene investigator with the BCA. Wesley's dark hair had turned snow white. He wore it long and slicked back. The color matched his two-day beard. His lean, nearly emaciated frame was in stark contrast to the muscular one Santana remembered.

Wesley gave Santana a dead-eyed stare before recognition showed in his hazel eyes. "John Santana."

"How you doing, Joe?"

"I've been better. You?"

Santana detected the strong odor of alcohol on Wesley's breath. "I've been better, too."

Wesley gave an understanding nod. "I try to avoid listening to or reading the news. Most of it's bad and filled with paranoia. But I did hear about your lady. Sorry."

Santana nodded while he waited in uncomfortable silence for Wesley to invite him in. Finally, he said, "Got some time to spare?"

"Time is pretty much all I've got now. So I choose not to waste it on things I can do nothing about."

"This won't take long, Joe." Santana nodded at the briefcase in his hand. "I'd like you to take a look at some photos for me."

Wesley's weary eyes shifted to the briefcase and then back to Santana. "I gave all that up. Just like I gave up my marriage, my kids, and nearly my life." His eyes momentarily flamed with an intensity that had, at one time, burned like a hot fire, Santana thought. Then the flame died, leaving nothing but the cold ash of dark memories in his eyes.

"I just need advice, Joe."

"Okay. Here's the best advice I can give you. Find another job that doesn't hollow you out like a cancer, a job that doesn't destroy you and everyone around you, something that doesn't leave you with nightmares of the monsters you hunted. Save yourself, John, and those still close to you."

Santana stuck his foot between the frame and the door as Wesley tried to close it.

"Didn't you hear what I just said, Santana?"

"I heard. But you haven't heard what I have to say."

"If it's about the cave killings, I don't want to hear it."

"Thought you didn't listen to the news."

"I stopped the paper. Next task is throwing out the TV. Only need a radio to catch sports."

"Two women are dead, Joe."

"And there's more to come," he said.

"Then help me. I'll keep you out of it."

"You wanted to keep me out of it, you wouldn't be knocking on my door. Now move your foot before I break it."

Santana pulled his foot back but held his right hand against the door. "My mother was murdered when I was sixteen, Joe, and my girlfriend just recently. I've been stabbed and shot and nearly died."

"And your point is?"

Santana removed his hand from the door. "Here I am, still doing my job."

Wesley held his eyes on Santana's for a long moment before closing the door.

Santana considered knocking again and then changed his mind. Instead, he walked out to the driveway, where Wesley's Range Rover was parked, and tried the driver's side door. It was open.

Removing a manila envelope from his briefcase, Santana placed it on the front seat along with his business card. Then he locked and shut the door, got into his own vehicle, and drove away, his hands tight on the wheel, the headlight beams illuminating the yellow stripe in the road, his eyes fixed on the asphalt that merged with the endless darkness of the universe.

* * *

Later that evening Santana decided to skip his run and workout. Tests the medical staff at Regions had conducted showed his vitals were normal, yet he felt lethargic and sleepy, a possible lingering effect from having inhaled the methane gas.

He took Gitana for a short walk and then went down to his boathouse, where he got a cold bottle of Sam Adams from the refrigerator and a folding lawn chair and a pair of Bushnell binoculars from a cabinet. He opened the bottle and the chair on the dock and sat down with sigh. Fatigue had set in. He stifled a yawn.

Gitana lay down with a sigh beside him. Her eyes were half-closed, communicating pleasure that he was home and with her. When she sighed and lay down with her eyes wide open, he'd learned from experience that she was communicating disappointment. The disappointing sigh was the guilt trip she laid on him when he wasn't going to play with her.

The setting sun painted the horizon a bright orange and laced the underbellies of the cumulus clouds with a pink hue. A cool but light breeze shook the yellow leaves on the birch trees that studded his back yard.

No matter which way he figured it, Laurie Baldwin was the piece that didn't fit the puzzle. She didn't work for the NTSB and had no apparent involvement with the Blue Skies investigation. Yet, instinctively, Santana felt that her death was connected in some way to the deaths of the others.

Santana unbuckled his belt, which held the pancake Kydex holster and his Glock 23. He slid the holster out of the belt loops and set it on the dock beside him. Then he buckled his belt again. He'd worn a gun for so many years that he felt naked without it, as if he'd forgotten to put on his underwear.

He kept a smaller Glock 27 in the nightstand near his bed and another in a holster attached to the underside of the dining table. He carried the Glock he kept in the nightstand with him whenever he ran with Gitana or went out for the evening.

His thoughts shifted to Natalia and how long it had been since he'd seen her. Tonight he would write her an e-mail. He'd refused to let her come and see him. The risk was too great.

He drank and scanned the river with the binoculars. A few power and sailboats were scattered on the water, and in the near distance, a small catamaran. Santana held the binoculars on the catamaran. As it approached on a close reach toward his dock, he recognized the brunette woman sailing it.

"Ahoy," Deborah Russell called, steering to windward, slacking the mainsheet until the cat slowed to a crawl and came to rest ten yards off the dock. Water dappled her wet suit and dampened her face and hair.

Gitana sat up and huffed, her tail wagging.

"Didn't know you sailed," Santana said.

"I used to race when I was a kid." She gestured at her catamaran. "Mostly Hobie sixteens. They're still a lot of fun to sail at any age." She smiled. "The daggerboard makes it easier to maneuver out of a marina and sail upwind. Tacks really well. But I can't get too close to your dock. That's one downside with a daggerboard. You sail much?"

"I've sailed some. But I'm more of a powerboat guy."

"Right," she said. "You've got a boat in the Hudson marina."

"The *Alibi,*" he said.

"Cute. Fits with the detective, huh? You ever want to sail before it gets too cold, let me know. I have an extra wet suit. Should fit you."

Santana didn't ask why she had a wet suit his size, maybe for an ex-boyfriend—or a current one.

"How's Gitana?" she asked.

Upon hearing her name, Gitana huffed again and wagged her tail furiously.

Santana tipped his beer bottle toward her. "Good as ever," he said.

"You doing okay?"

"How do you mean?"

"Well, I heard the story about you saving the guy in the sewer pipe on the local news."

Santana hadn't heard the news and didn't care to. Crime reporters from the media outlets would be trying to contact him for a quote or comment. He'd tried again to turn off his department cell phone after arriving home, but it wouldn't shut down. He planned to take it to the SPPD radio shop, which is located in the police annex across 10th street from the old police headquarters, when he had the time.

"I heard the guy you saved, Albert Greer, was wanted in connection with the murder of that young woman found in the cave. You're a hero."

Santana looked at her but offered no response.

Chapter 18

At seven the next morning, Santana's department cell phone rang. When he answered, a gravelly voice said, "What if I told you I burned the photos you left in the envelope on the front seat of my Range Rover yesterday?"

"Then you'd be lying, Joe."

"Pretty sure of yourself, huh, Santana?"

"No more than you."

A long silence ensued. Then Joe Wesley said, "I'm going fishing. If you want to talk, be at my place in one hour, or you'll miss the boat. And I mean that literally."

* * *

One hour and fifteen minutes later, Santana was seated in Joe Wesley's pontoon as the boat left the dock. The sky was ice blue, and the leaves on the trees along the shoreline blazed with red and gold. Wesley sat in the captain's chair behind the windshield and wood grain dash panel. The twenty-five-foot pontoon had a live well cooler, rod holders, a fish finder, and aft casting chairs, where Santana sat.

"Thought it appropriate today that we go after northern pike," Wesley said above the purr of the ninety-horsepower Evinrude outboard.

"I'm assuming you know where to look."

"They're most likely concentrated in and around deep water, where weeds are more likely to survive into late fall than those far up in the shallows. The larger ones hide in deep water to attack bigger fish like walleye or large-mouth bass." He trained his eyes on Santana. "Pike are ambush predators," he said with a maniacal look on his face and a gleam in his blood-shot eyes.

Once Wesley found a weedy spot on the lake, he cut the engine. "You fished for pike before, John?"

"Never."

"Well, they're notorious for playing with your bait. Sometimes they'll hit it and simply let go without actually running with it. Don't try and set the hook till the fish actually tries to run with the bait. If you lose a pike, don't reel in right away; go slowly. The fish might actually strike it again."

"What bait are we using?"

"In thick weeds, I'd use a tandem spinnerbait or a jerkbait. But in scattered weeds like this, we'll go to a shallow-running crankbait. Just so you know, we can't harvest pike between twenty-four and thirty-six inches, and only one pike larger than thirty-six inches."

"Then what's left for you, Joe?"

He grinned. "We'll see who catches what."

While they fished, they talked baseball and how the Twins had tanked this past season. Then the topic shifted to football and the Vikings and what chance the team had of reaching and winning the Super Bowl. Wesley was much more knowledgeable about baseball and football than Santana and followed the teams more closely. Santana preferred soccer and the World Cup matches.

"Soccer?" Wesley said.

"We call it football in South America. You know, because it's played with the feet."

"You can call it anything you damn well please," Wesley said. "I'd just as soon watch paint dry." He shook his head and let out a long, deep laugh.

Through it all Santana tried to concentrate on the beautiful fall day and the pike lurking in the weeds around the boat. But he could not totally forget the reason he'd come to see Joe Wesley and the violence and ugliness that followed him like a shadow.

By noon Santana had caught and released three pike. Wesley had caught and released four of approximately the same size. Santana placed their rods in the holders while Wesley opened a cooler. They sat at a table in the shade of a canopy and ate roast beef sandwiches. Wesley drank from a bottle of Budweiser, Santana a can of Coke.

"Tell me about the photos," Santana said, pointing to the manila envelope on the table.

"Heard you might've caught the perp who killed the Baldwin girl."

"Maybe."

"You're not sure?"

"That's why I'm here, Joe."

Wesley finished his beer and removed the crime scene photos from the envelope. The first photo showed the interior of the sandstone cave, where the body of the second victim, Laurie Baldwin, had been found.

Wesley studied the photo and then shifted his gaze to Santana. "In order for me to understand what happened to the vic," he said, "I need to know everything you can tell me about her."

"She was a junior at St. Catherine's College in St. Paul," Santana said. "She was a light drinker and didn't use drugs. According to her mother and friends, her boyfriend was out of town deer hunting when she was abducted from the convenience store where she worked on weekends and two nights a week. His alibi checked out."

"So she worked nights at a 'stop and rob,'" Wesley said, using the common law enforcement term for convenience stores.

"She did."

"Almost all convenience stores only have one person working the night shift," Wesley continued. "What about the security cameras?"

"The store camera that's attached to the wall above and behind the counter showed someone dressed in jeans and a hoodie entering the store at eleven ten. I assume it's a male by the way he walks."

Wesley nodded. "But we can't completely rule out a woman, John, even though there have been many more male serial killers than females throughout history. When I was working for the Bureau, we figured about seventeen percent of all serial homicides were committed by women. Since women commit around ten percent of total murders in the US relative to men, women represent a larger percentage of serial murders than all other homicide cases."

"Pretty much defies the popular understanding of serial murder," Santana said.

"Pretty much," Wesley said. "Holds true with African-American males as well, the largest racial minority group among serial killers. They represent about six percent of the population, but twenty percent of the total serial killings. We've got Hispanic and Asian American serial killers, too. Unfortunately, serial killers span all racial and ethnic groups."

Santana considered what Wesley had said. Then he continued with his explanation of the Laurie Baldwin investigation. "So the perp walks up and down the aisles of the convenience store and then picks up a carton of milk from the back and some bread from the front. He pays for the items and exits the store. A few seconds after he leaves, at eleven seventeen,

Laurie Baldwin comes around the counter and goes out the front door. She never returns. No one else enters the store till eleven twenty-five. Unable to locate a clerk, the customer calls 911. He's not a suspect in her disappearance."

"I take it there are no cameras in the lot."

"Correct. So we have no idea why Laurie Baldwin decided to leave the store. But she left her car behind, which indicates she either willingly or unwillingly got into someone else's vehicle."

"Any witnesses?"

"No. The customer who called 911 reported seeing a white or gray van leaving the lot as he was driving in. It's eight minutes between the time Laurie Baldwin left the store and the time the customer entered."

"Long enough for her to be overpowered or forced at gunpoint into the van," Wesley said.

"She might have known her abductor, Joe, which is why she left the store. Or maybe he created some kind of disturbance that lured her out the door."

Wesley nodded. "The scenario you're describing was not an impulsive act. Everything indicates that the UNSUB was a cautious, organized killer," he said, using the acronym for unknown subject. "It's likely that he's been in this store before to learn where the camera was situated. He reduced his risks as much as possible by wearing the hoodie and canvassing the store to make sure he was the sole customer."

"Someone could've come into the store while he was there."

"True. But risk-taking is part of the thrill. The fact that Laurie Baldwin's car was not taken is further evidence that this UNSUB was organized. He drove to and from the store in his own vehicle, possibly the van the customer described. He likely rigged the van in some way to contain her."

"You mean like tape or shackles?"

"Yes. Had her car been missing, we could assume that he arrived on foot or public transportation. That would be a sign of disorganization." Wesley pointed to the photo on the table. "The crime scene in the cave is like an artist's canvas. Predators often like to preserve it in some fashion, so they can return later to relive the crime. Looking at the location, it's obvious that he prepared beforehand, another sign of organization. He was familiar with the cave and was comfortable there."

"Albert Greer could be the perp in the Baldwin killing," Santana said. "I found a receipt from the towing company where he worked in her bedroom and her class ring under the mattress in his bedroom."

"The ring's a possible trophy," Wesley said. "The towing receipt puts the two of them together at some point. I'd look for a murder kit, too. Nearly every serial killer I've come across has one. The type of bag chosen and the items placed into it reveal a great deal about a killer's approach to murder, his sense of identity, and his imagination."

"The skeleton of the first vic, Kim Austin, was also found in a cave," Santana said.

Wesley shook his head. "I can't profile a killer if the only evidence is a skeleton. Do we know how she died?"

Santana pulled a second photo out of the envelope showing the Kim Austin crime scene and turned the photo toward Wesley.

"Notice any similarities, Joe?"

Wesley peered at the photo forensic techs had taken. "Dagger through the palm of each vic." Then he looked at Santana, his eyes now lit with intensity. "You're Catholic, right?"

"I was."

Wesley gave a slow nod as though he understood. "It's tough believing in a loving God when you spend this life in a shit storm of violence and death."

"You ever see something like this before, Joe?"

"This level of violence? Sure. But if you're asking if I've seen this exact scene before, no, I haven't. You question Albert Greer yet?"

"He was on a ventilator yesterday. I called the hospital this morning. He's breathing on his own now. Once he's out of intensive care, I'll question him."

Wesley was quiet for a long beat as he thought about what Santana had said. "Typically, a predator who abducts someone like Laurie Baldwin wants his victims alive, John. His whole purpose is to have complete control over another person, to make the victim helpless, so he can do as he pleases. His power is in his ability to inflict pain, to make the victim suffer while she's in his control. He wants his victim to show fear, which indicates weakness. Fear gives him pleasure."

"We don't have any evidence of torture in the Austin murder," Santana said.

Wesley thought about it for a time before replying. "Even though the crime scene is similar, if there's no evidence of torture in the death of Kim Austin, then it's possible that she was killed by someone else. Time-wise, the killings are far apart. That doesn't mean that the same person couldn't have killed both women."

"Laurie Baldwin died from a massive cerebral edema," Santana said. "The ME believes an ice pick, or something similar, perforated her vertebral artery. There were postmortem multiple sharp force injuries to the neck that nearly decapitated her."

"Indicates severe rage," Wesley said.

"No evidence of multiple stab wounds in the Kim Austin killing."

Wesley nodded his head.

"Any thoughts on what the UNSUB in the Laurie Baldwin killing does for a living?" Santana asked.

"I've met successful people who display all the characteristics of antisocial personality disorder—what we'd call psychopaths—in politics, banking, investment, medicine, sports, television evangelism, and law enforcement. The difference is, most don't become serial killers."

"They just prey on society in other ways."

"They do. But unlike psychotics, psychopaths are not out of touch with reality. They don't experience delusions or hallucinations. They're rational and aware of what they're doing and why they do it. It's a matter of choice. But you won't find a definition in the official handbook of mental health, the *Diagnostic and Statistical Manual of Mental Disorders*. Both psychopaths and sociopaths are defined as having an antisocial personality. The predator we're dealing with is not a sociopath."

"Why not?"

"Well, both lack empathy. But a psychopath doesn't have a conscience. If he lies to you so he can steal your money, he won't feel any moral qualms, though he may pretend to. He may observe others and then act the way they do so he's not discovered. A sociopath typically has a conscience, but it's weak. He may know that taking your money is wrong, and he might feel some guilt or remorse, but that won't stop his behavior."

"Any suggestions as to what to do next?"

"Well, first off, open that cooler beside you and hand me another beer. And get a Coke for yourself."

Santana retrieved the cold drinks and handed the beer to Wesley.

He unscrewed the cap and took a long swallow. Then he wiped his mouth on his sleeve and squinted at Santana. "You ever have nightmares, John?"

"All the time."

"I thought if I quit looking at evil, removed myself from it, I'd be able to leave it all behind."

"It doesn't work that way," Santana said.

Wesley nodded and drank more beer.

Santana continued. "Albert Einstein once said, 'The world is a dangerous place to live; not because of the people who are evil, but because of the people who don't do anything about it.'"

"That why you wouldn't take no for an answer yesterday?"

"That's part of it." Santana watched the small smile lines form at the corner of Wesley's mouth. "You believe that, Joe?"

"I did once. Not anymore."

Santana didn't ask Wesley what had changed his mind. He knew.

"My experience has taught me a lot," Wesley said. "Much of it I wish I could forget." He leaned forward. "But the most important and depressing lesson I've learned is that there are no limits when it comes to what one human being can do to another, especially when it involves sexual behavior. The darkness of human nature, John, is as infinite as the universe. Evil exists whether good men do something about it or not. And nothing is going to change that."

Wesley drank some beer and burped. Then he leaned back and gazed at the water. "The predator who tortured and killed Laurie Baldwin is already making plans and looking for new targets."

"Where's his Achilles heel?" Santana asked.

Wesley focused his eyes on Santana again. "Most psychopaths I've known are narcissists, especially sexual criminals. You can take it to the bank that sooner or later he'll begin to believe that he's invincible. He'll start taking unnecessary risks. The need for excitement will push him in search of a bigger adrenaline rush. That's when he'll make a mistake."

"And until then?"

"Let me put it to you this way. If somebody wants somebody bad enough, it's nearly impossible to stop. I don't care how much security you have or how much money. If a predator wants you and has the time and the patience, an opportunity is going to present itself. And there's nothing you or I can do to prevent it."

Chapter 19

That afternoon while Santana was at his desk in the Robbery/Homicide Unit, catching up on his paperwork, he received a call from Carol Baldwin.

"What can I do for you, Ms. Baldwin?"

"It's too late now. You had your chance."

Santana could hear the frustration and anger in her voice. "What chance was that?"

"You could've left that piece of trash, Albert Greer, in the sewer, Detective. Let him die in his own methane gas chamber. But you chose to save his life. I hope you're happy."

"We don't know for certain that Greer is responsible for your daughter's death."

"We know his history."

"How's that?"

"He was charged with sexual assault before. He's registered as a sex offender."

Santana figured the news media had leaked that information. "So you're saying I should've left him in the sewer to die."

"You'd have done all of us a favor."

"What if Albert Greer is innocent?"

She laughed. But it was a bitter, hollow laugh. "Albert Greer has killed before."

"There's no evidence of that at this time."

"Kim Austin," she said.

"I will bring your daughter's murderer to justice, Ms. Baldwin. Whether it's Albert Greer or someone else."

"Don't make promises you can't keep, Detective," she said and hung up.

* * *

Later that afternoon, Albert Greer was moved from the intensive care unit at Regions Hospital to a private room. Before going to the hospital to interview him, Santana and Hawkins wanted to talk to Greer's friend, Cory Brown. A check with the Computerized Criminal History System revealed no arrest records for Brown.

They located him at the technical college he attended. The three of them sat in plastic chairs in a large cafeteria beside a wall of windows facing a quadrangle sprinkled with red and yellow leaves.

Cory Brown was a young African-American man with a pudgy face and body and short hair. He had long sideburns that connected to a narrow line of hair along his jaw, often called a chin strip beard. His black-framed glasses with thick lenses were held securely in place by an adjustable eyeglass cord. His half-eaten lunch on the table in front of him consisted of a ham and cheese sandwich on white bread, a package of Doritos corn chips, and a can of Mountain Dew.

"What do you want to see me about?"

"Take a guess," Kacie Hawkins said.

His gaze transferred to hers. "Albert Greer?"

"Bingo."

"We did some cave exploring together. That's all."

"Who found the skeleton?"

"Albert saw it first. We thought maybe someone was trying to trick us. You know, for Halloween. But the more we looked at it, the more it looked real. I said we should call the police."

"Had you ever been in that cave before?"

Cory Brown shrugged. "We could've been. Can't say for sure."

"You know a woman named Kim Austin?" Santana asked.

"No, I don't." He thought for a time. Then his eyes lit with recognition. "Wait a minute."

"You do know her."

"No. But I remember the name. See, me and Albert been invited on a local TV show. I heard the name from the producer who called us. We're doing a special Halloween show. Her body was found in a cave, like Laurie Baldwin's."

"Tell us about Laurie Baldwin," Santana said.

"Hey," Brown said, waving his hands. "Only thing I know about her is, she's dead. Like the lady named Kim."

"How well did Albert know Laurie Baldwin?"

"Who said he knew her?"

"I just did."

Cory Brown gave Santana an unsteady smile. "I don't think he did."

"So Albert never mentioned her name?"

Brown scratched his neck. "Don't recall that he did."

"You ever go in the Food Mart on Grand Avenue with Albert?"

"I guess I have."

"No guessing, Cory."

"Okay. I've been there."

"Did Albert or you ever speak to the pretty brunette clerk behind the counter named Laurie?"

"Oh," he said, his eyes widening with feigned surprise. "That's the Laurie they found in the cave."

Santana leaned forward until his face was within six inches of Cory Brown's. "Let's cut the bullshit. Unless you want to be considered an accessory to Laurie Baldwin's murder." Threats, Santana knew, often worked with a reluctant witness.

"I had nothing to do with it."

"With what?"

"Her murder."

"You mean Laurie Baldwin's."

"Yeah."

"Are you saying Albert Greer did?"

"I don't know, man. Like I said, Albert isn't my best friend."

"But you hang out with him," Hawkins said.

"Don't mean nothing," he said. He met Santana's eyes again. "I told you all I know. I saw her in the convenience store when I went in there with Albert."

"Did Greer talk to her?"

"Yeah."

"About what?"

"Just small talk."

"That's all?"

"He asked her if the late model car parked out front was hers. I remember it looked like a piece of junk. She said it was hers. I think Albert might've said that he worked at the towing company down the block. If she ever needed help or parts, he could get her a deal."

"So why did you and Albert go back to the cave where Kim Austin's body was found?" Hawkins asked.

"Just to look around again."

"Maybe for more bodies?"

Brown shook his head. "I didn't want to go into that cave. Didn't want to go in the cave where the other lady was found either."

"So you two were also in the cave where Laurie Baldwin's body was found?" Santana said.

"Not me. Just Albert."

"When was he there?"

"The day before yesterday."

"On the day Laurie Baldwin's body was discovered by the parks employee?"

"That day, yeah."

"Albert told you he was in the cave the day Laurie Baldwin's body was found?"

Cory Brown nodded.

* * *

On the way to Regions Hospital to interview Albert Greer, Hawkins and Santana listened to the news on the radio, which was dominated by Greer's capture and the growing suspicion that he was a serial killer responsible for the murders of two women in the Mississippi caves in the last six months.

Callers demanded justice for Kim Austin and Laurie Baldwin. Based on their comments, "justice" meant Albert Greer should be convicted without an admission of guilt or a trial.

"Crackpots are always the first to crawl out from under their rocks," Hawkins said.

Based on experience, Santana knew Hawkins felt comfortable expressing her views to him. Like any good partners, they had shared much with each other over the years. Santana understood she would give her life for him, as he would for her, if the situation ever called for it. Their bond was one that would not easily be broken.

A uniformed officer stood outside Albert Greer's private hospital room. They held up their badge wallets before entering the room.

Greer, dressed in a hospital gown, was sitting up in bed, two pillows behind his back propping him up. His eyes widened with apprehension when he first saw the two detectives.

"Why are you here?"

"You owe me a new pair of shoes, Albert," Santana said.

Greer seemed confused for a moment. Then he nodded and said, "Serves you right for chasing me."

"You know why we're here, Albert," Hawkins said.

Greer's gaze shifted to the newspaper lying open in his lap. The headline read

SUSPECT IN BALDWIN MURDER APPREHENDED

Then Greer looked at Santana, a lopsided smile on his face. "Got my name in the paper again."

Santana stood on one side of the bed, Hawkins the other. He said, "You ever been in the Food Mart, Albert, near where you work?"

"I stop in there on and off."

Santana stepped closer to the bed. "You ever talk to Laurie Baldwin? The pretty brunette who worked behind the counter?"

Greer pulled the sheet up to his neck as if for protection. "Maybe."

"There's no *maybe* about it, Albert," Hawkins said. "Either you did or you didn't."

Greer's eyes shifted back and forth between the detectives. "I should have a lawyer here."

"You haven't been charged with anything yet," Santana said. "Not even fleeing from a police officer. But that can change —fast."

Greer thought about it. "Okay. So maybe I talked with her some. She was pretty. But she was a bitch."

"Because she wouldn't go out with you?" Hawkins said.

"She didn't know what she was missing."

"Maybe you talked about her car," Santana said. "Maybe you suggested if she needed a tow or auto parts, you could help her out."

"Where did you hear that?"

Neither Santana nor Hawkins responded.

"I know," Greer said, his face twisting in anger. "Cory told you, didn't he?"

Again the detectives offered no response.

"Well, so what?"

Santana pointed to the newspaper. "So that makes you a suspect in her murder."

"Just 'cause I knew her?"

"You also knew the cave where her body was found."

"I never been in that particular cave before she was found there. Ask Cory."

"We already did."

Greer's eyes flicked between the two detectives. "Well, maybe I've been there before. They all pretty much look the same. But I never go into caves alone."

"That's not true, Albert," Santana said.

"Says who?"

When neither detective responded, Greer said, "Cory told you, didn't he?"

"You were in the second cave the day Laurie Baldwin's body was found, Albert."

"Doesn't mean I killed her."

"Doesn't mean you didn't, either," Hawkins said.

"You like swords, Albert?" Santana asked.

Greer's face twisted in confusion.

"You have an awful lot of video games involving swords."

He shrugged. "So?"

"You own a sword?"

He shook his head.

"You're not lying to us again, are you, Albert?"

"No."

"Laurie Baldwin had a receipt from the towing company where you work. You towed her car."

"She couldn't get it started after work one night. I towed it to a garage and had it repaired."

"How did Laurie Baldwin get home that night, Albert?" Hawkins asked.

"I gave her a ride."

"How did you acquire her high school ring?" Santana asked.

Greer looked down at his hands. "What're you talking about?"

"Her class ring. The one you hid under the mattress in your bedroom."

Greer mumbled something.

"What's that, Albert?"

"She gave it to me," he said. "For helping her with her car."

"You sure you didn't take the ring off her after you killed her?" Santana said.

Greer looked away.

"You were in the second cave the day Laurie Baldwin's body was found, Albert. You sure you didn't take anything while you were there? Like maybe Laurie Baldwin's class ring?"

He shook his head.

"Why didn't you call the police when you found her body?" Hawkins asked.

"'Cause maybe you be thinking I killed her—and the other woman."

"You mean Kim Austin."

He nodded.

"You're a sex offender," Hawkins said.

His gaze turned inward as he considered Hawkins' statement. "I already talked about that with your partner."

"But you still like to strong-arm the ladies, right, Albert?"

"Those are your words, not mine."

Greer looked down at the newspaper once more before his gaze focused on the detectives again, his eyes shining with a sudden intensity.

"Okay," he said. "You're right. I killed 'em both."

Chapter 20

On Thursday morning, Santana and Pete Romano met with James Nguyen, the criminal division director from the Ramsey County Attorney's Office. The criminal division screened cases presented by detectives and determined whether criminal charges were warranted. They also handled appeals and post-conviction hearings. But their main responsibility was to prosecute all adult felonies in Ramsey County.

Nguyen was second-generation Vietnamese, the largest Asian immigrant population in the city after the Hmong from Laos. He was a short man with dark hair and skin, high cheekbones, and double eyelids, typical of many of the Vietnamese, who had immigrated to St. Paul after the Vietnam War.

He was seated next to Santana in one of the small chairs in front of Romano's desk in the Homicide Unit. Nguyen, as usual, wore a tailored dark suit and tie over a white shirt, and small dark-framed glasses. His hands were folded in his lap.

"The department's getting a helluva lot of pressure to charge Albert Greer for two murders," Romano said, looking at Santana and then Nguyen.

Santana wanted to say, "Since when did the media start running the department?" but he knew that would create an unnecessary conflict with Romano. And he needed Romano on his side, at least for the time being.

"By his own statements, we can place Greer at the crime scene the same day Laurie Baldwin's body was discovered," Romano said. "My detectives also found her class ring in his possession. Greer admits to meeting her and to towing her car one night and giving her a ride home. He's also a registered sex offender."

"What about DNA?" Nguyen asked Santana.

"Greer's DNA exists in CODIS," Santana said, referring to the acronym for the FBI's Combined DNA Index System. "The BCA lab is looking for matching DNA on Baldwin's clothing."

"But Greer's already admitted to being at the crime scene and to killing Baldwin and Kim Austin," Romano said, turning his attention to Nguyen. "What more do you need, James?"

Because he had "prosecutorial discretion," Nguyen had leverage over Romano and the department. Santana knew Nguyen would look at all the circumstances of a case, including Greer's past criminal record, in deciding whether and what to charge. Nguyen could file a murder charge, something less severe, or he could decide not to file any charges at all. Santana figured Nguyen was unwilling to risk his perfect record unless he was certain he could win the case.

Santana said, "According to the ME, Laurie Baldwin was killed with a sharp, pointed instrument to the right side of the brain."

"That doesn't sound like something an amateur would do," Nguyen said.

"What about the wounds to her neck?" Romano asked.

"Postmortem," Santana said. "When Kacie and I questioned Greer about the murder, he told us exactly what he'd seen in the cave. But when we asked him how he killed both women, he wouldn't, or, more likely, couldn't tell us. Tanabe nearly missed the small wound in the right side of Baldwin's head during the autopsy. There was no mention of a similar wound in Kim Austin's autopsy report. Typically, a murderer would strike with his dominant hand. Greer is left-handed. That fact, together with the autopsy report, leads me to believe Greer didn't kill Baldwin or Austin."

Romano's lips parted and his eyes widened in surprise. "But Greer confessed to both murders."

"I think he confessed for the publicity."

"What?"

"Greer doesn't have much self-esteem, Pete. I think he's trying to capitalize on all the publicity being generated by the murders. I doubt he's responsible for either woman's death."

"But how did he get her ring?"

"He was in the cave the day Laurie Baldwin was murdered. I believe he took her ring when he discovered her body."

"Is Greer crazy?"

Santana shook his head. "I don't think so. Confused would be a better term. He has this fantasy life in his head. Part of that fantasy is that Laurie Baldwin was his girlfriend."

"Dozens of people confessed in the infamous Black Dahlia case," Nguyen said. "Dozens did the same with the Lindbergh kidnapping and the murder of JonBenét Ramsey. Some people put themselves in the limelight out of a pathological need for notoriety. Others have an unconscious need to deal with residual guilt for other sins."

"I doubt that Greer thought this through," Santana said. "I checked with his former high school guidance counselor. His IQ is in the mid-seventies."

Nguyen nodded calmly and faced Santana. "Still, it's very hard to convince the public that a defendant who confessed to both murders is innocent. If you want me to pursue charges in the Baldwin killing, Detective, I'll review your report."

Nguyen would base his initial charging decision on the arrest report Santana sent to him. His willingness to plea bargain, how much bail would be required, the outcome of preliminary hearings—where hearsay evidence was often admissible—and trial tactics would also be based on Santana's reports. While not leaving the decision to charge totally up to Santana, Nguyen's unspoken message was clear. If Santana thought he had enough evidence to prosecute, then he should send him his reports.

"There's something else at work here, Pete. I'm just not sure what that something is, and until I know, I can't let it go."

Nguyen stood and looked at Romano. "You and I will have to deal with the media and those in the public who believe Greer is guilty of both murders. As for your detective . . ."

Santana waited until Nguyen was out the door before he said, "I need to go to Washington, DC, Pete."

Romano stared at Santana for a long moment, his forearms resting on the arms of his chair. "What does DC have to do with Laurie Baldwin's murder?"

"I'm not sure just yet."

"So I'm supposed to send you based on a hunch?"

"The answers to Kim Austin's murder might be in DC."

"*Might,*" Romano said.

Santana offered encouragement. "You worried about the Bureau?"

Romano's cheeks colored. "I don't give a damn what the FBI wants. This is our investigation."

"There were four members of the systems group investigating the Blue Skies crash," Santana said. "Kim Austin is dead and Paul Westbrook has disappeared. The other two NTSB members, Cathy Herrera and Barry McCarthy, refuse to discuss the case with me. They live in DC. So does the investigator-in-charge, Terry Powell."

"Any idea why they won't talk to you?"

"They're afraid."

"Of what?"

"The truth."

"Which is?"

"That's what I need to find out."

"What makes you think they'll talk to you now?"

"I can be persuasive."

"If the Bureau thinks you're continuing to harass the NTSB employees, they'll raise holy hell."

"You worried about Branigan?" Santana asked, referring to the chief of police.

"I run the Homicide Unit the way I see fit."

Despite his firm tone, Santana believed that Romano would cave to pressure from those above him or the Bureau if things got too hot. But he knew Romano was at least temporarily on his side now that FBI Agents Ted Lake and Jack Gaines had interfered. He only had to remind Romano of it once more.

"Why would the FBI want updates, Pete?"

He shrugged. "I don't know and neither do you."

"Maybe they don't want us to find out what actually happened in the Blue Skies crash."

"Why not?"

"If I knew that, I might know who murdered Kim Austin and her mother, and why."

"Did you discuss all of this with Hawkins?"

Santana gave a nod. "I phoned her last evening."

"I don't have the budget to send you both."

"I understand."

Romano thought about it. "I hate it when the Bureau threatens us. And I hate pompous assholes like Ted Lake and Jack Gaines."

"I don't like them either, Pete."

Romano jabbed an index finger at the murder book on his desk. "I read your initial reports. You spoke to a DC homicide detective named Lyman Grady. You have problems with him, or his lieutenant, give me a call. I want Kim Austin's murder solved soon. And by soon, I mean yesterday."

* * *

Gray clouds mottled the dusky sky that evening as Santana walked through the wooded area behind his house. Gitana followed on his heels.

Deborah Russell lived in a contemporary two-level home. Lights were blazing through the wall of windows that faced the river.

Santana rang the buzzer. Moments later, Russell opened the door. She was dressed casually in jeans, a University of Minnesota sweatshirt, and white athletic socks. She held a dishtowel in her hands.

"Hello, neighbor," she said with a smile. Looking down at Gitana, she said, "And 'Hello' to you too, beautiful." Gitana wagged her tail.

Santana would have wagged his if he'd had one.

Deborah Russell gestured toward a stack of three cartons in the kitchen behind her. "Come on in. I'm still unpacking. Hope you don't mind the mess."

"That's all right. I just have a favor to ask."

"Ask away."

"I need to go out of town for a couple of days and wondered if you could watch Gitana. I hate to ask, but . . ."

"No problem," she said. "I'd be happy to look after her."

"She's very self-sufficient. I'll leave her a couple of bowls of food and water. She only eats when she's hungry. And with the doggy door, she can let herself out to the dog run. I've fixed the lock on the gate."

"She's certainly welcome to stay here. I'm home all day and this weekend."

"It's up to you, but there's no obligation for her to stay with you."

"Nonsense. I'd love the company. She can run with me if you don't mind."

"That would be great."

"Just drop her off before you leave. I'm up early."

"Thanks again. I've got a late morning flight. I'll see you before I leave for the airport."

"Looking forward to it," she said.

Chapter 21

The following morning, after leaving Gitana with Deborah Russell, Santana caught a 10:20 a.m. flight out of the Minneapolis airport and arrived in DC at 2:00 p.m. After checking into his hotel, he met his contact from the Criminal Investigation Division, Detective-Sergeant Lyman Grady. He and Grady were seated in a booth in the Florida Avenue Grill on 11th and Florida.

"Oldest soul food restaurant in the world," Grady said with a smile. "Been in business since 1944."

Santana peered at the autographed photos of politicians and celebrities lining the walls and then at the menu in his hands. "What do you recommend?"

"Well, you can get the great breakfast all day. But I'm partial to the fried pork chops smothered in onion gravy."

"I'll try the Salisbury steak."

"Good choice. You get the onion gravy, too."

Santana wasn't thrilled with the idea of the gravy but decided to stick with the steak anyway.

Grady got the waitress' attention and placed their orders. "I'll take a cup of black coffee."

"A Coke," Santana said.

Grady cocked his head as the waitress took their menus and departed. "Not a coffee drinker?"

Santana shook his head.

"My lieutenant said you were originally from Colombia."

"Uh-huh."

"I thought that you . . ."

"All drank coffee?"

"Yeah."

"You're from the south, right, Grady?"

"Louisiana. Still carry a bit of an accent after all these years. You got a bit of one, too."

"So how come you didn't order chitterlings?"

"Point taken," Grady said with a wide grin.

He was a big man with large, thick-fingered hands and a head that was as bald and shiny as polished black glass.

"Been to DC before, Detective?"

"First time," Santana said. "How easy is it to get around?"

"It isn't. Unless you want to spend hours in gridlock, best to use the Metro. Could take thirty minutes just to get across town, even in a cab. Then you got the damn motorcades that can tie up traffic." Grady shook his head in disgust.

"How long have you been with the Metro Police?"

"Nearly twenty years. Hope to make it to twenty-five, when I can get out, but don't know if I can."

"How come?"

"MPD used to be a great place to work. The job was interesting to recruits because DC is a big city with lots of challenging calls. Plus, we often interact with the alphabet of federal agencies, experience you might not get elsewhere.

"But the departmental culture is punitive now and not designed for aggressive police work like it was when I signed up for the job. Don't get me wrong. I still love the job, but we've lost the vice unit, and officers are detailed to high-visibility stationary posts where they're no longer able to work cases. We're hunters, Santana. We patrol. That's why they call it 'patrol.'"

Santana had no desire to get into a lengthy discussion about the politics of Grady's department. He'd seen it firsthand in his own department. He changed the subject.

"So you know the city."

"Well enough. DC is what we call a company town, the company being the federal government. The MPD serves as the local police department, with county, state and federal responsibilities, and is under a municipal government, but we operate under federal authority. So even when the economy, unemployment rates, and the housing market tanked during the last recession, the city stayed pretty stable."

"Politicians take care of themselves first."

"Damn right. Then we've got the shifting demographics. The black population is less than fifty percent now. Lots of young people, mostly white, live in the city. Median age is below thirty-four. Whites are moving into the traditionally black neighborhoods in the Northeast and Southwest, driving up costs. That doesn't sit well with the longtime residents."

"Like you?"

He nodded. "You want to climb in this department, you got to stay above the political fray, if you get my drift, Santana. But we've got one of the largest income gaps between rich and poor in the country. That's like pouring lighter fluid on a smoldering fire."

Santana figured Grady's experience wasn't much different than that of cops in most departments, where political connections were often more important than competence. But he wanted to focus on the case.

"Your captain brief you on why I'm here?"

"Kim Austin," he said.

Their waitress dropped off the Coke and coffee and hurried away.

"The Blue Skies crash made headlines in the *Post* and the *Times,*" Grady continued. "It wasn't long after the NTSB investigation began that the conspiracy nuts started with their terrorist theories. Others thought it was suicide by pilot."

"You have an opinion?"

"Don't know enough about the crash to have one. But I'm guessing you do."

"I think Kim Austin's murder has something to do with the crash."

"What's the connection?"

"I don't know. But maybe what we're hearing about the crash isn't exactly what happened."

"That'd mean the NTSB plans to falsify the final report. Not something they're known for doing."

"Maybe their final report will be a conclusion drawn by the majority of accident investigators. Doesn't mean they were right. I'd like to read Kim Austin's report. Or Paul Westbrook's."

"He one of the investigators?"

Santana nodded. "He resigned from the department and disappeared."

Grady rubbed his dimpled chin with the fingers of his left hand. "I'm not much into conspiracy theories, Santana."

"It's not a theory that Westbrook has disappeared and Austin is dead."

Grady thought a moment before he spoke again. "A few years ago on Halloween, a guy was found stabbed to death in a vacant lot in the Barry Farm projects. My partner and I caught the case. We find the vic's wallet empty and figure it's a robbery gone bad. But then we find a note taped to the back of a street sign. It's a riddle written in rhyming poetry about a murder that leads us to another note taped behind a second sign. Now we're thinking maybe we got a serial killer taunting us, and we're gonna find another body if we just follow the clues."

"What's your point?"

"I'm getting to it. Later, we discover that a local boys' club had organized a Halloween murder mystery game for teens and had hidden clues in the area. It'd rained the night of the game, and some of the notes weren't picked up. So there was really no connection between the vic and the notes with the clues. We eventually caught the perp. But we wasted time looking for a connection that didn't exist."

"So you're saying the notes were nothing more than a coincidence."

Grady sipped some coffee and said, "Turned out to be."

"And Paul Westbrook's disappearance has nothing to do with Kim Austin's murder."

"All I'm saying is that our investigation could've run off the rails if we'd continued to focus on the notes instead of going with our initial conclusion of a robbery. Sometimes, at first glance, events appear to be connected to a crime but end up being nothing more than a coincidence.

"Look at it this way, Santana. There are all kinds of opportunities for coincidences to happen. When you consider all the people you know and all the places you go and all the places they go, chances are good that you'll run into someone you know, somewhere, at some point."

Grady drank some coffee and went on. "You know how many people need to be in a room before there's a fifty-fifty chance that two of them will share the same birthday?"

Santana shook his head.

"Twenty-three. That's all. Mathematicians call it the 'birthday problem.'"

"Statistics can't explain anything other than chance or probability," Santana said. "Ever hear of a woman named Violet Jessop?"

"No, I haven't."

"She was a stewardess who worked for White Star Line."

"Company that built the *Titanic*."

Santana nodded.

"Was she one of the survivors?"

"She was. But she was also on the *Olympic* ocean liner when it collided with the *HMS Hawke* the year before. Four years after she survived the sinking of the *Titanic*, she was on the White Star's *Britannic*, the sister ship, when it also sank. She survived all three disasters. What's the probability for something like that? Probability or chance isn't enough for me. I learned a long time ago to trust my intuition. I'm much better when I pay attention to it. Maybe you should take a look at Westbrook's disappearance."

Grady removed a spiral notebook from an inner pocket of his sport coat and turned the pages until he found what he was searching for. "Westbrook's parents died in a plane crash when he was twelve."

"Was he placed in foster care?"

Grady shook his head. "He lived with his grandparents till he went off to college at MIT, where he majored in engineering. Grandparents passed a few years later."

"So we have to believe that Westbrook decided to resign from his job and disappear with no explanation, a month after Kim Austin disappeared."

"I'll admit it doesn't smell right."

"Was Kim Austin's place searched?"

"Everything was placed in storage a couple months after her disappearance. Her apartment was cleaned and rented out. Mother is paying the storage fees."

"Not anymore."

"Why not?"

"She was murdered. Likely by the same person who killed and buried her daughter."

"You're tweaking my curiosity, Santana."

"What about Westbrook's credit cards?"

"Far as I can tell, he hasn't used one since he disappeared."

"Hard to live off the grid without using a credit card."

"You have enough cash, you can get by for a while," Grady said.

"Maybe longer if you have help. Any girlfriend or fiancée in the picture?"

"Not that I'm aware of. Looks like you're out a limb here, Santana."

"I've been out there before."

Grady paused and sipped his coffee. His eyes shifted momentarily off Santana, as if he were mentally running through the repercussions of the investigation. "Say you're right," he said. "Someone might not like you poking around. They take a saw to that limb you're on, you could be in for a long fall."

"I'm not asking for you to get involved, Grady. All I need is some help."

"Yeah," he said with a self-amused smile. "My lieutenant is gonna love it. Now that the department is about five hundred officers short of what the city council approved."

The waitress appeared with their meals.

After she left, Grady said, "Where you staying?"

"At the Courtyard Washington Capitol Hill."

"That's a block from the Navy Yard/Ballpark Metro station."

"Our budget is short as well, Grady. I don't have authorization for an unlimited stay."

"I hear you."

"Did you get the e-mail I sent before leaving Minnesota?"

Grady took a piece of paper out of his coat pocket and pushed it across the table. The phone numbers and addresses for Cathy Herrera, Barry McCarthy, and Terry Powell were listed on the paper.

"Thanks," Santana said. "Any other information you have on them would be appreciated."

"I'm working on it."

"You have my personal cell phone number?"

"You sent it with your e-mail. What's your plan?"

"I want to meet individually with Herrera, McCarthy, and Powell. But first, I'd like you to take me to Paul Westbrook's condo."

"I've got a search warrant," Grady said. "But you be careful what cages you rattle, Santana."

Chapter 22

Paul Westbrook lived in a newer Capitol Hill condominium on Pennsylvania Avenue. The condo had hardwood floors, a floor-to-ceiling glass window, nine-foot ceilings, and lots of open space for a studio.

Santana took Westbrook's bedroom. Grady took the living room and kitchen.

Sloppy. That was Santana's first impression. Unmade bed. Clothes stuffed in the dresser drawers and tossed on the closet floor. The ones on hangers weren't pressed.

He squatted in front of the open closet door and checked all the pants pockets. In one he found a crumpled ticket stub dated six months ago to a Hieronymus Bosch exhibit at the National Gallery of Art in DC, but nothing else.

If Westbrook had disappeared voluntarily, he hadn't taken much with him. There were no scraps of paper in the wastebasket. Nothing related to the Blue Skies crash. No plane, train, or bus tickets. No brochures for foreign countries.

The medicine cabinet in the messy bathroom yielded no clues as to Westbrook's whereabouts. A small wastebasket was empty.

He found Grady in the kitchen, going through the cabinets.

"Anything?" Santana asked.

Grady shook his head. "How about you?"

Santana showed him the ticket stub from the Bosch exhibit. "You might want to tag and bag this."

"You think it's important?"

"I don't know that it isn't."

Santana gave it to Grady and then looked under the sink for the proverbial plastic trashcan. It was there, but it, too, was completely empty.

He scanned the condo one more time. "Anything strike you as unusual, Grady?"

"Not much in the way of cooking utensils. Must not be much of a cook," he said in a bewildered tone of voice.

"What I meant was," Santana said, "you look around, you see quite a mess. Dirty dishes tossed in the sink. Stove top hasn't been cleaned."

"Yeah," Grady said. "Westbrook sure wasn't a neat freak."

"And yet, you see any paper around?"

"You mean like newspaper?"

"I mean like any paper."

"Can't say I do."

"I find that strange," Santana said. "A guy this careless with his clothes, dishes, you'd think he'd be the same way with his trash."

"A man thinking of dropping off the grid might not want to leave anything behind that could provide a clue as to his current location."

"He might not," Santana said.

* * *

Back in his hotel room, Santana called Barry McCarthy and got his voicemail. Then he called Cathy Herrera and discovered that she'd taken a leave of absence. Santana wondered if her leave had anything to do with his pursuit of the truth.

He called the investigator-in-charge of the Blue Skies crash, Terry Powell, and was surprised but pleased when Powell agreed to meet him later.

The clock in Santana's hotel room read 5:15 p.m. when he heard a knock on the door. Looking through the peephole, he recognized the familiar face on the other side of the door. He opened it and said, "Hello, Rita."

Rita Gamboni smiled.

"This is a surprise," he said. But on further reflection he thought, *Maybe it isn't.*

"Are you going to invite me in?"

"Sorry," he said, gesturing for her to enter.

She strode into the room and gave him a hug. Then she stepped back and adjusted the lapels on the traditional dark blue suit worn by those working in government jobs. Underneath her suit coat, a 9mm Glock rested in the holster clipped to her belt. Her short white-blonde hair had always reminded Santana of the *monas de ojos claros* he used to see in Riosucio, Colombia. No one seemed to know where the families of the blue-eyed blondes had come from in that town in the Caldas region of the country, whether they were perhaps German or Basques from Northern Spain.

"Have you had dinner?" she asked.

"I had a late lunch."

"How about a drink then? I know a good place close to here, if you're up for something different."

"Lead the way," Santana said.

Gamboni took him to the Tune Inn, a neighborhood bar in the middle of a stretch of row-house restaurants, bars, convenience stores, dry cleaners, and bank branches.

The Tune Inn had a long bar and chrome and black booths and bar stools. A chandelier made of antlers hung from the wood-beamed ceiling. The brick and dark wood-paneled walls were covered with sports and political memorabilia and deer heads. They both ordered a glass of New Belgian Fat Tire Ale, one of the eight drafts on tap. When the ale arrived, Gamboni raised her glass for a toast.

"What are we drinking to?"

"Old times," she said with a smile.

"To old times."

They touched glasses and drank.

"Good?" she asked.

"Very."

As their eyes connected, his mind flashed back to their times together as patrol officers and lovers, before Rita became a homicide detective—and before she married and divorced, and then became the SPPD's first female Homicide commander.

"I heard about Jordan," she said. "I'm sorry."

Santana nodded and took another drink. He set his glass on the table and said, "Is that why you've come?"

"That and because I wanted to see you."

"You knew I was in town."

"Word travels fast."

"I'll bet it does when you're with the FBI."

A quick smile passed over her lips. "I'm no longer working as a liaison between the department and the agency on the Safe-Streets Initiative."

"Good to know all the streets in St. Paul are safe."

She frowned. "The money dried up, John. The program was successful."

"As far as it went."

She looked at him a moment longer, her cheeks red with embarrassment or anger. Then she swallowed a sip of her drink before speaking again. "The Bureau offered me a position as a full-time agent. I won't be returning to the department."

"I didn't think you would."

"Why not?"

"You were never interested in being assistant chief or chief. It was time to move on to something else."

"What about you?" she asked.

Once he'd shared nearly everything with Rita Gamboni, including the circumstances of his mother's death and the revenge he'd inflicted on the two men responsible for it. But he and Rita had gone their separate ways over the past few years. He no longer felt close to her, though, to be honest, he still had —and always would have—feelings for her.

So he chose not to share the misgivings he'd had about his job since Jordan's murder, and the emotional and physical price he felt he'd paid for his years in Homicide.

"I'm satisfied doing what I'm doing," he said.

"Are you really?"

He shrugged. "I need a mission, a purpose."

She peered at her glass of beer and then at Santana again. "Maybe you could find it doing something else."

"Like what, Rita? Working for the feds?"

She shrugged. "Why not?"

"I don't think so."

"The Cali cartel and the Estradas are finished."

"So says our government."

"It's a very significant thing to take down what was once considered the biggest drug trafficking organization in the world, John. And because they're no longer in business, Colombia is safer. You should be pleased about that."

"Criminal gangs now run the trafficking businesses, Rita. And if you think this means the assassins sent by the Estrada family will stop coming for me, you're wrong. As long as one of them is still alive, they won't stop till I'm dead."

Gamboni shook her head in frustration and drank some beer.

"Why are you really here, Rita?"

"What do you mean? I told you why I'm here."

"It's not by coincidence that I'm in Washington, DC, and so are you."

"I'm working here, John."

"So am I."

"I don't—"

He held up a hand in a stopping gesture. "On a case," he said. "And I think you know what that case is."

She inhaled and let out a breath. "The Blue Skies crash."

"Your two buddies, Ted Lake and Jack Gaines, came to see me and Pete Romano."

"They're not my buddies."

"But you know them."

"I know who they are."

"Did Lake send you to see me?"

Her complexion darkened again. "No, John. He didn't."

"So why is the FBI so interested in my investigation that they'd send my former Homicide commander to talk to me?"

"The Bureau didn't send me, John." She leaned forward in the chair. "I came because I wanted to see you. Is that so difficult to understand?"

"Two birds with one stone."

"That's not fair."

"Isn't it, Rita? How fair is it that you're using our friendship to solicit information?"

She crossed her arms and gave him a hard look, a look he'd seen from her on more than one occasion as his superior—and as his lover.

"So what does that particular flight have to do with your murder investigation?" she asked.

"You already know the answer to that question. Kim Austin is dead, and Paul Westbrook resigned and has disappeared. Both were part of the Go-Team investigating the Blue Skies crash. And Kim Austin's mother, Elisha, is also dead. Probably to keep her quiet."

"Quiet about what?"

"Maybe you can answer that for me, Rita."

"The flight crashed because of pilot error."

"You're sure?"

"Well, I wasn't part of the investigation, but before crashing, the plane had drifted far off course. It ran out of fuel. Whose responsibility is that? And who's to say that Kim Austin wasn't murdered for a reason that had nothing to do with her job or the flight, or that Paul Westbrook is dead?"

"If he's not dead, Rita, then where is he? And why did he suddenly disappear?"

"I don't know. But it's a stretch to say that Austin's murder and Westbrook's disappearance are related."

"You wouldn't have said that if you were still working for the SPPD instead of the feds."

"That's not true, John, and you know it."

"What about Austin's mother?"

"There you go," Gamboni said. "Her mother had nothing to do with the crash investigation."

"Except that her daughter might have told her something, or she overheard something, that someone wants to keep quiet. Or maybe she never was told or heard anything, but someone couldn't take the chance."

"It's all speculation."

"Maybe."

"I'm trying to help you out," she said.

"How? By getting me off the case?"

"By saving you from embarrassing yourself. You're looking in the wrong place."

"You've studied the case."

"Not Austin's murder. But I've looked at the agency's report on the Blue Skies crash. Believe me, if there was something missing or something that didn't fit, I'd tell you."

"Would you, Rita?"

She stared at him for a long moment and then cocked her head as though she were looking at a never-before-seen object. "You've changed, John."

"How?"

"You're so distant . . . so . . . cold."

"Maybe I'm not the one who has changed, Rita."

Gamboni stared at him. Then she slid out of the booth and stood up.

"Was it something I said?"

She was about to respond when they both sensed someone approaching the booth and turned to look.

"Hello, John." Reyna Tran, dressed in high-heeled black boots, jeans, and a cowl-neck sweater that matched her blue eyes, stood with her hips cocked and one hand on her slim waist.

Santana glanced at Gamboni and then looked back at Tran.

Tran held out a hand. "Hello, Rita. I'm Reyna Tran."

Gamboni shook her hand. "Have we met?"

"No. But John spoke of you when we had lunch in Chicago recently."

"He did?"

"Yes." She smiled at Santana, comfortable with the lie she'd just told. "But I had no idea he and I would both be here in Washington at the same time. What a coincidence." She focused her eyes on Gamboni. "Could I buy you both a drink—or are you leaving?"

Gamboni took a step back, as if blown by a strong wind. "I am," she said. "Good night, John." She turned on her heels and left.

Tran looked at Santana. "I hope I didn't interrupt something."

Santana slid out of the booth and stood. "I was just leaving too, Ms. Tran."

"Was Rita upset?"

"That's none of your business. And how did you know her name?"

"I'm familiar with many of the Bureau's agents in town."

Santana wondered if that were true, or if there was something else at work here. He started for the door.

"I'm afraid you're upset, too, John. Let me buy you a drink."

"I'm on my way out."

"I'll tag along."

Outside on the sidewalk Santana stopped and faced Tran. "Have you been following me?"

"Now why would I do that?"

"I haven't a clue."

"Well," she smiled shyly, "you are the detective."

"What's that supposed to mean?" Santana's response was louder than he'd intended. People passing by turned their heads and stared.

Reyna Tran hooked her arm through Santana's elbow and said, "It's a beautiful evening. Let's walk."

Chapter 23

As they moved away from clusters of people, a light breeze carried the scent of Reyna Tran's Opium perfume.

"What is it you want, Ms. Tran?" Santana asked.

"Nothing—besides keeping you safe."

"I can protect myself."

"Can you?"

"I've been doing it since the age of sixteen."

"Ah, yes, after your mother's unfortunate murder. But there are other forces at work now, John."

"I've asked you not to call me that."

"Do you still consider me a suspect in Kim Austin's death?"

"I'm not sure."

"Yes, you are. You know I had nothing to do with her death."

Santana hadn't drawn that conclusion yet, but either way, he had no desire to encourage a relationship.

They walked awhile before stopping at a corner as a bus passed by. A sign on its side encouraged Washingtonians to celebrate the 500th anniversary of the death of Dutch painter Hieronymus Bosch by viewing his *Death and the Miser* painting at the National Gallery of Art in DC. Santana remembered the ticket stub from the National Gallery of Art he'd found in a pants pocket in Paul Westbrook's bedroom closet.

"I'll take your silence as a 'Yes' to my question," Reyna Tran said. "So if I'm no longer a suspect, I see no reason why we can't be friends."

"I don't need another friend."

"Everyone can use another friend, John." She squeezed his arm. "Come on, I'll buy you a drink."

Santana looked at his watch.

"Are you meeting someone?" Tran asked.

"Yes."

"One of the NTSB investigators from the Blue Skies crash?"

"Why would you suspect that?"

"Why else would you be in DC?" she said.

He still had nearly two hours before he was supposed to meet Terry Powell. He could go back to his hotel and watch TV or go with Tran.

"Come on," she said with a smile.

"Just one drink," he said.

Reyna Tran took him to the Barrel, a low-ceilinged, softly lit bar with a lot of exposed brick, reclaimed wood, and a concrete bar Santana estimated was at least sixty feet long. Glass shelves running the length of the wall behind the bar were filled with bourbon and whiskey bottles. They sat at a high-top table near the front entrance.

"Drinks made from bourbon are their specialty," Tran said.

"I'm not much of a bourbon or whiskey drinker. I'll order a draft beer."

"Come on, live dangerously."

"I already do."

Tran leaned closer to him. "There are two kinds of people in this world, John. Those who have drunk an Old Fashioned and those who have not."

"Put me in the latter category."

"We're going to change that tonight."

Reyna Tran ordered two Old Fashioned cocktails with bourbon rather than rye whiskey. Then she rested her elbows on the table and her chin in her hands. "You need protection."

"You keep following me around, I may need protection from you."

"Oh, don't be silly."

"I'm deadly serious, Reyna."

"That's so nice."

"What is?"

"Calling me by my first name. That's what friends do."

"You learned that, did you?"

"Well, of course. Didn't you?"

"But it came naturally to me. You do it so you can blend in with the rest of society."

She smiled. "Don't we all want to *blend in*, as you call it?"

"Some of us more than others. Personally, I'm comfortable in my own skin. I'm not uncomfortable being alone. And neither are you."

"Do go on," she said. "I enjoy hearing about myself."

"All right. You realized as a child that you were different in some way. You thought differently and made different decisions. Very soon you began to understand that unlike other children, you weren't so affected by emotions. You thought it was because you were so much smarter than everyone else."

"This is so fascinating, John. Please continue."

"You learned at an early age to look for clues to recognize the emotions that others were actually having. You learned to mimic emotions to please others, so you wouldn't stand out. You learned how to create relationships that were beneficial for you. You often lie. You have a need for excitement and a desire to control others. But you can't help yourself, Reyna."

"And why is that?"

"You're a sociopath."

Her smile widened. "And you know this because . . ."

"I've come across a number of them in my career."

"Have you?"

He nodded. "It's possible that there are many female sociopaths who live what looks like a normal life from the outside, like you, Reyna. They're content to just blend in and do what normal people do."

"I knew the first moment we met that you were a perceptive man, John. I think that's what attracted me to you—besides the looks, of course. I hope this doesn't mean we can't become good friends."

"I doubt that's possible."

"Not all sociopaths are serial killers."

"I know that."

The waitress arrived with their drinks. Tran waited until she departed before raising her glass in a toast. "To friends," she said with a bright smile.

Santana drank.

* * *

On the walk back to his hotel from the bar, Santana was thinking about the bus with a sign on its side advertising the 500th anniversary of the death of the famous surrealistic Dutch painter Hieronymus Bosch, and his *Death and the Miser* painting, which was displayed at the National Gallery of Art, and the ticket stub from the museum exhibit in a pants pocket in Paul Westbrook's DC condo.

When he returned to his hotel, Santana checked his watch. He still had time before he needed to leave for his interview with Terry Powell in Georgetown. He went to one of the computers off the lobby to search for references about the Bosch exhibit.

According to art historians, *Death and the Miser*, like many of Bosch's 15th century paintings, represented the inevitability of death and the choice Christians had between Jesus and sinful pleasures. The miser in the painting chooses a bag of gold offered by a demon over salvation.

Reflecting about the Bosch painting on the computer screen triggered a long-forgotten childhood memory at the Prado Museum in Madrid, Spain, where Santana's parents had taken him on vacation. One Bosch painting in particular had stood out: *The Garden of Earthly Delights*.

A Google search provided numerous links to the painting and to varying interpretations and underlying messages. After five hundred years, the true meaning and bizarre symbolism of the painting still confounded viewers and art historians.

The Garden of Earthly Delights is a triptych—meaning that it consists of three parts, or panels. Santana remembered how surprised he'd been at the sheer size of the painting in the Prado. It measured about thirteen feet by seven feet when all three panels were open.

Looking at the painting, he recalled that Bosch's narrative begins on the outside panels with the creation of the world. When the painting is opened, the story continues, left-to-right, with Adam and Eve in the Garden of Eden. The center panel, from which the painting takes its name, is filled with male and female nudes and a fantastical variety of animals, plants and fruits. The right-hand panel is the only one set at night and is divided from bottom to top into three tiers, Earth, Purgatory, and Hell. In the bottom tier, representing Earth, Santana saw a figure with a dagger through his palm.

He wanted to spend more time studying the painting, but he needed to get to Terry Powell's house.

He shut down the computer and went into the lobby, where he learned from the concierge that there was no Metro in Georgetown, where Powell lived. He could take the Metro to the Foggy Bottom/GWU stop and walk fifteen minutes to M Street NW in Georgetown. He needed the exercise, but he was uncertain how far Powell's residence was from there, so he took

Uber instead. His destination turned out to be a white brick row house in the East Village.

Santana sat at one end of the couch in the living room that had a high ceiling, wood-burning fireplace, and built-in book-shelves filled with hardcovers and paperbacks. The room was dimly lit by one low-wattage bulb in a lamp on an end stand.

"Here's your Coke," Powell said, handing him a can. "Hope you didn't want a glass."

"The can is fine." Santana took a long swallow.

Terry Powell sat on the other end of the couch. He was a fiftyish, heavyset man with a wreath of white hair on the sides and back of his scalp and a white, walrus mustache. He wore a pair of round eyeglasses, a blue plaid snap-front western shirt, khakis, and cowboy boots.

Santana drank from the can of Coke as his eyes scanned the living room. There were no photos of Powell or anyone else. He wondered if Powell was single or divorced and had no children.

"Nice place you have here, Mr. Powell."

"I like it," he said. "But you didn't come here to talk about interior decorating."

"No. As I said on the phone, I have some questions about the Blue Skies crash."

"But you're a homicide detective."

"I am."

"Then what does the Blue Skies crash have to do with Kim Austin's death?"

"I was hoping you could tell me, Mr. Powell."

He sipped some coffee without responding.

Santana prompted him again. "What did the systems group conclude regarding the cause of the crash?"

Powell hesitated a moment as his eyes darted around the room. Then they seemed to focus on the cover of a *National Geographic* magazine on the coffee table.

"Pilot error," he said.

"You don't believe that."

His dark eyes peered into Santana's, but he offered no response.

Santana drank more Coke and set the can on a coaster on the coffee table. "Tell me what you know."

"Nothing, really."

"You were the investigator-in-charge. You read all the team reports. Tell me everyone agreed that the crash was caused by pilot error."

Powell looked quickly over his shoulder, as if he were being watched.

"Waiting for someone?" Santana asked.

Powell shook his head.

Santana reached for the Coke can on the coffee table, but the can seemed to turn soft, like a wax sculpture melting under a flame. His hand slid by the Coke can and knocked over Powell's coffee cup.

"Something wrong?" Powell asked, staring at him, his expression caught between concern and guilt.

Santana tried to speak, but the mumbled words made no sense. The colors on the walls were dissolving and running together now. He felt nauseated and dizzy, as if he were drunk.

"I'm sorry," Powell said. "Just do what they say." He stood. "You'll be fine in a few hours."

Santana started to rise and caught Powell by the arm, but he pulled away.

Falling sideways on the coffee table, Santana felt the glass give way beneath him as he crashed to the floor. He tried to rise to his feet but collapsed again, pieces of broken glass slicing into his side.

He heard the front door bang open and saw two men enter. One was a stocky, muscular man; the other was taller and leaner. Both were clothed all in black, with hoods over their heads and gloves on their hands. The stockier man carried a long, thin rattan cane in his hand, the leaner one a coiled rope.

The stockier man carrying the cane squatted down in front of Santana and exhaled a breath that smelled of something familiar. "There's nothing in DC for you but trouble, Detective," he said. "We'd ask you nicely to fly back to jerkwater where the rest of the apple knockers live, but I doubt you'd listen. Maybe after tonight, you'll take the request seriously."

Santana got to his hands and knees and began crawling around the man in front of him, toward the front door.

The stocky man stood and said, "Wrong move, partner."

The cane whipped out of the air and stung him across the back. A second blow slapped across his rear, sending needles of pain up his spine. The leaner man taped Santana's mouth with duct tape, wrapped the rope around Santana's neck, and straddled him.

Santana drove his fist into the man's groin. Heard him scream. Felt the rope around his neck loosen and fall off.

He struggled to his feet. The stocky man grabbed him by the collar with his left hand and threw a right toward Santana's belly.

Instinct and muscle-memory from hours working on the heavy bag kicked in. Santana blocked the punch with an elbow and drove a one-two punch into the man's gut. He felt the man go limp and fall forward.

Santana broke away from him and crashed into the kitchen, tipping over chairs, scraping dishes off the table. He stumbled down a long set of steps and through an open door into a garage.

Getting to his knees, he tore one end of the duct tape away from his mouth. He slammed the door behind him. He rose to his feet, held his arms out to his side for balance, and stumbled forward, smashing into a tall garbage bin and knocking over a broom along the wall.

Santana fumbled for his gun in its holster. Then he watched helplessly as the Glock fell from his hand and clattered on the concrete floor. As he bent down to retrieve it, he nearly tipped over.

His fingers found the broom handle instead of the gun. With both hands, he twisted the handle until it came loose.

The door flew open and slammed against the wall.

Face to face with the stockier man, Santana drove the end of the broom handle into the man's gut. Then he swung the broom handle as if it were a baseball bat and cracked it into the side of the man's head, toppling him into the garbage bin and onto the floor.

With the floor beneath Santana pitching forward and back like the deck of a ship in a stormy sea, he dropped the broom handle and lurched toward a door that opened onto a red brick patio in back of the house. Staggering through an open gate, the duct tape hanging from his cheek, he reeled down the street. A hazy iridescence clouded his eyes and muted the headlights before him, the lights fading as he wobbled forward and fell into a welcoming darkness.

Chapter 24

When Santana opened his eyes, he realized he was lying underneath the covers in a comfortable bed, looking into the face of Reyna Tran.

She was seated on the edge of the bed, clothed in a long red dragon silk robe. Small smile lines formed at the corners of her mouth.

As he attempted to sit up, a sharp pain shot up his spine.

She pushed him gently back on the pillow. "Relax, John. You need to rest."

His head ached. He felt hung over. "Where am I?"

"The guest bedroom in my condo in DC."

"How'd I get here?"

"You don't remember?"

Santana thought about it and then shook his head.

"What do you remember?"

"I . . . I went to Terry Powell's row house in Georgetown. He was the NTSB investigator-in-charge of looking into the Blue Skies crash."

"Was he there?'

"Yes."

"What happened after that?"

Santana shook his head. "I . . . I don't know."

"We picked you up in the street."

"We?"

"One of my security men was with me."

"So you were following me?"

"One of my men."

Lifting the sheet, he realized that he was wearing nothing under the covers except his boxer briefs and a gauze bandage on his side. He dropped the sheet and saw that his clothes were draped over the back of a loveseat against one wall.

Tran patted his cheek and said, "You have a very nice body, John. But it's not the first one I've had the pleasure of seeing." She stood, slid a cigarette out of a package on the nightstand, and lit it with a slim lighter. Then she went to a window and pushed back a dark curtain. Dim light filtered into the room.

"How long have I been out?"

"All night. I suspect you were drugged."

Santana guessed Powell had given him Rohypnol. The new version of the pill had a liquid blue center so if it was slipped into someone's drink, the dye would make clear liquids turn bright blue and dark drinks turn cloudy. The blue center had been added because of the number of sexual assaults associated with the drug's being given without the victim's knowledge. But the color change was hard to detect in a dark room or in a dark beverage.

Reyna Tran let go of the curtain and turned toward him, exhaling a small cloud of smoke. "Someone hit you across the back with a hard object. Could've been a cane or broom handle. You have some bruising on your back and cuts on your side. I removed some small pieces of glass from the cuts."

Closing his eyes, Santana concentrated his thoughts on the previous evening. He remembered placing the phone call to Terry Powell from his hotel room and how surprised he had been when Powell had agreed to meet with him. Now he saw himself sitting on the couch beside Powell, though the image was distorted, as if he were peering through a smudged lens. In the background, he detected two faceless shadows moving toward him before the image dissolved.

"I think two men came into the house," he said to Reyna Tran.

"We didn't know that or realize that you'd been beaten when we picked you up. Only after your clothes were removed." She smiled and gestured toward his clothes. "Our concern was getting you to safety. The blows left reddish welts and bruises on your back. They'll last a few days. But there's another problem."

"What?"

Tran walked to the dresser on the far wall and stubbed out her cigarette in an ashtray. She picked up a folded newspaper and brought it to Santana. "Take a look."

He unfolded the newspaper. His heartbeat jackknifed when he read the headline in the *Washington Post*:

NTSB ACCIDENT INVESTIGATOR FOUND MURDERED
SUSPECT SOUGHT

Terry Powell, an NTSB accident investigator, was found shot to death early this morning in his Georgetown row house. Police are releasing few details, but department sources have indicated that Mr. Powell may have been beaten before being shot. A gun believed to be the murder weapon was recovered.

Detectives remained on the scene throughout the night and into this morning. Neighbors told police that a male in his late thirties or early forties was seen fleeing from the row house around 10:30 p.m. Police described the suspect as wearing a dark sport coat and slacks. Anyone who may have seen this person or who has information is asked to contact police.

Mr. Powell had worked for the NTBS for fifteen years. He had recently been in charge of the team investigating the crash of Blue Skies Flight 624.

Santana set the newspaper in his lap. "I didn't kill him."

"I could care less," she said. "It's the police I'm concerned about. Your Glock is missing."

Santana wondered if he could trust Detective-Sergeant Lyman Grady of the Metropolitan Police Department. But before he considered contacting Grady, there was something else that needed his immediate attention. "If I was given Rohypnol, it doesn't stay in the system long, Reyna. I need a blood sample taken."

"No problem," she said, as if it were a common request. "I know a doctor who makes house calls."

"In this day and age?" Santana remembered that medical house calls were commonplace in Colombia when he was growing up. He wondered if that were still the case today.

"For the right people," Tran said.

"You mean those rich and powerful enough to afford it."

"They're the right people," she said with a smile.

"But we need to follow the chain of custody, or the blood sample will be inadmissible."

"Contacting the police isn't the best idea."

"I'll need my cell phone, Reyna. And your address."

She retrieved his phone from a pocket in his sport coat and brought it to him. She recited her address and said, "There's a bottle of Aleve on the nightstand with a glass of water. I'll call the doctor."

"Before you go, take some photos of my wounds."

Pain stung the bruises on Santana's back and the glass cuts in his side as he sat up. He squeezed his eyes shut, sucked in air through his nose, and held his breath for a moment. The very act of breathing caused him discomfort. He released the air slowly, hoping that this relaxation technique would dull the pain. He swallowed two pills and washed them down with the glass of water while Tran took photos of the bruises on his back and, after loosening the gauze, photographed the cuts in his side.

Then he set the glass on the nightstand, propped up the pillows behind him, and carefully leaned back as she handed him his phone and left the room. Santana checked the messages on his voicemail first. He'd left his SPPD cell phone at home and taken only his personal phone, in order to avoid hassling with the department over what were business calls and what were personal calls on his phone bill when he returned home.

There was one voicemail. It was from Lyman Grady.

Maybe you heard that Terry Powell, one of the NTSB investigators you wanted to interview, was found murdered in his house last night. Give me a call.

Santana pushed the CALL BACK icon. The detective-sergeant answered on the second ring.

"Grady, it's Santana."

"Where you been?"

"Recovering."

"You sick?"

"Not exactly. We need to talk."

"So go ahead."

"Not on the phone." Santana gave him Tran's address.

"This wouldn't have something to do with Terry Powell's murder, would it?"

"It would," Santana said. "And make sure you bring a gunshot residue kit with you."

Santana dozed off and then was awakened when the bedroom door opened. Reyna Tran entered, followed by a small, darker-skinned man Santana thought might be from India. In one hand he carried a leather bag. "This is Dr. Raman," Tran said. "He'll take the blood sample."

The man bowed his head slightly as he stood near the edge of the bed.

"We need to wait," Santana said.

"Till the detective arrives?" Tran said.

"Till then."

"I hope you know what you're doing."

Ten minutes later the doorbell chimed. Tran left the room and returned with Lyman Grady.

His wary cop eyes shifted from Santana to Tran, then to the doctor and back to Santana. He read from a business-sized card in his hand. "You're Reyna Tran and run a security company?"

"That's right."

Grady shifted his gaze to Santana. "What's going on?"

"I was at Terry Powell's house last night."

Standing at the foot of the bed with his hands on his wide hips, Grady nodded, as though he had expected the admission. "I'm not assigned to the case."

"Maybe you should be."

"You kill him?"

"No. Someone is setting me up."

"How many times you heard that excuse from a perp, Santana?"

"More than I care to remember."

Grady gestured toward Raman. "Who's he?"

"I'm Dr. Raman," the Indian man said with a British accent. "I'm here to draw blood from Detective Santana."

Grady cocked his head and looked at Santana.

"I was drugged last night," Santana said. "Rohypnol, I think. I'm giving you a blood sample."

"Who's to say you didn't take the drug yourself?"

"Who's to say I didn't kill Powell?"

"Exactly."

"You'll have to take my word for it, Grady."

"That's pretty thin."

Santana punched in his security code and held up his iPhone. "Video this," he said to Tran, handing her the phone. She took it and stepped back where she could get a full view.

When Raman was finished, he handed the tube to Grady.

"You're giving me the blood sample?"

"Have it analyzed," Santana said.

Raman pointed to the tube. "The detective's name and today's date are written on the label attached to the tube."

"Did you bring the gunshot residue kit?"

Grady nodded and held it up for Santana to see. "No use checking your hands for GSR. It's been more than six hours since the shooting."

"Check my clothes."

Tran stopped the video. "Everything is recorded here," she said, holding up the phone.

"Keep it running while Grady checks my clothes for GSR," Santana said.

Grady looked at him. "This is supposed to be a chain of custody?"

"It's all we've got for now."

"You mean it's all *you've* got," Grady said.

"Except for my word."

"I don't know you well enough to trust that your word is good, Santana."

"There's something else," Reyna Tran said.

Santana wasn't sure what she was talking about. By the look on Grady's face, he wasn't either.

She walked to the dresser and pointed. From his position on the bed, Santana couldn't see what she was pointing at.

She looked at Grady. "It's the duct tape John had taped across his mouth. Have it checked for touch DNA and then run the results through CODIS," she said, referring to the national Combined DNA Index System. "If the perp didn't use gloves when he first handled the duct tape, he probably transferred skin cells when he handled it or touched it."

They waited while Grady slipped on a pair of latex gloves, bagged the duct tape, and checked for GSR from Santana's jacket and shirt with adhesive lifters. "What you've got in your hand is proof that I was drugged, and that I didn't fire my weapon," Santana said. "And if the DNA pans out, we might have the name of one of the men who attacked me."

"Rohypnol can be detected in the blood several hours after ingestion," Raman said. "We may be past that point now. But a metabolite of Rohypnol can be detected in the blood and urine for upwards of forty-eight to seventy-two hours after taking the drug." He looked at Santana.

"All right. I'll give you a urine sample."

"Splendid." From his medical bag, the doctor pulled out a urine specimen cup and gave it to Santana.

"You seem to know an awful lot about Rohypnol, Doctor," Grady said.

"Unfortunately, I have seen far too many victims of this crime."

Chapter 25

After Santana had provided a urine sample and gotten dressed, he went downstairs to the living room. The pain medication had alleviated some of his discomfort—but not all of it.

He sat next to Tran on a couch in a living room that had a high ceiling, rosewood furniture, and dark hardwood floors. Tran had changed into red suit with a short skirt. Her long dark hair was slicked back and tied in a high ponytail that hung nearly to her waist.

Lyman Grady sat in a cushioned chair opposite them with a pen and spiral notebook in hand. His taupe suit coat and slacks were wrinkled, and his moss-colored striped tie was loosened around his thick neck.

Santana went through the night before again. As he spoke, he tried to remember more details, but just when he thought he had something, it disappeared like blown smoke.

"You remember having a drink," Grady said, "but nothing after that?"

"Nothing."

"Perhaps I can help," Tran said.

Santana and Grady looked at her.

"Have you ever been hypnotized?" she said to Santana.

"Not that I'm aware of."

"We've used it a few times in our department," Grady said.

Tran shifted her gaze to him. "Is that so, Detective?"

Grady nodded.

"Was it helpful?"

"It was."

Tran faced Santana. "I've done it numerous times," she said.

Santana was wary. "Hypnotically induced testimony isn't admissible in Minnesota courts. That's why I don't use it."

"Ah, but your Supreme Court did say that it's an extremely useful investigative tool. Especially when a witness is enabled to remember verifiable factual information that leads to the solution of a crime."

"How do you know that?"

"How do I know many things, John? I'm well-read and smart."

Grady said, "I know federal courts have permitted the use of this testimony."

Tran nodded. "Why shouldn't they? Hypnosis affects only the credibility of the witness and not the witness's competence or the admissibility of his or her testimony."

"But hypnotically induced testimony isn't admissible here in Maryland," Grady said.

Santana shrugged. "I don't even know if I can be hypnotized."

Tran looked at him with a humored expression. "Why don't you let me try? It might be the only way to remember the details from last night."

"Or the only way to save your hide," Grady added.

"Okay," Santana said.

Tran got up and closed the blinds over the window. Then she went into the dining room and returned with two hardback chairs. She set one directly in front of the other and sat down in the chair opposite Santana. She gestured for him to sit in the other one.

Santana gave Grady his iPhone. "I want you to take video of this, Lyman."

"Set the phone on one of the bookshelves where you have a clear view, so your hands are free," Tran said. "But please don't speak until I ask you to." Grady did as requested.

Once Santana was seated, Tran said in a soft, soothing voice, "To begin, I want you to rest your arms limply on your thighs, like this." Tran demonstrated the relaxed position for him.

He followed her instructions, though doubts about the effectiveness of hypnosis lingered in his mind.

"Now I want you to focus on my right hand, John. In a moment I'm going to bring my hand up in front of your eyes like this." Tran raised her right hand up just above his eyebrows with the index and middle finger in a V position. "When I do, I'll pass my hand down in front of your eyes." Tran brought her hand down slowly, one finger moving down over each eye. "Keep your eyes fixed on my fingers. As I bring my hand down, let your eyelids close. Do you understand?"

"Yes," Santana said.

Tran raised her right hand to a pointing V position just above Santana's eyebrows, so he had to look up at an angle to see her bright red fingertips. "Okay," she said. "Focus your eyes on my fingers."

Santana did as directed.

"Now I'm passing my hand down in front of your eyes, and as I do, let your eyelids close."

Santana followed her hand down, watching one finger moving down over each eye until his eyes closed.

"Now that your eyelids are closed, I want you to relax every muscle and nerve in and around your eyelids. I want you to relax them so much that they wouldn't work even if you wanted them to."

She waited for a time, letting Santana relax as instructed.

"When you know that you've relaxed your eyelids so much that they wouldn't work even if you wanted them to, go ahead and try to open them."

Santana was surprised to discover that his eyelids felt as heavy as lead. He couldn't open them.

She paused for a few seconds before continuing. "That's good, John. Now, stop trying to open your eyes and just relax. I want you to go deeper."

Santana felt as if his whole body were numb.

"I'm going to raise your hand now. I will do it by grasping your right thumb in my fingers like this."

He felt her grasp his right hand between the thumb and index finger. "As I lift your hand," she said, "just let it hang limply in my fingers. Now I'm raising your hand."

Santana felt his hand lift.

"Let it hang limply. That's good. Now when I drop your hand, let it drop like a wet, limp rag. When your hand touches your body, you will feel a wave of relaxation from the top of your head all the way down to the tips of your toes. Your present level of relaxation will double."

As his hand fell onto his thigh, Santana felt a sensation like that of an ocean wave wash over his whole body.

"Now, we'll do the same thing with your left hand."

Once more, Santana followed her directions. When she was finished, his body felt like it was encased in ice, though he wasn't cold.

"Your body is relaxed now, John, so I'm going to show you how to relax your mind. Listen very carefully. The next time I touch your forehead, I want you to begin counting very slowly from one hundred backward like this: One hundred, deeper asleep, ninety-nine, deeper asleep, ninety-eight, deeper asleep, and so on. By the time you reach ninety-five, you will find those numbers disappearing. You will find your mind has become so relaxed that you'll just relax them out of your mind."

"All right," Santana said. His voice sounded as if it came from another person.

"Get ready now, three, two, one . . ."

Santana felt her tap his forehead.

"Begin counting."

Santana said, "One hundred, deeper asleep . . . ninety-nine, deeper asleep . . ."

"Good, John."

"Ninety-eight, deeper asleep . . . ninety-seven, deeper asleep . . ."

"Start relaxing the numbers out of your mind, John."

"Ninety-six, deeper asleep . . . ninety-five, deeper asleep . . ."

"Let them fade away completely now."

Santana stopped counting.

"That's fine. You've relaxed your body. You've relaxed your mind. You've gone into a much deeper state of hypnosis."

Santana felt as if he'd fallen asleep without losing conscious awareness of things around him. He noticed that his breathing had slowed way down. He felt a pleasant, almost euphoric state of peace, and a sense of distance from where he was in the physical world.

"Detective Grady is going to ask you some questions about last night now, John. I'll be right here, but you can talk to him as if you were talking to me."

"All right," Santana said.

"You can ask him questions now, Detective Grady."

Grady cleared his throat. "You told me you went to Terry Powell's house last night."

"Yes," Santana said.

"Why did you go there?"

"To ask Powell about Kim Austin's murder and the Blue Skies crash."

"Had you spoken with Powell before about Austin and the crash?"

"No, I hadn't."

"What did you think Powell could tell you?"

"He was the investigator-in-charge. I think Powell knew that the NTSB report was not forthcoming. And I think he knew that Kim Austin felt the same."

"And that's why Powell was killed?"

"Yes," Santana said.

"Did Terry Powell serve you something to drink at his apartment?"

"Yes. A Coke."

"What happened after you drank some Coke?"

"Nothing . . . at first. Then I began feeling really dizzy."

"Did you suspect that you'd been drugged?"

"I did. But I knew for certain I'd been drugged when Powell said, 'I'm sorry. Just do what they say. You'll be fine in a few hours.'"

"You're positive that's what he said?"

"Yes."

"What happened next?"

"Powell stood up. I grabbed him, but he pulled away. I fell onto the coffee table and broke the glass. Then two men came in the front door."

"Could you see their faces?"

"No. They were wearing hoods."

"Then what happened?"

Santana could see it all again in front of his eyes now, as if he were watching a movie on the backs of his eyelids. He explained to Grady how he'd been beaten by the stockier man with a cane but managed to escape, and how he'd passed out on the street in front of Powell's row house.

"You should check the end of the broom handle for DNA," he said. "I hit the stocky guy pretty hard with the handle. There's probably blood on it."

"I'll talk to forensics. Was Powell alive when you last saw him?"

"Yes, he was."

"Who do you think the two men who attacked you worked for?"

"I don't know for sure. But they set me up for Powell's murder."

In his mind's eye, Santana saw the stockier man's hood-covered face leaning close to his. The man's voice saying *with a slight Southern accent,* "There's nothing in DC for you but trouble, Detective." And then Santana recalled the smell on the man's breath.

Butterscotch.

"The two men," Santana said.

"Yes?" Grady replied.

"They were from the FBI."

"What?"

"Their names are Ted Lake and Jack Gaines. Gaines is the one I hit with the broom handle. Lake I punched in the groin." Santana had a warm feeling about that.

"I thought this hypnosis works," Grady said.

"It does," Tran said.

"Well, Santana is confused."

"I'm not confused at all, Grady," he said. "I'm sure they were the two who attacked me. I remember Gaines' butterscotch breath and Southern accent. Just match the DNA on the handle with his."

"And exactly how am I supposed to do that?"

"You'll think of something, Grady. Might have Gaines' or Lake's DNA on the duct tape as well."

There was long pause during which Santana didn't know exactly what was going on.

Then Grady said, "What happened to your gun?"

Santana told him how he'd dropped it in the garage. Then he said, "If I can learn what actually happened to flight six twenty-four, and why the FBI and NTSB—or some other government agency—wants the true cause of the crash kept from the public, I might be able to solve Kim Austin's murder."

"Do you have any other questions, Detective Grady?" Reyna Tran asked.

"No."

"Now, I'm going to count from one to five, John, and then I'll say, 'Fully aware.' At the count of five, your eyes are open, and you are then fully aware, feeling calm, rested, refreshed and relaxed. You will remember everything you've told us."

"All right."

"One. Slowly, calmly, easily you're returning to your full awareness once again. Two. Each muscle and nerve in your body is loose and limp and relaxed, and you feel wonderfully good. Three. From head to toe, you are feeling perfect in every way, physically perfect, mentally perfect, emotionally calm and serene.

"Four. Your eyes begin to feel sparkling clear. On the next number I count, your eyelids open. You are fully aware, feeling calm, rested, refreshed, relaxed, invigorated, and full of energy.

"Five. You're fully aware now. Eyelids open. Take a good, deep breath and fill up your lungs, and stretch."

Santana looked at Tran and then Grady. "How long was I out?"

"Thirty-five minutes," Tran said.

Santana peered at his watch. He'd felt certain that it was no more than ten minutes.

"You know Ted Lake and Jack Gaines?" Grady asked.

"They're FBI agents."

Grady nodded and wrote in his notebook.

"How are you feeling, John?" Tran asked.

"Great," he said.

Grady stood and held out a pair of handcuffs. "I hope you're still feeling good after talking with my lieutenant."

Chapter 26

Lieutenant Bernie Clark's office at the Metropolitan Police Department in DC was as plain and as grim as a military barracks. The lone photo on the wall was a large framed shot of Clark shaking hands with the President.

A thin manila folder lay underneath Clark's folded hands. A paperweight of Martin Luther King Jr.'s head sat atop a neatly arranged pile of reports to his left.

Clark wore a navy blue tie and a stiffly pressed white shirt with gold badges and a gold MPD insignia pinned on each side of the collar. The white shirt was in stark contrast to his ebony skin. His black hair was cut close to his head and sprinkled with gray. Clark's appearance and meticulously clean office suggested a military background. His muscular physique indicated he lifted weights and kept himself in good shape for a man Santana estimated was in his late forties or early fifties.

Santana sat in a hardback chair directly in front of the desk. He kept his posture as straight as possible so that his bruised back was slightly away from the backrest. Lyman Grady sat in a chair to his right. Santana's cell phone lay on the desk.

They had listened to the hypnosis recording Grady had made. Clark had also viewed the photos of the bruises and cuts on Santana's back and side, and had made a phone call to Pete Romano at the SPPD. Santana had spent another thirty minutes bringing Clark up to speed on his investigation into the death of Kim Austin.

When he'd finished, Clark trained his dark brown eyes on him. "Your commander seems to think you're an honest man, Detective. Apparently, he considers you his top homicide detective. That's the good news."

"And the bad?" Santana asked.

"Sometimes good, honest men commit terrible crimes."

"Did Romano tell you I was stupid?"

Clark cocked his head. "No, he did not."

"Then if I shot Powell to death, why would I leave my gun at the crime scene?"

Santana saw Grady nodding his head. "Doesn't makes sense, Lieutenant," he said.

"I didn't realize that I'd assigned you to this case, Detective-Sergeant Grady."

"Well, you didn't. But seeing as I have evidence possibly exonerating Santana . . ." His voice trailed off, as though he didn't know what else to say.

Clark's gaze drifted from Grady back to Santana. "I'll tell you why you left your gun at the scene, Detective. Panic."

"Right," Santana said. "After I shot Powell, I panicked. But I still took time to beat myself on the back before leaving the scene."

"Perhaps it was Powell who struck you while defending himself."

"With what?"

"The broom handle."

"Where was that found?"

Clark opened the folder on his desk and removed the crime scene photos. He sifted through them and said, "In the garage."

"Just where I dropped it. You'll find my prints on the broom handle. Why would my prints be there?"

"Because you took the broom away from Powell before shooting him." Clark held up a photo. "Powell's body was found in the garage. So why shouldn't I believe that he fled for his life and fought you off with the broom handle before you fatally shot him?"

"And my motive was . . .?"

Clark sat back in his chair, tented his hands, and considered Santana's response.

"Maybe we should wait for the lab tests on the drugs, the gunshot residue, and DNA, Lieutenant," Grady said.

Clark let out a slow, weary breath. "We all know that a negative result can mean that the GSR deposited on Santana's clothing wore off. No one knows for certain how long it remains. And wiping the hands on anything, even putting them in and out of your pockets, can transfer GSR off the hands."

"Except that it remains longer on clothing than on hands," Santana said. "And it can also prove that I was nowhere near the gun when it was fired."

Clark was silent for a time, his eyes focused on Santana, as if he were taking his measure. "You expect us to believe two men from the FBI attacked you?"

"The DNA on the end of the broom handle belongs to FBI agent Jack Gaines. The agent with him was Ted Lake."

"Anything else about the Kim Austin murder case you care to share with me, Detective?"

"You heard the tape recording. You know what I know. What are you going to do about it, Lieutenant?"

Clark sat forward again and leaned his elbows on the desktop. "I'll tell you what I'm not going to do, Detective Santana. I'm not going to jump to conclusions."

"You have all the evidence you need."

Clark sat quietly for a time. Then he sat back in his chair and said, "One of the uniforms interviewed a neighbor of Powell's who said she saw a dark car speeding from the scene shortly after you left the premises."

"Why didn't you tell me that before?" Santana asked.

"Because I wanted to hear your narrative, Detective. And because it doesn't mean that those were the same two men you say attacked you."

"Did the neighbor get a license number?"

"Partial."

"And the car?"

Clark shook his head. "Dark four-door sedan is all she saw."

"You know I didn't do this, Lieutenant."

"What I know are the facts," he said. "And the facts still point to you."

At that moment Clark's door opened and FBI agents Ted Lake and Rita Gamboni walked in.

Gamboni glanced at Santana, but he couldn't read her blank cop face.

Clark said, "Who are you two? And what the hell are you doing barging into my office?"

Lake held up his FBI credentials. "We're taking Detective Santana with us," he said.

Clark rose. "Over my dead body."

"It's a matter of national security, Lieutenant," Lake said.

Clark pointed an index finger at Santana. "This man is the prime suspect in a murder."

"If you have a concern, take it up with your chief." Lake motioned to Santana. "Let's go."

Santana stood. "You want to cuff me?"

Lake smiled and shook his head. "I don't think so. But if you run, I'll shoot you."

They left the building and got into a silver Chevy Tahoe. Santana sat in the back seat. Gamboni drove, and Lake sat in the passenger seat.

"Where we going?" Santana asked.

Lake turned in his seat and faced Santana. "The airport."

"What for?"

Lake pulled a folded piece of paper out of an inner pocket of his suit coat and handed it to Santana. It was a plane ticket to Minnesota.

"Hope you enjoyed your stay, Detective," Lake said.

"What about my clothes?"

"Your clothes are in your suitcase in back. We took the liberty of packing for you."

"My investigation isn't finished here."

"Oh, I'm afraid it is, Detective, unless you want us to take you back to Lieutenant Clark's office. I'm sure he'd be delighted to see you again."

"What happened on that Blue Skies flight, Lake? What's the Bureau hiding?"

"John," Gamboni said, looking in the rearview mirror. "We're doing you a favor. Don't screw it up."

"You know I didn't kill Terry Powell, Rita."

"I know that. But not everyone believes you." She nodded at Lake.

"For the time being, as a favor to Rita," he said, "I'll hold off judgment concerning your guilt or innocence."

There was something in Lake's statement that led Santana to believe he was bowing to Gamboni's judgment not out of respect for her experience, but because of his feelings for her. Santana wondered if she felt the same about Lake.

"How's your groin, Ted? Sore?"

Lake's face colored with embarrassment. "I don't know what you're talking about."

"And where's Gaines? Nursing the wound in his head where I cracked him with the broom handle?"

Santana could see Gamboni staring at him in the rearview mirror. "Maybe you and Gaines killed Terry Powell," he said to Lake.

"Stay away from the NTSB employees," Lake said. "I warned you before. I won't warn you again."

"I go where the investigation takes me."

"No one from the NTSB killed Kim Austin."

"How can you be sure of that?"

"Trust me," Lake said. His grin was meant to be reassuring but had the opposite effect.

"If you don't believe Ted," Gamboni said, "then believe me."

"I know there's a connection between that crash and Kim Austin's death," Santana said. "And I'm going to find it. No matter whose toes I have to step on."

"I think your commander and chief might have something to say about that," Lake said.

Chapter 27

Tim Branigan had been a very competent detective while working in Fraud and Forgery and later in Homicide before becoming assistant chief of the Major Crimes and Investigations Division. Most recently, Branigan had become chief of police.

He had the dark hair and eyes associated with the Black Irish and their Iberian ancestors, rather than the stereotypical fair hair, pale skin, and blue or green eyes. He favored black and navy blue suits and dark-colored shirts with vertical lines, the choice of clothes designed to make his thin, five-foot-eight-inch frame appear taller than it actually was.

He'd moved into the larger chief's office, but the ceremonial plaques, awards, and family photos were much the same as those that had decorated his former office. Branigan still had a life-sized sculpted raven on the corner of his desk, a reminder to all who entered that his surname had come from a very famous Irish clan and meant the descendent of the son of the raven.

"It's a beautiful fall afternoon, Detective," Branigan said as Santana stood in the doorway of his office. He took off his suit coat and hung it over the back of his high-back leather chair. "Let's take a walk, shall we? You probably need the exercise after your plane ride this morning."

It was an Indian summer afternoon with a temperature in the low seventies, no wind, and a high blue sky marked only by the contrails of two airplanes overhead.

There was a dry season and a rainy season in Santana's boyhood home of Manizales, Colombia. After arriving in Minnesota at the age of sixteen, it had taken him a number of years before he appreciated Minnesota's four seasons and the beauty in the death of the leaves in fall and their verdant rebirth in spring. But despite the wonderful fall day, the numbing cold deadness of winter lurked like a long shadow darkening the landscape.

Santana walked with Branigan to the Bruce Vento Regional Trail near the LEC. The seven-mile-long asphalt trail led through an abandoned rail corridor that connected the Bruce Vento Nature Sanctuary with Swede Hollow and Phalen Park to the north.

Santana had once worked a case in which a body was found along the trail. But it was another case he remembered now, a case involving the murder of a high-priced escort from Costa Rica, a case that had involved the former assistant and now chief of police, Tim Branigan.

"How was your plane ride back from DC this morning?" Branigan asked.

"Fine," Santana said, though his sore back had made the trip uncomfortable, despite the pain medication he'd taken.

Branigan had left a message on Santana's voicemail asking to see him as soon as he was back in Minnesota. Santana was certain of the meeting's purpose. The FBI had contacted Branigan. But Santana still had some leverage because of Branigan's involvement with the escort—and he intended to use it, if necessary.

The air was musty with the scent of dead leaves that crunched under their feet. Two women dressed in T-shirts and shorts jogged by them, followed by a similarly dressed woman on a bicycle.

"You got yourself in quite a mess in DC," Branigan said.

"It was a setup."

"That's what Agent Lake told me."

"Did you also talk to Gamboni?"

"Yes, I did. You should be thankful both agents took your side."

"They didn't do it out of the goodness of their hearts," Santana said.

"Why then?"

Santana stopped along the side of the trail and looked at Branigan. "You know why, Chief. Because I didn't kill Terry Powell, and Ted Lake knows it."

"Because he was one of the men who attacked you at Powell's."

"Yes. Lake and Jack Gaines."

"That's certainly not standard procedure for the FBI."

"We don't know what the FBI is capable of. And I doubt their supervisors ordered the attack."

"Why would they attack you?"

"They want me off the Kim Austin case. Threatening Pete Romano didn't work. Now they want you to intervene."

Branigan pursed his lips and began walking again.

"I need to talk with Cathy Herrera," Santana said. "And Barry McCarthy."

"Ted Lake mentioned they were two of the NTSB employees you were to avoid."

"Doesn't that make you curious, Chief? Because it sure makes me curious."

"We've had this talk once before, Detective."

"And what talk was that?"

"About your insistence on going your own way, of not being a team player, despite the consequences."

"Someone once said that since the dead can't cry out for justice, it's the duty of the living to do so for them."

"And you feel the only way to solve Kim Austin's murder is to badger the NTSB."

"I'm not *badgering* anyone," Santana said. "I'm simply asking questions and expecting answers."

"Maybe you just don't like the answers you're getting."

"And maybe the answers I'm getting are untruthful."

Branigan stopped again and looked at Santana. "I can't always protect you."

"Can't or won't?"

Branigan took in a deep breath and exhaled. "I'm perfectly aware of the understanding we have between us, Detective. I'm not proud of what I did. But my wife and I were separated at the time. I admitted that seeing the escort was a mistake. A mistake I have to live with the rest of my life. But what I resent most of all is having to relive that mistake every time I have dealings with you."

"You were the one who brought it up."

"Don't take me for a fool, Detective. I know perfectly well that you'll continue to blackmail me as long as it serves your purpose."

"You've got it wrong, Chief."

"Have I?"

"This isn't about blackmail, as you put it."

"What would you call it then?"

"No one is perfect. We all make mistakes. Believe me, I know."

"Yes, I believe you do."

Santana detected compassion in the chief's words rather than animosity. Branigan was well aware of Jordan Parrish's death.

"Like you said, Chief. We have an understanding. I keep my mouth shut."

Branigan snickered. "And I keep granting you favors."

"You're not doing me any favors by helping me solve one and possibly two murders."

"The FBI can make both our jobs . . . difficult."

"When I solve this, they'll get off our backs."

"I wish I shared your confidence."

They walked in silence for a time before Santana said, "I need another gun."

Branigan stopped and waited for a male jogger to run by before he spoke again. "The thing is, you're a damn fine detective. Romano believes you're the best we have. Trouble is, you're also a constant pain in the ass."

"I'll take that as a compliment."

"Take it any way you want. I just hope you know what you're doing. For both our sakes."

* * *

After leaving Swede Hollow, Santana called Kacie Hawkins to debrief her about his trip to DC.

"Why don't you come by?" she said. "You've never been to my home. I could rustle up some dinner."

Santana preferred to go home and relax after his trip, but he felt he owed his partner the courtesy of accepting her invitation. She'd been especially kind and supportive since Jordan's death and had invited him for dinner on a number of occasions. Turning her down once again when he had no legitimate excuse would be rude and disrespectful.

"I'll pick up some wine."

"No need to, John."

"It's my treat," he said.

Kacie Hawkins had recently sold the small stone Tudor she'd lived in on St. Paul's East Side and purchased a two-story Craftsman with hardwood floors, oak woodwork, and a wood-burning brick fireplace in St. Anthony Park, near the University of Minnesota's St. Paul campus and the Minnesota State Fairgrounds. The secluded area with a small-town feel is about three miles from a completely separate suburb of northeast

Minneapolis also called St. Anthony. Santana knew that Hawkins had saved for a long time to purchase the house in the upscale area known for its hills, curving streets, and Tudoresque business district, as well as for its international students and faculty connected to the university.

She'd grown up with a single mother in the Englewood neighborhood on the south side of Chicago, an area of high poverty and higher crime. Santana thought it remarkable that while most of her childhood friends had ended up on the wrong side of the law, she had resisted temptation and peer pressure and had chosen a career in law enforcement.

While Hawkins attributed much of her success to her strong-willed mother, who had instilled in her a set of good values, Santana believed that her success was due to resilience; her ability to recover after a setback or a challenge, a belief that no matter the mistakes, she could try again. Having a home in a nice, safe, quiet neighborhood was Hawkins' testament to her resilience.

Santana believed that he and Natalia were also resilient. After the deaths of their parents, when they both were still young, they could have chosen the wrong path. There was easy money to be made working for one of the cartels in Colombia. Now Natalia was a doctor, and like Kacie Hawkins, Santana had chosen a career in law enforcement.

But his choice—his resilience—was once again being tested.

Not knowing what Hawkins had planned for dinner, Santana brought a bottle of Chardonnay and one Cabernet Sauvignon.

Hawkins, dressed in jeans and a bright orange T-shirt, gave him a hug and directed him to the tan three-piece sectional in front of the fireplace while she went out to the kitchen.

Her favorite singer, the late Marvin Gaye, was singing "What's Going On?" on her DVD player. A gray cockatiel with bright orange cheek feathers was perched in a large cage in one corner of the room, occasionally whistling along with the music.

Hawkins turned the volume down when she returned from the kitchen with two bottles of Sam Adams. She gestured with a bottle toward the birdcage and said, "That's Smokey."

Smokey gave a wolf whistle and said, "Hello."

"Clever," Santana said.

"With patience, you can teach a male lots of things," she said with a chuckle, handing Santana a beer.

"Are you talking about birds or males in general?"

She winked. "What do you think?"

"I think you might be right."

"Good answer," she said.

He drank some cold beer. "You went out and bought Sam Adams?"

"I always keep a few of your favorites handy just in case you ever changed your mind and came by."

"Here I am."

"Finally," she said, sitting down on the sectional.

"Hey, you just moved in."

"You were never inside my old house either."

Santana had no retort for that. Come to think of it, he'd never invited her to his house.

"So what about DC?"

He drank some Sam Adams and then summarized what had happened at Terry Powell's residence and how he'd been set up for Powell's murder.

"You could've gotten yourself killed," Hawkins said.

"But I didn't."

"You can't keep pressing your luck, John. And what's with Ted Lake and Jack Gaines?"

"And what is the FBI hiding, Kacie?"

Santana drank more beer and let his gaze fall on the big-screen television above the fireplace, the framed photos of

Kacie and her mother on the end tables, the purple African violet in a yellow pot on a table near the front window, and a framed photo of Kacie and him on the coffee table in front of the sectional.

The photo had been shot from a slight distance and from the waist up. Santana had his right arm around Hawkins' shoulder and she an arm around his waist. They were smiling broadly as they stood in front of a white wall filled with framed police and sheriff patches from the Twin Cities and from federal law enforcement such as the ATF and US Customs. They were dressed in their standard work clothes: dark slacks, white shirts, and sport coats. Santana, as usual, was wearing a tie.

"Remember where that photo was taken, John?" Hawkins asked, following his gaze.

"Rita Gamboni's going-away party," he said. "At Alary's."

"Yes. Gamboni was leaving her commander position to take the liaison position with the FBI."

"She came to see me while I was in DC," Santana said.

"What did she want?"

"I think she wanted information about our investigation."

"Maybe she wanted to see you *and* to get information," Hawkins said.

Santana shrugged. "Could be."

"What did you tell her?"

"That the FBI knew there was a cover-up involving the Blue Skies crash."

"I'm sure she was happy to hear that."

"It gets worse. When Rita and I went out for a drink, we ran into Reyna Tran."

"The woman from Chicago?"

"Yes."

"What was she doing there?"

"She has an office in DC."

"How did it get worse?"

"I think Gamboni thought there was something between Tran and me."

"Is there?" Hawkins asked with a sly smile.

"I don't date sociopaths."

"Reyna Tran is a sociopath?"

"Uh-huh. But she helped me out of a jam in DC."

Santana told Hawkins how hypnosis had helped him remember the sequence of events that had taken place that night.

"Jesus, John. How could you let Reyna Tran hypnotize you?"

"I couldn't recall exactly what had happened at Powell's house."

"You trust Reyna Tran?"

"As far as I know, she's been straight with me."

"Yeah," Hawkins said with a shake of her head. "*As far as you know*. Letting her hypnotize you was a risk."

"It was worth it."

"You hope," she said. "And then there's the FBI. You counting on Rita to help you?"

"She's all I've got. Ted Lake sure as hell won't help."

"Rita might not help you after the way you treated her."

"She convinced Ted Lake to help her get me safely out of DC. But the FBI knows something about the Blue Skies crash, Kacie. Something they don't want us to find out."

"You have any idea what that *something* is?"

He shook his head. "Afraid not. What about the passenger lists on flights leaving Minneapolis the day the security conference ended?"

"I'm checking the names. Of course, someone could've driven here and back to DC."

"That'll be harder to track."

"Speaking of passenger lists," Hawkins said. She stood up and went to the dining room table, where she picked up a small stack of papers and brought it back to the living room.

She handed the papers to Santana and then sat down beside him.

Six pages were stapled together. In the upper left-hand corner of the first page was the Blue Skies logo. Underneath the logo were the words: TP 624 PASSENGER MANIFEST. There were four columns on each page. The first column contained a number. In the second column was a passenger's name. The third and fourth columns contained each passenger's nationality and age. The names were listed alphabetically.

Circled in red in the middle of the first page was the name Brian Devlin.

Santana looked at Hawkins. "Who's Brian Devlin?"

"A corporate raider."

"Meaning?"

"Well, from what I read and understand, he's an investor who buys a large number of shares in a corporation whose assets he thinks are undervalued."

"So?"

"So Devlin recently bought lots of shares of Cyber Security Systems."

"That's David Knapp's company."

Hawkins nodded. "A large share purchase would give Devlin significant voting rights. He could then push changes in the company's leadership and management. Theoretically, that would increase share value and generate a substantial return for Devlin when he sold his shares."

"Couldn't Devlin also downsize operations or liquidate the company?"

"Yes, he could. According to his bio, he has liquidated companies in the past."

"That might make David Knapp very nervous," he said.

Hawkins canted her head and thought a moment before replying. "If the downing of the Blue Skies flight wasn't an act of terrorism, then . . ."

"Maybe someone wanted to kill someone on board that plane."

Hawkins' eyes lit up. "You mean David Knapp killed everyone on board just so he could kill Brian Devlin? That's insane."

"Quite possibly. But when I was growing up in Colombia, an Avianca flight from Bogotá to Cali was blown out of the sky five minutes after it left the airport. Pablo Escobar, the head of the Medellin cartel, planned to kill César Gaviria Trujillo, who was running for President of Colombia. But Gaviria changed his plans and didn't get on the flight. All one hundred seven people on board were killed, as well as three people on the ground. Two Americans were on board. The bombing so angered the Bush Administration that President George H. Bush sent in ISA to help track down Escobar."

"That's the secret government agency Reyna Tran told you about."

"And the agency that David Knapp once worked for."

"You really believe Knapp had something to do with the Blue Skies crash?"

"He had a motive. And remember, the focus of the security conference that Kim Austin attended was DNA, hacking, and encryption. Knapp's company deals with hacking and encryption technology. Maybe Kim Austin knew how Knapp brought down that plane. Maybe that's why she ended up dead."

"You think Knapp killed Austin?"

"He's another suspect. What's one more murder after you've killed hundreds? I'll ask Tran if she knows anything more about David Knapp and Brian Devlin."

"The Dragon Lady? Again?"

"Profiling is what she does."

"Among other things," Hawkins said.

* * *

That night Santana dreams of a beautiful garden filled with luscious plants, fruits, and naked figures. There are no children or old people, only young men and women. Santana realizes he is naked as well, yet he feels happy and content rather than ashamed and embarrassed.

Directly ahead a woman lies within a transparent shield.

In the distance a woman is bathing naked in a fountain as a man rides on horseback around it.

Then the mood darkens, and the garden becomes a ravaged landscape lit by the glow of a fire. Prison-like city walls are etched in inky silhouette against the flames. A blade slices between two enormous ears that are pierced by an arrow. A dagger impales a man's hand. A man's head supports a disk populated by demons.

A wolf attacks a knight lying on the ground. As the knight turns his head, Santana sees his own face, sees the wolf's teeth, bloody with torn flesh, reaching for his neck . . .

The image jarred Santana awake. His heart was pounding; his hands were sweating. He sat up in bed, wiped his palms on his thighs, and waited until his heartbeat slowed.

Gitana, lying at the foot of the bed, raised her head and stared at him. He'd picked her up at Deborah Russell's house after his dinner with Kacie Hawkins.

It was near dawn, and slivers of light pierced the darkness behind the blinds covering the sliding door. He got out of bed and padded across the hardwood floor to the sink in the bathroom, where he washed his face with cool water and toweled off. Then he went to the nightstand beside the bed, retrieved his dream journal and a pen, and sat with his back against the headboard. He closed his eyes for a time, remembering the strange and unusually surrealistic images in the dream that had awakened him.

Santana had been a fan of surrealism since his boyhood days in Colombia and had studied the works of André Breton, considered the father of the cultural movement that began in

Paris in the 1920s. Surrealist artists like Salvador Dalí used the unconscious mind as a means to unlock the power of imagination, typically through the bizarre juxtaposition of distinctly different images.

But what truly interested Santana were the surrealists' accounts of dreams. Two objects that could never be juxtaposed in reality often became so in a dream. One of Santana's favorite writers was Gabriel Garcia Márquez, whose stories and novels often juxtaposed the normal and the dream-like. And interpreting his dreams was something Santana had practiced and written about in his journals since he was a child.

The images in his most recent dream were familiar. He'd seen them in the Bosch painting entitled *The Garden of Earthly Delights*, once as a child, and most recently on a hotel computer in DC. When he'd visited the Prado Museum in Madrid with his parents, he'd been too young to understand the meaning of the famous painting. But the images had remained in the depths of his subconscious for all these years. Something about this current case had now drawn them to the surface. He was certain that there were hidden meanings in the objects and faces in his dream, meanings that might help him solve the murders. What was his subconscious trying to tell him?

He wasn't much of an artist, so he used words to describe the images in his dream journal, adding his interpretation after each description.

The face of the woman in the bubble was certainly that of Kim Austin. Like the woman in the painting, her lips were sealed, indicating, Santana thought, that she carried a secret. One he hoped would help him solve her murder.

The dream image of a man on horseback circling a fountain in which a naked woman was bathing wasn't difficult to interpret. Freud, whose dream interpretation had a profound influence on surrealism, would say that Santana had a repressed sexual desire for Reyna Tran, even if his conscious mind denied it.

The two enormous ears cut in half by a blade represented Albert Greer.

Santana recalled from his Google search of the painting that arrows represented words, in that as they traveled from one place to another, they could be misinterpreted. Words could also mislead people. Santana believed that Albert Greer had misled him regarding Kim Austin's and Laurie Baldwin's murders. He wondered if the arrow also represented Trevor Dane, since Dane had practiced archery.

Santana figured the disk on the man's head stood for the disks from David Kaplan's security conference.

The man with the dagger through his hand symbolized Kim Austin and Laurie Baldwin.

If Santana was the knight being devoured by a wolf, then who, he wondered, was the wolf?

Chapter 28

Early that same morning, city lights shimmered under the gray stare of a dead sky as Santana drove north toward Grand Marais, Minnesota. He took Gitana and a thermos of hot chocolate with him.

He'd purchased a dog hammock that attached to the headrests and hung between the front and back seats. It provided a comfortable nest and extra support while keeping her from falling into the foot well on a quick stop. The hammock was also supposed to block her from getting into the front seat, but she was big enough to step over it. On occasion, she would place her front paws on the console between the front bucket seats, where she would stare out the windshield or lick Santana's ear.

He was thankful that Deborah Russell had looked out for Gitana after she'd gotten out of her dog run and while he was in DC. Even though he'd repaired the gate, he was sure, if he asked, Russell would dog-sit her again. But he felt better with Gitana along for the ride instead of leaving her alone once more.

He'd learned long ago to trust his intuition, and it was telling him that he needed to stay close to her. Besides, she enjoyed trips in the car and had never gotten sick or claustrophobic. She would listen to him talk, though she wasn't much of a conversationalist, preferring to sniff the air through a slightly open back window.

Knowing he would need energy for the nearly four-hour drive, he'd fixed a traditional Colombian breakfast from the

Paisa and Antioquia region of his native country called *calentado,* a dish made from leftovers of reheated rice, beans, and potatoes. Along with the *calentado,* he ate an *arepa* with cheese, a *chorizo,* fresh fruit, and hot chocolate.

About halfway to his destination, Santana pulled off the highway at a rest stop overlooking the city of Duluth. He used the restroom and then let Gitana out to do her business and to give her some exercise.

He'd taken two Aleve after breakfast, which had dulled the pain in his back. Looking in the mirror this morning, he'd noticed that the bruises were now purple in color.

His personal cell phone rang while he watched Gitana tracking a scent.

"You never called before leaving Washington."

"Hello, Reyna. How did you get my personal number?"

"When you were in my guest bedroom in DC."

"I don't recall giving you permission to snoop on my phone."

"I don't recall you asking me to help you in DC."

"Point taken," Santana said. "Why the call today?"

"I was worried about you, John."

"I'm fine."

"They didn't charge you with Terry Powell's murder?"

"Not yet."

"Thank God."

"You're not a believer."

"Of course not," she said. "But it's what people often say in this situation."

"The FBI drove me to the airport."

"You weren't given a choice to leave?"

"I wasn't."

"Where are you now?" she asked.

"Outside Duluth. I'm on my way to see Cathy Herrera."

"One of the accident investigators?"

"Yes."

"Oh, you're such a bad boy. The feds will be so upset with you."

Santana could hear the mischief in her voice. "If they find out," he said.

"I won't tell."

"I know you won't, Reyna. I owe you."

"Yes, you do."

"But I need another favor."

"Oh, good," she said.

Santana told her what he needed. Then he and Gitana got back in the SUV and headed north.

The harbor village of Grand Marais sits on the edge of Lake Superior at the base of the Sawtooth Mountains, near the Boundary Waters Canoe Area and Superior National Forest. Santana had set his ETA for noon and had left the Twin Cities before rush hour, stopping just the one time outside of Duluth.

Once he'd learned in DC that Cathy Herrera had taken a vacation, he suspected she'd gone to her cabin near Grand Marais in northern Minnesota. Early last evening he'd called the outdoor shop owned by Herrera's brother. After identifying himself as a St. Paul homicide detective and saying that he needed to talk with Herrera regarding the Blue Skies crash, he'd confirmed that she was, indeed, staying there. Having learned that there was no phone at the cabin, Santana had gotten directions and decided to make the drive.

He gassed up his SUV in Grand Marais and then followed the GPS coordinates and Siri's voice, which directed him to turn off the state highway and onto a dirt road that narrowed as it wound its way through a dense forest, the branches scraping the sides of his SUV. At the end of the mile-long, winding road, a plank board shack sat in the shadow of tall pines. Along the right side of the cabin was a large portable generator. An outhouse sat on the opposite side. A red Jeep Cherokee was parked beside it.

Shutting off the engine, Santana got out of his Explorer and opened the back door for Gitana. The crisp air smelled of woods and wet fern and humus. A glint of sunlight flared off the windshield of his SUV. He told Gitana to "empty," the command word signaling her to urinate, and then walked up the stone path and knocked on the front door of the cabin.

When the door opened, Santana saw the Mossberg 500 twelve-gauge shotgun Cathy Herrera held in her hands. The barrel was pointed directly at his chest.

Santana raised his hands and said, "Take it easy."

She glanced at Gitana, standing beside Santana, and then focused her gaze on him again. "Who are you and what do you want?"

"Detective John Santana. St. Paul PD."

"Show me some ID."

Santana reached carefully into a leather jacket pocket, removed his badge wallet, and showed her his ID.

"How'd you find me?"

"I'm a detective. It's what I do."

Cathy Herrera studied Santana's face, her deep-set dark eyes unblinking. She had an olive complexion and cheeks slightly pitted by acne scars. Her ebony-colored hair was cut short and curled at the ends. A long-sleeved denim shirt hung over her waist and down to her jean-covered thighs.

She looked at Gitana again and back at Santana. "Your dog?"

"Her name is Gitana," Santana said.

Herrera held the shotgun with one hand and stroked Gitana's head with the other. "She's beautiful."

"I've come a long way, Ms. Herrera. I'd like to talk to you about the Blue Skies crash."

He could see the momentary confusion and nervousness in her face. She gripped the shotgun with both hands once more. "I don't know anything more than what I've already told you."

"I think you do. That's why you're hiding out up here."

"Who says I'm hiding out?"

"You asked me how I found you. People who are hiding from something or someone ask that question. They also point shotguns at people who knock on their door."

"I can't help you."

"I think the NTSB and the FBI know something about the crash, something they don't want the public to know. One of your colleagues is missing and two of them are dead, Ms. Herrera. You could be next."

"You said *two* are dead. Who's the other one besides Kim Austin?"

"Terry Powell."

She let out a quick breath but kept her grip on the shotgun. "Terry's dead?"

"I'm afraid so."

"When?"

"He was murdered two days ago." Santana didn't mention that Powell was killed immediately after he'd talked to him.

"My God," she said.

"I can protect you, Ms. Herrera, but I need to know what you know about the crash."

"It's all been in the newspapers and online."

"Not all of it," Santana said.

She thought a moment and then lowered the shotgun and said, "Come in."

Santana and Gitana followed her inside.

On the walls were collections of whitetail antlers, some with names and dates scribbled on index cards alongside, orange hunting caps hanging from nails, and a gallery-like presentation of dated snapshots. There were two sets of bunk beds, one set under the windows on each of the walls to Santana's left and right, and on a countertop in the kitchen were enough pots and pans to feed a small group of hunters.

"My brother uses this as a hunting shack," she said.

"You hunt?"

"Ever since I was a kid."

She pressed the shell latch on the camo-pattern Mossberg, unloaded the seven shells from the magazine, and placed them on the kitchen table. Then she depressed the slide release, racked the slide, and ejected the eighth shell from the chamber. She stood the shotgun in a corner and grabbed a flannel jacket off a hook on the wall.

"Are we going somewhere?"

"I want to show you something." She led him out of the cabin, closing the door behind her. "It's only about a half-mile from here."

"What is?"

"A year ago a CRJ200—that's a small commuter airliner—went down, killing all forty-five passengers and crew aboard. I was one of the investigators." She slipped into her coat and retrieved a package of Pall Malls and a lighter from an outer pocket.

"Was the plane off course like the Blue Skies flight?"

She lit the cigarette and dropped the lighter back into a pocket. "No. It was weather related." She fished in a jacket pocket and brought out a cell phone. "Give me a minute," she said, dialing a number as she walked away.

Santana could hear her talking in a low voice to someone but couldn't clearly make out what she was saying.

Then she disconnected and returned to him. She took a long drag on her cigarette and said, "This way."

Santana wondered whom she'd called, and if he could trust her. Terry Powell had drugged him. Maybe Cathy Herrera had something special planned for him, too.

He felt the new Glock in the belt holster under his jacket for reassurance, and then he and Gitana trailed Herrera as she zigzagged between stands of spruce and tall white pine. The air, fresh and cool, smelled of pine and damp leaves and smoke from her cigarette. The stillness surrounding them reminded Santana of a cemetery and was broken only by the sound of snapping twigs and the crunch of leaves underfoot. High above the canopy of trees and the shadowed floor of the forest, the hollow dome of sky held no color at all.

They walked between a broken-down rail fence and continued on for a quarter mile. Santana could see an open space ahead, like the end of a long tunnel. Ducking his head under a low-hanging branch, he and Gitana followed Herrera through the last trees into a flat field he estimated was two hundred yards wide and long.

All that remained of the CRJ200 crash were fire-blackened trees stripped of their branches, charred stumps, patches of new grass, and burnt, upturned soil.

Herrera stopped and smoked her cigarette, contemplating.

Fifty yards ahead Santana could see the impact point, where over twenty-five tons of airliner had slammed into the earth.

"The plane came down at a steep angle," she said.

Santana felt a chill run down his spine, like ice water. He could only imagine the overwhelming sense of terror and panic that must have overtaken the passengers and crew as the doomed airliner plunged toward earth, the plane rattling in the turbulence as the angle of descent became more severe.

"What about the Blue Skies crash?" he asked.

Cathy Herrera stubbed out her cigarette in the black earth, and as they continued walking, she told Santana the details of the doomed Blue Skies flight from takeoff until it crashed into the Pacific Ocean.

"Flight 624 was scheduled to depart from Narita Airport in Tokyo, Japan, on Thursday, February 18th, at 5:25 p.m.," she said. "Barring complications, the flight to Los Angeles would take it across the lonely stretches of the north Pacific and the International Date Line and to a safe landing at LAX on

Wednesday, February 17th at 12:00 p.m. There were 217 passengers and crew aboard the 767-300."

As they stopped beside the blackened trunk of a pine tree, Herrera continued.

"Because of the ten-hour flight time, two complete crews were required, each consisting of one captain and one first officer. Blue Skies designated one crew as the 'active crew' and the other as the 'relief crew.'

"The active crew consisted of fifty-seven-year-old Captain Edward Turner and forty-two-year-old First Officer Patrick Sheridan. The relief crew was composed of fifty-three-year-old Captain James Parker and thirty-eight-year-old First Officer Dean Wilson."

"What do you know about the pilots?"

"Captain Turner was a veteran pilot who had been with Blue Skies for more than thirty-five years and had accumulated approximately twenty thousand total flight hours, more than sixty-three hundred of which were in the 767. Captain Parker had nearly as much experience."

"Had they flown this route before?"

"Turner had a couple of times."

They walked on for a time before Cathy Herrera spoke again. "The eastbound flight system from Japan to North America consists of four numbered tracks, one, three, fourteen, and fifteen. The Blue Skies flight was assigned track one, the northernmost track.

"Before boarding, Captain Turner reviewed with dispatch the current weather reports and flight plan. I imagine Turner was especially careful because, as I said before, he'd flown this particular route on only two previous occasions.

"Once in the cockpit, he loaded the flight plan into the aircraft's computer. First Officer Sheridan read the plan out loud from the computer as Turner cross-checked each point against the flight plan for accuracy. The points were latitude/longitude intersections called waypoints. The flight took off right on schedule. Once they were airborne, Captain Turner climbed to thirty-three thousand feet, and the 767 sailed over the Pacific.

"One hour out of Narita, far from land-based radar stations, First Officer Sheridan fixed their location using the global positioning system and then used the long-range high-frequency radio to report their position to Oceanic controllers. Their positions were based on the charts he'd prepared and the course he'd plotted. He and First Officer Sheridan continued reporting their position via HF radio every forty to fifty minutes, annotating the time at their current point and ETAs to the next point on the chart, so he could read them to air traffic control."

"When did the relief crew take over?"

"There's no formal procedure specifying when each crew flies the aircraft, though it's customary for the active crew on Blue Skies to make the takeoff and fly half the flight. The relief crew then assumes control of the aircraft until about one to two hours before landing, at which point the active crew returns to the cockpit and takes control.

"According to the cockpit recorder, four hours into the flight, relief Captain James Parker and relief First Officer Dean Wilson replaced Turner and Sheridan in the cockpit."

"Both at the same time?"

She shook her head. "No. Each crewmember staggers the relief between individual pilots by a few minutes so one pilot can thoroughly brief the other as to their current position and status of the aircraft.

"Turner and Sheridan were back in their seats as the flight neared the US and Point Bravo, their last reporting point. Oceanic controllers then handed it off to Los Angeles Center ATC."

"Air traffic control."

She nodded. "Sheridan reported that they had reached Point Bravo. When there was no response from LA Center, he notified Oceanic controllers that he couldn't raise LA."

"The first sign that something was wrong."

"Yes. About a minute later, Turner communicated that a Global 747 had just crossed their path heading east. Oceanic controllers responded that the only Global 747 flight they had that day was a flight from Hawaii to LA. Turner and Sheridan realized now that they were off course and decided to follow the 747 toward LA. They also figured they were approximately one thousand miles from LA, or about two hours' flight time. And they only had about one hour's worth of fuel left. Given that gauge readings are often not precise, Turner had to ditch the aircraft in about thirty minutes to make sure he wouldn't run out of fuel. Once the engines quit, so would the hydraulics—and any chance he had of a controlled landing. Oceanic control contacted the Navy and asked if there were any ships in the area. If there were, it would be desirable to set down near one. Unfortunately, there were none in the immediate area."

"So what did Turner do?"

"He turned the aircraft toward LA and declared an emergency. Then he called the head flight attendant up to the cockpit and told her to go back and get Captain Parker. When Parker came up to the cockpit, he and Sheridan and Turner tried to figure out what had gone wrong."

"Did they figure it out?"

"No. They alerted the cabin crew to prepare for ditching. Turner planned to touch down on the windward side and parallel to the waves and swells. He adjusted the flaps to forty degrees for the slowest airspeed.

"As the aircraft descended below five thousand feet, the circuit breakers were pulled to stop the warning horns from sounding. The landing gear and APU switches were turned off, and the outflow valve switch was closed to prevent water from entering the airplane."

"These are all standard operating procedures?" Santana asked.

"Right from the manual," she said. "Prior to five hundred feet, both ground and terrain proximity switches were turned off. At three hundred feet the 'Brace for Impact' command was given. In order to land properly, Turner had to maintain airspeed at VREF."

"Sorry," Santana said.

"My apologies, Detective. VREF is the final landing approach airspeed target with the airplane configured for landing. If a pilot slows too much on approach, the airplane can stall and hit short of the runway. Flying too slowly in windy conditions can also change the approach airspeed into an unexpected stall. But carrying too much airspeed on approach leads to floating and a long landing that can send you off the far end of the runway.

"Unfortunately, there was only open water and no runway, but the VREF concept is the same. Turner had to maintain a two hundred to three hundred feet per minute rate of descent until the start of flare." She held up her hand, palm toward him, before he asked the question.

"The flare follows the final approach phase and precedes the touchdown and roll-out phases of landing. In the flare, the nose of the plane is raised, slowing the descent rate, and the proper attitude is set for touchdown."

"So what happened?"

"The ocean was a bit rough that day. The data recorders indicate that Turner did everything by the book—right up to the end."

They stopped beside the impact crater, and Herrera looked up into Santana's eyes.

"So how did the flight get so far off course?" he asked.

Herrera put her hands in the pockets of her windbreaker and stared at the crater. Without looking at Santana, she said, "Someone could've tampered with the global positioning system."

"Who?"

"I'm not sure. Maybe terrorists."

"And the NTSB has a different view."

"I don't know what view they have. They haven't released the final report." She took a deep breath and let it out slowly. "To tell you the truth, Detective, I don't know what to believe anymore."

"But you suspect the NTSB will disagree with your interpretation."

"It wasn't initially my interpretation. It was Kim's."

"Did Terry Powell feel the same way?"

"Not at first. But I think later he had his suspicions."

"What about Paul Westbrook and Barry McCarthy?"

"Barry's the kind of guy who goes along to get along. He didn't have an opinion one way or the other."

"And Paul Westbrook?"

"Paul was adamant that pilot error caused the crash."

"So he and Kim Austin disagreed."

"Yes."

"If pilot error wasn't the cause of the crash," Santana said, "how did someone take over the flight path?"

"Let's walk back, and I'll explain it to you," she said.

Chapter 29

Cathy Herrera asked as they headed through the woods again toward her cabin, "Have you ever heard of something called a 'spoofing attack,' Detective?"

Santana shook his head.

"It's a situation where one program successfully masquerades as another by falsifying data. In the case of the Blue Skies flight, there's a high probability that someone hacked into the navigation system and altered the GPS signals to confuse the system and steer the plane off course."

"How could they do that?"

She pointed to the sky. "All GPS signals are sent from satellites to Earth without any authentication or encryption. You could use a GPS spoofer to feed erroneous information to the autopilot. As far as the spoofing itself, it's easy as long as the person has enough expertise."

"What's a spoofer?"

"Any earth-bound transmitter, even a weak one, could easily overpower real GPS signals. To create the spoofed signals, the hacker would use a GPS simulator on the planned diverted route and record them. Then they'd just have to play back the simulation record and transmit it. The power of the counterfeit signals is then gradually increased. After taking control of the plane's GPS unit, the spoofer induces a false trajectory that deviates from the flight's desired trajectory."

"Wouldn't the pilots notice?"

"Not if it was done gradually and over a long period of time. The ten-hour flight from Japan to LA would be perfect. Of course, the diverted heading would have to be roughly similar to the expected heading. So if the pilots know they're going north, and the diverted heading is south, they'd immediately realize something was wrong. It wouldn't work if the pilots knew the route well. The hacker would start to influence the heading and the pilot would see the unexpected heading and get confused."

"There was an experienced crew onboard," Santana said.

"But not on this particular route. If it was a domestic commercial flight or at least had a flight plan with 'flight following' activated, air traffic control would probably notice it. Even a private pilot, if he's requested 'flight following,' will get notified by ATC if he starts to deviate significantly from the planned route. That's why a diversion would be most effective if it was an international flight or going through uncontrolled air space.

"Say the spoofing attack starts an hour out of Narita, far from land-based navigation stations," she said. "The flight crew would have to start position reporting with their long-range HF radios. They'd have GPS fixes to report from their flight plan as they headed eastward.

"Let's say their first reporting point is ABC followed by DEF, GHI, etc. They'd report the points and, of course, they'd be in error, but air traffic control would plot them in the correct position, not aware of the error. With a slight data error to the right, the flight would be far southwest of LA after ten hours. But this kind of attack would only work if you knew ahead of time the aircraft's planned route and speed."

"Say you're right," Santana said. "How could this happen?"

"The FAA is replacing the current system with the Next Gen system, which tracks every plane in flight using GPS data rather than traditional radar. But with Next Gen the location data passed between the plane and the control towers is unencrypted and unauthenticated, leaving them open to potential hacker attack."

"And you came to this conclusion on your own?"

"No. Kim was the one who concluded that a GPS hacker attack was a real possibility. But once she explained it to me, it made perfect sense."

Santana understood the NTSB's and the FBI's concern. "If word got out that hackers or terrorists were diverting airliners or bringing them down in the ocean," he said, "the airline industry could collapse, not just here, but worldwide."

Herrera nodded. "The FAA would ground all international flights till the Next Gen system was fixed. That's why the NTSB is pushing for pilot error as the cause. Think of the impact on the economy, not to mention the money the government is spending to implement the Next Gen system. People need to know this kind of thing is possible."

"But if a terrorist group like ISIS did bring down the plane, wouldn't they claim credit for it?" Santana asked.

"That's the part that makes no sense," Herrera said. "If terrorists weren't responsible, then who was, and why?"

When they reached the cabin, Herrera said, "Are you hungry, Detective Santana?"

"I am. I haven't eaten since breakfast."

"I don't feel safe leaving the cabin, but I could rustle up some sandwiches and coffee."

"You wouldn't happen to have some hot chocolate?"

"I believe I do. Come on in."

While Cathy Herrera brewed a pot of coffee, heated some water on the stove for Santana's hot chocolate, and made tuna fish sandwiches, Santana went out to his SUV and returned with one of Gitana's dishes, which he filled with cool water.

"Potato chips and paper plates are in the cupboard above your head," Herrera said.

When the two of them were seated at the kitchen table, Santana said, "Paul Westbrook was the group leader for the systems team on the Blue Skies crash."

"He was."

"I understand his parents were killed in a plane crash when he was twelve."

Herrera's eyes lit up with surprise. "How do you know that?"

Santana looked at her without comment.

"Oh, right," she said. "It's what you do."

Santana nodded.

"Well, Paul never liked talking about that."

"You think it affected him much?"

"How do you mean?"

"Emotionally."

"I'm sure it did. You lose your parents when you're young, it obviously affects you, don't you think?"

"You really never get over it," he said.

Herrera gazed at him in silence for a time before she spoke again. "Your parents were killed when you were young?"

"They were."

"Plane crash?"

"Something else."

Herrera started to say something and then stopped, as if she'd thought better of it. "Is that why you became a detective?"

He nodded.

"Paul never said exactly why he became an accident investigator. But I believe it had something to do with his parents' deaths."

"Why did you become an investigator, Ms. Herrera?"

"I sort of fell into it. Now I wish I'd chosen another line of work."

"Like what?"

"I enjoyed psychology classes in college at Penn State and combined a psychology major with courses in mathematics and science. Later, I received a National Science Foundation fellowship to attend graduate school at the University of Michigan, where I studied social psychology."

"Which is?"

"Studying how people's thoughts, feelings, and behaviors are influenced by others. Let me show you something."

Herrera retrieved a small notebook and pen from a purse and tore out two sheets of paper. Sitting down again she drew a vertical line on one sheet of paper. On the second sheet she drew three vertical lines of varying lengths. She labeled the three lines, A, B, and C. Then she pushed the two sheets of paper to the center of the table. "Which line, A, B, or C, matches the line on the first sheet of paper?"

At first glance Santana thought there must be some trick to the question since it appeared obvious to him that vertical line C was the same length as the line Herrera had drawn on the first sheet of paper. He hesitated a moment longer to make sure and then said, "Line C."

"Correct."

Santana shrugged. "What's the point?"

"Asch's paradigm."

"Never heard of it."

"In the nineteen fifties Solomon Asch recruited a group of eight male college students. Only one of the eight was the actual subject. The other seven participants were actors who knew the true focus of the study."

"Which was?"

"How individuals went along with or resisted a majority group and the effect of such influences on beliefs and opinions." She pointed to the drawings on the papers. "In this particular experiment, how one subject would react to the actors' behavior."

"But the two lines with the same length were easy to choose," Santana said.

She smiled. "You had no peer pressure, Detective. See, the actors were introduced to the subject as other participants. Like you, each student viewed a card with a line on it, followed by another with three lines labeled A, B, and C. Each participant was then asked to say aloud which line matched the length of that on the first card. Prior to the experiment, all actors were given specific instructions on how they should respond to each card presentation. They would always unanimously make one choice, but on certain trials they would give the correct response and on others, an incorrect response. The group was seated in such a way that the subject always responded last."

"So what happened?"

"Well, with no pressure to conform to actors, the subject answered correctly nearly one hundred percent of the time. But when the actors deliberately chose the incorrect answer, a third of the subjects conformed. Only twenty-five percent consistently resisted majority opinion."

"People are often swayed or manipulated by others," Santana said.

"That happens a lot in your work?"

"More than it should."

Herrera mulled over Santana's response and then continued. "Asch found there were three distinct groups of subjects. Those who conformed to the majority on at least half of the trials were reacting with what he called a distortion of perception. They were a minority who believed that the actors' answers were always correct.

"Most of the subjects who yielded on some of the trials expressed what Asch termed distortion of judgment. They concluded that the majority must be right. Asch determined they had low levels of confidence.

"The final group of subjects who yielded on at least some trials exhibited a distortion of action. They knew what the correct answer was, but conformed with the majority group simply because they didn't want to seem out of step by not going along with the rest."

Santana said, "So what you're suggesting is that the members of the systems group assigned to investigate the Blue Skies crash were all pressured to say pilot error was the cause."

"Distortion of action," she said.

They ate quietly until Herrera broke the silence. "You ever have that feeling on a case, Detective?"

"What feeling?"

"What your eyes see is a distortion of reality."

"Sometimes," he said.

"So you go with your gut instinct. What you know to be real, to be factual, right?"

He nodded. "What about the other accident groups?"

"They never disagreed that the cause was pilot error."

"And you conformed with the majority simply because you didn't want to seem out of step by not going along with the rest," Santana said.

"Yes." She looked away in embarrassment. "But everything changed for me after Kim disappeared," she said.

"You felt her disappearance had something to do with the Blue Skies crash."

"I did."

"You think someone from the NTSB is responsible for Kim Austin's murder?"

"I don't know."

Santana could hear the frustration in her voice.

"But now Terry and Kim are dead," she said, "and I'm up here hiding."

"Did anyone from the FBI pressure you?" Santana asked.

She shook her head.

"Another government agency?"

"You mean like the CIA?"

"Maybe the CIA or the NSA or some other agency we don't even know about."

"No."

Santana told Cathy Herrera what had happened to Terry Powell and to him in DC.

"I'm so sorry," she said.

"Not your fault."

"I don't know why Terry would drug you."

Santana didn't want to spook her by implicating the FBI. Then again, he was investigating Kim Austin's murder. It didn't take a genius like Reyna Tran to figure out he'd come to DC to question Powell, Herrera, and McCarthy about the Blue Skies crash. Maybe they'd had Powell's residence staked out. He wondered if anyone had followed him up here as well.

Someone knocked on the cabin door. Gitana, lying at Santana's feet, barked and got up.

"You expecting someone?" Santana asked.

"I am." Herrera stood, went to the door and opened it.

A lean man dressed in a green mock turtleneck, jeans, and dusty brown hiking boots entered, a leather shoulder bag over one shoulder. A stocking hat covered most of his long, reddish brown hair. He wore a pair of wire-rimmed glasses and had a small dent between his upper lip and left nostril. Santana recognized him from the photo Herrera had sent.

"Detective Santana, meet Paul Westbrook," she said.

Chapter 30

As the three of them sat around the table, Santana's gaze slid from Herrera to Westbrook. "How long have you been staying here?"

"I got here this morning," Westbrook said. "I went into town before you arrived."

Santana figured that the phone call Herrera had made when they had first left the cabin to walk to the crash site was to Paul Westbrook. But he asked Herrera to verify it just to make sure.

She nodded. "I told Paul that Terry had been murdered. We wanted to know who you were and that it was safe."

"Who has the most to lose if word got out that the downing of the Blue Skies flight was a terrorist act?" Santana asked.

"The airline industry, of course," Herrera said.

"That's obvious. But maybe we're thinking too broadly."

Herrera trained her eyes on Santana. "What do you mean?"

"The airline industry would obviously be affected," he said. "But Blue Skies would be the biggest loser if consumers thought they were at least partially responsible."

"Same difference," Westbrook said.

"Maybe not," Santana said. He looked at Herrera. "You mind taking Gitana out for a walk?"

"Why?"

"I want to ask Mr. Westbrook some questions."

"About what?" Westbrook asked.

Herrera stood and grabbed her coat. "Come on, Gitana," she said. "Let's get some exercise."

After they'd left the cabin, Santana said to Westbrook, "Why did you quit working for the NTSB?"

"I'd been thinking about a career change for quite a while."

"What do you plan on doing?"

"I'm not sure yet. I've saved some money. I don't have to rush into anything."

"Where have you been the last few months?"

"Traveling."

"You haven't been using your credit cards."

"You've checked."

"The DC police did."

"Well, I like to pay cash rather than interest on my cards. Why?"

"Kim Austin disappeared and turned up dead. You disappeared. We thought you might've met the same fate."

"Fortunately, I haven't."

"I understand you and Ms. Austin argued about the cause of the Blue Skies crash."

"I wouldn't say we argued. It was more of a disagreement."

"You don't think someone spoofed that airliner."

"Impossible."

"Really?"

"Highly unlikely."

"Why do you think Ms. Austin came to that conclusion?"

"I have no idea."

"What were you doing at the security conference in St. Paul?"

"Terry Powell asked me to talk to her."

"Regarding?"

"Kim wanted the spoofing attack included in her report. Terry knew that we were friends. He asked me to speak to her one more time to see if she'd change her mind. I also like to keep up on the latest technology trends."

"Did she change her mind regarding the crash?"

"She told me she'd think about it."

"And that was the day she disappeared."

Westbrook shrugged. "I guess so."

"How did you find out Kim Austin was missing?"

"Terry Powell told me she never showed up for work."

"Anyone you know who'd want to harm her for any reason?"

"Well, Kim told me at the conference that she thought she was being followed."

"Did she have any idea why someone would be following her?"

"Because she disagreed with the NTSB's conclusion about the crash. She thought the government was after her."

"But you agreed with the government's position that pilot error caused the crash, Mr. Westbrook. So the government wouldn't be after you."

"I never said they were."

"Yet here you are, hiding with Cathy Herrera."

"I'm not hiding. I came to see her. But now that Terry and Kim have been murdered, I'm a little paranoid."

Santana drank some hot chocolate. Then he changed course. "You visited the Hieronymus Bosch exhibit at the National Gallery of Art in DC."

Westbrook's eyes opened wide in surprise. "How do you know that?"

"Pretty familiar with Bosch's paintings, Mr. Westbrook?" Santana asked, ignoring Westbrook's question.

"Not really."

"What made you visit that particular exhibit?"

He thought for a moment before replying. "A friend of mine wanted to go."

"Ever seen *The Garden of Earthly Delights*?"

"Is that a painting?"

"Probably Bosch's most famous one."

"Huh. I'll have to look it up sometime."

"You do that, Mr. Westbrook."

"What does a Hieronymus Bosch painting have to do with the Blue Skies crash?"

"Maybe nothing," Santana said.

Westbrook nodded his head.

"But I'm going to find whoever is responsible for Ms. Austin's murder," Santana said.

"You have any idea who it might be?" Westbrook asked.

"No," Santana said. "But I hope to soon. In the meantime, I need your cell phone number in case something comes up."

Westbrook recited his number as Santana added it to his Contacts list.

Santana stood and went to the door and called to Herrera and Gitana, who were playing in the woods.

When Herrera entered the cabin, Santana asked for her cell phone number.

"Sometimes it's hard to get reception up here," she said.

"What provider do you use?"

"AT&T," she said.

Santana looked at Westbrook.

"The same," he said.

Santana looked at Herrera. "Why don't you come to the cities with me?"

She shook her head. "I'm safer here."

If I found you, someone else could, he wanted to say, but he didn't want to frighten her more than she already was. Besides, he didn't know who, if anyone, was looking for her.

"What about your job?" he asked.

"I still have some vacation time coming. But I can't hide forever. I'll have to return to DC soon and take my chances."

"You two best be careful."

Herrera gestured toward the shotgun in the corner. "Someone tries to get in here, they'll get a load of lead."

Santana had no doubt she meant it.

* * *

It was about an hour before sunset when Santana headed back to the cities along Highway 61, the highway once made famous in a Bob Dylan song. He was trying to get his mind around the possibility that some person or some group had deliberately steered Blue Skies Flight 624 off course, killing everyone on board.

He was moving along the two-lane blacktop at fifty miles an hour when he felt the SUV accelerate. Backing off the gas, he peered at the speedometer and realized it was still climbing.

He stepped on the brake pedal and felt no resistance as it thumped against the floorboard. He pumped the pedal fast and hard four times to build up brake fluid pressure, but it was futile. The Explorer continued to accelerate—58 . . . 59 . . . 60 . . .

He glanced behind him. Thankfully, Gitana was stretched out on the dog hammock instead of sitting next to a window, looking out, where a sudden turn could send her tumbling.

Santana shoved the gearshift into neutral. Hit the emergency flashers. Gripped the steering wheel with both hands. Took a breath and let it out slowly. *Stay relaxed,* he told himself.

His options were limited.

From his defensive driver training, he knew that switching off the ignition would silence the racing engine, but it would also make the Explorer more difficult to maneuver. In the worst-case scenario, it could lock the steering wheel, and he would lose complete control.

The road was flat. There were no hills or inclines to slow the vehicle. He scanned the landscape for small trees. If he had to hit one to stop, there was a good chance he would survive the impact when the airbag deployed, but it was too dangerous a calculation with Gitana unprotected in back. He dismissed the idea.

If he could manage to safely get to the right shoulder, he could scrape the Explorer against the guardrail, using the friction to slow it down. He would need to come in at a shallow angle and gently rub the car against it.

Suddenly, the windshield wipers came on, and then the radio blasted music. He tried turning off the radio and then stopping the wipers, but it was futile.

He glanced at the speedometer. With the Explorer in neutral, the needle was gradually dropping back from 70. As Santana lifted his eyes, he realized he was coming up fast on a slow-moving car in front of them. Too fast.

He considered aiming for the car's bumper, but if he didn't hit it squarely, the impact could send the unsuspecting car careening out of control. Farther ahead, a fully-loaded logging truck was rounding a bend, coming toward him on the opposite side of the road. He had to make a split second decision: try to pass the car and risk hitting the semi-truck head-on, or try for the shoulder and risk losing control.

As he eased the wheel to the left and the Explorer crossed over the no-passing stripe, Santana glanced at the old man hunched over the wheel of the Chevy as his SUV shot past.

The logging truck had cleared the bend in the road and was bearing down on him now. Santana heard the loud bleat of the semi-truck's horn. He saw its trailer begin to sway as the driver applied the brakes and moved toward the shoulder.

Tightening his grip on the steering wheel, he guided the Explorer toward the right lane. It was going to be close.

The Explorer flew by the semi in a gust of wind so close that it ripped off the Explorer's side view mirror. After barely clearing the trailer, he was into the bend in the road.

Santana felt the right side wheels momentarily lift off the pavement. He kept the wheel straight, resisting the urge to over-correct. The Explorer settled back down again as the bend straightened into a long stretch of road, the engine continuing to race even as the SUV began to slow. With his left foot Santana gradually depressed the parking brake pedal. Jamming it down would lock up the rear wheels, sending the Explorer into an uncontrollable skid.

Keep the vehicle pointing straight ahead. Jerking the steering wheel to the left would cause the left front tire to strike the raised edge of the pavement at a sharp angle, triggering a roll-over or a swerve into oncoming traffic.

He steered the Explorer toward the right shoulder, pressing the emergency brake all the way down. As the inside tires moved off the asphalt, the treads dug into the grass and gravel on the shoulder. Stones rattled in the wheel-wells.

The speedometer read 50 . . . 49 . . . 48 . . .

He was gaining control. No need to rub up against the guardrail to slow the SUV.

Gradually, the Explorer rolled to a stop. He shoved the gearshift into park and shut off the engine. His heart thumped in his chest. He exhaled a long breath.

The old man in the Chevy, still hunched over the wheel, passed him doing maybe 35 mph.

Santana had heard of the throttle on some cars sticking. Lawsuits had been filed. But he doubted there was something wrong with the Explorer.

If it were possible to spoof a plane, would it also be possible to spoof a vehicle?

Chapter 31

Santana sat in the Explorer by the side of the road for ten minutes with the emergency lights flashing, letting go of his paranoia, before he called AAA Roadside Assistance on his cell.

It took forty-five minutes before a tow truck arrived from Silver Bay. Twenty minutes later, the Explorer was hooked up, and Santana was seated in the middle of the passenger seat of the truck, Gitana to his right—fortunately, the driver liked dogs—as they headed back toward Silver Bay, Duluth, and finally, to a Ford dealership in White Bear Lake on the northern edge of St. Paul, where he paid the driver and left the Explorer, and he and Gitana drove home in a Taurus loaner.

He was hoping for a quiet, relaxing evening. However, his paranoia returned the moment he entered his driveway and saw the lights on in his house, and the black Mercedes S-Class sedan parked in front of his double garage door.

Anyone entering should have triggered the alarm system. But if someone had broken in, why would they turn on the lights and leave their car in the driveway?

Santana stopped the Taurus near the end of the driveway. Took his Glock out of his holster. Grabbed his Maglite from the center console. Got out and told Gitana to stay. He kept to the shadows and made his way to the Mercedes. The windows were darkly tinted, making it difficult to see inside the car, even with the flashlight.

Santana followed his Glock to the back door of the house and then lowered his gun. A sign taped to the inside of the door read

WELCOME HOME, JOHN
COME IN AND HAVE A DRINK

When he walked into the living room, he saw Reyna Tran sitting on the couch across from the fireplace. Birch and oak logs sizzled and snapped in the flames. Beside her was either a very large black purse or small overnight bag.

Not in a million years, Santana thought.

She raised a cocktail glass. "Would you like an Old Fashioned? I brought a bottle of bourbon."

"What the hell, Reyna? I could've shot you."

"I knew you could read. Would a burglar leave you a sign?"

"How did you get in without tripping the alarm system?"

She gave him a crooked smile. "Really, John. Your system is good. But I'm better."

"That's comforting."

"I can offer you some suggestions on improving it if you'd like."

"What are you doing here?"

"You asked me for information on Brian Devlin."

"I mean *here*. In my house?"

"I wanted to see where you lived. I'm glad I decided to come. You have some holes in your security system."

Santana turned and headed for the back door.

"Where are you going?"

"To get Gitana from the car."

"Who's Gitana?"

"My golden retriever."

"I love dogs!" she called as Santana went out the door.

After he parked the Taurus in the garage, Gitana followed him into the house and went directly to Reyna Tran.

"What a beautiful, friendly animal," she said, petting Gitana's head.

"She likes everyone."

"Thank you for the compliment."

Santana hung up his jacket in the front closet and set his holstered Glock on the kitchen counter.

Tran came into the kitchen and stood next to him. She was wearing a tight-fitting red sweater dress that showed off her figure and a pair of black boots. Her black hair fell loosely down her back. He could smell her Opium perfume.

She gestured to the bottle of bourbon on the counter. "Could I make you an Old Fashioned?"

"I'll stick with a Sam Adams."

He filled Gitana's food and water bowls and got a bottle of Sam Adams from the refrigerator. Then he went into the living room and sat down in a heavy cushioned chair opposite Reyna Tran. He was tired from the long drive up north and back and from the stressful hack on his Explorer. His patience was running thin.

"To good friends," Tran said, raising her glass in a toast.

She didn't seem to mind when Santana didn't reciprocate.

"I really don't appreciate your breaking into my home, Reyna. I should have you arrested."

She set the cocktail glass on the side table beside the couch and held out her hands, palms up. "Please, cuff me."

"I'm serious," he said. "I feel like I'm being stalked."

She thrust out her lower lip in a pouting gesture. "I'm hurt."

"Is that supposed to bother me?"

"Of course. We're friends."

"No, we're not."

"But I've helped you."

"Yes, Reyna. You have. But friends don't always expect something in return. You do something for someone simply because they're your friend."

"That makes perfect sense." She opened the large purse on the couch beside her and retrieved a folded sheet of paper. "And because we're friends, I'm about to help you again," she said.

Santana let out a breath and drank some beer. Reasoning with her was like trying to reason with a five-year-old.

"But before we talk about the information I have for you," she said, "what did Cathy Herrera have to say?"

"You're asking me to trust an admitted sociopath."

"How many have you known, John?"

"I haven't really *known* any. I've just arrested some for crimes they've committed."

"Now's your opportunity to actually know one. We're not all evil."

"I'll be the judge of that."

"Oh, come on," she said. "If I *was* really involved in this whole sordid affair, I would've had you killed long ago."

"That easy, huh?"

"I've certainly had my opportunities."

"I thought we were friends."

"Exactly. And friends don't kill each other. Well, most friends. So . . ."

Santana summarized his conversation with Herrera. Then he told her how someone had hacked into the electronic system in his Explorer.

"Someone really does want you out of the picture."

"You wouldn't have any idea who that someone is, would you?"

"Do I detect a hint of irony in your voice, John?"

"It was hard to miss."

She waved off his sarcasm. "I certainly want to keep you around. But whoever got control of the electronic systems in your SUV has other ideas." She finished her drink and said, "I need a refill. How 'bout you?"

"I'm good."

She got up and went into the kitchen like she owned the place.

Gitana, having finished her dinner, stretched out in front of the fireplace.

Santana drank more beer.

"Vehicles are more advanced, but that doesn't mean they're immune to hacks," she said, sitting down on the couch again, fresh drink in hand. "All this technology comes at a cost."

"That being?"

"Hackers can infiltrate car electronic systems through security holes." She smiled. "Like I infiltrated your home security system."

Santana tried to think of where the "holes" in his home security system were but came up empty.

"One entry point for hacking a vehicle is the OBD II port," she continued. "It's basically the Ethernet jack for your car."

"And that's located where?"

"Usually below the dashboard on the driver's side. It's the car's command center and connects to all of the different computer systems. Mechanics often plug directly into it to retrieve diagnostics for the car's emissions, mileage, and engine errors."

"But no one plugged directly into my Explorer's port," Santana said.

"True. But hackers just have to find a hole somewhere within one of the networks to plug into a vehicle's control system, and then they have access to everything."

"So where's the hole?"

She sipped her drink before replying. He could see the blood-red imprint on the lip of her cocktail glass.

"You really should try an Old Fashioned, John. They're excellent."

"The security holes, Reyna."

"You're no fun." She gave him a coy smile.

"Come on," he said. "Quit playing around."

She sighed. "If you insist."

"I do."

"Well, there's a lot of code in a typical car. Much of it comes from different vendors, which makes it nearly impossible for automakers to know all the software inside their vehicles. When code from one device communicates with code from another device, software conflicts create security holes. Hackers use these holes to enter your vehicle's system. We in the security industry call this type of hack a 'zero-day exploit.' Once hackers find the hole, they have wireless control through the Internet. The hacker can send commands through your entertainment system to your dashboard functions, steering, brakes, and transmission, all from a laptop that can be across the country."

"Automakers are aware of this?"

"Of course they are. It's their nightmare come true."

Santana shook his head in frustration and drank the last of his beer.

"Look, John," she said in a more serious tone. "I've been in this business a long time. Things are changing. Rapidly. We used to think about information security as confidentiality and privacy. For years, we've been trying to prevent data theft. Anyone who has had data stolen and used for identity theft can tell you what a nightmare that can be. Remember the Ashley Madison breach?"

He nodded.

"All those husbands and wives who were cheating on their spouses and thinking they were safe." She shook her head and chuckled. "How about the Sony Pictures data theft in Hollywood? Hackers stole personal information about employees and their families, information about executive salaries at the company, copies of then-unreleased Sony films. Now we have Russian hackers trying to influence elections."

"What about a possible hack of the Blue Skies flight?"

Setting her drink on the coffee table, she unfolded the sheet of paper she'd removed from her purse. "I profiled everyone on that flight, except for the children."

"Of course," he said sarcastically, feeling his blood get hot. "Children."

"Makes you angry, huh?"

"But not you."

"It's not about anger. It's about finding the people who did this."

"I'm not like you, Reyna. I can't turn off my emotions. Or maybe you never had any to turn off."

"This doesn't help."

"What doesn't?"

"Turning your anger and frustration on me. I didn't bring this plane down." She pointed to the sheet of paper on the coffee table. "But maybe the information on this paper can help us find out who did."

"Us?"

"I want to know as badly as you."

"Why?"

She leaned forward, resting her elbows on her knees and her chin in her hands. "Curiosity, mostly. But whether you believe me or not, I want to help you, too."

He couldn't tell if she was serious or not. But she'd helped him in the past. Still, he wondered what she really wanted.

"So what do you have?" he said.

She tapped the couch cushion beside her with the long nail on her index finger. "Come sit beside me."

"What for?"

"You think I might bite?"

"Maybe."

She smiled. "I saw your workout room. A big strong man like you afraid of me?"

A shot of panicked adrenaline shot through his bloodstream. "How long were you here before I arrived?"

"Not long."

"You drove from Chicago?"

"Certainly not. I used my company's Lear jet. Takes about an hour. Then I had to rent a car and drive out here, which took nearly as long. You do live quite a ways out of town. I imagine that's intentional."

Santana hadn't thought about her going through his house, looking at his personal and private things. "You didn't go through my closets and drawers, Reyna, did you?"

"I might've looked a teensy bit." She made the universal gesture with her thumb and index finger indicating a little bit. "Mostly, I just walked through the rooms. I wanted to get more of a sense of you."

"Great."

"You've been in my place. And slept in my guest bedroom."

"You put me there. And don't get any ideas, Reyna."

"What's fair is fair." She reached into her purse and pulled out an expensive-looking white lace baby doll negligee and G-string panty. "I brought my sleepwear just in case."

"I don't think so."

"Are you sure?"

"I am."

"Still too close to Jordan's death?"

Santana felt the heat of anger again. "You don't know anything about her, Reyna. So leave it alone."

Most people would have been stung by his angry outburst, he thought, but not Reyna Tran. He watched her face for some recognizable expression. There was some expression there, but he wasn't sure what it was.

"Sorry," she said with a shrug—and without remorse. "You can't blame a girl for trying. I'll be in town the rest of the week, meeting with clients, if you change your mind."

She folded the negligee and panties and put them in her purse. Then she took out a small laptop computer, placed it on the coffee table, and pressed the power button. Holding up the sheet of paper, she patted the cushion next to her again.

"I want you to look at this while we talk. Okay?"

He hesitated.

"We're focusing on the case now."

"Okay," he said.

He got up, went to the refrigerator for another Sam Adams, and then sat down beside her. Weariness was overtaking him now.

"You're already aware that Brian Devlin was rumored to be interested in purchasing large shares of Cyber Security Systems stock. The company owned by David Knapp. But you're not aware of something else."

She did a quick Google search and found Blue Skies Airlines on the NASDAQ stock market website.

"What are you searching for?" he asked.

"Companies know who all their shareholders are, John. Individuals must disclose when their ownership exceeds five percent. Companies and hedge funds must disclose when their ownership exceeds ten percent."

Santana watched as Tran clicked on the "Holdings" link in the left sidebar and then on "Institutional Holdings." Two pie charts were displayed showing "Ownership" and "Active Positions." Farther down the page were the names of all stockholders listed by date of purchase, shares held, change in shares, percentage change, and value in 1,000s. The list ran from those who held the largest number of shares to those with the smallest number.

"Let's see if we recognize any of the shareholders," Tran said in a voice filled with excitement.

As she scrolled through the long list, Santana could see that investment firms, large banks, asset management companies, teacher retirement systems, and law firms owned the majority of the Blue Skies shares.

Then she stopped and pointed to a name halfway down a page. "Cyber Security Systems," she said. "Notice the date when Knapp's shares were purchased."

"He bought all his shares of Blue Skies stock after the crash."

"When the share price was very low," she said. "The share price has made up some of that loss. If Blue Skies has no major problems in the near future, the share price should continue to rise."

"So Knapp will make money."

"Lots of it," she said. "If Knapp was involved in hacking the airliner, he's counting on the government not releasing the true cause of the crash to the public. Many people would be reluctant to get on a plane if they thought the control systems could be hacked, leading to a disaster like the Blue Skies crash. But more importantly, the FAA would ground every international flight until the problem was solved. Imagine the economic hit the airline industry would take, not to mention the global economy."

"So Brian Devlin, the corporate raider, is dead and no longer a threat to take over Cyber Security Systems. Blue Skies shares have begun to rise. Both occurrences benefit David Knapp." Santana thought for a moment. "Is there any other way Knapp could've benefitted from the crash?"

"Oh. I love your way of thinking, John. It's so devious."

"I'm not sure that's a good thing."

"You mean thinking like a sociopath."

"I've dealt with enough of them."

"Yes," she said, patting him on the arm. "I imagine you have."

Chapter 32

While Reyna Tran surfed the Internet for more information on David Knapp's security company and made a few phone calls, Santana went into his kitchen to fix something to eat. He hadn't eaten since his lunch at Cathy Herrera's cabin, and the two bottles of Sam Adams had given him a slight buzz and a growling stomach.

He grilled two Copper River salmon and fried two *empanadas* and a half-dozen *papa criollas.* The small, yellow, creamy potato was Santana's favorite and the most popular potato in Colombia. They were often difficult to find outside of Colombia, but he could buy them at El Burrito Mercado, a Hispanic grocery store on St. Paul's West Side. When fried until they were tender, their paper-thin skin burst open like tiny balloons when bitten into.

Reyna Tran came out to the kitchen and leaned against the center island. "My, aren't you the handy one. Do you do laundry and windows as well?"

"No one to do it for me."

"Poor boy," she said. "How 'bout some wine with dinner?"

"In the rack," he said, pointing to the six-bottle wine rack on the far end of the counter. "Glasses are in the cabinet above it."

She chose a Pinot Noir, uncorked it, and poured two glasses. She set them on the dining table and then located plates, silverware, and napkins.

"Where are the candles?" she asked.

"In a cabinet, where they'll remain."

"Well, it's good to know that you actually have some."

Santana decided not to ask why.

When they were comfortably seated, Tran said, "This is so nice of you to fix me dinner."

"I was hungry. It would be impolite to eat in front of you, Reyna."

"How romantic," she said without a trace of irony.

They ate and drank in silence for a short time until she spoke again. "I made some calls. Word on the street is that David Knapp's company is overextended and has a high debt load."

"Meaning Knapp could use some cash."

She nodded. "There's nothing illegal about him buying stock."

"Except if he was somehow involved in the Blue Skies crash, Reyna."

"That might be difficult to prove."

"Murder sometimes is."

She ate some salmon and sipped her wine. "You asked if there was another way David Knapp could've made money off the Blue Skies crash."

"You have an idea?"

"What if he shorted Blue Skies stock?"

"How would he do that?"

"Well, if he anticipated negative events that would impact the stock, a short position would give him a way to make even more money—assuming his outlook was correct."

"Like if he knew the Blue Skies airliner was going to crash."

"Yes. Historically, the stock market trends upward. That means short sellers have to swim against the tide. But if you short a stock at the right time, you can make a bundle."

"But he bought stock after the crash," Santana said. "After the share price fell."

"Yes, he did. But he also may have made a short sell transaction before the crash. When you short a stock, you borrow it from a broker rather than buy it."

"What?"

"If Knapp knew the share price of Blue Skies stock was about to slide, he would borrow the stock from a broker at, say, one hundred dollars per share. Most brokers require you to borrow shares before they'll even accept your short sell order. When a broker fills a short sell order for you, another investor agrees to buy the shares at one hundred dollars per share. When the stock drops to seventy-five dollars, Knapp buys back the shares and returns them to the broker. Knapp makes twenty-five dollars per share. The broker collects interest on the loan and a commission for lending the shares."

"So Knapp could've made money both before and after the crash."

"He could've made a killing," Tran said.

"In more ways than one." Santana ate some salmon and digested what he'd just learned. "You said Knapp would short a stock through a broker."

"That's right."

"You happen to know the name of his broker?"

"A man named Trevor Dane."

"Dane?"

"You know him?"

Santana withheld the fact that Trevor Dane was Kim Austin's ex-boyfriend. He still wasn't sure he could trust Reyna despite all the help she'd provided.

"I've met Dane," he said. "Could we check Knapp's short sells on NASDAQ?"

"Firms are required to report their short positions as of settlement on the fifteenth of each month," she said. "A compilation is published eight business days after. Prior to 2010, the public could download the daily and monthly short sale volume files for free. Since then the short sale files are only available for download on the secure NASDAQ Trader FTP site, and for a fee."

"Looks like I'll have to talk to Dane."

Tran leaned forward and rested her chin in a hand. "If David Knapp was responsible for the Blue Skies crash, how are you going to prove it?"

"I'm not sure just yet," Santana said. "But if Knapp's guilty, I'll find a way."

* * *

Later that evening, after Reyna Tran had left, Santana went upstairs to his bedroom and sat at his desk in front of his computer and digital video recorder. He hit playback and then stopped the footage at 5:05 p.m. as Reyna approached the front door of his house. He saw her look up at the camera mounted high above the door. She had a smile on her face as she waved and then blew a kiss. A moment later she entered the house without the alarm activating.

Santana let out a sigh and sat back in his chair. He was aware that either suppressing the alarms or creating multiple false alarms that would render them unreliable could subvert home alarm setups. He just hadn't known how it was accomplished.

At dinner, Tran had explained that no matter what the brand or where they were sold, all the top-brand wireless alarm systems relied on radio frequency signals sent between door and window sensors to a control system that triggered an alarm when any of these entryways were breached. The signals were sent any time a tagged window or door was opened, whether or not the alarm was enabled.

However, when enabled, the system tripped the alarm and sent a silent alert to the monitoring company, which contacted the occupants and/or the police. But the systems failed to encrypt or authenticate the signals being sent from sensors to control panels—the same problem that existed between GPS satellites and airliners—making it easy for someone to intercept the data, decipher the commands, and play them back to control panels at will, which Reyna Tran had done.

According to Tran, false alarms could be set off using inexpensive software. She was able to copy signals from up to 250 yards away, though disabling his alarm required closer proximity of about ten feet from his home. Even moderately sophisticated burglars, she'd explained, could use a software defined radio, which allowed them to suppress the alarm as they opened the door, do whatever they wanted within the home, and then leave like they were never there.

Santana knew he would have to upgrade his security system. He hated to ask Tran what she suggested, but reluctantly he had to admit that she knew what she was talking about when it came to security systems—and other matters.

Gitana had come upstairs after him and was now stretched out on her belly on his bed, looking at him. Her presence reminded him of her escape from the gated dog run behind the house and the leaf that had apparently blown over the camera, blocking the view of the confined area.

He wondered now if someone, using a software radio device similar to what Reyna Tran had described, had entered his house. As far as he could tell, nothing had been moved or stolen, though he hadn't done a complete search.

Tran had also been in his house for an hour before he returned from Grand Marais. There was no telling what she'd looked through or what she might have left behind.

Santana stood up and began searching each room in the house, starting with his bedroom. He looked under every chair and table, in every drawer and cabinet, under the beds and living room furniture, in the lamps. It took him an hour and a half.

He found no listening device or bug. That didn't mean there wasn't one. They were so small now that he could have missed it. He wouldn't feel secure again until he'd picked up a bug detector.

His thoughts returned to David Knapp and the possibility that Knapp had used GPS spoofing to bring down the Blue Skies airliner for financial gain. Sending that many people to their deaths simply for monetary gain was difficult, but not impossible, to comprehend. Pablo Escobar had done the same, though for different reasons, and with a bomb instead of the latest technology.

Any doubts Santana had regarding the power of GPS spoofing had dissipated after the hijacking of his Explorer's control systems. If someone could do it to his SUV, they might have done something similar to Flight 624.

When FBI agents Ted Lake and Jack Gaines had attacked him in Terry Powell's house in DC, it was more evidence that he was on the right track regarding the cause of the Blue Skies crash. But Santana doubted that Lake and Gaines had killed Terry Powell and then framed him for Powell's murder. Lake and Gaines were jerks, but not cold-blooded killers.

Someone else had killed Terry Powell and Kim Austin.

Was that someone David Knapp?

Chapter 33

Early the next morning, Santana received a call from Sergeant Lyman Grady in DC.

"You up, Santana?"

Santana rolled over and peered at the time on his digital radio. It was six o'clock. "I am now."

"I just got the DNA results on the broom handle."

Santana sat up in bed.

"You were right about the FBI agents," Grady said. "The DNA on the broom handle belongs to Jack Gaines. DNA on the duct tape is Ted Lake's."

"How did you get their DNA?"

"I followed them. When they stopped at a Starbucks, I confiscated a discarded coffee cup from each."

"Great work, Lyman."

"When I ran a background check on Gaines, I discovered he was from my home state of Louisiana. He worked as a police officer in New Orleans before joining the Bureau. Louisiana is one of the few states that require its officers to provide genetic samples. So Gaines' DNA exists in the Louisiana database as well. I called in a favor from a lab tech friend of mine. Since the Terry Powell murder investigation has stalled, it looks like I need to schedule a chat with Mr. Gaines and Mr. Lake from the FBI. Appears they might be our prime suspects."

Santana laughed. "I'd love to be there for that interview."

"Bet you would."

"I find anything connected with Powell's murder, I'll let you know," Santana said.

"You do that, Santana. And stay safe."

"You, too, Lyman."

After disconnecting, Santana took a shower and ate breakfast. Never one to take many pills, he passed on taking more pain medication. The bruises on his back were still sore but tolerable.

Before driving to the LEC, he stopped at the Ford dealership. They had replaced his side view mirror and run a series of tests on the engine and brakes. Everything checked out fine.

While he was at the dealership, he phoned Pete Romano and told him he would have to miss the regularly scheduled weekly murder meeting because of "car trouble."

Romano wasn't pleased. Santana promised he would talk with Romano later. "I expect a full report on your progress," Romano said before disconnecting.

Santana then called Kacie Hawkins to explain the reason for his absence. An hour later, she was waiting for him at her desk in the LEC. He sat beside her and told her about his trip to Grand Marais and his discussion with Reyna Tran about David Knapp.

When he finished, Hawkins sat silently looking at him for a time like she didn't recognize him. Then she just shook her head.

"What?" he said.

"I should've been with you."

"Nothing you could've done about the hack of my SUV."

"Maybe not. But you'd better watch your step with the Dragon Lady. Who knows what she's up to?"

"I hear you."

"You think David Knapp is our man?" Hawkins asked.

"It's definitely possible. Suppose Kim Austin told Trevor Dane that she believed spoofing caused the Blue Skies crash rather than pilot error. Dane casually mentions Austin's conclusion to his client, Knapp. He's worried because he did spoof the flight in order to kill Brian Devlin, the corporate raider who was about to take over his company."

"Circumstantial evidence," Hawkins said.

"There's more. Knapp knows Kim Austin has signed up for his company's security conference in St. Paul. He steals the dagger from Trevor Dane's office, gets Austin alone, kills her, and then frames Dane for the murder."

"But why bury Austin in a cave along the Mississippi River where her body might never be found?"

"If her body is never found, Knapp's in the clear. If it is found, we start looking at Trevor Dane as the prime suspect. The dagger impaled in Kim Austin's hand either belonged to him, or it was exactly like the one he owned. He dated Austin. She was upset with him for pawning the watch he gave her. A piece of the pawn ticket found under her remains belonged to Dane. He's into surrealism, even if he doesn't have any reproductions of a Bosch painting."

"Again, all circumstantial evidence," Hawkins said.

"True. But in either case, Knapp is in the clear."

"So what's next?"

"Let's start with Trevor Dane."

"You want me to call his office? See if he's in?"

"Good idea."

As Santana stood up from his chair, Pete Romano waved for him to come into his office. Santana glanced at Hawkins and then shrugged when she mouthed, "What's up?"

Romano was sitting on the edge of his desk when Santana entered. "Chief wants to see you."

"How come?"

"He didn't say."

Santana rode the elevator up to Tim Branigan's office on the sixth floor. It took him only a moment to figure out the purpose of the meeting when he stood in the doorway to Branigan's office and saw Ted Lake, Rita Gamboni, and Branigan all seated on the black leather sofa at the far end of the room to his left.

"Ah, Detective Santana," Branigan said. "Come in. Have a seat."

Gamboni was gazing at Santana, but when he returned the gaze, her eyes shifted off him.

Santana looked at Branigan. "What's this all about, Chief?" he said, knowing full well what the answer would be.

Ted Lake snickered. "Don't act stupid, Detective."

"I'll handle this," Branigan said, shooting Lake a hard look.

"I hope you do a better job handling this, Chief, than your Homicide commander."

"Ted," Gamboni said. "This won't get us anywhere. Let's hear what John . . . Detective Santana has to say."

"Fine," Lake said. "I'm sure the detective has an explanation as to why he disobeyed our directive to stay away from the NTSB employees."

"Detective?" Branigan said. His eyes were fixed on Santana.

Santana wasn't sure whether he saw support or helplessness in them. Either way, he wasn't about to grovel at Ted Lake's feet, especially after speaking with Lyman Grady. He had leverage now, and he was happy to use it—though he was in no hurry.

"Terry Powell and Kim Austin are dead," he said. "What NTSB employees are you talking about?"

"The one you failed to mention, Detective. Cathy Herrera."

Santana wondered how Lake knew he'd talked to Herrera. Agents were either tracking him, or Lake had spoken with Herrera. Lake could be bluffing, Santana thought, but he doubted it. Rather than getting caught in a lie, Santana spoke the truth, though he decided to leave Paul Westbrook out of the discussion. He wasn't sure if the FBI knew Westbrook was alive and staying with Herrera.

"I talked with Herrera for the same reason I gave you before," Santana said. "I go where the case takes me."

Lake threw up his hands and looked at Branigan. "There you go, Chief. Your detective disobeyed a direct order."

Branigan's eyes were trained on Santana and not on Lake. Santana knew the chief was weighing the costs of supporting him or supporting the FBI.

Branigan took a moment before turning his head in Ted Lake's direction. "It wasn't *my* direct order, Agent Lake. You don't order my detectives around."

Lake seemed surprised and at a loss for words before he recovered. "The Blue Skies crash is a federal matter, Chief Branigan. Your department, and your detective, are causing problems by meddling in our investigation."

"What investigation?" Santana said.

As if on cue, everyone's head turned toward him.

"Our investigation," Lake said.

"Your investigation is already over, *Ted,*" Santana said, purposely using Lake's first name. "You don't want me on this case because you're afraid I'll find out what actually caused the crash."

"Pilot error," Lake said.

"You both know that's bullshit," Santana said, looking at Lake and then at Gamboni.

"Easy, Detective," Branigan said. "Why don't you tell us what you have?"

Santana was tempted to ask Gamboni to explain what the FBI already knew, but he couldn't put her on the spot.

"Spoofing," he said.

"What?" Branigan said.

Santana spent the next twenty minutes explaining what Cathy Herrera had told him regarding the likely cause of the crash. "How's that possible?" Branigan said when Santana finished.

"It isn't," Lake said.

"It happened to my SUV, too," Santana said. He told them how he'd nearly been killed on the drive back from Grand Marais.

"A car is one thing," Lake said. "An airliner is something else."

"It sure is," Santana said. His eyes locked on Gamboni's.

She gave a little nod and turned toward Lake and Branigan. "John's right, Chief."

Lake jerked as though he'd been given an electrical shock. "Rita. What're you doing?"

"It's time we worked together on this, Ted."

Lake gave a small laugh. "You don't know what you're doing."

"Yes, I do."

"There's a lot riding on this, Rita."

Santana understood the meaning behind Lake's words. He knew Gamboni understood as well.

"I'm fully aware of that, Ted. Maybe it's my background in homicide. But I want this case solved, whatever the ramifications."

Lake nodded but remained silent.

"How come Jack Gaines isn't here with you, Ted?" Santana asked, wanting to take the focus off Gamboni.

Lake looked at him. "Agent Gaines is working another case."

"How's his head?"

"What'd you mean?"

"Don't act stupid," Santana said, using Lake's own words against him. "The Metropolitan Police Department in DC found Jack Gaines' DNA on the broom handle I hit him with, and your DNA on the duct tape you put over my mouth. You and your buddy Gaines are now the prime suspects in Terry Powell's murder."

Lake stood. "This meeting is over as far as I'm concerned." He strode toward the door. Then he stopped and looked back at Gamboni. "You coming, Rita?"

Lake's jaw was hanging open so wide Santana thought he might trip over it on his way out. "Say 'Hi' to Gaines for me, Ted."

Gamboni stood slowly, looked back at Santana, and followed Lake out the door.

Chapter 34

Kacie Hawkins was seated at her desk when Santana returned to the Homicide Unit. "What did Branigan want to see you about?"

Santana told her.

"Nice to hear that Gamboni is on our side," Hawkins said. "She's always had guts and integrity. But you know how the FBI is, John. Rita can't be on their side *and* ours. She goes against Ted Lake, she could lose her job."

"I think Agent Lake has much bigger things to worry about."

"Like what?"

Santana told her about the DNA on the broom handle and duct tape.

Hawkins burst out laughing. "You're kidding me."

"I'm dead serious."

Hawkins stopped laughing. "But those assholes hurt you."

"It was worth it. You get ahold of Dane?"

"He's in his office."

"Good," Santana said. "Let's see if we can shake something loose."

* * *

Trevor Dane was seated behind his desk in his office when Santana and Hawkins walked in. "Detective?" he said, looking up from his computer screen. "Or is it *Detectives*?"

"This is my partner, Detective Hawkins."

Dane rose from his chair and reached across his desk to shake Hawkins' hand.

"Mr. Dane," she said with a nod—and without offering her hand.

Dane put his hand down, an awkward smile on his face.

"Have a seat," Santana said.

Dane hesitated a moment, as though unaccustomed to taking a directive, especially in his own office, and then eased himself into his chair.

"Are you two going to sit down?"

"We'll stand," Santana said. "Why did David Knapp short his Blue Skies stock?"

"Who said that he did?"

Santana leaned forward and rested his hands on the edge of the desk. "If you know something about the Blue Skies crash, Mr. Dane, you'd better tell us now."

Dane's cheeks darkened. "Hey, I'm just Knapp's broker. He tells me to buy or sell a stock, I do it."

"No questions asked?"

"As long as the transaction is legal."

"You own stock, Mr. Dane?"

"Of course."

"Ever short any of it?"

"Not for my personal gain."

"Not even Blue Skies stock before the crash?"

"No," he said with a vigorous shake of his head.

"You wouldn't mind proving that, would you?"

"Not at all." He tapped the keys on his computer, printed out three sheets of paper, and handed them to Santana. "A summary of my portfolio for this year," he said.

Printed on the paper were colorful pie charts and graphs tracking investments. Hawkins scooted next to Santana so she could read along with him.

Santana quickly scanned each page. He saw no Blue Skies stocks in Dane's portfolio.

"Is this all your current investments?"

"It is."

"What about David Knapp's portfolio?"

"He'll have to give you permission," Dane said. "Otherwise, you'll need a warrant. But you're welcome to take those pages with you."

The surrealistic paintings on the wall reminded Santana of the Bosch paintings and his discussion with Paul Westbrook.

"You ever meet a man named Paul Westbrook?"

"I did. Kim introduced me to him here at the office. I used to manage her investments before our relationship soured. Westbrook was looking for some investment advice."

"Was he here on more than one occasion?"

Dane thought about it. "A few times, as I recall."

"Do you manage his portfolio?"

Dane shook his head.

"Are you familiar with *The Garden of Earthly Delights* by the Dutch painter Hieronymus Bosch?"

"I've heard of the painter but have never seen any of his work. Why?"

"You might find it interesting."

"I'll check it out."

"You do that, Mr. Dane."

Back in their sedan, Hawkins said, "Maybe Dane's clean."

"Maybe," Santana said.

"What was that Bosch thing all about?"

Santana told her of his dream and the possible meaning behind the images.

"You scare me sometimes, John," she said. "The way your mind works. All this dream stuff."

"You don't dream, Kacie?"

"Of course I do. But I mostly forget my dreams seconds after waking up."

"You should write them down in a journal."

"I'd only write down the good ones."

"And what are they about?"

She smiled shyly. "What do you think, Detective?"

"Let's stick with the case," Santana said.

* * *

David Knapp lived in a gated community off Dell Road in the southwestern suburb of Eden Prairie, approximately eleven miles from downtown Minneapolis. Traffic rarely flowed smoothly along Interstate 494, and this day was no exception. The thirty-minute drive from the LEC took forty-five minutes.

A NO TRESPASSING sign on the front of a stone gatehouse and a security officer who monitored cameras and every vehicle that entered greeted Santana and Hawkins. The guard wore a black shirt, trousers, and a ball cap with a Cyber Security Systems logo. Apparently, Knapp's company provided security for the whole gated community.

Santana told the guard whom they were here to see. The guard checked a sheet on the clipboard he held in one hand. Then he gave Santana directions and waved them through.

Despite the added sense of security and privacy a gated community provided, they weren't as popular around the Twin Cities as in some other parts of the country, like Florida and California. Many Midwesterners thought such housing epitomized elitism and was unnecessary and pretentious. David Knapp was obviously not one of them.

His brick and stone mansion was set far back from a quiet, tree-lined street. The mansion had a manicured lawn and shrubbery and a long cobblestone driveway, which led to a triple garage and a circular drive set around a fountain in front of the house.

Santana and Hawkins followed Knapp through a dining room with vaulted ceilings and mahogany floors and into the living room, where they sat in a grouping of red leather wing chairs. Outside the French doors to Santana's right was a wood deck that overlooked a pond and the golf course.

Knapp gestured with the cocktail glass he held in one hand. "Can I get you two anything to drink?" he asked.

Santana glanced at Hawkins, who shook her head. "We're good," he said.

Knapp settled into a seat opposite them. He was casually dressed in tan khakis and a dark green polo shirt.

"I see you provide security for the community," Santana said.

"It's more about privacy than security. But that's not why you drove all the way out here to see me. So let's get to it," he said, directing his question at Santana. "I've got a plane to catch early this evening."

"Tell us about Brian Devlin," Santana said.

Knapp was about to take a drink and then paused, the cocktail glass halfway to his mouth. His eyes shifted from Santana to Hawkins and then back again. He nodded his head, as if confirming a thought, and drank from the glass.

Setting the glass on the coffee table, he said, "Brian Devlin is—or was—a corporate raider who was looking to take over my company."

Santana was surprised that Knapp was so straightforward. "We're aware of what Devlin did for a living, Mr. Knapp. We're wondering if his occupation got him killed."

"Devlin died in a plane crash. How is that related to his occupation, other than he was a frequent flyer?"

"You know what 'spoofing' is, Mr. Knapp?"

"Of course I do."

"What if the Blue Skies crash wasn't an accident?"

"Everything I've heard in the media points to pilot error. Now if you know that something or someone was responsible for the crash, I suggest you contact the FBI."

"You bought stock in Blue Skies shortly after the crash."

"So what? I buy and sell lots of stock. At least my broker does."

"So maybe you had Trevor Dane short Blue Skies stock because you knew something was about to happen to that flight," Hawkins said.

"You're way off base here, Detectives. Neither I nor anyone in my company had anything to do with that crash."

"You ever short Blue Skies stock?" Santana asked.

"I'm not a gambler. Too conservative for that."

"Are you willing to prove that?"

"I'd be happy to contact Mr. Dane and have him prove it to you."

"We'd appreciate that, Mr. Knapp," Hawkins said.

Santana had been watching Knapp for any tells, but he seemed confident and self-assured in his answers. Maybe he was an accomplished liar, but Santana didn't think so.

Knapp peered at the gold watch on his right wrist. "I need to go, Detectives. You have any more questions, call me."

* * *

By early evening the rain that had fallen periodically all day had subsided. Gray, purple, and pink clouds hung like strips of colored paper along the sunburned horizon. The temperature was in the mid-forties, and with a light wind blowing out of the west, it was a perfect evening for running.

Santana tried to clear his mind of all the complexities of the cases he and Hawkins were working, but his thoughts kept returning to the victims for whom he was seeking justice.

His instincts told him the deaths of Kim Austin, her mother, and Terry Powell had something to do with the Blue Skies crash. Clearly, someone had spoofed his Explorer. He was inclined to believe Cathy Herrera's version in which spoofing had caused the crash. But, he admitted to himself, there was another possibility.

He could be wrong.

Despite Herrera's insistence that spoofing had brought down the airliner, the FBI and other accident investigators might have it right. Pilot error could have caused the crash, which meant that he and Hawkins had spent days chasing a dead end.

Perhaps they were no closer to solving the murders than they'd been the first day of the investigations. For his and his partner's sake—and more importantly, for the victims' sake—he hoped that all their efforts hadn't been wasted.

Darkness had swallowed all the light by the time Santana was halfway home—running easily, his muscles warm and relaxed, and his skin moist with sweat, despite the cool temperature—when Gitana suddenly stopped running beside him and looked behind her, ears pricked.

Santana slowed and then stopped as well when she didn't move. "What is it, girl?"

She looked at him for a moment as her feathered tail waved, then stared into the distance again and raised her nose into the air, picking up a scent.

He figured she'd heard something that he couldn't. He wasn't sure if it was an animal, perhaps another dog, or maybe something else, but he knew that something, or someone, was behind them. He felt for the compact Glock 27 he carried in the kidney holster on his waist when he heard the slap of footsteps on the pavement.

Gitana huffed as her tail began wagging.

"Hello, there," a woman's voice called.

Out of the darkness Santana recognized Deborah Russell jogging toward them.

She halted in front of Gitana and squatted down to pet her. "Hope I didn't alarm you. It gets dark so quickly now this far north. I'm not used to it."

"That's right," he said. "You're new to Minnesota."

"Yes," she said, standing. "I'm not looking forward to my first winter here. It must've been a shock to you, too, being from Colombia."

"How did you know I was from Colombia?"

"Must have read it in the newspaper. Apparently, they often refer to you as the 'Detective from Colombia.'"

"My claim to fame."

"That must be it," she said, beginning to jog in place. "Do you mind if we run? I don't want to cool down too much."

"Let's go."

The three of them ran along the asphalt road in silence before Santana said, "How about coming over for dinner tomorrow night at six thirty? I owe you for taking care of Gitana for me."

"No need to pay me back," she said. "It was a pleasure. She's such a good dog."

"I'm happy to have you come over."

"All right. Tomorrow night is fine."

"Tomorrow night it is," Santana said.

After his run, Santana took a shower and then ate a grilled steak with mashed potatoes and a cold bottle of Sam Adams.

He'd just finished cleaning the kitchen and putting the dirty dishes in the dishwasher when his SPPD cell phone rang. The caller ID read "Unknown." He let the phone go to voicemail.

When he saw that the caller had left a message, he listened to it and then pressed the "Call Back" button. He heard a few clicks on the line before the call went through.

"Were you busy?" Rita Gamboni said.

"I didn't recognize the number."

"It's new."

"Thanks for your support this afternoon," he said. "Ted got a little upset."

"He's really not a bad guy, John. Once you get to know him."

Santana wondered how *well* Gamboni knew him.

"Are you busy?" she asked.

"Not at the moment."

"Well, I'm in the area and was wondering if I could drop by."

"Kind of far from the city, aren't you, Rita?"

"I had dinner in Stillwater."

"With Ted?"

"Can I drop by or not?"

"I'll be waiting," Santana said.

* * *

Gitana was thrilled to see Rita Gamboni, whining and licking and carrying on like she did whenever Santana left her for more than a day.

"I'm glad someone is happy to see me," she said, handing Santana her suede jacket.

"Something to drink?" he asked, hanging the jacket in the front closet.

"Red wine would be good."

Santana poured two glasses of Cabernet and brought them into the living room, where Gamboni was seated in the cushioned leather chair near the fireplace, stroking Gitana's head. Her red lipstick matched her turtleneck sweater. Her dark jeans matched the black holster and Glock on her hip.

"Haven't changed the place," she said, taking a sip of wine.

"I like it the way it is," he said, sitting on the couch.

She nodded and sipped more wine, her blue eyes fixed on his. "How are you doing?"

"Fine," he said.

"I'm not making small talk, John."

"I know. I just don't like discussing it."

"You loved her?"

"Yes," he said. "I still do."

"You'll never forget."

"No. I never will. But Jordan's death got me thinking."

"About what?"

"My job. My future. At least what's left of it."

"You're resourceful," she said. "You've survived till now. The Cali cartel is no more. Your job is who you are."

He smiled and drank some wine. "Maybe I'm more than my job."

"Yes, you are. But I know this much about you. You need to believe in something."

"I believe in justice."

"So tell me how you achieve the justice you so desire without your badge and your gun?'

"Maybe along with justice, I need some peace, Rita. Some time to heal."

Gamboni thought for a while. Drank some wine. Petted Gitana. "You said you've been thinking about your job and your future. What does that mean, exactly?"

"I've sacrificed a lot. Lost most of those closest to me. Even before that, I lost my parents. All I have left now is my sister and my dog."

Gamboni looked at him for a long moment without speaking before her eyes came off his.

"Ted Lake and Jack Gaines are in a world of trouble," he said.

She locked eyes with him again. "I don't understand why they attacked you in DC."

"It's a guy thing, Rita."

"What are you talking about?"

"Ted has the hots for you."

Her cheeks reddened with embarrassment. "He does not," she said, unconvincingly.

"He knows you and I were involved."

"So what?"

"I'm just offering you a guy's perspective."

"So he beat you up because you and I were once lovers?"

"I wouldn't characterize it like that."

"Why not? We *were* lovers."

"I was referring to the 'beating up' part."

She exhaled an exasperated breath. "As long as I live, I'll never understand men's thinking."

"Well," he said, "if we're going to get into gender specific thinking—"

"Hold it right there before you get yourself in trouble."

He toasted her with his glass of wine and drank. Then he said, "Is the FBI still blaming the Blue Skies crash on pilot error?"

"That or terrorists."

"Really?"

She shook her head and let out a breath. "No," she said, as her eyes found his again. "I can't lie to you. There's no evidence it was a terrorist attack. And something this big, this dramatic, whatever terrorist group was responsible would be telling the world about it. You know that."

"Yes, I do. I'm also guessing that you and your colleagues have no leads."

Gamboni looked at him without responding.

"Let me rephrase that," he said. "You have no leads that you're willing to share."

"If we had something concrete, I'd share it with you. I want this solved as much as you do."

"And you'd like to hear what I think—or rather, what I know."

"You have a lead?"

"I believe that whoever murdered Kim Austin, her mother, and Terry Powell was responsible for bringing that plane down."

"They were killed to keep them quiet?"

"As a member of the Go-Team, Kim Austin had access to all the flight data information."

"As did all the accident investigators."

"But the NTSB and FBI pressured everyone to conclude it was pilot error and not GPS spoofing."

"The Bureau never pressured anyone."

"You don't know that, Rita."

"Okay, maybe I don't. So everyone but Kim Austin went along with the report?"

"She saw the holes in the Next-Gen system, mainly the lack of encryption between satellites and aircraft. And it's going to happen again, Rita. Someone or some terrorist group is going to figure it out."

"If what you suspect is true," she said, "you can understand why the NTSB and FBI would be reluctant to let the public know how and why that plane crashed."

Santana looked at her for a time before he said, "Where's the justice in that, Rita?"

Chapter 35

The following morning at the LEC, Santana stopped by Bobby Jackson's office. Jackson was the SPPD's computer forensics examiner.

"I've been having trouble shutting down my department cell phone," Santana said. "It also has low battery life and feels hot."

"You hearing any background noises and clicks while you're making a call?" Jackson asked.

"Maybe once or twice."

"If you're having issues with shutting your phone down and hearing clicks, I'd say your cell phone could very well be compromised. Have you checked your data usage lately?"

"No, I haven't."

"Log into your mobile account and view your past invoices. See whether there has been a drastic increase in your online data usage."

"How come?"

"If someone has access to your cell phone, it means they'll be able to get to all of your apps and Internet browsers. If they're able to manage your apps using the Internet, you'll definitely see an increase in downloaded and uploaded data. Plus, these spy applications transmit information to another location via the Internet twenty-four hours a day, seven days a week."

"But my cell phone has never been out of my possession."

"Doesn't need to be," Jackson said. "Anyone can purchase an inexpensive cell phone spy app online for about seventy bucks. The app works by remotely accessing data from the target phone—in this case, your phone—and displaying that data on their cell phone, tablet, or computer. They can spy on your cell phone without being anywhere near it and see virtually everything that takes place, including text messages, calls, GPS location, photos, videos and e-mails. All of this without ever having your phone in their possession."

"That's crazy, Bobby."

"It gets worse," Jackson said. "The app has a stealth camera feature. They can secretly take a picture using your cell phone's camera and have that picture sent to their phone. Think of it this way: you have your phone in your hands, and I'm monitoring your phone from mine. I send a command to your phone telling it to take a picture. The program snaps a picture on your phone and then automatically sends that picture to me. I can now view that picture on my cell phone."

"I don't believe this."

"Believe it, brother. But that's not all the app can do. It has a 'listen to surroundings' feature. Whoever bugged your phone can activate your microphone, allowing them to hear everything that's going on around you. It's as if they were standing there beside you."

"This is all legal?"

"Far as I can tell. And the technology actually does have some legitimate purposes."

"Such as?"

"Suppose parents want to monitor their children, make sure they're not in danger or hanging out with the wrong crowd. Employers could also use the app to monitor the activity of employees on company-owned devices."

"That's comforting to know. Maybe the department has bugged my phone."

Jackson laughed. "Welcome to the age of paranoia, Detective."

"Not sure I want to be a part of it," Santana said.

"Don't think you have much choice, unless you're completely off the grid. You know, those who have questionable motives can misuse any type of technology, Detective."

"Might be something the department should look into."

"I've already discussed it with the brass. But we'd need probable cause and warrants before we could use this technology. Anyone outside the law doesn't have to worry about the legal consequences. At least not yet."

"Could I be tracked if my location services were turned off?"

"Sure, an IP address will give away someone's location down to a city or zip code level. Your Internet provider has logs that keep track of your IP address and user association. Given a time and an IP address, the department could find out the account the device was registered under even if a person had a dynamic IP that changes from time to time."

"So what should I do about my department cell phone?"

"Get yourself a new one," Jackson said.

* * *

Santana left Jackson's office and drove directly to the SPPD radio shop to get a new phone. Per department policy, he had to write a report detailing what had happened. Then he was given his replacement.

Santana returned to his desk, sat down beside Kacie Hawkins, and said, "My department cell phone was bugged."

"How?"

He repeated what Bobby Jackson had told him.

"That's unbelievable," Hawkins said. "I better check my usage. You have any idea who bugged it?"

"Maybe," he said. "Let's take a look at the DVDs from the security conference again."

"Because you dreamt about disks in your dream the other night?"

"Yes. But also because when we viewed them before, we were focusing on Kim Austin. I want to focus on someone else."

"Who?"

"Reyna Tran."

"It's about time," Hawkins said.

Santana ignored her comment and watched the computer screen as she inserted the first DVD and scrolled ahead to the exact time when Kim Austin and Reyna Tran were talking.

"Keep going," Santana said.

The camera panned to the right.

"There's Paul Westbrook," Hawkins said.

The camera swept past Westbrook and then reversed course and panned to the left. When it came back around to where Westbrook had been standing, he was gone.

"We've seen this before."

"Keep it running," Santana said.

They watched until the first DVD ended.

"I didn't see anything different than we saw the first time," Hawkins said.

"What's on the second DVD?" he asked.

"Another conference room. But I don't recall seeing Kim Austin anywhere on it."

"You were focusing on Austin at the time. What about Reyna Tran?"

Hawkins considered it. "I believe Tran was on the second DVD."

"Let's take a look."

Hawkins ejected the first disc and replaced it with the second one. The second conference room had a similar setup as the first room, except that the camera was stationary rather than panning. They could see conferees milling about, chatting with one another in pairs or in small groups, or looking at the conference brochure.

"Stop!" Santana said.

Reyna Tran was entering the conference room.

"Okay," he said. "Run it forward a bit."

"There," Hawkins said, freezing the frame.

Tran was talking with Paul Westbrook.

Hawkins glanced at Santana and then stared at her computer screen. "Look at that, John," she said.

"Tran is touching Westbrook on the arm."

"Exactly," Hawkins said. "If a woman is talking with you casually at a party or a bar, or at a security conference like this, and she finds a reason to touch you, she's sending you a signal. It's the oldest, most obvious trick in the book. It's not something a woman usually does unless she's flirting."

"Or unless she knew Westbrook," Santana said.

"It's possible," Hawkins said. She started the DVD playing again and then abruptly stopped it. "Look how close Tran is to Westbrook. She's definitely in his personal space. When a woman enters your space or brushes past you with a glance and a smile, she's flirting."

"Run it back a few frames and play it again."

Hawkins did as he asked.

Santana studied the screen with more focus now. "Stop it right there."

Hawkins did and then swiveled her chair to face him. "What do you see?"

"Tran came up to Westbrook."

"Yes. She made the approach. And did you notice as they were talking, she was playing with her hair?"

"More flirting," he said.

Hawkins nodded.

They watched the rest of the second DVD but found no other instances of Reyna Tran or Paul Westbrook.

Santana got up from his desk chair. "You have Westbrook's bio handy?"

Hawkins shuffled through the folders on her desk until she found the one she was looking for and held it up.

"What year did Westbrook graduate from MIT?" Santana asked.

Hawkins opened the folder and scanned it until she found the date. When she told him, he paged through his notebook. Then he looked up at Hawkins. "Reyna Tran attended MIT that same year."

"So they knew each other."

"Definitely a possibility," Santana said. He took out his new SPPD cell phone.

"Who you calling?" Hawkins asked.

"Reyna Tran."

Tran answered on the second ring.

"You still in town?" Santana asked.

"Hello, John, so nice of you to call. I am in town."

"We need to talk, Reyna."

"Why so serious?"

"I'll tell you when I see you."

"Oh, I love mysteries."

"Then you're going to love this one," Santana said.

* * *

Reyna Tran was waiting for Santana at the Dock Café in Stillwater, on the shore of the St. Croix River. They sat under a canvas umbrella at a round table on the large brick patio. Santana could see upriver to the historic Stillwater Lift Bridge that connected Minnesota and Wisconsin.

The sky was bright blue, the temperature near seventy. A gentle westerly breeze ruffled the colorful leaves on the trees.

"What a lovely fall day," Tran said.

"This isn't a social visit, Reyna."

"I have meetings all afternoon and need to eat. I'm sure you're hungry as well. Can't we talk and eat at the same time?"

"You're not going to like what I have to say."

"Are you going to hurt my feelings?"

"I don't think that's possible."

She smiled a little and sipped her lemonade from a straw. "You are in a bad mood, aren't you?"

Santana followed her gaze to the Venetian gondola carrying a couple along the shoreline. The gondolier wore the traditional straw boater with a red ribbon around the crown, a blue-and-white striped-shirt, and black pants. Santana wished he were on his own boat rather than immersed in a murder investigation.

"That's what we should be doing," Tran said as her gaze fell once again on him.

"How is it you knew I was in DC, Reyna?"

"I didn't know. I just happened to run into you."

"Coincidence, huh?"

"I have an office there."

"And how did you know I was at Terry Powell's house?"

"Because I had you followed."

"You were worried about me."

"Yes, I was. And I still am."

Santana laid his new cell phone on the table. "I think you bugged my department cell phone."

"Now why would I do that?"

"Because you wanted to track my progress on the Kim Austin murder case. And because you, and not David Knapp, had something to do with the Blue Skies crash."

"Oh, John. I'm so disappointed in you."

"Likewise," Santana said. "How much Blue Skies stock do you own, Reyna?"

"None."

"You steered me toward Knapp with the short sell theory and because he bought shares of Blue Skies after the crash."

"I didn't steer you toward anything," she said without a hint of anger. "You came to *me* for help. Not the other way around, remember? You have your own theory as to how and why the airliner was brought down. I had nothing to gain by Brian Devlin's death, or Kim Austin's, for that matter. David Knapp sure did."

"But your company would gain if Knapp's company went out of the security business."

"I can think of much easier methods of putting him out of business, if that was my intent."

Santana wasn't going to ask what those methods were. And he had to admit that what he was describing was a convoluted plan for getting rid of Knapp. Still, Reyna Tran was a sociopath. In order to understand her, he had to *think* like her. In the past he'd put aside his doubts and trusted her out of necessity. Now doubts plagued him.

"So tell me about Paul Westbrook."

"What do you want to know?"

"You knew him at MIT."

"Yes."

"Why didn't you tell me that before?"

"Paul and I weren't close. Besides, I didn't think it was important."

"Don't lie to me, Reyna. You knew he was one of the accident investigators in the Blue Skies crash. And you knew I've been investigating that crash and the murders of Kim Austin and Terry Powell."

She let out a sigh. "Are you making any progress?"

"What else do you know that you're not telling me?" he said, ignoring her question.

"Nothing of importance."

"What did you talk to Westbrook about at the security conference?"

"We didn't have much time to chat."

"Did he talk to you about the Blue Skies crash?"

The waitress arrived with Tran's strawberry chicken salad.

"You sure you don't want anything to drink, sir?" she asked Santana.

"Water's fine," he said. He waited until the waitress left before addressing Reyna Tran again. "Did Westbrook talk to you about the crash?"

Tran took a bite of her salad and sipped her lemonade. Then she patted her red lips with a napkin. "No. Why would he speak to me about it?"

"Did he talk to you about Kim Austin?"

"No, he did not."

"I realize I'm asking a sociopath, but would you say Paul Westbrook had mental health issues?"

"Just because I admit to being one," Tran said, "doesn't mean that I can see those tendencies in others."

"Sure you can, Reyna."

"Well, I don't recall Paul having emotional problems at MIT. He was a bit of a narcissist and very secretive. I can't tell you anything about his sexual behavior."

"What about his behavior at the conference?"

"He was a bit agitated and paranoid."

"About what?"

"He didn't say, and I didn't ask."

"Did you know that Westbrook's parents were killed in a plane crash?"

"Yes, I knew that."

"Do you know what airline they were flying?"

"Blue Skies," she said.

Santana felt an adrenaline rush. "How bright is Paul Westbrook?"

"He went to MIT, so he's bright. Not as bright as me, of course."

"Is Paul Westbrook bright enough to have brought down that airliner?"

Reyna Tran set down her fork and folded her hands on the table. "Now that is a very interesting thought."

Chapter 36

When he returned to the LEC, Santana debriefed Kacie Hawkins on his conversation with Reyna Tran.

"You still think she's innocent?" Hawkins said.

"She's not innocent and probably never was. But is she guilty of murder or spoofing the Blue Skies flight? I doubt it."

"I don't know why you trust her, John."

"Well, until she gives me a reason not to . . . "He shrugged.

"So what about Westbrook?" Hawkins asked. "Up until recently, he's been missing."

"Has he?" Santana set his department cell phone on his desk and pointed to it. "Every time we receive a call, our cell carrier takes note of the incoming telephone number, the time, date, and duration of the conversation, and—because the call is sent through a network of cell towers—our location."

Hawkins smiled. "If we got Westbrook's mobile phone records, we'd know where he's been the last six months."

"We'll need a warrant," Santana said.

"We should request location logs from Google as well," Hawkins said. "If Westbrook used Google Maps on his smartphone, they'll have his location history as part of their Timeline feature."

"I didn't know that feature existed."

"Most people probably don't. Google not only stores the information about your location, but also analyzes it. They know where we work, where we live, where we work out, where we spend most of our time and money, our GPS travel patterns, and how we commute."

"In other words, pretty much everything about us," Santana said.

"Yes. And if we're also using Google photos, they'll link our pictures to a specific day and location. The good news is, their current policy is to comply with law enforcement requests for the data."

"Let me check on something else," Santana said. He dialed Lyman Grady's cell phone number in DC.

Grady answered after three rings. "What's up, Detective?"

"Did Paul Westbrook have any large deposits in his checking or savings accounts approximately six months ago?"

"Give me a minute," Grady said.

Santana waited while Grady shuffled through some papers.

"There isn't one large sum," Grady said. "But there are a series of smaller five-thousand-dollar deposits in his checking account over the course of five months."

"What's the total?"

"Comes to . . ." Grady paused. "Wow! One hundred grand."

"Thanks, Grady."

"What's going on with Westbrook?"

"I'll let you know." Santana disconnected and looked at Hawkins. "Paul Westbrook deposited one hundred thousand dollars in his checking account over the last five months."

"Where did he get that kind of money?" Hawkins asked.

"I'm betting he shorted Blue Skies stock. Let's write up a warrant for Westbrook's cell phone and Google history and take it to Judge Will," Santana said.

Hawkins chuckled. "Good old 'always will.'"

Judge Franklin Will had been given the moniker "Always Will" in the Homicide Unit because of his propensity for signing warrants. But Santana knew that he and Hawkins would have to show probable cause that Westbrook had committed or was about to commit a crime. He felt reasonably certain that they could convince Judge Will. He wouldn't have felt as confident with other judges he'd dealt with in the past. But he had credibility with Judge Will and had never let him down or made him look bad. That tipped the scales of justice in the judge's eyes.

Santana focused his thoughts on his old cell phone, wondering if Paul Westbrook had bugged it. Whether he had or not, Westbrook's cell phone history would tell Santana where he'd been the last six months. He was at the security conference in St. Paul near the time of Kim Austin's disappearance. Had he been in in DC when Terry Powell was shot to death?

* * *

As Santana was driving home late that afternoon, his personal cell phone rang. He recognized the number and considered letting the call go to voicemail before he changed his mind and answered.

"Hello, Reyna."

"I'm heading back to Chicago first thing tomorrow, John. Let me take you to dinner tonight."

"I don't think so."

"Why not?"

"Look, I appreciate all the help you've been."

"Then do me the favor of letting me take you to dinner."

"I already have dinner plans."

"I'd hate to leave town and not see you."

"You talk as if we're romantically involved. Which we're not."

"Trust me," she said. "You'd definitely know if we were."

"Thanks for the warning."

"I'll be in your area. I'll call you later."

"No need to, Reyna. We can say our—"

She hung up.

* * *

Deborah Russell came over that evening at 6:30, just after the sun had disappeared below the horizon. Santana let her in the back door, feeling the bite of cold air despite his thick cotton sweater and jeans.

"I brought a blueberry pie," she said. "I'm not real handy in the kitchen, so I bought this at the bakery."

"Thank you," he said, carrying the pie into the kitchen and setting it on the counter.

She followed. "Nice cold night for a fire," she said, gesturing toward the logs crackling in the fireplace. "Last I heard, the temperature had fallen to near forty degrees."

She wore a slim, quilted ivory vest over a black turtleneck sweater, blue jeans, and light blue Adidas running shoes. The scent of musk and vanilla fragrance in her perfume was strong.

"Hope you like beef stroganoff," he said.

"Sounds great. Can I help with anything?"

"You could slice up the lettuce and veggies for the garden salad. Everything is on the counter. There's a knife in the butcher block. The beef is almost ready."

She slid the knife out of the wooden block and touched the blade with her index finger. "Sharp," she said with a smile.

While she sliced the lettuce, carrots, tomatoes, cucumbers, and onions, Santana walked into the living room, where Gitana was lounging on a rug in front of the fireplace, and added a log to the fire.

When the salad was ready, he poured two glasses of Merlot and brought them to the dining table. Deborah Russell served the salad.

"To good neighbors," she said, raising her glass in a toast.

Santana nodded and drank.

Logs crackled and hissed in the fireplace as the wood split and released steam.

"What would you have been if not a detective?" she asked.

"A doctor."

"That's interesting."

"How so?"

"Both doctors and detectives are in the problem-solving business. What killed the patient or who killed the victim?"

"But doesn't a doctor save lives?"

"So, too, a detective by getting the perpetrator off the streets."

"I suppose that's true," Santana said.

After finishing the salad, Santana served the stroganoff. She poured more wine.

"This stroganoff tastes delicious," she said. "You're quite the cook."

"Not really."

"Well, my culinary skills are limited, so I appreciate a good home cooked meal once in a while. The wine is excellent as well."

"You eat out a lot?"

"Too much. Thankfully, all the running keeps the extra weight off."

"You run every day?"

"I try to."

They ate in silence for a time before she said, "Seems like you're doing well in your job. I would think it's difficult outsmarting killers. You must be very bright."

"More of an opportunist," he said.

"What does that have to do with solving a crime?"

"Many times the perpetrator makes a mistake. A good detective has to take advantage of the opportunity when it presents itself."

"Well," she said with a wave of her hand, "solving crimes is not something I'd be any good at."

"Experience helps."

"Yes, but seeing the awful things we humans do to one another on a daily basis. It would be too stressful for me. And there is an endless supply of criminals."

"There is that," Santana said. "You get rid of one and two more take his place."

"Bad weeds never die," she said with a smile.

Santana felt his heartbeat increase. Blood roared in his eardrums. He tried to keep his emotions in check and not to overreact to her last statement, but his body hummed like a taut wire. He took a deep breath, exhaled and said, "Why did you decide to become a jury consultant?"

She cocked her head and thought for a time. "I like studying human behavior."

"Such as?"

"Analyzing mannerisms and verbal and non-verbal responses."

"Have you picked up any cues from me?"

"Oh, no. I don't mix business with pleasure."

"Hard not to."

"Would you like more wine?"

"I'm fine."

Santana kept his eyes fixed on her. "*Mala yerba no muere,*" he said.

"*Sí,*" she answered.

"I thought you didn't speak Spanish."

She looked at him, a glass of wine in her hand. "Huh?"

"Only someone from Colombia would know the phrase 'bad weeds never die.'" He reached for the Glock under the table.

Deborah Russell set the wine glass on table. "It isn't there," she said, pulling his Glock out of her right vest pocket and pointing it at him.

"You've been in my house."

She smiled and nodded. "Of course."

"Who are you?"

"Think about it, Detective. You know who I am. You've known since you were sixteen and murdered the sons of Alejandro Estrada. From what I understand, you may have killed him, too. But it matters little to me."

Santana's heart thumped against his ribcage. His mouth was dry. His palms were slick with sweat. "You kill a police officer in the States, you're going to have a hard time getting out of the country."

She smiled. "Whatever you choose to believe is fine with me. I come and go as I please. Today I am Deborah Russell in the USA. Tomorrow I am someone else, somewhere else."

"What happened to my neighbors?"

"They are on vacation. One that, unfortunately, will never end."

She switched the Glock to her left hand, pinched the blue contact lens in her right eye with her index finger and thumb, and removed it. Then she switched the Glock back to her right hand and removed the contact in her left eye.

"Never could get used to these things," she said, looking at him now with eyes that were as dark and as empty as a deep, dry well.

"You killed Laurie Baldwin."

"I've killed many, but not her."

"You've got no reason to lie."

"Not now."

Santana hoped that if he could keep her talking, she would make a mistake. But he knew the odds of that were slim to none. "You do this for the money?"

She shook her head. "Money allows me to travel, to live wherever and however I want. But the real enjoyment, the real excitement comes in getting to know the victim. You fascinate me, Detective. You're a very guarded person, hard to get close to."

Santana said nothing.

"Most men want to get me in the sack very quickly, which makes my job so much easier. Your resistance surprised me. I suspect it has something to do with the death of Jordan Parrish."

"Or maybe I'm a good judge of character."

"Perhaps better than most men whose brain is between their legs."

"I imagine you know all about me."

"I spend a great deal of time getting to know my new friends," she said.

"Victims would be a more accurate term."

"Is that how you see yourself, Detective? Because I'm certain my client doesn't see you as one."

"I'm guessing your client isn't a victim. Especially if he or she belongs to a cartel in Colombia."

"My job is not to judge," she said. "I merely carry out the sentence."

"You let Gitana out of her dog run."

She stood up. "Anything else you want to say in the time you have left?"

"You going to shoot me?"

"Not unless I have to."

"What then?"

"You're going to have an accident. It helps keep the police off my trail." She motioned with the gun. "Get up."

"What if I don't want to?"

"Then I'll shoot that mutt of yours before I put a bullet between your eyes."

Santana had no doubt she would. He stood up.

The front doorbell rang. Gitana barked, got up, and headed for the door.

"Who's that?" Russell said in a calm voice.

"I don't know."

"Get rid of them. And remember, if you try anything stupid, the first shot takes out your dog."

Santana walked to the door. "Sit, Gitana," he said. She sat.

Santana glanced at Russell. She was standing off to the side, out of sight from the door, the Glock aimed at him.

He figured he could make a break for it once he opened the door. Russell would get off at least one shot. She could miss, which was highly unlikely, unless he was quick enough. If he were hit, it might not be a fatal wound. But all of it was fanciful thinking. If he made a break for it, Russell, or whatever her name really was, would surely kill Gitana. And depending on who was at the door, she would no doubt kill them as well. He would have to wait—and hope—for a better opportunity.

He chose not to hit the switch for the outside light as he opened the door.

No one was there.

Gitana got to her feet and peered out the door.

Santana looked at Russell. She cocked her head and mouthed, "What?"

He shrugged his shoulders.

Russell came forward slowly, waving the Glock at him to move out of the way.

Santana backed away from the open door. Gitana, sensing something was amiss, followed him.

Russell glanced quickly around the doorframe and then at Santana.

"Drop the gun!"

They both looked toward the open back door through which Reyna Tran had entered. She was now standing in front of the fireplace with a small, slim, but powerful Glock 36, .45-caliber automatic handgun expertly held in a two-handed grip.

Santana said, "Gitana, down!"

She looked at him and then lay down.

Russell smiled and pointed Santana's Glock at his head. "Who are you?" she said to Tran. She stood at an angle so she could see both Santana and Tran.

"A friend," Tran said. Her blue eyes were lit with an intense, excited light.

Russell kept smiling. "Good to have friends."

"I doubt you have any."

Santana felt that the two of them had made some sort of instant symbiotic connection.

Russell remained silent for a time, her gaze jumping back and forth between Tran and Santana. Then she said, "We are that way, aren't we?"

"I don't think so," Tran said. "You're definitely a psychopath. A soon to be dead one, if you don't put down that gun."

"I see this as more of a standoff," Russell said.

"Someone once told me," Tran said, "that a woman with a gun in her hand isn't necessarily as dangerous as the gun in her hand."

"You think you can get off a shot before I put a bullet in the detective's head?"

"I can get off a number of shots with one pull of this trigger."

Russell laughed. "Time to call it a day," she said as she began backing toward the front door. "I will see you again, soon, Detective."

"Stay where you are," Tran said.

"Let her go, Reyna," Santana said.

"Let me kill her, John. I can put a bullet through her frontal lobe and into her motor cortex. She'll be dead from the neck down before she can pull the trigger."

Santana had no idea how good a shot Tran was, but even if she was an excellent one, she might miss her small target area, allowing Russell to pull the trigger. "Too much of a risk," he said.

Russell kept backing away, Santana's Glock in her hand, still pointed at his head. "Listen to the detective," she said to Tran as she stepped back onto the front stoop.

Tran moved slowly toward her, the Glock in her hands trained on Russell.

Santana dove for cover behind the open front door.

Russell fired at Tran and leapt out of sight. Tran exhaled a loud breath as the bullet knocked her down.

Gitana jumped up at the sound of gunfire.

"Reyna!" Santana yelled.

He drove his shoulder into the door, slamming it shut and throwing the dead bolt. Then he was by Tran's side. He could see where the bullet had penetrated her clothing just over her left lung. Her eyes were squeezed shut in pain, but he could see no blood.

"Reyna."

Her eyes blinked open. "Don't let her get away, John."

He called 911 on his cell. "Hang on," he said, squeezing Tran's hand.

"Go now," she said.

"I'll stay with you."

"No. Go after her. I'm wearing a vest."

Santana felt for the vest and then picked up Tran's gun.

"Hurry," she said, touching his cheek with her fingers.

"Stay!" he ordered Gitana as he ran out the back door, pulling it shut behind him.

He had no plan as he raced into the darkness, other than to stop Russell. Permanently.

Chapter 37

Santana threaded his way between the trees that studded his backyard, running in the dim light from a crescent moon that sliced a thin black patch out of the night sky. He could hear the river lapping against the shoreline, see the darkness behind the windows of the house where his neighbors had once lived and had, presumably, died.

Reyna Tran hadn't fired a shot, so he had six .45 caliber rounds in her Glock 36, plenty of stopping power if he didn't waste his shots or miss his target.

He'd already lost a gun in DC, and now a second one to Russell. He aimed to get this one back.

He cut to his right when he cleared the tree line and sprinted along the side of his neighbor's house, anger and adrenaline fueling his drive, his eyes adjusting to the pale light.

Before reaching the front edge of the house, he stopped and peered around the corner. Seeing no car in the driveway, he wondered if Russell had already made her escape, or if she'd even retreated here after fleeing from his house.

As he crossed the asphalt driveway in front of the garage door, he heard the roar of a car engine and the squeal of tires. He jerked his head to the left and then dove forward as the wooden garage door shattered into pieces and a car screeched out of the garage and blew past him, barreling down the driveway.

Santana rolled onto his shoulder and up onto his right knee. With his heart hammering, he swung around, gripped the

Glock in both hands, and rested his left elbow on his left knee, waiting until the car slid to a stop. Then he opened up, firing three rounds into the dark sedan, the gun kicking in his hand as bullets exploded with loud bangs, shattering glass and thumping into metal, each shot echoing in the night air.

He saw the muzzle flash from her gun before he heard the shot and a thud as a bullet slammed into the wood siding behind and to the right of him.

Diving onto his stomach, he fired another round as Russell thrust the car into drive. Tires screamed against the asphalt as she hit the gas pedal and the car shot forward, leaving a cloud of gray smoke in its wake as it flew down the road and out of sight.

Santana got to his feet and inhaled a deep breath, letting it slowly out of his lungs, trying to calm his racing heart and steady his nerves.

Then he ran back to his house as an approaching siren wailed in the distance.

Reyna Tran was seated in a chair at the dining table, petting Gitana, who turned when she saw Santana and came quickly to him, her tail wagging.

"Did you get her?" Tran asked.

Santana shook his head.

"You didn't pursue?"

"Too much of a head start. And I didn't call it in either."

"Why not?"

"All I saw was a dark, late model sedan. I have no idea where she's headed. Wherever it is, I'm sure she has another vehicle close by and a contingency plan."

"You should've let me kill her, John."

"You needed a perfect shot."

"I've made them before."

Santana didn't ask her to elaborate. "You all right?"

"I'll be fine." She gestured toward the Kevlar vest on the floor at her feet. "Technology. It's not all bad."

Santana came to the table and sat down in a chair beside her. The siren was getting close.

"How did you know something was wrong?"

"When I came around back to surprise you, I saw Russell through the window holding a gun on you. I got a Kevlar vest out of the trunk of my car and then created a diversion by ringing the front doorbell and coming in the back."

"You're lucky I left the door unlocked."

"No, *you're* lucky."

"A case could be made for that, I guess."

"I've got a deep bruise on my chest," she said. "It hurts to breathe."

"The bullet's impact might've broken a rib."

She smiled. "Want to take a look?"

"I'll let the paramedics handle it."

She kept smiling at him without speaking.

"What?" he said.

"You do care about me, don't you?"

"I owe you."

"That's not the same thing as caring."

"And you know the difference?"

"In your case, yes," she said.

Santana could hear the siren dying as the paramedics pulled into his driveway.

He stood. "You'll feel better soon, Reyna."

"You know this isn't over," she said.

"What do you mean?"

"You'll see her again, John. Believe me. A professional like her has a contract to fulfill. If she doesn't honor it, she's out of business. But you know that, don't you?"

Santana said nothing.

"You'd better be ready," Tran said.

* * *

While Santana served his mandatory three-day administrative leave for an officer-involved shooting, the St. Paul PD worked with the Washington County Sheriff's Department and the Bureau of Criminal Apprehension.

Reyna Tran spent the night in the emergency room at Regions Hospital. X-rays indicated bruised but not broken ribs. Detectives from the OIS team, Internal Affairs, and Homicide interviewed her.

At her request, Santana picked her up at the hospital the next morning and drove her to the airport, where her security personnel were waiting to help her with her luggage and to board her Lear jet. One of them had returned her rental car.

She sat in the passenger seat of his Ford Explorer and looked into his eyes. "I can't watch out for you all the time."

"No need to," he answered.

"You will be careful."

"Of course."

She laughed and then her face twisted in pain. "It hurts to laugh. Hurts to do just about everything. Otherwise . . ." she smiled.

"You're my friend, Reyna."

"Yes. I suppose I am. That's better than your enemy."

"I won't forget what you've done."

"Believe me, I won't let you. And remember to upgrade your security system."

"I will."

She leaned forward and kissed him lightly on the lips.

He did not resist.

"Good-bye for now, John Santana," she said.

* * *

Santana drove to Karen Wong's 19th century brownstone in the Crocus Hill neighborhood for his required OIS meeting with the department's psychologist. Clients used a separate private entrance to her office. He sat in a comfortable cushioned chair in front of Wong's black lacquer desk.

Wong was an attractive Asian woman with a heart-shaped face and black hair cut even with the nape of her neck. She wore it brushed across her forehead so that it drew attention to her large brown eyes.

"It's good to see you again, Detective, even if the circumstances that bring you here are unpleasant."

"Firing my gun wasn't unpleasant," Santana said. "Not hitting my intended target definitely was."

"In the past we've talked about the guilt you carry."

"Yes, we have."

"Would you like to talk more about it?"

He shook his head. "I have a request."

"What is it?"

"It's about my dog," he said.

* * *

That evening Santana sat on the couch in his living room with a glass of red wine and with Gitana by his side. He was hoping he and Hawkins would soon have Paul Westbrook's cell phone location data. It could link Westbrook to the murders of Kim Austin and her mother, and to Terry Powell.

But Laurie Baldwin was still the outlier. As far as Santana knew, she'd had nothing to do with the Blue Skies crash. If there was a copycat killer, he or she must've had inside information about the Kim Austin murder scene. Albert Greer had told the press about the dagger through Austin's palm, so a copycat would've known that. But no one, to Santana's knowledge, had been told that that both Austin and Baldwin had been struck on the head with an object. Either that key piece of information had been leaked, or the killer had been present at both crime scenes.

Santana got up from the couch, took a yellow legal pad and felt tip pen out of a drawer, and sat down at the kitchen table with what was left of his wine. He began writing the names of those who had been present at Kim Austin's crime scene. He and Hawkins were the first names on the list, followed by Gina Luttrell, the SPPD district supervisor, and Reiko Tanabe, the ME. Two forensic techs that worked with Tanabe had been present. Santana recognized their faces but didn't recall their full names. In the morning at the LEC, he would have to look at the crime scene log in the murder book. Thinking of the log reminded him that Rick Paukert, the young, enthusiastic SPPD patrolman who had asked about becoming a detective, had been the first officer on the scene. Paukert had also shown up at Laurie Baldwin's crime scene, though after the parks employee had discovered her body. Santana circled Paukert's name. He would need to look into Paukert's history and record with the department before drawing any conclusions. Rob Wallace, the forensic anthropologist, was the final name Santana added to the list.

If anyone had leaked information about Kim Austin's crime scene, Rob Wallace and his inflated ego would be a likely candidate. He was always looking to promote himself, given the opportunity.

Before going to bed, Santana checked the private e-mail account he and Natalia used. She'd left him a message in the draft file saying that she missed Colombia and was planning to fly from Barcelona to Manizales to visit one of her childhood friends.

Santana felt a rush of adrenaline. She would be risking her life, and he wouldn't be there to protect her. He typed a return message in the draft file urging her not to go.

* * *

Santana was back on the job and in Pete Romano's office Monday morning of the following week.

"Thanks for completing your reports while you were on leave, Detective," Romano said.

"Nothing else to do."

"I understand you've also completed your visit with Karen Wong."

"I have."

"I hope it was productive."

Santana smiled but offered no reply.

Romano placed his hands flat on the desk and said, "Your neighbors' bodies were found in a basement deep freezer. ME said they were both shot at close range. And by the way, that pie she brought to your house was laced with benzodiazepine. A piece of that would've put you to sleep long enough for her to do whatever she wanted."

"Anything on her prints?"

"We got a good set off the wine glass and sent them to Interpol. Turns out the woman who attempted to kill you is Karina Rojas, also known as the Wolf. She grew up in Venezuela, the daughter of a wealthy landowner and oil executive. She was educated in London and Paris.

"When Hugo Chavez came to power, her father was murdered and her family impoverished. Rumor has it she attempted to assassinate Chavez, but was unsuccessful. That was her one and only failure, according to authorities that have tracked her for years. Rojas is the prime suspect in the murders of at least fifteen individuals in a dozen different countries. You're lucky to be alive, Detective."

"I thought she was responsible for the Laurie Baldwin copycat killing, Pete. But she wasn't."

"How do you know?"

"She told me."

"And you believe her?"

"What's one more killing to her? If she was responsible, she would've said so."

"Well," Romano said, "we located a stolen van we believe was used in the Baldwin kidnapping and murder."

"Where?"

"It was parked in a downtown ramp. Forensics dusted for prints. We find the perp, we might be able to get a match."

"Any murder kit?"

Romano shook his head. "Where does that leave us?"

"I'll tell you what I think," Santana said.

Chapter 38

By early that afternoon, Santana and Hawkins had obtained Paul Westbrook's phone records and Google location data. They tracked his movements and locations for the last six months using Google Timeline. By entering the year, month and date, they knew exactly where he'd been on a particular day and whether he'd walked or driven. All the information was overlaid on a map of the area. A solid line tracked every movement from place to place.

"We already know, based on the security video, that Westbrook was in town when Kim Austin was murdered," Santana said, looking at Hawkins.

"According to Google, he drove to the parking lot near the caves," she said. "No doubt with Kim Austin's body. He was also at Terry Powell's house the night Powell was murdered."

"Look at the time, Kacie. It was after Reyna picked me up."

Santana grabbed his cell phone and called Cathy Herrera. She answered on the first ring.

"Are you still at the cabin in Grand Marais, Ms. Herrera?"

"Yes. Why?"

"Where's Paul Westbrook?"

"He left this morning. Said he was headed for the Twin Cities."

"Do you know why?"

"He didn't say. I told him it was safer to remain here, but he said he had something important to do and then he'd be back."

"Stay close to your phone, Ms. Herrera. Don't let anyone into the cabin except someone from the sheriff's department."

"What about Paul?"

"Especially him."

"What's going on?"

"I don't have time to explain everything now. Just please do as I say."

"I can protect myself."

"I'm sure you can protect yourself, Ms. Herrera. But I'll contact the Cook County Sheriff in Grand Marais and apprise him of the situation. They'll send someone out."

"One other thing," she said. "I was in town when Paul left. My shotgun is missing."

"That's good to know," Santana said.

He used the browser on his cell phone to find the phone number for the Cook County Sheriff's Department in Grand Marais and dialed. When he had the sheriff on the line, he explained the situation and requested a squad be sent to Herrera's cabin.

Santana disconnected and swiveled his chair to face Hawkins. "Reyna Tran told me something interesting the other day."

"Her again," Hawkins said.

"Westbrook's parents were killed in a Blue Skies crash."

"I think I know where you're going with this, John."

Santana logged on to his computer and Googled Blue Skies crashes. Peering over his shoulder, Hawkins said, "What are you looking for?"

"This," Santana said, pointing to the computer screen.

20 Years Ago Today, Blue Skies Flight 247
Crashes After Takeoff from MSP

The Crash Left 144 People Dead

On October 21, 1997, Blue Skies Flight 247 crashed shortly after taking off from Minneapolis/St. Paul Airport.

A total of 139 passengers and 5 crewmembers were killed.

The flight was headed to California when it left the gate. The DC-9 Super 82 pilots forgot to conduct their pre-flight checks. As a result, the warning system never turned on. This led to the plane's wing flaps failing to extend prior to takeoff. As the plane rushed down the runway, it lifted only 40 feet off the ground.

It then crashed onto Interstate 494 and struck vehicles, killing two people on the ground. The plane broke apart and burst into flames as it hit an overpass. There were only two survivors from the crash, the co-pilot, Greg Manning, and 6-year-old Chelsea Erickson. (See interview with her below.)

The National Transportation Safety Board conducted a full investigation of the crash. Their final report determined that the probable cause of the accident was the flight crew's failure to use the taxi checklist to ensure that the flaps and slats were extended for takeoff. Contributing to the accident was the absence of electrical power to the airplane takeoff warning system, which thus did not warn the flight crew that the airplane was not configured properly for takeoff. The reason for the absence of electrical power could not be determined.

The flight's captain, Stuart (Stu) Pearce, was an experienced pilot with 28 years with the airline. The flight's first officer, Greg Manning, had logged more than 8,000 hours of flying in his career. Fellow pilots described the two as "competent and capable."

A black granite memorial was built in 1999 to commemorate the victims. It sits at the top of a hill at Post Road and I-494.

Family, friends, and loved ones of the victims will gather today to remember those lost 20 years ago.

> **The memorial vigil will begin at 1:26 p.m., the time the crash occurred, at the memorial site, located at Post Road and Interstate 494.**

"Stuart Pearce," Santana said.

Hawkins looked at him. "What about it?"

"Stu," he said. "Ring any bells?"

Hawkins shook her head. Then her eyes opened wide. "Stu. That was the name of Laurie Baldwin's father."

Santana nodded. "Carol Baldwin said her husband was killed in an accident when Laurie was a baby. She was twenty years old when she was murdered."

"Couldn't be," Hawkins said. "Could it?"

Santana checked his notebook for Carol Baldwin's phone number and dialed. When she answered, he told her who was calling.

"Have you changed your mind about Albert Greer murdering my daughter?" she asked.

"How did your husband, Stu, die, Ms. Baldwin?" Santana asked, ignoring her question.

"What does his death have to do with my daughter's murder?"

"Maybe everything," Santana said. "Was your husband a pilot for Blue Skies airlines?"

She didn't reply.

"Ms. Baldwin."

"Yes, he was."

"Twenty years ago today," Santana said, "Blue Skies flight 247 crashed. Your maiden name is Baldwin. You went back to it after your husband's death."

There was a long silence before she spoke again. "Stu was a good man and a good husband. But I couldn't allow my daughter to suffer because of his mistake."

"I understand."

"You said his death has everything to do with my daughter's murder. What did you mean?"

"Trust me, Ms. Baldwin," Santana said. "If I'm right, you'll know very soon."

When Santana disconnected, Hawkins said, "Westbrook killed Laurie Baldwin."

"Yes. Westbrook wanted Laurie Baldwin's mother to suffer like he suffered when he lost his parents."

"Because of Stu Pearce's mistake."

"Exactly."

"But why wait twenty years, John?"

"I think it took that long for Westbrook to plan how he was going to carry out his act of revenge on Blue Skies airlines and the people he held responsible. He was ready on the twentieth anniversary of the crash."

Hawkins nodded. "What's the address of the Food Mart where Baldwin was kidnapped?"

Santana searched through his notebook until he found it.

"Let's check his Google location data," she said.

Two minutes later, they had their answer.

"We can place Westbrook at each of the crime scenes," Hawkins said. "The murders of Terry Powell, Kim Austin and her mother, and Laurie Baldwin are all connected in some way to Blue Skies airlines."

Santana grabbed his cell phone.

"Who you calling?" Hawkins asked.

"Trevor Dane."

When Dane answered, Santana identified himself. Then he pushed the speaker button on his phone and said, "You told Detective Hawkins and me that Paul Westbrook asked you for some financial advice."

"That's right."

"Did Westbrook ask you about short selling stock?"

Dane hesitated.

"Paul Westbrook murdered Kim Austin and tried to set you up to take the fall, Mr. Dane."

"Yes," Dane said. "Westbrook asked me about short selling stock."

Santana thanked him and disconnected. "I'm wondering whatever happened to the co-pilot who survived the Blue Skies crash twenty years ago, Kacie."

Hawkins found a number of links on Google for Greg Manning, the co-pilot, prior to 2000, then nothing. "Manning dropped off the grid," she said.

The few links she did find after the crash explained how the co-pilot had been burned over forty percent of his body in the crash. The fire had seared his lungs so that he needed an oxygen tank to breathe. Manning had also suffered a broken spine, leaving him paralyzed from the waist down. Having been blamed for the crash along with the dead pilot, Stu Pearce, Greg Manning had retreated from the public eye.

Santana opened his notebook and flipped through the pages until he found what he was searching for. "Glen Morgan lives next to Elisha Austin," he said. "I interviewed him the day we discovered her body. He'd been badly burned and uses an oxygen tank to breathe and a wheelchair to get around because he's paralyzed from the waist down. He also told me his house had been broken into."

"You think Greg Manning and Glen Morgan are one and the same?" Hawkins said.

"I do. And I think Paul Westbrook planned to kill Morgan the same day that he killed Elisha Austin. But when he broke in, he discovered Morgan wasn't home. Cathy Herrera told me Westbrook left her cabin this morning with her shotgun and was driving to the Twin Cities. Guess where he's going?"

* * *

Santana looked up Glen Morgan's phone number in his notebook and called him.

"I don't get many calls," Morgan said when Santana identified himself. "You kind of surprised me."

"Are you alone?" Santana asked.

"Pretty much all the time," he said.

"I want you to lock your door, Mr. Morgan. And don't let anyone in till we arrive."

"What's going on?"

"I'll explain when we get there."

"Does this have something to do with my neighbor's murder?"

"Possibly."

"Her daughter worked for the NTSB."

"She did."

Morgan went quiet.

"Are you still there?" Santana asked.

"You know about my past, don't you Detective?"

"I do."

"I've tried putting it behind me, but I never can. The guilt is always there."

"I know the feeling, Mr. Morgan," Santana said, thinking of Jordan.

"I just want people to leave me alone."

Not wanting to get into a discussion about Morgan's past, and worried that Paul Westbrook would get there before he and Hawkins, Santana said, "We'll be there soon."

Morgan hung up.

Santana now knew what had caused the hopelessness and despair he'd heard in Morgan's voice the first time they had spoken and again today. Survivor's guilt.

* * *

A light rain was falling as Santana drove past Glen Morgan's house, took the first right and then another, and stopped in the alley behind the bungalow.

Hawkins got out of the sedan and peered through a window into the garage. "Van in here with a handicapped sticker," she said, looking at Santana. "Probably Morgan's."

"I didn't see Westbrook's Land Rover parked out front or here in the alley."

"You sure he's driving a Land Rover?"

"He was when I met him at Cathy Herrera's cabin."

"Maybe he hasn't arrived yet," Hawkins said.

"That's my guess."

"How do you want to do this?"

"I'll park the car on the next cross street and come back. Wait here for me."

"Roger that," Hawkins said.

Santana drove to the end of the alley, parked along the curb on a side street, and retraced his route. Hawkins was waiting by the garage.

"Cover the back door, Kacie. I'll go around the front and clear the rooms. If Westbrook is here, we'll find out real quick. I think he has a Mossberg shotgun with him that he took from Cathy Herrera's place. Don't take any chances if he comes your way. This guy is dangerous."

Hawkins smiled and tapped the butt of her Glock resting in her belt holster. "I'll be waiting."

Santana unzipped his raid jacket and slid his Glock out of the holster. Opening the gate in the chain link fence that enclosed the back yard, he angled to his right. He saw no bowls or leashes in the back yard indicating Glen Morgan owned a dog, nor had he seen or heard one when he'd first spoken to Morgan on the front porch.

There were two windows along the north side of the house. Santana held his Glock in his gun hand, the barrel pointing skyward. He pressed his back against the siding and peered into the first window. Between the curtains he could see a wheelchair near a door on the far wall and the bottom half of a double bed under the window. A man was lying on the bed. Santana assumed it was Glen Morgan, but because the bed was against the near wall, he could only see Morgan from the waist down.

He moved quickly to the second window and peered through it into the living room but saw no one.

Rain was falling harder now. Santana stepped onto the front porch. He could see that instead of locking the front door as he'd requested, Morgan—or someone else—had left it partially open.

Santana stood against the right side wall, with his gun close to his body, and gave the door a solid push with his left hand. As it opened away from him, he took a step backward, so that his back was once again against the wall. Not wanting to step into the doorway and fully expose himself, he took small sidesteps, moving to his left in a semi-circular motion around the doorway entrance, clearing the room in small slices before he quickly stepped through the entryway and into the room, moving to his right, giving a quick glance over his left shoulder to make sure no one was hiding behind him.

When he had cleared the living room, he closed the front door and moved down the hallway until he reached the bedroom on his left.

Glen Morgan was sprawled on his back. Beside him on the bed was a Smith & Wesson .38 Special snub-nose revolver. Morgan's head lay back against the wall, his eyes staring blindly at the ceiling. It appeared that he'd held the gun barrel under his chin and pulled the trigger. The round had exited from the crown of his head and patterned the sheetrock on the wall with red streaks.

Santana knew Morgan was dead, but he felt the disfigured man's neck for a pulse. Then he bowed his head and knelt down beside the bed, not to pray, but because he would now bear the burden of this man's death, as Morgan had carried the anguish and guilt of the DC-9 crash with him for twenty years.

If he hadn't called Morgan to warn him, Santana thought, perhaps the man would still be alive. Perhaps if he'd only asked if Morgan was at home and hadn't engaged him in a conversation, the former co-pilot would be alive.

Santana was certain that Morgan had relived the fateful day of the crash in many nightmares and in his waking hours, as Santana had relived Jordan's death. He was certain that, like him, Morgan had wondered countless times how and why he'd survived while so many innocent victims had perished. He was sure that Morgan had replayed the events leading up to crash over and over in his mind, imagining what he should have done to prevent the tragedy, as Santana had replayed the events leading up to Jordan's death.

Morgan had finally succumbed to the weight of it all when he realized that his name would surface again in the media once they discovered that the son of two of the victims of the DC-9 crash was out to kill him.

There was little consolation for Santana in the knowledge that, if Glen Morgan wanted to commit suicide, there was nothing Santana could do to prevent it. He stood and looked once more at Morgan's sightless eyes before turning away.

After clearing the rest of house, he let Hawkins in the back door. "Where's Morgan?" she asked.

"Follow me."

Santana led her into the bedroom.

"Oh, Jesus," she said. "Suicide?"

"That would be my guess. Survivor's guilt finally got to him."

"Because of the plane crash?"

Santana nodded.

"What about Westbrook?"

"We wait," he said.

Chapter 39

Thirty-three minutes after entering Glen Morgan's house, Kacie Hawkins called out to Santana. "Westbrook's coming."

Santana, who was watching the front door, hustled into the kitchen. Outside one of the curtained windows, Paul Westbrook was parking his Land Rover in the alley beside Morgan's garage.

"He's got the shotgun," Hawkins said.

"Let's make it easy for him," Santana said. "Leave the back door unlocked."

They moved out of the kitchen and found cover, Santana in Morgan's bedroom, Hawkins in the bathroom across the hallway.

A minute later Santana heard the back door open with a squeak. He heard Westbrook's shoes on the tiled kitchen floor, then the creak of a floorboard as he worked his way down the hallway.

Santana saw the barrel come through the bedroom doorway before Westbrook appeared. He grabbed the barrel with his left hand and stuck his Glock into the surprised face of Paul Westbrook, just as Kacie Hawkins put the barrel of her gun against the back of Westbrook's head.

"Drop the shotgun!" Hawkins said. "Now!"

Westbrook released his grip.

Santana pulled the shotgun out of Westbrook's hand and said, "Get down on your knees! Clasp your hands behind your head!"

Westbrook did as he was told.

Hawkins cuffed him and read him his rights.

"Been waiting for you," Santana said when she finished.

Westbrook's eyes were trained on Glen Morgan's lifeless body on the bed.

"Too late," Santana said. "But you're going down for the others."

Westbrook lifted his eyes to Santana. "What others?" he asked.

* * *

While Kacie Hawkins ushered Paul Westbrook through booking, Santana debriefed Pete Romano and talked with forensics. Then he met Hawkins in one of the interview rooms, where she'd taken Westbrook.

Santana said, "What were you doing at Glen Morgan's house with a shotgun, Mr. Westbrook?"

Westbrook held Santana's gaze but offered no response.

"You broke into Glen Morgan's house with a loaded shotgun," Santana said. "That's taking a direct step toward killing Morgan, a textbook definition of attempted murder."

"He was dead when I got there," Westbrook said, stabbing a finger at Santana. "It's impossible to murder a man who's already dead."

A good lawyer could offer up an impossibility defense, Santana thought. But Terry Powell was another matter, as were the victims of the Blue Skies crash, Kim and Elisha Austin—and Laurie Baldwin.

"Let's concentrate on Terry Powell."

"Terry? I had nothing to do with his death."

"Then what were you doing at his house the night he was shot to death?"

"I was never there."

"According to your cell phone location data, you were."

Santana could see by the furrows in Westbrook's forehead that he was trying to work out a reasonable explanation.

"You shot Powell with my gun after I left and framed me for the killing."

"It doesn't make sense that I'd kill Terry. He thought the Blue Skies crash was due to pilot error. He was on my side."

"You had to get me off the case. The best way to do that was to frame me for murdering Powell."

"Good luck proving it, Detective."

"You were also in the parking lot near the Mississippi caves the day Kim Austin disappeared. You were at Elisha Austin's house the day she was murdered. And you were at the convenience store the night Laurie Baldwin disappeared. Coincidence? I don't think so."

"Why would I kill Kim?"

"You murdered her because she suspected that you had something to do with the downing of the Blue Skies flight." Santana recalled how Kim Austin's lips were sealed in the surrealistic dream he'd had, as though she knew a secret. "Kim Austin knew Glen Morgan was actually Greg Manning and told you, without knowing the possible consequences. That's another motive for killing her."

"Right," Westbrook said with a sneer. "And her mother?"

"I thought at first that when Kim Austin's remains were discovered, you had to make sure that she hadn't told her mother anything that could implicate you in her daughter's murder. But I wasn't sure why you'd wait six months before killing her. I'm thinking now that you killed Elisha Austin because she saw you snooping around Glen Morgan's house and asked what you were doing."

Westbrook sat perfectly still, his lips forming a tight, thin line.

"You'd been to Trevor Dane's office with Kim Austin when she introduced you to him. You knew he had surrealistic paintings. After visiting the Bosch exhibit in DC, you checked out his other work, including *The Garden of Earthly Delights*. You attempted to frame Trevor Dane for Austin's murder by stealing the dagger he owned and using the symbolism in the Hieronymus Bosch painting."

"I don't know what you're talking about."

"You asked Dane for financial advice on how to short sell stock. That's where you got the hundred thousand in your bank account."

"You'll never prove any of this," he said. But his voice lacked conviction.

"You kidnapped and murdered Laurie Baldwin because her father, Stu Pearce, was piloting the Blue Skies plane that crashed, killing your parents. He, along with Greg Manning, also known as Glen Morgan, forgot to conduct their pre-flight checks. You wanted to put Blue Skies out of business and maybe the whole airline industry by spoofing the flight. You also wanted us to find Laurie Baldwin's body so we'd think we were dealing with a serial killer. That's why you didn't bury her body, like you buried Kim Austin's."

"That's a lot of killing, Mr. Westbrook," Hawkins said. "Why don't you tell us about it?"

Westbrook kept silent.

"Hard to carry all that guilt with you," Santana said. "And we can add your attempt to kill me by spoofing my SUV near Grand Marais. I think you planned to murder Cathy Herrera as well. But you changed the plan when I showed up at her cabin."

"You've been a busy boy," Hawkins said.

Westbrook looked across the table at them, his face without expression.

"I wonder what forensics will find on the laptop computer in your Land Rover," Santana said.

Westbrook's complexion turned as pale as the white walls. "I want a lawyer," he said.

* * *

Santana phoned Lyman Grady in DC and gave him the information he had on Westbrook. Grady assured Santana that he and his forensic team would try to match the unidentified DNA found in Terry Powell's house with Westbrook's DNA. With any luck, they might find evidence that would link Westbrook to Powell's murder.

Before leaving the LEC late that afternoon, Santana spoke with Pete Romano.

"What about Paul Westbrook?"

"The BCA is testing for his DNA on the pillow used to suffocate Elisha Austin. The DC police found some unidentified DNA in Terry Powell's house. They're attempting to match it with Westbrook's. The location tracking on his phone puts him at both sites the days of the murders."

"Nothing linking him to Kim Austin's death?"

"That's tougher. We've got no murder weapon or DNA—yet. But when forensics searched Westbrook's Land Rover, they found a toolbox containing duct tape, rope, leather gloves, and a titanium ice pick."

"A murder kit."

"Yes," Santana said. "I believe Westbrook used the ice pick to murder Laurie Baldwin. And his DNA is probably in the van that was found in the downtown ramp. Prints might be there as well."

"Westbrook's going down for at least one, if not more, murders," Romano said.

Santana nodded. "And the Blue Skies crash?"

"You know as much as I do, John. It's up to the FBI and NTSB as to whether they'll pursue charges against Westbrook."

Santana thought about what he was about to say before he spoke again. "I'd like to take my remaining vacation time, Pete."

Romano nodded his head. "I read Karen Wong's recommendation in the report she filed. You've earned it. When would you like to go?"

"I need to get my boat stored for the winter. Then, as soon as the paperwork is completed, I'll leave."

"Enjoy yourself," Romano said. "Rest up. We need you."

When Santana returned to his desk, he told Kacie Hawkins of his impending vacation.

She stared at him for a long moment before replying. "You're coming back, aren't you?"

"That's the plan."

"An unequivocal 'Yes,' instead of an ambiguous response, would've been more reassuring," Hawkins said.

"I just need some time, Kacie."

"I hear you." She reached out and gave him a hug. "Stay safe."

"It's a vacation."

"Right," she said. "In Colombia. What could possibly go wrong?"

* * *

That evening Santana called Rita Gamboni in DC and told her about his plans.

"Please stay in touch," she said.

"I will."

"Telling me about your plans isn't the only reason you called, is it?"

"What's the Bureau doing about Paul Westbrook and the Blue Skies crash?"

"Investigating."

"And how long is that going to take?"

"I don't know."

"Forensics will find evidence on Westbrook's computer. Then the Bureau and NTSB will have to decide whether to make the information public or bury it, like all the bodies Westbrook left in his wake."

"I'm afraid the Bureau will stick to their story. There's too much riding on it, John."

"You mean the possible collapse of the airline industry."

"And the global meltdown that could follow."

"Why am I not surprised? How's Ted Lake?"

"Not so good. He and Jack Gaines might lose their jobs."

"*Might*?"

"There's some politics going on," Gamboni said.

"What a shock."

"I heard about the shooting at your house," Gamboni said, changing the subject. "You think Karina Rojas was hired to kill you by the remaining members of the cartel?"

"It was probably Angel Estrada, one of Alejandro Estrada's stepsons. You recall I killed his sister, Elena, after she shot me."

"And you're going to Colombia."

"I have to make sure Natalia is safe. Besides, it's where I lived for nearly half my life, Rita."

"Just make sure it isn't where you die," she said.

Chapter 40

Three days later, Santana and Gitana took a Delta flight from the Twin Cities to Atlanta, where they caught a second Delta flight to Bogotá, Colombia.

Large jets, such as the 757 they flew from Atlanta, couldn't land at the La Nubia airport in Manizales because of the short runway and the regularly occurring fog, rain, and wind. For the one-hour-and-fifteen-minute flight over the Andes, they took an Avianca turboprop Fokker, and even the smaller, noisy aircraft could only land during daylight hours.

Santana considered flying from Bogotá to the airport in Pereira, which could handle larger jets. He could rent a car and drive the thirty-two miles to Manizales. But he remembered from his childhood that the airport in Pereira was a mess. By all accounts it hadn't changed during his years in the States. Plus, he was anxious to get to Manizales to see his sister.

Santana never cared much for flying, especially in a small turboprop, which was often at the mercy of wind currents over the snow-capped Andes. Thinking about a possible spoofing attack—and recalling the survivors of the Uruguayan flight that crashed in the Andes in 1972 who were forced to eat the flesh of the dead in order to stay alive—did little to bolster his confidence. Gitana, on the other hand, slept like a baby most of the way. Santana was grateful to Karen Wong for granting his request for Gitana to be his emotional support dog, thus allowing her to fly with him.

Santana stayed at the dog-friendly Quo Hotel in a suite with a large bedroom, living room, and open kitchen. The modern hotel just outside the heart of Manizales was equipped with an iPad that controlled the lights, TV, and window shades. He liked the idea of having a kitchen but was disappointed to discover there were no cooking utensils.

He slept well for the first time in weeks, despite his excitement about seeing his sister again. She was staying at a friend's house in Manizales. They had agreed to meet that morning at the bronze statue of the settlers who had founded the city in the mid-1800s.

When Gitana had been fed, Santana ate breakfast in the hotel dining room. A waiter brought him a copy of *La Patria,* the daily newspaper in Manizales. Above the fold on the front page, Santana was stunned to read that Angel Estrada, believed to be a member of the former Cali cartel, had been killed in an auto accident.

Santana reread the headline and the story once more. A smile came to his face as he sat back in his chair. Maybe, just maybe, his days of waiting for a cartel assassin to strike were over. Then he thought of Karina Rojas and Reyna Tran's warning. Rojas was still out there. She would honor her contract regardless of Angel Estrada's death. That was the code of an assassin hired by the cartel. If she didn't honor the contract, she would never be hired, or trusted, again.

He finished his meal and directed a cab driver to take Gitana and him to Los Colonializadores, the beautiful park that sat on a ridge high above the city in the Chipre barrio, where he and Natalia had grown up and gone to school.

The October sky was gray and overcast—typical for this time of year and the 6,500-foot altitude—the early morning fog shrouding the city like a gray veil.

Manizales was noted throughout Colombia for its numerous private and public universities, and Santana could see students walking to classes and sitting in the countless cafés along Avenida Santander.

Once they were out of the cab, Gitana, fascinated by all the new scents, had her nose to the ground, but Santana hurried her along, anxious to get to the statue and to see his sister.

To the east, north, and south he could see the city nestled up against the western side of central Cordillera. Far below to the west were the green valleys, rivers, and coffee plantations.

Santana's heart beat faster as they neared the statue and he saw the tall young woman with the beautiful face dusted with freckles, the shoulder-length auburn hair, and the glistening hazel eyes.

Natalia waved as he approached and ran toward him. He gathered her in his arms and held her close. He could hear her crying softly against his shoulder.

"I missed you," she said, speaking in Spanish.

He took her face in his hands and wiped the tears off her cheeks. "I missed you, too, *Gato,*" he said, using the Spanish pet name for "Cat" that he'd called her as a child.

Gitana barked and tried to get between them.

"And I know who this beautiful girl is," Natalia said, bending down to hug Gitana and receive her kisses.

"She never gets enough attention," Santana said, beginning to get into the flow of speaking his native Spanish again.

When she stood again, her eyes locked on his. "I am so happy to see you. But you should not have come."

"I am your big brother. I have to look out for you."

"And who looks out for you?" Natalia asked.

They took a cab to a flower shop and then to the San Estebán cemetery, where their parents were buried.

The sun-bleached headstones, crosses, tombs, and crypts were arranged in an ever-expanding circle around a tall statue of the crucified Christ and an altar where priests celebrated Mass. The fog had lifted. From this vantage point, Santana could see the towering steeple of the Cathedral de Manizales, the water tower in the Chipre neighborhood where they had grown up, and in the far distance, the snow-capped peak of the dormant Nevado del Ruiz volcano.

They found the Baroque tomb containing the burial vaults of their parents and both sets of grandparents.

Gitana was calmer in the cemetery, as if she knew they were in the place of the dead.

Santana knelt down, Gitana sitting on one side of him, Natalia on the other. She placed the bouquet of flowers Santana had purchased against the cool marble tomb and said a prayer.

As he listened to his sister, he hoped that this would someday be his final resting place, as he'd requested in his will. His mother had wanted the family to be together.

After they left the cemetery, Natalia took Santana and Gitana to her friend Paula's house, where they spent the afternoon catching up.

That evening, while Paula babysat Gitana, Santana and Natalia ate dinner at the very nice Vino y Pimienta restaurant.

They talked about Angel Estrada's death and about Jordan Parrish for a time, Natalia holding Santana's hand across the table as he spoke of his feelings for her and the difficulty he was having coming to terms with her loss and moving on with his life.

"Your sorrow is written in your face," Natalia said, squeezing his hand. Then, sensing his reluctance to talk more about Jordan, she switched subjects. "Your last case," she said. "You never sent me an e-mail about how it ended."

Santana summarized what had happened and expressed his doubts that Paul Westbrook would ever be prosecuted for downing the Blue Skies airliner.

"I should call you *Gato,*" she said. "You are the one with nine lives."

Santana smiled and wondered how many lives he had left.

"You could have been killed, Juan. This woman, Reyna Tran, do you have feelings for her?"

"Only as a friend."

"Can someone like her have friends?"

"I still have my doubts, but we will see."

"Now that Estrada is dead and the Cali cartel is finished, you should come and see me in Barcelona," she said as they drank from their glasses of wine. "I have a large flat and two bedrooms. I am close to the beach. And you could bring Gitana."

"I might do that," he said.

"I am spending the day with Paula. We are going to the cathedral in the morning."

"You cannot go there alone."

"You mean without you."

Santana nodded.

"It has been fixed up. And it is much safer climbing the Polish Corridor to the top."

The steps and steel spiral stairway leading to the top of the spire had been given the name to pay homage to those impacted by Hitler's invasion of Poland during World War II, when the cathedral was completed.

"Well, I have no desire to climb up that far," he said. "But I will come along."

"You can leave Gitana with Paula's daughter. She will take good care of her."

He raised his wine glass. "To tomorrow," he said.

* * *

Santana left Gitana at Paula's house and followed Natalia and Paula to the cathedral just after a morning thunderstorm ended. Having to travel only a short distance, they arrived before the crowds.

La Catedral Basílica de Nuestra Señora del Rosario, or the Cathedral Basilica of Our Lady of the Rosary, is located in the Plaza de Bolívar, which is in the center of Manizales. A bronze statue of Simón Bolívar with the head of a condor overlooks the plaza. Opposite the Bolívar statue is the neo-Gothic cathedral with its five spires, steeply pitched roofs, and Gothic arches.

From a distance, Santana always thought the square concrete structure, with its dull gray columns and concrete walls and roofs designed to protect it from earthquakes, looked like a gigantic stone. It was the second tallest cathedral in South America, just five feet shorter than the Basílica del Voto Nacional in Quito, Ecuador, and could seat up to five thousand people.

Having climbed the spire as a young teen on a dare, he had no intention of doing it again. He was quite content to once again see the beautiful canopy supported by columns over the main altar, the large stained glass windows, and to remember the Masses he'd attended with his parents and Natalia when they were children. He sat in a pew behind Natalia and Paula while they prayed, his eyes scoping the faces of the visitors, looking for something out of the ordinary.

The three of them took an elevator up to the second floor, where there was a large outdoor café on the roof offering a great view of the surrounding city and mountainside. While they were all seated at the table, he caught sight of a woman's face out of the corner of his eye.

Turning quickly in his chair, he saw her from behind as she left the coffee shop and returned to the cathedral. She was wearing a black raincoat and black fedora.

It couldn't be, he thought. But the woman had looked an awful lot like Karina Rojas, *el Lobo,* the Wolf. Curiosity got the best of him.

He stood, told Natalia and Paula he would be right back and to stay where they were, and hurried into the cathedral, where the crowd had increased considerably.

His eyes scanned right and left and then settled on a group of twenty or so people on the opposite side of the cathedral. They were following a man speaking in Spanish out a door and onto the roof. *A guided tour*, he thought.

Near the middle of the single file line, he saw the woman in the raincoat and hat.

He crossed the floor quickly and caught up to the end of the line and then stopped.

There was no way off the spire. She would have to come back the same way she'd gone up. He could wait here until the tour returned and get a good look at her. Satisfy his curiosity.

But the tour could last for an hour or two, depending on the speed and condition of the tourists. He didn't want to waste the day standing here, especially if he was wrong and the woman wasn't *el Lobo*.

The tour cost five dollars. He would have to get in line and buy a ticket, and then wait for another group to form. He figured he could avoid the hassle and delay by tagging along at the end of this group until they reached the dome. He could get a good look at her there. If he was wrong about the woman, he would head back down. And if he was right . . .

Santana took a deep, relaxing breath and let it out slowly as he stepped outside the door and onto the narrow concrete steps along the moss-covered roof ridges. There were handrails and a security cage around the steps, but he still felt a rush of adrenaline as he moved across and then climbed up the roof at a steep forty-five-degree angle, his sweaty hands gripping the cold handrails. The city of Manizales and the surrounding area spread out far below him, but he didn't look down. He kept his eyes fixed on the steps ahead. Fortunately, he was in good shape. Climbing this many steps in a high altitude was a challenge.

The caged corridor was so narrow that the group had to proceed in single file. At the top of the stairs, he turned right onto an even narrower walkway that took him back across the roof and through a small doorway. To his left was a short set of stairs that led up and into the wide circular dome.

There was considerably more room here, and the people on the tour had spread out. Some stood on the bottom steps of the Polish Corridor, the bright orange winding steel stairs that led up inside the spire and out to an enclosed 360-degree walkway where visitors had a spectacular view of the city and surrounding hills.

Directly ahead of Santana in the center of the dome were three metal rails, the top rail about five feet high, surrounding an opening that was covered by wooden boards. The opening, called the *falsa cúpula*, or false dome, led straight down to the main floor of the cathedral far below. A symbol of the Corpus Christi, damaged in an earthquake in 1999, had once covered the opening. Santana remembered as a child looking up from the main floor of the cathedral and seeing the symbol.

His eyes swept the dome now, searching for the woman in the black raincoat and hat.

The tour guide had stopped on the first landing of the stairs and was speaking to the group scattered below him about the historical significance of the dome.

The winding staircase was wider than the steps outside along the roof ridge—two average-sized people could squeeze past each other—and had three-foot tall handrails on both sides, but there were no safety cages surrounding it as it spiraled upward like a corkscrew.

The woman in black couldn't have gone up ahead of the guide. Yet Santana saw no one in a black raincoat and hat.

Along one wall, he could see what remained of the old wooden steps boxed in by wooden planks that had once been used to make the precarious climb. To his right was a balcony enclosed by safety bars. Stuffed in the corner, he could see a black raincoat and hat.

He was certain now that his eyes hadn't deceived him. *El Lobo* was here.

As the group began climbing the winding stairs, Santana drifted along behind them, trying to get a good look at the faces of the women up ahead of him. He walked in the middle of the stairs, taking his time, preferring to stay as far away from the railing as possible.

When he reached a landing near the top, a mustachioed young man in a black ball cap and long-sleeved yellow-and-black soccer jersey was leaning over the top railing, taking a photo of the dizzying drop to the dome floor below.

Santana passed him and then stopped. He'd only glanced at the man, but in that second his cop eyes had spotted the slight scar running just below the man's right cheekbone to under his bottom lip. Only it wasn't a man. Santana been so focused on the women in the group that he'd ignored the possibility that *el Lobo* had disguised her appearance.

He spun around to face her, but the Wolf was waiting.

She lunged toward him with her arms outstretched and shoved him backward hard, sending him crashing against the railing. Off balance, he tried to right himself as she bent over, grabbed one of his ankles, and lifted his leg.

Santana turned his upper body as she flung his leg over, frantically grabbing the top railing with both hands, holding on with everything he had, his heart thumping wildly in his chest, his body hanging in empty space. As she leaned over the top railing, a malevolent smile on her face, he looked up into the deep pools of darkness that were her eyes. Then she went for his right hand, trying to pry his fingers loose.

Santana felt his grip loosening. With all his remaining strength, he pulled upward as if he were doing a chin-up. Tightening his hold on the railing with his left hand, he let go of the railing with his right and in one swift motion seized a fistful of her jersey.

She stepped back and grabbed his hand, trying to break his grip, but he yanked her forward as he slid back into empty space, slamming her waist into the railing.

Unable to resist the full weight of his body pulling her down, she toppled over the railing and slipped past him as he let her go, tumbling like a diver as she fell, never uttering a sound.

Epilogue

A solitary man sat in a wicker chair at a *chiringuitos*, or beach bar, in Barcelona, Spain. He was drinking a glass of white Cava and watching tanned young women in bikinis play volleyball on the sand in front of the bar. Behind the young women, the Mediterranean Sea glittered, and white sails shone like bleached bones under the sun's bright rays.

The man had been sitting at a table for over an hour, eating *tapas* under the canopy and gesturing for the waitress when he wanted another drink. A golden retriever was lying on the floor beside him.

A young boy sat on the sand near the restaurant, watching intently as the man washed down the *tapas* with what Catalonians called "Spanish champagne." Beside the boy was a blanket filled with three rows of Panama hats that he sold to help support his mother and siblings. The hats were white with different colored hatbands.

It was near the end of the tourist season, and the man piqued the young boy's curiosity—though he did not offer to sell the man a hat. The man with the dog had a detachment, an attitude of solitude bordering on menace, about him.

He wore a long-sleeved V-neck cotton shirt with the sleeves rolled up to his elbows and had a neatly trimmed, heavy dark beard. He had neck-length wavy black hair, which he parted in the middle, and a trim but muscular body. On his left wrist he wore a gold watch, and on the right, a wide leather wristband.

The boy had noticed the long, jagged white scar on the back of the man's right hand the first time that he saw him in the bar and wondered how he had gotten it. But it was the man's intense ice blue eyes that held the boy's attention. They did not appear to focus on anything, yet seemed to track everything. The boy, having had some interactions with authorities, had seen those types of eyes before. He surmised that the man had been, or was, a policeman.

Over the past few weeks, as the boy observed the man's skin quickly darkening under the warm Spanish sun and the white cotton shirts he favored, he thought he might be from India. But then he had heard the man order a drink and food in Spanish and knew by his accent that he was Hispanic, though not from Spain. He guessed somewhere in South America, perhaps Colombia, as there were many Colombians working and living in Barcelona now.

The man came to the bar with his dog on most days, but a woman had accompanied them on occasion. She was tall like the man and very pretty, with shoulder-length auburn hair and clear hazel eyes. At first the boy thought they were lovers, but as he observed their interactions and heard bits of their conversations, he concluded they were related, most likely brother and sister.

When the volleyball game ended and the women scattered, the sun was nearing the horizon. Now the boy watched as the man paid his bill, swallowed the last of his drink, stood, put on a pair of aviator sunglasses, and strode out of the bar and onto the sand, his dog walking with him. He wore faded jeans cut off just above the knees and a pair of huarache sandals. Even though he had drunk quite a few glasses of Cava, he walked naturally and with purpose.

He glanced down at the boy as he passed, following the beach toward the city.

The boy watched him for a moment and then got to his feet and prowled in the direction of the restaurant, as he did not want to call attention to himself. His eyes quickly scanned the empty chairs, looking for the waitress who had served the man his drinks.

When he saw no one watching him, he moved like a cat to the table where the man had been sitting and snatched the remaining *tapa* from the plate. Stuffing it quickly into a front pocket of his shirt, he turned and saw two teenagers standing beside his blanket. Both were heavy-set. They wore dirty jeans, shabby tennis shoes, and white tank tops. Their heads were shaved. Tattoos covered their arms.

They were members of the Mara Salvatrucha, or MS-13. Older friends of the boy had told him the MS-13 was one of the most dangerous and violent criminal organizations. The king of Spain had spoken out against the Latin American gangs, which were a mounting threat in Spain, where economic hardship and high unemployment had left many young people feeling marginalized.

The boy had seen these two before and knew they had no intention of buying a hat. They were after what little money he had. He considered running but realized he had no chance. They were bigger and faster and would soon run him down. Angry that he had fled, they would beat him before taking his money.

Swallowing his fear, the boy approached the blanket, his hands in his front pockets, the money he had made today clutched in the palms of his hands. He waited for the two to make their demands. Then he saw their eyes shift away from him as a long shadow engulfed them.

The man from the restaurant had returned, the dog beside him.

He removed his aviator sunglasses and slipped them into a case clipped to his belt. His eyes studied the gangbangers and then came to rest on the boy.

"I would like to buy one of your hats," he said.

One of the gangbangers started to object, but when the man stared at him, he quickly shut up.

"Is there a problem?" the man said, turning to face them, his legs spread evenly apart, fists clenched by his sides.

The boy did not fear the man, but he could sense fear in the air and see it in the eyes of the Mara Salvatruchas. It was not a fear of being beaten, though it was obvious by the man's size and threatening presence that the MS-13s stood no chance against him. Rather, the fear the boy saw in their eyes was recognition that the man possessed no fear of harm, or injury—or even death.

The MS-13s looked at one another and then turned and walked away.

The boy looked up into the man's eyes and saw something else in them now.

The man smiled.

"What hat would you like?" the boy asked in Spanish.

The man pointed to one with a black hatband. "*¿Cuánto cuesta*?"

After the boy retrieved the hat, he told him the price. The price the boy quoted was considerably less than he usually charged. But the man had prevented a robbery and saved the money the boy had earned today. He was more than willing to give him a break in the price.

The man asked politely if he could try it on for size.

"Sí," the boy said, embarrassed that he had forgotten to ask the man's hat size. It fit the man's head perfectly. The man smiled again and gave the boy a banknote.

"Sorry," the boy said. "I do not have change for this amount."

"Keep it," the man said. He pointed to the *tapa* in the boy's shirt pocket. "And get yourself something to eat."

The man turned and began to walk away with his dog when the boy said, "Tell me something, please, *Señor*."

The man stopped and looked back at the boy.

"Are you a policeman?" the boy asked.

"I was once," the man said.

"Will you ever be one again?"

"Perhaps," the man said. He waved as he walked away.

The boy watched the man for a long time as the sun sank lower on the horizon, the shadows grew longer, and the man grew smaller and smaller in the distance, until he disappeared in the last glittering rays of sunlight.

Acknowledgments

Thanks to: Captain David Burns, Sun Country Airlines, and Tim Lynch, Homicide Commander, St. Paul Police Department (Ret.), for sharing their knowledge and expertise.

Special contributions were made by the following, without whom this book would not exist in its present form: Abigail Davis, Linda Donaldson, Lorrie Holmgren, Peg Wangensteen, Jenifer LeClair, Dave Knudson, and my terrific editor, Jennifer Adkins. Thank you all for your time and suggestions regarding the manuscript.

Many thanks to my beautiful wife, Martha, for her love and inspiration.

Thanks to my growing family of readers for your wonderful support and e-mails.

AN INVITATION TO READING GROUPS/ BOOK CLUBS

I would like to extend an invitation to reading groups/book clubs across the country. Invite me to your group and I'll be happy to participate in your discussion. I'm available to join your discussion either in person or via FaceTime, Skype, or the telephone. (Reading groups should have a speakerphone.) You can arrange a date and time by e-mailing cjvalen@comcast.net. I look forward to hearing from you.

Not Sure What to Read Next?
Try these authors from Conquill Press

Jenifer LeClair: The Windjammer Mystery Series

Rigged for Murder
Danger Sector
Cold Coast
Apparition Island
www.windjammermyseries.com

Chuck Logan

Fallen Angel
Broker
www.chucklogan.org

Brian Lutterman: The Pen Wilkinson Mystery Series

Downfall
Windfall
Freefall
www.brianlutterman.com

Steve Thayer

Ithaca Falls
The Wheat Field
www.stevethayer.com

Christopher Valen: The John Santana Mystery Series

White Tombs
The Black Minute
Bad Weed Never Die
Bone Shadows
Death's Way
The Darkness Hunter
www.christophervalen.com

For more information on all these titles go to:
www.conquillpress.com

CPSIA information can be obtained
at www.ICGtesting.com
Printed in the USA
LVOW03s0800080817
544183LV00001B/1/P